Praise for Ryan Steck

"[A] strong debut. . . . The suave yet vulnerable lead and propulsive narrative will keep readers hooked. This is an auspicious start for Steck."
PUBLISHERS WEEKLY on *Fields of Fire*

"Done exceptionally well. Steck's debut actually gives us two bangs for the buck, hitting on a pair of classic thriller tropes in the same volume. . . . His command of battle scenes and the warrior mindset is exceptional. *Fields of Fire* reads like Nelson DeMille seamlessly blended with the likes of Brad Thor, Brad Taylor, or Jack Carr, and is not to be missed."
PROVIDENCE JOURNAL

"This breathtaking debut thriller . . . [is] well done, with crisp writing that produces the always desired yet rarely achieved sensation of 'being there.' The author's concise style and clean prose get the reader engaged in the characters as well as the story line from page one. The adrenaline-fueled pace does the rest. The result is a book that won't allow the reader to walk away before the story is finished."
READER VIEWS on *Fields of Fire*

"*Fields of Fire* is going to be a hit that fans of the thriller genre will quickly gravitate to and love. Steck's Matthew Redd will be around for a long time, captivating readers with each page. Make sure you thriller readers grab yourself a copy of this one—you won't regret it."
BEST THRILLER BOOKS

"Ryan Steck's *Fields of Fire* busts out of the chute with nonstop action and it never lets up until the final page. A magnificent debut with a terrific sense of place in Big Sky Country and a hero to root for in Matthew Redd."
C. J. BOX, #1 *New York Times* bestselling author of *S.*

"Ryan Steck hits it out of the park with his debut, *Fields of Fire*. Part military thriller, part spy novel, part good old-fashioned Western—Matthew Redd has cemented himself as the go-to man in a bad situation. It starts off with a literal bang and never lets up, with an ending that will leave readers scrambling for more."

BRAD TAYLOR, *New York Times* bestselling author of *End of Days*

"The stakes—and tension—don't stop building until they explode into a denouement readers will never forget. The debut thriller of the year."

KYLE MILLS, #1 *New York Times* bestselling author of *Enemy at the Gates*, on *Fields of Fire*

"You know Ryan Steck as the Real Book Spy. Now get to know him as the author of *Fields of Fire*, his debut thriller featuring Marine Raider Matthew Redd in a battle that will leave you speechless and begging for more. Lock and load!"

JACK CARR, Navy SEAL sniper and #1 *New York Times* bestselling author of *The Devil's Hand*

"The Real Book Spy becomes the real spy. Action! Suspense! And the introduction of former Marine Raider Matthew Redd, a formidable new hero who doesn't like being told no. Ryan Steck's *Fields of Fire* kicks off an exciting new series. Check it out."

BRAD MELTZER, #1 *New York Times* bestselling author of *The Escape Artist*

"Ryan Steck's *Fields of Fire* breathes fresh life into the thriller genre with his hero Matty Redd, a hard man forced to fight for those he loves in the harsh wilderness of Montana. A compelling premise strongly executed. Fans of C. J. Box and Vince Flynn will anxiously await the follow-up to *Fields of Fire*."

MARK GREANEY, #1 *New York Times* bestselling author of *Sierra Six*

"An iconic character is born. . . . This compelling debut will linger in your thoughts long after turning the final page."

K. J. HOWE, executive director, International Thriller Writers, and bestselling author of *Skyjack*, on *Fields of Fire*

"Ryan Steck has gone from writing about thrillers to writing a first-rate thriller himself. All you have to do is start reading about his new hero named Matthew Redd to understand. This is a book that does exactly what books like it are supposed to do: keeps you turning the pages to find out what happens next. And spoiler alert? Every time you think you know, you don't."

MIKE LUPICA, *New York Times* bestselling author of *Robert B. Parker's Payback* and *Robert B. Parker's Stone's Throw*, on *Fields of Fire*

"A flawless story with a stellar cast of memorable characters—Ryan Steck's stunning debut, *Fields of Fire*, is a twisty, electrifying thriller reminiscent of the very best of Brad Thor that will keep readers flipping pages well into the night."

SIMON GERVAIS, former RCMP counterterrorism officer and bestselling author of *The Last Protector*

"Thriller fans, debuts don't get better than this. Explosive from page one and rarely letting up, *Fields of Fire* heralds the arrival of hard-charging, even harder-hitting Marine Raider Matthew Redd to the genre's pantheon of mesmerizing franchise heroes. First-time author Ryan Steck writes with the expertise of a seasoned pro and delivers 1,000 percent. Get your hands on this book!"

CHRIS HAUTY, nationally bestselling author

"*Fields of Fire*, Ryan Steck's long-awaited debut novel, is loaded with action, emotion, and plenty of authentic details. I could not put it down!"

NICK PETRIE, author of *The Runaway*

LETHAL RANGE

RYAN STECK

LETHAL RANGE

A MATTHEW REDD THRILLER

Tyndale House Publishers
Carol Stream, Illinois

Visit Tyndale online at tyndale.com.

Visit Ryan Steck online at therealbookspy.com.

Tyndale and Tyndale's quill logo are registered trademarks of Tyndale House Ministries.

Lethal Range

Cover photograph of mountains by David Mullins on Unsplash.

Cover photograph of clouds by Kenrick Mills on Unsplash.

Cover designed by Dean H. Renninger

Edited by Sarah Mason Rische

Published in association with The John Talbot Agency, Inc., a member of The Talbot Fortune Agency, LLC, 180 E. Prospect Ave. #188, Mamaroneck, NY 10543.

Lethal Range is a work of fiction. Where real people, events, establishments, organizations, or locales appear, they are used fictitiously. All other elements of the novel are drawn from the author's imagination.

For information about special discounts for bulk purchases, please contact Tyndale House Publishers at csresponse@tyndale.com, or call 1-855-277-9400.

Library of Congress Cataloging-in-Publication Data

A catalog record for this book is available from the Library of Congress.

ISBN 978-1-4964-6291-6 (HC)

ISBN 978-1-4964-6292-3 (SC)

Printed in the United States of America

29   28   27   26   25   24   23

7   6   5   4   3   2   1

To the love of my life, Melissa.
There is nobody I'd rather do life with than you.
Thank you for all that you do for me and our children.
I love you more than words.

And to baby Derhammer.
You are loved more than you know, little one.
Uncle Ryan can't wait to meet you!

"If you would
revenge yourself,
dig two graves."

WILLIAM ELLIOT GRIFFIS (1876),
PARAPHRASING A TRADITIONAL JAPANESE PROVERB

ONE

For the moment, things were quiet, but they wouldn't stay that way for long.

The drone was about the size of a hummingbird and just as quiet as it flitted from tree to tree, hiding behind branches until its operator determined that it was safe to continue moving. A sharp-eyed observer on the ground would have no difficulty distinguishing the tiny remote vehicle from an actual bird. Fortunately, the target area appeared to be clear of observers, sharp-eyed or otherwise.

Half a kilometer away, in the rear cargo area of a panel van emblazoned with the logo of a floral delivery service, four men huddled around a twelve-inch iPad Pro, watching the feed from the drone's 4K high-definition video camera. Three were sworn agents of the US Federal Bureau of Investigation, assigned to a rapidly deployable international

1

counterterrorism unit—a fly team. The remaining man—dark-haired with a broad chest and biceps that strained the fabric of his black long-sleeved Under Armour T-shirt—was working under an exclusive contract to the bureau and was, by virtue of his experience and superior training as a former elite Marine Raider, the field leader of the fly team's eight-man tactical operations unit. His name was Matthew Redd.

The screen of the iPad showed the back of the villa—a sleek, modern structure of glass and steel that was conspicuous against the rugged rocky hills overlooking Port de Pollença. The floor-to-ceiling glass walls afforded the villa's occupants an unobstructed view of the bay to the east but also provided the four men in the van an unobstructed view of the house's interior.

"There." Redd stabbed a finger at the screen. "Back it up a couple seconds."

The man holding the tablet—the team's intelligence analyst, Special Agent Sean "Mac" Fleetwood—tapped the screen, then used the slider to reverse the playback until Redd called out, "Freeze it. Can you zoom in?"

The frozen image showed a sitting room, appointed with a large sectional and two overstuffed chairs, and as the picture was magnified, it revealed two figures seated therein. One of them, clearly male, sat on the sectional, looking out, his face fully exposed to the camera. The other person occupied one of the armchairs, which was positioned opposite the sectional. As a result, the person's back was to the window. Despite the camera's astonishing resolution, all the men in the van could see of the second person was a luxurious mane of thick flaxen hair.

"Is that him?" asked a third man, Special Agent Bryan Tanaka.

Redd stared at the screen for several seconds. He was the only member of the fly team to have seen the subject in person—in fact, he had actually brunched with the man the previous year—but his familiarity was of the face-to-face variety.

He shook his head, uncertain. "It might be."

"*Might be* isn't going to cut it with Kline."

"I know," Redd sighed. "Go back to the live feed. Let's see if we can get a different angle." He reached up to activate the microphone headset attached to his tactical radio. "Damon, when am I going to be able to hear what's going on in there?"

The voice of Special Agent Damon Jones squawked in his earpiece. "Sending you the feed right now, boss."

Jones was presently perched in a tree farther down the hillside, just beyond the wall that delineated the edge of the villa's lot, painting one of the big windows with the invisible beam of an infrared laser. The laser was part of a sophisticated eavesdropping device that read the vibrations on the window glass the same way that a phonograph stylus read the almost-microscopic deviations in the groove of a vinyl record and transformed them back into sounds—specifically, into a remarkably faithful rendering of the conversation taking place inside the villa.

A pop-up window appeared on the tablet with a link to the audio player. Fleetwood tapped the pop-up to accept the invitation, and a noise like rushing wind filled the interior of the van. After a moment, the static abated, replaced by the sound of someone talking.

". . . want to do about Regeneron?"

Redd closed his eyes to focus on the voice, paying more attention to its timbre and cadence than to what was actually being said. It was a male voice, with a hard-to-pin-down European accent.

"That sounds like Giroux," Fleetwood whispered.

Redd raised a finger, requesting silence.

Then a different voice sounded. "Let's hold on to it for now. The pendulum always swings back."

Redd's eyes snapped open. "That's him," he said without a hint of reservation. "That's Anton Gage."

✖ ✖ ✖

Fifteen months earlier, all that Redd knew about Anton Gage was that he was the Elon Musk of biotechnology research. Not merely an innovator, though he was certainly that. Nor just obscenely rich, the handsome and charismatic Gage had achieved a level of celebrity that money alone couldn't buy. Rather than pursuing grandiose dreams of space travel and planetary conquest, Gage had focused his attention on a more grounded and immediate concern, namely finding a way to feed the earth's growing population through genetically engineered, high-yield, drought- and disease-resistant cereal crops.

Or so he had claimed.

In reality, Gage's solution to ending world hunger was not to make more food, but rather to reduce the number of hungry mouths to feed. His tinkering with the genome had been part of a radical plot to decrease birth rates in the developing world.

Although Gage himself had not initially been on anyone's radar, the FBI's counterterrorism division had become aware of another key figure in the plot, a mysterious bioweapons scientist known only by the code name Willow. A team of Marine Raiders had been sent to capture Willow at his research lab in Mexico, but a highly placed mole in the bureau alerted the scientist to the danger. Acting under Gage's orders, Willow had not only escaped but had arranged a lethal reception for the Marines, killing the entire squad . . . save one.

Matthew Redd.

Redd's guilt at having let his team down was exceeded only by his anger toward the man who had, albeit with the best intentions, prevented him from accompanying the ill-fated mission. That man, Gavin Kline, was now in charge of the FBI's Intelligence Directorate and, as such, was Redd's boss, at least insofar as his activities with the fly team were concerned.

Kline was also Redd's biological father.

Theirs was a troubled relationship. Redd's mother, who had died when Redd was a child, had kept Kline in the dark regarding the existence of his son. When he finally learned the truth, being a father was the last thing the career-focused Kline had time for. Rather than make room in his busy life, Kline had instead handed young Matthew off to an old war buddy, a Montana rancher named Jim Bob Thompson—Redd had always called him J. B.—to raise as his own.

Redd did not blame Kline for the death of his team, but neither did he entirely forgive the FBI director. There was a gulf between the two men that, at least as far as Redd was concerned, could never be bridged. The only thing that really bound them together was the hunt for Anton Gage.

Although Redd had ultimately thwarted Gage's scheme, the billionaire himself had escaped, fleeing the country. Gavin Kline, acutely aware of his son's tactical prowess, as well as his burning desire to balance the scales of justice, prevailed upon Redd to join the fly team on an ad hoc basis, which was why Redd was now sitting in the back of an ersatz delivery van five thousand miles from home.

As eager as he was to see justice done, what Redd really wanted was to be finished with the hunt. To get back home to Montana, where the work on his ranch was piling up even faster than the bills. More importantly, home was where Emily and little Matthew Jr. were waiting for him.

He still remembered what he'd said when Kline had first tried to recruit him to the fly team.

"I'm not like you. Gavin. I'm not going to abandon my wife and son to chase bad guys."

He had meant to wound with those words, but it had also been the truth.

The sting of loss had begun to fade, first as his love for Emily, his high school sweetheart, was rekindled, and then with the arrival of their son. He was no longer compelled by a desire to carry out some Old Testament retribution—an eye for an eye, a soul for a soul—upon Anton Gage. There wasn't enough room in his heart for both love and the kind of hate required to keep a man on the path of vengeance. In the end, he had taken Kline up on the offer more out of a sense of unfinished business than anything else.

Now, after months of relentless searching, the target was at last in the crosshairs. Forty-eight hours earlier, a wire transfer from a flagged Cayman Islands account had set alarm bells ringing at FBI headquarters. The funds had been electronically transferred to a bank in Palma on the Spanish island of Majorca. The man who made the withdrawal had been identified as Jean-Paul Giroux, believed to be Gage's financier. After leaving the bank, he had gone directly to a villa on the other side of the island, where, it was also believed, his employer was presently hiding out.

Kline had immediately ordered the fly team into the field and begun the not-inconsiderable chore of coordinating with Spanish authorities. Redd, who had been home in Montana when the word went out, had been forced to travel by commercial air. Although the team had a twelve-hour head start on him, he hit the ground running.

Confidence that they had indeed run Gage to ground was high, but not absolute. Neither Kline nor the Spanish government would authorize further action without 100 percent positive identification. As the only person on the team—and quite probably in the entire bureau—to have met Gage face-to-face, Redd's presence was doubly important.

Without another word, Redd drew back from the huddle and exited the vehicle. Once outside, he took out his bureau-issued Iridium satellite phone and called Kline.

"It's him," Redd said as soon as the connection was established.

"You're sure?" Kline asked.

It was an unnecessary question, and Redd had to bite back a sarcastic reply to that effect. Instead, after taking a moment to compose himself, a moment that could easily be attributed to signal lag, he said, "You don't forget a voice like that."

In fact, it wasn't just the sound of Gage's voice that Redd recognized but everything about the way the man communicated. His languid, self-assured, supremely arrogant persona. "It's him," Redd repeated.

"Because we can't afford to get this wrong," Kline went on. "We're on thin ice with the Spanish government as it is. They'd prefer to handle this themselves."

This time Redd answered with silence, which stretched out to several seconds before Kline finally spoke again. "All right, what's your plan?"

"We keep it KISS." KISS—"keep it simple, stupid"—was Redd's standard operating procedure. The fewer moving parts in a plan, the less chance for catastrophic failure. "We'll wait until oh-dark-thirty, then go in under cover of darkness." Redd shot a glance at his watch, which he had adjusted to local time during the long flight to Barcelona. "It's about three thirty here. That gives us nine hours to recon the objective. Figure out what kind of security he's got. And it gives you plenty of time to clear any bureaucratic hurdles."

Kline seemed to consider this for a moment, then came back. "All right. I'll get to it, but—and I can't stress this enough—under no circumstances are you to go kinetic without a green light from me. Understood?"

"Yeah," Redd answered with all the respect he felt Kline deserved, and then rang off without further comment.

In Redd's opinion, Kline was being overly cautious. It was a common tendency among those who left the operational side of things to become bureaucrats. There was nothing more pathetic than a door kicker turned bean counter.

An excess of caution was not Redd's only concern, however. Gage could not have avoided detection, never mind capture, for as long as he had without help. Whether because of loose security procedures among international law enforcement agencies or information supplied by highly placed double agents, Gage had managed to stay several steps ahead of his pursuers. There was good reason to think that looping in the Spanish authorities might inadvertently tip Gage off to the fact that the net was finally closing around him.

Redd shoved the sat phone into his pocket and climbed back inside the van. "Anything to report?"

Fleetwood shook his head. "They're still talking shop. Moving money around. Secret hedge funds and stuff."

"Anyone else in there?"

"Doesn't look like it, but if he's got security, they might be laying low. Keeping quiet and unobtrusive."

While Redd considered this, Tanaka weighed in. "He might not have anyone. He knows we're looking for him. An entourage would just attract attention."

"That will make our job a whole lot easier," Fleetwood said.

"Nothing is ever easy," Redd said. "If we stroll in there expecting no resistance, we could get surprised real fast."

He quickly outlined the plan and timetable that he had given Kline, then added, "Let's pull the drone back for now. I don't want to take any chances on Gage or one of his men spotting it. We'll maintain audio surveillance only until it gets a little darker. Tanaka, see if you can find a floor plan for the villa online. It looks pretty open, but better to be sure. We've got the time. We're going to rehearse until we can do this blindfolded if we have to."

✖   ✖   ✖

With Fleetwood, Tanaka, and Jones maintaining surveillance on the villa, Redd made the forty-minute drive back across the island to a Spanish National Police Corps—CNP—training facility located in the general aviation area of the Palma airport, where the rest of the team was standing by. He found them in the shoot house, running through dry-fire entry exercises along with four shooters from the elite tactical Grupo Especial de Operaciones—GEO—the CNP's equivalent of the FBI's hostage rescue team.

Kline had negotiated use of the training facility as a staging area with the understanding that going after Anton Gage would be a joint operation. It was a political decision, not a tactical one, and while Redd knew that the GEO operators were every bit as competent as his own men, he was apprehensive about trying to coordinate with the Spanish team, especially on such short notice. Special mission units were successful because the individuals who comprised the teams trained together for hundreds of hours until they were as in tune with each other as the musicians in an orchestra. He had gone along with the arrangement up to this point because he didn't have a choice, but now that Gage's presence was confirmed, he faced the added challenge of figuring out a way to involve the Spanish police without actually involving them. He figured he had about eight hours to crack that nut.

Using the blueprints as a guide, Redd's team created a fairly accurate facsimile of Gage's villa in the shoot house, with plywood panels held in place by sandbags to simulate interior walls. Once that task was complete, they resumed their dry-fire drills, running through almost every conceivable variation of the anticipated raid. Redd would have preferred live-fire rehearsals with pop-up targets—simply shouting, "Bang, bang" did not prepare one for the noise and smoke and fury of going in hot—but time and circumstances, not to mention a limited supply of ammunition, necessitated restraint. He wasn't overly concerned about it. The team had spent plenty of time on the range, and he had drilled with them four days a month for the last nine months. They all knew what to expect. These rehearsals were just a matter of fine-tuning before going live.

They were into something like the thirtieth iteration when Redd got a call from Fleetwood.

The agent came right to the point. "We got a problem, boss. I'm gonna play you what we just heard."

There was the briefest pause, and then Redd heard Anton Gage's voice in his ear. "Let's hold on to the crypto for now. I've got a feeling the Chinese are going to reverse their position on that, and when . . ."

Gage trailed off, and then a new voice could be heard, a man's voice, low but urgent. "Sorry to interrupt, Mr. Gage."

The voice was not Giroux's, which meant there was at least one other person in the villa, possibly a bodyguard. Also, they now had independent confirmation that the man whose voice he'd identified was Anton Gage. Redd's satisfied grin slipped, however, when he heard the rest of what the newcomer had to say.

"We've just received word that this location is compromised."

"Compromised?" Gage's easygoing manner instantly transitioned to wariness.

"The FBI knows that you're here. They're already moving resources into place."

You've got to be kidding me!

Redd's nostrils flared as he fought to keep his temper in check. This was exactly what he knew would happen once the bureaucracy got involved. Someone had leaked information about the impending raid, and now Gage knew they were closing in.

"How long do we have?"

"Hard to say. We should leave immediately."

There was a brief pause and then Gage spoke again. "We're too vulnerable on the roads. Have the helicopter pick us up here. We can fly directly to the yacht."

"Helicopter?" Redd snarled as if spitting out a curse.

"That will take a while to set up," Gage's aide cautioned.

"How long?"

"An hour. Maybe a little longer."

"Do it."

Redd had heard enough. "Mac, come back."

The audio playback ended and Fleetwood spoke. "I'm here, boss. What's our play?"

"Get the drone back up. I need to know everything there is to know about that villa. How many hostiles, where they are, how they're armed." He took a breath, then added, "And be ready to move when we get there."

He hung up without further explanation and stepped back into the shoot house. "FRAGO!" he shouted, employing military shorthand for "fragmentary order," the term used when there was a minor change to the mission plan. "We're moving out now!"

After a moment of stunned silence, the fly team operators shifted gears, checking their weapons, securing equipment and ammunition that had been put aside during the rehearsals. The GEO shooters exchanged confused glances; then their leader, Alex Tomas, approached Redd.

"What is going on?" he asked.

His English was just a little better than Redd's Spanish, or as Tomas had derisively called it, "your Mexican." There were enough differences between Tomas's native tongue and the dialect Redd had learned during nearly a decade of living in San Diego and making weekend runs to Tijuana to make communicating in English the preferred option.

Redd debated trying to mislead the Spaniard. Given what he was planning to do, he certainly didn't need any interference from the local authorities, and he would never get a better chance than this to slip the leash. On the other hand, there were advantages to having the locals on his side. He decided to take a chance on them.

"Somebody warned Gage. He's planning to evacuate by helicopter in about an hour. If we're going to take him down, we have to move. *Now.*"

That explanation seemed to suffice. Tomas and the GEO team were door kickers like Redd and didn't need convincing. Tomas nodded and turned back to his men, urging them to follow the Americans' lead. Redd wondered if the phone call he was about to make to Kline would go as smoothly.

TWO

"Negative," Kline said flatly. "I'm sorry, but it's not going to happen. There's no way I'll be able to get approval inside of an hour. You have to stand down."

Redd's fist tightened around the sat phone handset. With an effort, he kept his temper in check. Kline's response was not unexpected.

Redd took a deep, calming breath and stared out the side window of the van as it sped along the Ma-13 motorway, one of two main highways that stretched across the island. Anticipating resistance, he'd put off making the call to Kline until they were on the move, with the two teams and all their gear loaded into a pair of unmarked passenger vans. The landscape flashing by outside reminded him of Southern California, which wasn't all that surprising since both locations were at about the same latitude and had a similar climate. But thinking about California made him think about his military service. And how it had ended.

He let the breath out, then gave the answer he had rehearsed. "It took us more than a year to find him. If he gets away now, we might not get that lucky again."

"He's not going to get away," Kline countered. "We'll be able to track every move he makes."

"You think he doesn't know that?" Redd's self-control slipped a little. He took another breath, then continued in a more even tone. "I'm not confident we'll be able to track him once he leaves that villa. There are too many ways he could slip the net. And somebody is feeding Gage intel about our operations. That's why he's been able to stay one step ahead of us. We won't get another chance like this."

"I understand your concerns, Matty."

Redd felt his cheeks go hot at the use of the juvenile nickname. His mother had called him that, despite his increasingly strident objections, until the day he found her dead with a needle in her arm. He hadn't minded it as much when Emily had called him that back when they were high school sweethearts, or when she did now, for that matter, but the list of people who could get away with calling him Matty was short, and Gavin Kline wasn't on it.

"But this is the way it has to be," Kline went on. "We can't risk an international incident." As if realizing how pathetic that sounded, he added, "You'll get another shot. I promise. Maybe sooner than you think."

Redd knew Kline wasn't going to budge. He managed, barely, to rein in his anger, and when he spoke, his voice was as flat and unyielding as steel. "You know what, Gavin? Don't sweat it. I'll take care of it."

Then he hung up and powered down the phone.

"So no go?" said Rob Davis, the team's weapons expert and Redd's second-in-command. Although Davis and the other men had only heard Redd's side of the conversation, their leader's reaction filled in all the gaps.

Redd shook his head. "We're driving on. I won't let Gage slip away again."

Davis, a senior FBI agent with more than fifteen years of experience, leaned in close, whispering so that only Redd could hear. "You know I'd follow you into hell, brother. But going rogue is not an option."

Redd managed a grim smile. "Don't worry. I've got it covered."

✗ ✗ ✗

They gathered at the ersatz floral delivery van, where Fleetwood updated them on the situation inside the villa. "We've confirmed four men, including Gage and Giroux. The other two might be bodyguards, but we can't tell if they're armed. There hasn't been much chatter from inside since they decided to bug out."

Redd nodded. "Any word on when that helo is going to show up?"

"Someone inside gave an ETA of twenty minutes. That was eight minutes ago. So if we're going to do this, we have to go right now."

Davis cleared his throat. "Redd, are you going to tell them, or am I?"

"Tell us what?" Tanaka asked.

Redd shot a frown in Davis's direction, then addressed the group. "Kline won't give us the green light. It's political."

The revelation elicited a round of murmured complaints, but Redd quickly silenced them with a raised hand. "We're not going to let Gage slip away again." He turned to Tomas. "We might not have the authority to go in there, but you do."

The Spaniard raised a suspicious eyebrow. "I am not certain about that. We were assigned to work with you, so if you don't have authorization, neither do we."

Redd waved his hand to dismiss the objection. "You're cops, right? Police officers? There's an international fugitive in that villa and he's about to escape. That's all the authorization you need. You and your men can go in. Detain Gage, keep him in custody until Kline sorts out the red tape. That way we avoid an international incident. We'll back you up, but strictly as observers . . . unless the situation calls for something more."

The individual members of the two tactical teams exchanged nervous glances. Finally Davis spoke up. "This doesn't exactly sound kosher, Redd."

"I'm not going to ask any of you to do anything illegal. And I'll take any heat that comes our way . . . But believe me, once we've got Gage in custody, nobody's going to care if we ignored some internal procedures."

There was another protracted silence. Redd could tell from the looks on his men's faces that he had failed to convince them.

"Guys, come on. He's right there." Redd stabbed a finger in the direction of the villa. "But we have to go. Right. Now."

Tomas clapped his hand against his thigh. "We'll do it. The thought of this . . . this scum Gage going free . . ." He shook his head. "But there are only four of us. I would humbly ask that my American friends, acting in their capacity as observers, of course, come in after us to secure the rooms as we clear them."

Redd nodded as he turned to Davis. "What do you say, Rob?"

Davis let out a heavy sigh. "Why not? I hear pensions are overrated anyway."

"Then let's do this." Redd broke from the huddle and reached inside the van to collect one last piece of equipment—an eight-pound Fiskars splitting maul. Hefting it, he turned to Tomas. "I'll get the door."

※　※　※

Unlike an ordinary neighborhood, the palatial residences that dotted the hills above Pollença existed in a state of mutual isolation, hidden behind privacy hedges and security walls. So despite the fact that it was late afternoon, the assault element was able to close in on the objective without attracting any attention. If anyone noticed the men in full tactical kit moving stealthily down the road, they did not come out to watch.

A twelve-foot-high stucco-covered wall surrounded the villa, and a steel gate blocked the driveway. An aerial survey of the compound with the drone had revealed security cameras trained on the gate, but there appeared to be no coverage along the walls. Working together, the assault teams surmounted the wall in a matter of just a few seconds. Once on the other side, Fleetwood and Tanaka set up an overwatch position to cover the gate, eliminating the only avenue of escape, while the others crossed the manicured lawn to the front entrance. There was no indication that anyone inside the villa had observed the covert entry, but every man on the ground knew that the apparent quiet might conceal an ambush.

They lined up to either side of the French doors, with the GEO team on the left and the fly team on the right. At a signal from Tomas, Redd stepped up and drew back the maul, ready to batter down the door, but then the leader of the Spanish team held up his hand, palm out, indicating that Redd should hold fast. Upon receiving an answering nod from Redd, Tomas reached out and depressed the thumb latch on the ornate entry handle. There was a faint click as the latch disengaged and the door opened a crack.

Unlocked.

Redd wasn't sure if that was a good sign or not, but Tomas didn't hesitate. He pushed through the doorway, followed by the rest of his team, suppressed Heckler & Koch MP5s at the high ready. Immediately after entering, each man turned in a different direction, covering his assigned sector of the room.

Redd held his breath, waiting for the sound of gunfire, suppressed or otherwise, but heard nothing. He took a second to slide the orange fiberglass handle of the maul through a carabiner clipped to his assault vest, then readied his own MP5 and headed inside after the GEO team, who were already stacking in preparation to move to the next room.

They moved as swiftly and silently as wraiths, entering every room, checking every closet and cupboard. Two minutes into the raid, Redd heard a shout from the next room—the sitting room on the far side of the villa, where they'd observed Gage and Giroux on the drone camera, if his mental map of the interior was accurate. It was Tomas, identifying himself as a policeman and ordering someone to get down.

Redd tightened his grip on his MP5, expecting the bullets to start flying, but the initial shouts were followed only by the scuffle of suspects being disarmed and restrained.

A beat later, Tomas called out again. "Clear!"

Redd advanced into the room, keeping the muzzle of his weapon down to avoid flagging the GEO operators, and saw them standing over four prone figures—facedown on the floor, arms and legs splayed in a demonstration of total submission. Tomas and another of his men were covering the detainees with their MP5s, while the other two were moving in to frisk and restrain.

They had done it, and without a single shot fired.

Redd fixated on the captive with the flowing mane of blond hair whose face was pressed against the luxurious Berber carpet and mostly hidden from view. As he stared at the motionless man, Redd's initial excitement at their success was pierced by a thin sliver of apprehension.

That was too easy. Something's not right.

After signaling his intention to Tomas, Redd moved in and knelt beside the blond man. Without saying a word, he reached down with one gloved hand, grasped the man's shoulder, and flipped him over, exposing his face to view.

It wasn't Anton Gage.

THREE

MONTANA

Not for the first time since leaving home, Emily Redd's gaze drifted up to the rearview mirror. The reflected image remained unchanged. The infant car seat, secured in the center of the Tahoe's middle row of seats, faced backward, which meant that all she could see from her present vantage was the back of the molded plastic safety seat. Its silent occupant was hidden from her view.

Emily brought her attention back to the road, her lips forming a quiet prayer.

Please be okay, baby.

She had first noticed the fever the previous afternoon when she picked Junior up from day care, sensing it with that preternatural attunement only a mother possesses and confirming with a quick check using a temporal artery thermometer: 38.7 degrees Celsius.

Normal body temperature was 37. It was a fever, though not yet a serious one.

As a medical professional—Emily was a nurse practitioner at the Stillwater County Health Center—she knew that mild fevers were not unusual in infants. A one- or two-degree rise in body temperature was their immune response to a host of different factors, and the condition often resolved without medical intervention. If she had been advising the parent of a patient, she would have recommended a dose of infant Tylenol every four to six hours and to check back in forty-eight hours or if the fever got worse—say 39 degrees or 102.2 degrees Fahrenheit.

But she wasn't a doctor advising a patient right now. She was a mother with a sick child.

She had, with some effort, tried to stay calm and follow the standard advice. She'd dosed little Matty with Tylenol—3.75 milliliters of the syrup solution—but twelve hours later, the fever had not come down, and Dr. Emily's influence over Mama Redd was down to zero. She'd put in a call to Junior's pediatrician in Bozeman and had taken the first available appointment.

Bozeman was a ninety-minute drive from the ranch, which was just north of Wellington. Wellington was the county seat and only real population center of any consequence in Stillwater County, which wasn't saying much. Trips to Bozeman, or north to Helena, were a routine part of living out in the sticks in Big Sky Country, and ordinarily, the miles flashed by while she indulged her favorite Spotify playlist or a new audiobook. Today it seemed to take forever.

Emily groaned aloud when she passed a sign that proclaimed "I-90 Junction 15 miles."

Fifteen more miles? I should be there already.

Once she reached the interstate highway, it would take her about twenty minutes to reach the city limits and, she knew from experience, another ten to reach the pediatrician's office. Half an hour, just to get to the waiting room, where she would no doubt be subject to another interminable delay, but at least she would be able to *see* her son, hold him in her arms. Not being able to see him was the worst thing about the drive. If Matthew had been here, she would have made him drive so she could sit with Junior, but he was off doing his FBI thing somewhere.

She didn't begrudge his decision to join the fly team. In fact, she had encouraged him to do it. It was good for him to keep a foot in the outside world. Matthew Redd was too big a man to be completely contained in Stillwater County. It was just that the timing was pretty lousy. Hopefully, this episode would pass quickly, and little Matty would be back to his normal, energetic self by the time Daddy got home.

Without thinking, she glanced in the mirror again.

Useless.

But this time her eye caught something else. A motorcycle coming up behind her. It definitely had not been there the last time she looked.

She glanced down at the speedometer. The Tahoe was cruising along just shy of eighty miles per hour. For the rider to have caught up to her, he must have been doing in excess of ninety. From the machine's profile, she could tell that it was not a sleek, aerodynamic racing bike—a crotch rocket, as her father called them—but a big cruiser, a "hog." Bikes like that weren't built for that kind of speed, certainly not for sustained periods.

She shook her head. There was a reason that many of the emergency room doctors she had worked with called motorcycle riders "organ donors."

The motorcycle continued to close, confirming her estimation of its size and configuration, but also affording her a look at its rider.

The man looked like something out of a Norse epic—a relentless berserker, possessed by battle fury. The hulking figure was not hunched over against the rush of air but rode with arms extended up to the grips of the bike's ape hanger handlebars. He wore no helmet, and his only apparent concession to safety was a pair of dark wraparound sunglasses. His copper-red hair and prodigious beard were pulled back taut by the fierce wind, his teeth bared in what was either a grimace of discomfort or a defiant grin.

"Maniac," Emily muttered, shaking her head again.

The rider kept advancing, devouring the distance separating them, and for the first time since spotting him, Emily felt a twinge of apprehension.

What's he doing?

She replayed the drive in her head, trying to recall if she had passed the motorcyclist back in Wellington and perhaps cut him off or done something else to warrant his ire. He wasn't there in her memory, but distracted as she was by little Matty's condition, it wasn't impossible.

She quickly considered her options, which weren't many. She could speed up and try to leave him behind, or she could slow down and encourage him to pass.

She didn't like option one. The Tahoe wasn't built for that kind of speed either, and she had Junior to think of. At higher speeds, there was a much greater likelihood of losing control. Small errors could magnify into cascading failures with catastrophic outcomes. A sudden swerve to avoid an obstacle might lead to a rollover accident.

On the other hand, if this was the beginning of a road rage incident, slowing down might be just what the biker was hoping for. But if the guy tried something, she could always floor it or, if things got extreme, use the Tahoe's superior size and stability as a weapon of self-defense.

With only seconds to decide, she made what she hoped was the safer choice and slid her foot from the gas pedal to the brake, tapping it without actually pressing down, hoping that the flash of brake lights would signal her intent. The bike was so close that any sudden deceleration might cause him to rear-end her. Even without applying the brakes, the big SUV immediately began to shed velocity.

As if anticipating her decision, the biker smoothly swerved left into the opposing lane and shot past her like she had come to a complete stop. As it passed, the roar of the bike's unmuffled engine, which had barely been audible when it was behind her, escalated to an apocalyptic crescendo that reverberated through the Tahoe and churned Emily's insides. As the decibels retreated, a new sound joined the cacophony—a shrill wail she knew only too well. Junior was now screaming his lungs out.

Emily bit back an oath that would have earned more than just a reproving look from her father, a longtime preacher, and tightened her grip on the steering wheel.

"Hush, little guy," she said, hoping the sound of her voice would be enough to calm him.

It wasn't, but the noise from outside was thankfully diminishing as the bike got out ahead of the Tahoe. As it had passed, she'd gotten a better look at the rider. In profile, she could not help but notice his immense size, which only reinforced her mental impression of a crazed Viking warrior. Although it was hard to be sure given that he was in a seated position, she thought he must be nearly seven feet tall, but unlike most tall men who tended to be thin, this man was thick with muscle. His black leather vest, the only thing covering his torso, left his tattooed arms bare, revealing biceps that looked almost as big as Emily's thighs. The back of the vest was adorned with an embroidered patch depicting a variation of the Jolly Roger, the classic skull-and-crossbones pirate flag, only in this likeness, the skull had flames in its eyes and the bones had been replaced by a piston and rod and a dagger dripping blood. A rocker across the top displayed the word *Infidels*, while a smaller square patch to the right of the image had just two letters, *MC*.

Outlaw bikers, whether affiliated with a "motorcycle club"—a clever euphemism for "gang"—or not, came and went from Wellington like the tide, and like the tide, their coming brought disruption and even destruction. Their appearance usually signaled an uptick in emergency room activity, from road accidents, violence, or worst of all, drug overdoses in the community at large. Trafficking in illicit substances—fentanyl was a new favorite, but meth was still in high demand—remained a primary enterprise for the outlaw bikers. It had been a couple years since Emily had seen a biker openly displaying his patch, and she wondered if this signaled the start of another cycle of biker activity.

She did not understand the quasi-romantic mystique surrounding motorcycle gangs, any more than she understood why people, especially men, tended to associate organized crime figures with masculinity. As far as she was concerned, they were a threat to public safety on a good day. Today the threat felt a lot more personal.

With the biker no longer behind her, she eased down on the brake, shedding even more forward velocity, and let the motorcycle increase its lead. No sooner had she done this than the motorcycle slowed abruptly and swerved back into her lane, cutting it so close that for a moment, the bike's rear wheel was eclipsed by the Tahoe's front end.

The close call sent a fresh surge of adrenaline through Emily. She pressed the brake a little harder, trying to give the biker even more of a lead, but as she did, the motorcycle's brake light flashed on—a cyclopean red eye, glaring a warning.

A cry slipped from Emily's lips as she jammed down on the brake pedal. There was a squeal of rubber on pavement that ended when the antilock brake system engaged, preventing the vehicle from going into a skid but also increasing the likelihood of plowing into the motorcycle. For a moment, all she could do was squeeze the steering wheel and pray.

Just when it seemed that a collision was unavoidable, the bike's brake light winked out, and the machine shot forward again. Emily maintained pressure on the brake pedal, bringing the Tahoe to a complete stop as the motorcycle sped away.

Shaken, with little Matty's shrieks reverberating in the close confines of the Tahoe's interior, Emily needed a moment to collect her wits.

You've got to move, she told herself. *You're stopped in the middle of the road. It's not safe.*

She drew in a shuddering breath and slid her foot over to the accelerator. As if influenced by her emotional state, the big SUV seemed sluggish in its response, mired in inertia. She realized the problem wasn't with the vehicle, but rather with her. She was barely pressing on the gas pedal. With an effort, she pressed harder, and the Tahoe gradually picked up speed.

But before the speedometer needle reached forty, she spotted the motorcycle in the distance. It still appeared to be moving, but only just, creeping along at twenty or twenty-five miles an hour.

It was almost as if the rider wanted her to catch up.

"Nope," she said aloud. "We're not going to do that again."

Her voice was calm, projecting a confidence she didn't feel. She squeezed the steering wheel again, steeling herself, and maintained pressure on the gas pedal, accelerating steadily, closing with the slow-moving motorcycle.

This time she would not back down. If the biker challenged her or dared her to a game of chicken, he would lose.

"Hang on, baby," she added, reflexively shooting another futile glance at the rearview mirror. Her soothing admonition fell silent. The mirror showed several more motorcycles approaching from behind. It was hard to say exactly how many, but they were traveling three abreast in at least two ranks, so at least six, but possibly a dozen or even more.

Emily's chest tightened; her blood felt like ice in her veins as she began to grasp the gravity of the situation in which she now found herself.

This is bad. This is really bad.

Her mind raced, searching for a way out as she said a silent prayer.

The gun?

There was a revolver—a Smith & Wesson .38—in a locked gun safe bolted into the center compartment. Matthew had insisted on it, calling it "roadside assistance." Emily was comfortable using firearms, less so with using them on humans or having them in places where little Matty might someday find them. But shooting while driving? That wasn't in her skill set. The revolver would only be useful if she came to a complete stop, and that was the last thing she wanted to do right now.

Call 911?

Her gaze flitted to the center console where her iPhone rested, plugged into the charger. With Siri, she could make the call without even touching the phone, but then what? Even if there was a sheriff's deputy or highway patrolman in the area, it would take a few minutes at the very least for them to reach her. She had only seconds to escape this trap.

Besides, she couldn't afford to divide her attention right now. No, her best choice—her only choice, really—was to reach a populated area where the bikers would be less likely to menace her. But despite her constant acceleration, the pack of motorcycles was closing in. Meanwhile the Tahoe was approaching the bike that had passed her, ridden by the man she thought of as "Berserker."

Emily kept her foot pressed down as a plan began to form. All she had to do was get past Berserker and then drive like mad for Bozeman. He was only about a hundred yards in front of her now. She could hear the throaty roar of his unmuffled engine, heard it rise a little in pitch as he throttled up, surging ahead just enough to slow the relative rate of her advance. Then, as if sensing what she was about to attempt, the biker swerved left, into the oncoming lane, then right, then back again in a serpentine undulation designed to prevent her from passing.

For a moment—only a moment—his strategy worked. Emily hesitated, easing her foot off the gas pedal. It was an instinctive response, the result of many years of trying to avoid collisions, but she quickly overcame it and floored the accelerator again, holding the wheel steady. She wasn't going to bother trying to pass Berserker. If he didn't get out of the way, she would roll right over him. Her only concession was to honk the Tahoe's horn in a single long blast as she closed the remaining distance.

She might as well have shouted into a hurricane. The horn's eruption was completely overwhelmed by engine noise—not from Berserker's bike, but from at least a dozen others. In the brief instant in which she had hesitated, the pack had made their move, swarming around the Tahoe on all sides.

She was surrounded. Three motorcycles had pulled up alongside to her left, and three more to her right, so close that, if they wanted to, they could have reached out and touched the SUV. Two more had raced ahead, bracketing Berserker and forming a picket line in front of her, while two ranks of two remained stationed at the Tahoe's rear.

Then, over the roar of the bikes and Matty's screams, came a new sound, one not so much heard as felt. It was a dull, insistent thud, like the beat of a bass drum, reverberating through her like a series of rapid-fire gut punches. The bikers were beating the Tahoe's fenders with their fists.

Had she been able to think straight, she would have realized just how much danger the bikers were putting themselves in with this display of force. Dividing their attention, removing one hand from the handlebars while trying to maintain a high rate of speed and a true course, and while separated from a larger vehicle by mere inches, was an extraordinary feat. And an extraordinary risk.

But thinking straight was impossible for her. Primal fear had elbowed her higher brain function aside. She couldn't think, couldn't act. She held on to the steering wheel, but her knees bent, pulling her foot away from the gas pedal. It was all she could do to keep from curling up in a fetal ball.

The Tahoe immediately began losing speed again.

A voice in her head, not her own but Matthew's, shouted, *Don't stop! Whatever you do, don't stop!*

But her body stubbornly refused to acknowledge. The Tahoe was slowing. Forty mph. Thirty-five . . . thirty.

The pounding intensified.

Do something!

A cry tore past her lips as she bludgeoned through the mental barrier and jammed her foot down on the accelerator. The tachometer needle leaped into the red as the V8 revved. She eased back a little, struggling to tune out the overwhelming sensory assault and stay focused on escape.

She turned the steering wheel to the left, into the path of the bikers hanging out there, but they easily swerved away, all the while keeping her at an arm's length. She swung in the other direction, but the bikers on the other side avoided her just as easily.

They were sending her a message. A taunt.

"We can do this all day."

But her attempt at fighting back had, if only momentarily, stopped them from pounding on the Tahoe's exterior, and that gave her a moment to think. She snatched the phone out of the center console and shouted, "Siri, call 911!"

Nothing happened. Evidently the device could not differentiate her voice from all the other noise.

She held the phone closer and tried again, shouting at the top of her lungs, and this time it worked. The display went dark and then showed the words *Calling 911 in* . . . followed by a five-second countdown. Emily held the phone to her ear. Over the din, she could just make out the trill of an outgoing call and then, harder to distinguish, the dispatcher's voice.

Emily didn't need to hear the woman on the other end of the line; she just needed to be heard.

"My name is Emily Redd. I'm heading south on the highway about twenty-five miles from Bozeman. I'm being attacked by a gang of bikers." She didn't know what else to say, so she just repeated her location and added, "They're trying to run me off the road."

She paused then and could hear the dispatcher's voice in her ear but still couldn't make out what was being said.

Suddenly, without any visible precursor, the bikes on either side peeled away, making broad U-turns and heading back in the direction of Wellington. Far ahead, Berserker had already come around and, a moment later, flashed past in the northbound lane. The roar of engine noise faded as the Tahoe, still cruising forward at about forty miles per hour, pulled away from the retreating pack. In a matter of seconds, the bikers were lost from view, vanishing like a nightmare upon waking. Only the memory of the encounter remained. In the near distance, Emily could see the exit that would take her onto I-90 east.

Junior was still wailing in the back seat, but his cries weren't loud enough to drown out the dispatcher.

"Ma'am, are you still there?"

As the adrenaline drained away, Emily wanted nothing more than to pull over, shut the car off, sag against the steering wheel, and cry her eyes out. Or maybe throw up. But she didn't dare stop.

What if they come back?

She maintained pressure on the gas pedal and, when she was able to catch her breath, spoke into the phone. "I'm all right now. You don't need to send anyone. I'll contact the sheriff's department and make a report."

"Ma'am, can you—?"

Emily ended the call, set the phone on the empty passenger seat beside her, and took the exit to Bozeman.

FOUR

Redd didn't linger on the scene to figure out what had gone wrong, how they had been duped, or more importantly, how Gage had been forewarned. Maybe he hadn't. Maybe the setup at the villa had been arranged out of an abundance of caution on Gage's part. Redd didn't think so. But figuring that out could wait until the fly team was back on friendlier ground.

Within an hour of the failed raid, the team was back at the shoot house, deconstructing the mock building of Gage's house and erasing any trace of their being there. Tomas, who had been surprisingly nonchalant about the gaffe, had volunteered to take the HEAT round—assuming responsibility for the raid and taking the Gage look-alike and the others into custody in order to give Redd and the FBI team time to get out of the country.

Eventually the truth would come out and there would be hell to pay, but at least they wouldn't get caught high and dry in a foreign country.

They were over the Atlantic when Kline found them. When Redd saw Kline's number on the display of his sat phone, he took a deep breath and readied himself to meet the director's wrath with a little righteous indignation of his own. But Kline didn't give him the opportunity.

"Your plane is scheduled to arrive at 11:20 a.m.," Kline snapped, skipping the usual pleasantries. "Be in my office by noon."

Before Redd could open his mouth to answer, a double beep sounded in his ear, signaling that the call had already ended.

Redd stared at the sat phone feeling equal parts relief and irritation. Relief at having postponed the inevitable chewing out a little longer and irritation at having been denied the chance to speak his mind.

Gage had known they were closing in and had set a trap for them—not a lethal trap, but rather one designed to embarrass the FBI. To make them think twice before trying to pursue him internationally. But where was he getting his information?

"Was that the boss?"

Redd looked up and met the gaze of Rob Davis, seated across the aisle. With an effort, he unclenched his jaw. "Yeah."

"What did he say?"

"Not much. He's pissed off, but so am I." He shook his head. "Don't worry about Kline. I'll take responsibility for what happened. I'll make sure he knows that I gave the order to go in over your strenuous objections."

Davis nodded slowly. "For what it's worth, I think you made the right call. Even if it did go pear-shaped."

Redd just grunted. He wasn't so sure he *had* made the right call, and the more he thought about it, the more obvious it was that they had been played.

And that *really* pissed him off.

The impostor bore only a passing resemblance to Gage, and even less of one once his blond wig was removed. There hadn't been time to establish his identity, but when Tomas had questioned him, it had been immediately apparent that the man was local. An actor with no actual knowledge of Gage's operation. The fact that he had kept his back to the window meant whoever had hired him had been aware that watchful eyes would be looking into the house. The critical piece of the deception—the conversation they had overheard, which had led to Redd's positive ID of Anton Gage—had been produced electronically, either with a recording or a live transmission from some other location. The very fact that the little dramatic production had been arranged in the first place strongly suggested Gage knew, or at least suspected, the FBI was closing in. But how had he known? Was there a leak? A mole?

To Redd, that was the most important takeaway from the failed raid. Gage had a source inside the bureau, and that was reason for real and immediate concern. Redd had, in his first tangle with Gage, exposed Kline's predecessor, Rachel Culp, as a traitor working for Gage, but that did not mean she was the only one. This time the only wound suffered had been to their pride. Next time they might not be so lucky.

If Kline was planning to light him up for a minor procedural breach, Redd was going to hit back. Hard.

Redd didn't try explaining any of this to Davis. He was still trying to work it out for himself. When the sat phone rang again, he accepted the call without even looking at the number and preempted Kline's next rant by speaking first.

"Gavin, just shut up and listen. We were set up. Gage knew we were—"

A voice that didn't belong to Kline cut him off. "Matt, it's Mikey."

It took Redd a moment to switch gears. "Mikey?" Then, because he knew his friend would never call unless there was a serious reason, he added, "What's wrong?"

✻ ✻ ✻

When he had returned to Stillwater County after so many years away, a ranch and a high school sweetheart were not the only things Matthew Redd rediscovered. Once he'd gotten over the culture shock of transitioning from a life of military discipline and camaraderie to the small-town lifestyle he had never imagined he would return to, he began to recall the things he had longed for during those first grueling days at boot camp. One of those things had been his friendship with Michael "Mikey" Derhammer.

Their friendship had begun not long after Redd came to live with his adoptive father, J. B. Like Redd, Mikey had grown up without a father, and that common experience, which in many ways isolated them from their peers in the small-town middle school they attended, formed the basis for a strong friendship that had lasted until high school.

Then, during Redd's junior year, J. B. had been laid up with a serious back injury, and Redd had felt compelled to quit school in order to work the ranch on his father's behalf. Because he had dropped out so abruptly, and because he was too proud to ask anyone for help, his closest friends—Emily and Mikey—thought he had simply ghosted them, and in a way, that was exactly what he had done. By the time J. B. got back on his feet, Redd had his GED and was ready for a change of scenery, so he signed on the dotted line, took the oath, and headed off to boot camp, thinking he'd never return.

Although his relationship with Emily had quickly rekindled following his return to Montana, Redd had initially been wary about reaching out to Mikey. Fortunately for both men, Emily was not about to let the years come between them. Mikey worked for her father, Elijah Lawrence, effectively managing his auto body shop now that the old man was mostly retired, and Mikey's wife, Elizabeth, was Emily's best friend, so there wasn't a chance that she would let the two men remain estranged. For Mikey, it was as if the Prodigal Son had returned. They had immediately reconnected, and all past sins were forgiven.

And so, when Redd explained that he would be spending part of every month back East doing some contract work for the government—the exact nature of the work had to remain a secret, even from his best friend—Mikey had made a solemn promise. "Don't worry about a thing. We'll look after Em and Junior."

Emily had just rolled her eyes. She didn't need "looking after," thank you very much.

Nevertheless, knowing that Mikey and Liz were there for his family helped put his mind at ease when he went away for training, and especially when his work with the fly team sent him into harm's way.

He never actually expected Mikey to call, though, and the fact that he had sent a chill down Redd's spine.

"They're okay," Mikey said quickly, answering the most important question first. "Just a little shaken up."

"What happened?" Redd's imagination was already running wild. A car wreck? Emily was a safe driver, but there were plenty of idiots on the road. He couldn't imagine what else it might be.

But if Mikey was calling instead of Emily, just how "okay" was she?

Then Mikey told him.

"She said they came out of nowhere. A dozen of them, all riding big hogs and wearing jackets that said Infidels on them. I've seen them around town a few times over the years but never heard of them causing any trouble with ordinary folks."

The description rang a bell for Redd, who instantly felt a ball of rage form in his stomach.

"They pulled up beside her and started beating on her rig," Mikey went on. "And this wasn't sitting at a stoplight, dude. This all happened while she was rolling down the highway. They rattled her cage. Put a good scare into her, but it doesn't look like they did any permanent damage."

No permanent damage?

Redd realized Mikey was probably talking about the Tahoe.

Biting back his fury, which wasn't really directed at Mikey anyway, Redd asked, "Does Sheriff Blackwood know?"

"I called him. He said he'd look into it, but he sounded kinda funny about it. I think these bikers have him a little spooked. They've never done anything like this before."

"Where's Em now?"

"I convinced her to stay the night. Her and Liz just got the boys to sleep." Mikey and Liz had a two-year-old son named Luke, and the families tried to arrange playdates for the boys whenever circumstances permitted, in hopes of creating an enduring friendship like the one shared by their parents. "She didn't want me to call you, didn't want you worrying while you're off saving the world," Mikey said a tad sarcastically, "but I thought you should know."

Redd nodded unconsciously. "I appreciate it. Can you put her on?"

"All right, hang on."

The silence that followed was the longest thirty seconds of Redd's life. Then Emily's voice sounded in his ear. "Matty?"

"Em, are you okay? Is Junior okay?"

"We're fine," she said.

He didn't think she sounded fine.

"I don't know what Mikey told you," she went on, "but it was nothing. I'm more concerned about Junior. He's running a little hot. Dr. Beech said to treat it with Tylenol, but it doesn't seem to be helping."

She was talking fast—too fast—a sure sign that she wanted to distract him from the real issue at hand.

"But I've got things under control, Matty. I don't want you worrying about us. Not when you're . . ." She hesitated a beat, presumably trying to come up with a euphemism to hide the nature of Redd's work from Mikey and Liz. "When you're in the field."

"I'm already on my way home." He did some quick mental math. It was possible to make the trip from DC to Bozeman in six hours, if the layover in Denver wasn't too long, but he had to factor in the time difference as well. "I'll be there by dinnertime at the latest."

"Well, that's great." Her sincere joy at this news quickly changed to wariness. Before leaving, he had told her that the op might last a week or more. A truncated timeline meant that things had either gone very well or very wrong, and she knew it. "Is everything okay? Did you—?"

"It's fine. I'll tell you about it later. I want you to stay with Mikey and Liz until I get back. I mean *stay there*. Don't go out for any reason."

"Matty, you're making a fuss over nothing."

Redd closed his eyes and took a deep breath before responding. "Please, Em. Do this for me."

There was a long silence, followed by a sigh. "If it will make you feel better."

"It will. Can you put Mikey back on?"

"Sure. Just a sec."

There was a faint rustling over the line, and then Mikey's voice. "Yo."

"Mikey, I need you to do something for me."

Anticipating the request, Mikey said, "You want Em and Junior to stay with us. You don't even have to ask, brother."

"Keep them *there*, Mikey. Don't let her out of your sight." He paused a beat, then added, "And keep a gun close. Just in case."

"You think we'll have trouble?" A hint of alarm intruded into Mikey's tone.

"I don't know. But I'll feel a lot better knowing that you're ready for it if it comes. I'll be back tomorrow evening."

"What are we talking about here, bro? This a handgun or shotgun kind of situation?"

"Both. Keep 'em handy. Again, just in case."

There was a slight pause. "You have a run-in or something with these guys?"

Redd thought back to the year before, when he threw one of the Infidels a beating, then told another to get lost before sunup the next morning. Now, more than anything, he wished he would have made good on his promise to ensure they left town.

"Something like that," Redd replied. "Said some stuff they didn't really care for. Might have body-slammed one of them into the ground."

"Man, you gotta learn to watch your mouth. Always did get you into trouble."

Redd suppressed a groan. His friend wasn't wrong, and being stuck on a plane wasn't helping.

"Matt . . . they're okay," Mikey said again, offering reassurance Redd had not asked for. "We'll take care of them."

"I know you will, Mikey. Thanks."

He ended the call, realizing only after the connection was broken that he had forgotten to tell Emily he loved her. Since they'd gotten back together, he had been almost superstitious about professing his love whenever they parted, however briefly, and ended every phone call with those three words. Some part of him believed that, if the worst happened and he caught a bullet on a mission or took a corner too fast or whatever, she would remember those last words.

He'd never imagined a world where she might be the one in danger.

He thought about calling her back but then shook his head.

You're being stupid.

Instead, he called a different number. After a couple cycles of ringing, a connection was established and he heard a slightly gravelly female voice issue from the receiver. "Sheriff's department. What do you need?"

"Maggie, it's Matt. Can you put me through to the sheriff?"

"Sure thing, hon. I guess I know what this is about. It's just terrible. Folks can't even drive on the roads anymore."

Maggie Aldridge, the department's receptionist and the sheriff's gate-keeper, could be counted on to provide editorial comment, solicited or not. Redd liked her well enough and usually appreciated her sometimes-sarcastic wit, but today he didn't have the patience for it.

"The sheriff, Maggie?"

"Okay, okay. Don't get your undies in a twist." There was a subtle quiet on the line and then another electronic trill, which ended a moment later, replaced by the gruff voice of Stillwater County's sheriff.

"Blackwood here."

"You wanna tell me what's going on over there, Sheriff?" Redd snapped, barely keeping his voice below a shout.

"Matthew." There was a note of weary resignation in Blackwood's tone. "We're still trying to make sense of it here, but I promise I'll get to the bottom of this."

"They attacked my wife. With my son in the back seat. How did you let this happen?"

"I don't have a crystal ball, Matthew." Now there was just a hint of defensiveness. "There weren't any warning signs."

Redd wasn't interested in excuses. "I'm on my way back from . . . a job."

Blackwood knew that Redd was doing contract work for the bureau and probably suspected that it had something to do with the ongoing search for Anton Gage, but was not cleared for operational details.

"Do you think you can keep my family safe from these maniacs until I get back?" he went on, making no effort to keep the acid from his tone.

"Matthew . . ."

"You and I are going to have a long talk about this as soon as I get home." Redd ended the call before Blackwood could respond and threw the sat phone into the seat beside him.

"Trouble on the home front?" Davis asked.

Redd winced, realizing too late that he should have found a more private place to make the call. "It's nothing."

"Didn't sound like nothing." When Redd did not respond, Davis went on. "'They attacked my wife.' That's what I heard. And from where I was sitting, it didn't sound like you were speaking figuratively. Now I know you've got this whole 'lone wolf' thing going on, but you're part of our team. If something happens to you, it affects us all."

Redd stared back at him, weighing his options. He genuinely appreciated Davis's expression of support, and part of him wanted to share, if only to put his outrage into words. On the other hand, if he told Davis about what had happened, there was a chance it might get back to Kline, and that was territory he had no desire to explore.

He decided to take a chance. "Em . . . my wife got harassed by a bunch of bikers on her way into Bozeman."

"Bikers?"

Redd nodded. "A gang called the Infidels."

Davis let out a low whistle. "Those are some pretty bad hombres."

"You've heard of them?"

"The bureau keeps an eye on them. They're one of the 'big five' OMGs."

"OMGs?" He figured it out before Davis could supply an explanation. "Let me guess. Outlaw motorcycle gangs."

Davis nodded. "Everyone knows about the Hells Angels. They'll always be numero uno on the list, even though they've mostly mainstreamed. I mean, they've even got a website. Most of these bikers are just in it for the lifestyle. They like being called outlaws, even if they don't actually break any laws. But then you've got guys like the Infidels who like living on the dark side."

"So not just a bunch of thugs having a midlife crisis?"

Davis shook his head. "Nope. They're every bit as organized and, in their own way, disciplined as a military unit. The Infidels mostly operate in the rust belt. Moving product—crystal, fentanyl, guns—across the Canadian border. Racketeering and prostitution, too." He cocked his head to the side and gazed back at Redd. "I wonder why they decided to mix it up with your missus."

"Do they need a reason? They're animals."

Davis frowned. "They generally stay in their own little world. They're violent, sure, but only with rival clubs or people who owe them money. As a general rule, they leave civilians alone. Nothing brings the wrong kind of attention to a criminal enterprise like attacking someone who's just minding their own business. I hate to ask, but is there a chance that your lady did something to piss them off? I mean, she's a doctor, right? Maybe they wanted her to get them some prescription drugs or something like that, or . . ."

Redd wasn't listening anymore. Davis's musings had brought back to the surface the memory that had been rattling around in his consciousness like a rock in his combat boot.

It had happened right after he'd come back to Wellington, right after he'd found out that J. B. had died—murdered on Gage's orders. He'd been shadowing a local ne'er-do-well, more out of curiosity than anything else, and had stumbled into the middle of a prostitution-slash-narcotics operation run by a couple biker dudes wearing Infidels patches. They tried to crack his skull, and he responded in kind, giving them a lesson in the cowboy way. After kicking the crap out of them, he'd given a warning.

"I'm sure you're going to want payback," he recalled saying. *"You should know that's a really bad idea. Before you even think about coming after me, just know that next time . . . I'll put a bullet right between your eyes and bury your body someplace nobody will ever find you."*

Was that what this was? Payback for what he'd done to two of their number?

In the insanity with Gage that had followed, he hadn't bothered to check back to make sure they were gone, but as he had not seen any of them in Wellington in the months since, he had assumed they'd taken his warning seriously.

Evidently they had just been biding their time, patiently planning their revenge.

Did I do this? Did my actions put Emily and Junior in danger?

Rage tunneled Redd's vision.

I should have just killed them. Buried them in the woods. No one would ever have known. He took a breath. *I warned them . . .*

Through the roar of blood rushing in his ears, he almost didn't hear Davis calling his name, and when the other man put a hand on his shoulder, trying to shake him out of his trance, it was all he could do to keep from taking a swing at him.

"Redd!" Davis gave his shoulder another shake.

"I'm fine." Redd shook himself free.

"I know that look. Don't lose your head over this. Believe me when I say you don't want to tangle with these guys. Not on your own."

Redd waved away the admonition. "I'm not going to do anything stupid," he said.

Deep down, though, he knew that was a lie.

FIVE

Anton Gage stood on the balcony of his suite on the twenty-fourth floor of the Holiday Inn–Cheraga Tower gazing out across the Mediterranean Sea. Despite being situated in one of the city's tallest buildings, the three-star hotel was a considerable step down for the man who had, barely a year before, ranked among the world's wealthiest. While he could have afforded better, even with his means now severely restricted, the Holiday Inn supplied a degree of anonymity that kept him well below the FBI's radar.

From his vantage near the top of the tower, Gage could see the cityscape spread out before him to the north and west, and beyond that, the darker expanse of the bay, dotted with the lights of vessels, some moving, others at anchor. Farther out, three hundred kilometers to the north, well beyond the horizon, lay the island of Majorca, where he had flushed out his pursuers, confirming the report that they were closing in on him. It had almost been too easy, he thought. He was able to bait them without ever personally setting foot on the island.

Maybe I gave the FBI more credit than they deserve.

Clean-shaven, with his hair dyed black and styled in a rather ordinary Ivy League cut, Gage now bore little resemblance to the body double who had impersonated him in the Majorca villa earlier that day. Even Matthew Redd would have been hard-pressed to pick him out of a lineup.

He felt no satisfaction at having outwitted the FBI agents. Living on the run was quickly burning through what was left of his hidden fortune and, even worse, exhausting the limited supply of favors he was owed by influential people. Maintaining the status quo was not a sustainable solution. He needed a win.

He continued looking out from the balcony, scanning the dark water until he saw a new set of lights moving above the sea—one red, one green—getting brighter as the aircraft headed landward. Gage watched its progress for several more minutes until he could distinguish the dull roar of the helicopter's dual turboshaft engines and the rapid thump of its rotor blades beating the air into submission. Only then did he turn away, heading back inside the unremarkably functional interior.

The noise of the helicopter's approach continued to grow louder as the aircraft entered the space directly above the tower and set down on the rooftop, whereupon the noise of the engine ceased, followed shortly thereafter by the buffeting of the rotor blades.

Several more minutes passed before a knock came at the door of Gage's room. He quickly went to open it and found two people waiting on the other side—an attractive blonde woman in an immaculate red business suit and a tall, uber-fit male attired in a navy-blue polo shirt and khaki cargo pants. Without waiting for permission, the latter pushed inside and began purposefully inspecting every room of the suite. Less than sixty seconds later, he returned to the entrance and nodded to the woman, who in turn tapped the discreet Bluetooth device in her right ear and said, "All clear." Then, as abruptly as they had come, the pair stepped back into the hallway. Gage, who had not moved a muscle or uttered a word, remained where he was, patiently waiting until another man stepped through the doorway.

The newcomer's confident stride faltered a little when he laid eyes on Gage, evidently surprised by the dramatic change to Gage's appearance. For his part, Gage would have recognized the other man anywhere, even if they had not been more than casual acquaintances. His face, bespectacled, bookish—some would say nerdy and they would not be wrong—appeared regularly on the covers of *Forbes* and *Fortune*, as well as *Wired* and *PC Magazine*. The onetime CEO of one of the world's most successful personal computing products empires, he had more than once claimed the title of the richest man alive, and even after losing much of his fortune in an acrimonious and very public divorce, he still ranked in the top five. He was also a member of a secretive cabal of men—twelve men—dedicated to solving global problems through direct action, and it was in that capacity that he was paying a visit to Anton Gage, who was also one of their number.

Gage had been waiting for this meeting for more than a year.

"Thanks for coming," Gage began, but the other man raised a hand to silence him.

"I don't have a lot of time to waste here," the man said, "so I'll keep this short. We met yesterday to discuss what to do with you."

Gage felt a chill go down his spine. "You can't . . . You have to at least give me a chance to defend myself."

The man regarded him sourly. "We don't have to do any such thing. After your spectacular failure, the only chance you deserve is to voluntarily fall on your sword." He paused a beat. "However, this is uncharted territory. We've never faced a debacle of this magnitude. The matter was put to a vote, and we were unable to reach a unanimous verdict, as outlined in the bylaws, so for the time being, you remain one of us. That said, given your somewhat-reduced influence on the world stage, you're going to have to earn your way back into our good graces."

The cold spike of adrenaline flooded out of Gage's veins, leaving him weak in the knees. Despite his determination to stay on his feet, he staggered sideways, steadying himself by placing both hands on the back of a chair. Yet relieved as he was by this evident reprieve, his indignation quickly rose to the surface.

"If I failed spectacularly, it is only because I dared to achieve something spectacular. Something to which the rest of you, as near as I can tell, have only paid lip service."

The visitor's nostrils crinkled a little, as if Gage's statement had fouled the air. "Evidently others among our number share that opinion. Which is why you're being given a second bite at the apple, as it were."

"A second bite?"

"Your plan was fundamentally sound. Our investigation into the affair has determined that the only reason you failed was because of sloppy security practices at your facilities, particularly the Montana facility. If you had kept a tighter rein on your people . . . to say nothing of your offspring . . . you would quite likely have succeeded."

Gage's cheeks went hot at the mention of his offspring. Both of his children had died as a direct result of Matthew Redd's interference, and while he had not shed many tears for his wayward son, Wyatt, Gage acutely felt the loss of his daughter. Hannah had been a woman worthy of his name.

Matthew Redd would pay for what he had done to Hannah.

"Hopefully you've learned from your mistakes," the man went on. "We want you to try again, and this time we expect complete success."

Gage shook his head slowly. "All samples of the cereal strains were destroyed, as was most of the research. It would take years to reproduce it all." *If it's even possible,* he did not add. The crucial developments had been produced by Rafael Caldera, aka Willow, who was now dead, along with nearly everyone on his research team.

The visitor gave him a hard stare. "So you're saying that you can't do it?"

Gage sensed the trap that had been set for him. If he answered truthfully, his usefulness to the Twelve, which was probably the only thing keeping him alive, would be at an end. On the other hand, if he committed to doing something that simply couldn't be done, it would only postpone the inevitable.

Thankfully, he had one last card up his sleeve.

He took a breath. "Realistically, I don't think the original plan will work now. Leaving aside the difficulty of trying to duplicate our research from scratch, the international community is now extremely wary of the long-term impact of GMOs on their food supply. However . . . there may be another way to achieve a comparable outcome. It won't be as elegant as what I originally envisioned, but it will yield results far quicker."

The visitor's eyes narrowed, zeroing in on Gage with a mixture of suspicion and interest. "I'm listening."

"In the course of our research, we developed several extremely virulent strains of cereal rust."

"Rust?"

"It's a type of mycelium. A fungal organism that kills grain crops before they can mature. Once rust is detected in a crop, the only recourse is to burn the entire field to prevent it from spreading. Our strain, in addition to being extremely prolific, is also resistant to heat. It can survive in the soil even after the field is sterilized and come back year after year."

The visitor nodded slowly. "Go on."

"A single widespread release of our genetically modified rust would remove as much as a billion bushels a year from the global food supply." Gage was not pulling these numbers out of thin air. This plan had been developed two years earlier as a fallback option just in case the primary research into sterility-inducing GMOs failed to produce the desired results. He'd been keeping it in reserve, waiting for the right moment to put it forward and redeem himself in the eyes of the Twelve.

"Most people don't realize how close we are to a tipping point when it comes to food security," Gage continued. "Crop yields have been trending down for years, while demand continues to grow. All it would take is a slight bump to send us over the edge.

"The knock-on effect would be an immediate spike in food prices across the board. Affluent countries would begin hoarding, which would further drive prices up, leaving the developing world to starve. Famine would only be the first domino. Food insecurity is the trigger for unrest, ethnic violence, and even civil war."

"You're proposing an accelerationist solution? Sacrifice a few million now in order to prevent the suffering of billions down the road?" Judging by the hungry look in the man's eyes, he had no moral reservations about the plan.

"It would at least be a wake-up call for mankind," Gage said. "From Malthus on, intellectuals have sounded the warning about overpopulation. When their predictions failed to come true, they were dismissed as Cassandras, while kings and robber barons congratulated themselves on their ingenuity in dodging the bullet. But it wasn't ingenuity. It was luck, and luck always runs out eventually. As unpleasant as it sounds, the only way to convince the world that we *must* maintain a sustainable population is by letting the population bomb detonate."

The visitor nodded slowly. "What sort of timetable are we looking at?"

"If I can get to the vault where we stored the mycelium strains, we could deploy in a matter of days. Once deployed, it will take a while for the fungus to propagate and spread. I'd say a few weeks before the effects are noticeable."

"If you can get to it? Where is this vault?"

Gage told him.

"Ah. I can see where that might pose a bit of difficulty."

The understatement would have been laughable were the consequences not so dire. "With the right amount of money in the right hands, I can get there. Staying undetected will pose a bit more of a challenge, but not an impossible one. The problem is that my resources are a bit . . . thin right now."

"Yes, I suppose they are." The visitor shot a glance at his smartwatch. "Your plan has merit, but the group will have to make the final decision. I will restore your access to the discretionary fund. That should give you a little more freedom of movement. Make whatever preparations you deem necessary, but do not execute until you hear back from me."

Gage nodded, hiding his smile. His days of wandering in the wilderness were finally at an end.

SIX

"What part of *stand down* did you not understand?" Gavin Kline snapped as Redd stepped through his office door.

Redd let the question hang as he crossed the room and sank into a chair opposite the other man. When he was seated, he looked Kline in the eye, maintaining contact for several seconds before answering. "I wasn't going to take a chance on Gage getting away again. It was the right call."

He did not point out that, because the Spanish police team had taken point and the fly team had been acting in an observational capacity, technically he had not disobeyed Kline. Beside the fact that it was a flimsy pretext at best, Redd didn't want to win the argument on a technicality. It was more important to speak his mind.

Or at least it had been until Mikey had called about Emily's encounter with the Infidels.

When he'd heard about the attack on his family, Redd's first impulse had been to blow off the meeting with Kline and catch the first flight west. The only reason he didn't was that catching the earliest flight would have meant a four-hour layover in Denver waiting for the connecting flight to Bozeman. He could catch a later flight and still make the connection, which meant there was time enough to face Kline's wrath and dish a little of his own.

"And yet Gage did get away." Kline's retort dripped with sarcasm. "You caused an international incident for nothing."

Redd shook his head. "You're missing the point."

"The point?" Kline's voice rose an octave. "I told you to stand down. That's the point, Matt. The only way this works is if you respect the chain of command. We're a law enforcement agency, and if you want to be a part of this team, you're going to have to respect the law. Did you even stop to think what would happen if Gage had been there? Do you want him skating on a technicality? Or asking the Spanish for political asylum? Because either one of those things could have happened, and then we'd be up the creek."

"The *point*—" Redd paused a beat to emphasize the word—"is that Gage knew we were coming. He set a trap for us."

"A trap that you walked right into."

"He knew we were coming," Redd repeated, stressing every word. "*How* did he know, Gavin?"

For the first time since Redd's arrival, Kline appeared to at least consider what Redd was saying. "It could have been somebody at State. Or someone on the Spanish side."

Redd shook his head again. "This took time to set up. It wasn't thrown together at the last second. There's a great big hole in your security. I don't know if it's a leak or a mole or something else, but until you figure out who or what it is, Gage is going to always be one step ahead of us."

Kline regarded Redd silently for a long moment. Finally he said, "It doesn't change the fact that you disobeyed a direct order. You're suspended."

At this moment, his future with the bureau was just about the last thing Redd cared about, yet the pronouncement felt like a slap. He couldn't help but hear an echo of the ignominious end of his military career. Kline had been responsible for that, too.

"Suspended? For how long?"

"Indefinitely."

"Are you firing me?"

"I don't know." Kline now seemed unable to meet his gaze.

Redd's fingers involuntarily curled into fists. With an effort, he unclenched them, then gripped the armrests of his chair and shoved to his feet. When he spoke, his voice was low, like the warning growl of a guard dog. "You know what I am . . . how I work. If you wanted somebody to do things your way . . . the FBI way . . . why did you even bother asking me to join the team in the first place?"

"You know, I've been asking myself the same question."

Redd threw his hands up, turned on his heel, and headed for the door. There was plenty more he wanted to say, but what was the point?

Kline's voice reached out to him, his tone almost conciliatory. "Matt, wait."

Redd stopped but didn't turn to look.

"Let's just give it a few days," Kline said. "If I still have this job when the dust settles, we'll talk about the way forward."

"Don't bother," Redd replied, then threw the door open and stalked out of the office.

✖   ✖   ✖

Gavin Kline stared at the empty doorway for almost a full minute after Redd's departure.

"Well, that could have gone better," he muttered.

There had been no alternative to the suspension. Justified or not, Redd had gone full cowboy on the sovereign soil of a friendly nation, and the State Department was out for blood. There was no way to insulate Redd from the blowback. The only question was whether State would be content with Kline's disciplinary measures or call for *his* ouster as well.

Redd had been right about one thing: Kline had known from the outset that Redd would chafe at the idea of doing things the FBI way. It had been a mistake to put him in charge of the tactical team, even with his special operations experience.

Redd was a sledgehammer, not a scalpel. His approach to any problem was direct, decisive, and usually destructive. Sometimes that was exactly what the situation called for, which was how Kline had justified bringing Redd into the fold as a contractor. But when a lighter touch was needed, Redd's usefulness, not to mention his judgment, was limited.

But then Redd's operational experience was not the reason Kline had hired him.

He knew how Redd felt about him and knew that he deserved the young man's scorn. He'd done the unthinkable—abandoned his own child. It didn't matter that he hadn't even learned of Redd's existence until years after his birth, didn't matter that he was not then nor now capable of being a good parent. None of those justifications mattered to Redd, and Kline knew it. But he had held on to the slim hope that, by keeping Redd in his professional life, they might eventually be able to have a different kind of relationship—if not father to son, then at least man to man.

He wasn't really surprised that it had blown up in his face. Redd was stubborn.

Must have gotten that from his mother, Kline thought.

He sighed and tried to think about something else.

"Gage knew we were coming. . . . How did he know?"

It was a fair question, and something about which he should probably be more concerned.

"A leak or a mole or something else."

Was Redd's assessment correct, or was he just trying to deflect blame for his screwup? Kline shook his head at the thought. Deflection wasn't Matty's style. He took responsibility for his mistakes, as well as for the mistakes made by others on his watch. If he said there was a leak, then it was at least worth looking into.

Kline took out his FBI-issued mobile phone and placed a call to Rob Davis, who answered on the first ring.

"Special Agent Davis speaking."

Kline resisted the impulse to laugh. He and Davis were on a first-name basis, and the caller ID would have revealed that it was Kline, so the formal greeting could only mean that Davis was worried his neck might be on the chopping block too.

"Relax, Rob. Just checking in with you."

"Okay" was the guarded reply. "We're on our way to the Office. Should be there in about fifteen minutes. Do you want me to come in once we're done unloading?"

The Office, Kline knew, was the fly team's nickname for their dedicated training facility at the FBI Academy outside Quantico, Virginia.

"No need. I just wanted to get your thoughts on something. Matthew told me he thinks we might have a leak somewhere. That Gage had advance warning about your operation. What do you think?"

"I think he's right. That whole setup had just one purpose—to embarrass us. Gage was thumbing his nose at us, which means he knew we were coming."

"Could someone there have been on his payroll? A local?"

"I guess it's possible, but the deception was pretty elaborate. They didn't just throw it together last minute."

Kline nodded. "Matt said pretty much the same thing. I'll look into it." He paused a beat, then added, "I know the operation didn't go off as planned, but that's not on you or the team. Once you're squared away there, take the rest of the day off. Take the boys out for pizza and beer, my treat."

"Thank you." Davis sounded hesitant.

"Something else on your mind?"

"What about Redd?"

"He's taking some personal time."

Kline was worried that the politically correct nonanswer would only make Davis more suspicious, but all the other man said was "I figured he would."

It was an odd reply, but Kline didn't press for an explanation. "We'll catch up later. Have fun tonight. That's an order."

"Will do."

As soon as the call ended, Kline placed another, this time to Special Agent Stephanie Treadway.

When he'd taken over the intelligence directorate, Kline had cleaned house, transferring out several senior agents whose loyalty to him was, at best, questionable. It was not that he was looking to surround himself with yes-men and sycophants. If anything, the agents he chose to fill the vacancies were more likely to question his decisions, keeping him honest. No, he'd carried out the purge because it was in the best interests of the bureau. His job—his *mission*—was too important for him to be worried about internal politics or who might be rooting for him to fail. And of all the agents who'd earned their way into Kline's inner circle, the one he counted on the most was Stephanie Treadway.

Treadway *was* a scalpel and Kline's go-to girl, especially when circumstances called for actions that were not strictly legal.

It had been she who, on Kline's orders, had posed as a California surfer chick in distress in order to prevent Matthew Redd from accompanying his Marine Raiders unit on an ill-fated mission into Mexico, saving his life and in the process destroying his military career.

That was something else Redd would never forgive Kline for.

Kline had made the desperate decision because he'd known that the mission was compromised, that the Marines were heading into a trap, but had lacked the authority to cancel the mission, which had been ordered by his predecessor, Rachel Culp. Later, Culp had been revealed as a mole, a double agent working for Anton Gage.

And if there was one mole, why couldn't there be another?

"Hey, boss," a cheery Treadway said when she picked up. "What's shakin'?"

"Are you hungry? I'm hungry. Let me buy you a burger."

SEVEN

MONTANA

The cloud of anxiety that had plagued Redd ever since the failure of the raid in Majorca began to lift as his plane made its final approach to Bozeman Yellowstone International Airport. Even though it was after dusk and there wasn't much to see, just knowing that he was back in Big Sky Country always improved his mood. And as he slid behind the wheel of the old F-250 Super Duty dually he'd inherited from J. B. and pulled out of the economy long-term parking lot, the anticipation of seeing Emily and little Matty again, of being home, brought a smile to his face.

The truck was a workhorse, even if it was fifteen years old, sun-faded, and spotted with rust. When he'd gotten the insurance check after totaling his beloved 2020 F-150 Raptor, he'd faced the choice of using the settlement—which did not even come close to replacement value—as a down payment on a new truck or using it to pay down some of J. B.'s debt. With a new wife and a baby on the way, it hadn't been a hard choice.

He had managed to acquire the salvage title to the Raptor, which now occupied a corner of Elijah Lawrence's back lot, and as soon as he and Mikey could make their schedules work, he planned to restore it to its former glory, but like so much else, a styling ride seemed a lot less important now that he was a family man.

The only real downside to using J. B.'s old relic as his primary vehicle was that it was built for work, not speed. At anything above sixty-five, it sounded like it might come apart at the seams, which meant the commute to and from Bozeman took a little longer. Emily always offered to drive him, but he hated saying his goodbyes at the airport.

His good mood was short-lived. As he was pulling onto I-90 west and trying to get the old truck up to highway speed, a motorcycle shot past in the leftmost lane. Even the brief glimpse he caught as the bike passed in front of his headlights was enough to reveal that it was not a customized Harley-Davidson but a fully outfitted Honda Gold Wing, painted a cheery metallic red, with matching trunk and panniers, and that the rider's expensive leathers were unadorned by motorcycle club patches. Nevertheless, the sighting was a reminder of the problems he was coming home to.

Oddly enough, the question of how to deal with the Infidels was not a source of concern. That was something that fell squarely inside his wheelhouse. While he had not worked out exactly what shape his response would take, he felt more than equal to the problem, much as a trained mechanic might feel confident in his ability to restore an automobile to working order without knowing exactly what repairs would be required.

What bothered him about the Infidels' harassment of his wife was the possibility . . . no, the likelihood that he was to blame. The idea that his past encounter with two bikers had precipitated the attack and put his family in danger left a sliver of guilt in his consciousness that worried its way deeper with every failed attempt to rationalize his earlier actions.

By itself, that would have been burden enough, but there was also the matter of the suspension of his contract with the FBI. Although training with the fly team was just a side gig, and a temporary one at that, he had come to depend upon the regularity of that paycheck. Those extra few dollars from the government, along with the travel vouchers and per diems, kept Matty Jr. in diapers and baby wipes and gave Redd and Emily some breathing room.

They'd get by without it, he knew. In fact, if things had gone differently in Majorca, he'd be in the same situation, but somehow ending his association with the bureau on Kline's terms and not his own felt like a tick mark in his personal loss column.

His failure to bring Anton Gage to justice was another.

He'd thought he was past wanting revenge for all the pain Gage had caused him, but the deception at the villa had ripped the scab off. J. B.'s murder, the ambush of the Marine Raiders in Mexico, the attempts on his own life, which had put Emily in danger as well . . . Gage had to be made to answer for those crimes. Until that happened, Redd knew he would never be able to move on with his life.

Only now, the hunt for Gage would go on without him. If Gage was eventually caught or killed, Redd would have only the satisfaction of a spectator, watching from the sidelines.

Maybe I should call Kline, he thought, *apologize for how things went down.* But he quickly dismissed that idea.

He stewed over all of this during the hour-plus drive back to Wellington, switching from one anxiety to the next like someone randomly flipping through the channels on a TV set. The trip seemed to take forever, but as he neared Wellington, he called Emily to let her know that he was close, and just hearing her voice was enough to banish the dark clouds once more.

Ten minutes later, he turned off Old Lausen Road, east of Wellington proper, and into the short gravel driveway that ended in front of the Derhammers' ranch-style house. As Redd pulled up alongside Emily's Tahoe, she appeared on the porch with Junior in her arms and all but ran to greet him. His homecomings were always a joyous occasion, but this time, by unspoken accord, the hug lasted just a little bit longer. So did the kiss.

"Okay, you two," Mikey called from the porch, breaking the mood. "Either come inside or go get a room."

Redd couldn't help blushing a little. Their reunions usually took place up at the ranch without an audience. Before he could respond, both Emily and Liz, who was standing beside her husband, simultaneously chimed, "Shut up, Mikey."

However, Emily did pull back, just far enough to hold little Matty out to him. "Somebody missed his daddy."

Although he was fussing, the baby's eyes lit up when Redd took him.

"Somebody's daddy missed him," Redd replied, hugging the infant to his chest. Even through the layers of fabric between them, Redd could feel the heat radiating off Junior's body. "He's burning up."

Emily grimaced. "He's due for another dose of Tylenol, but even alternating that with ibuprofen, I can't seem to get his fever to break. I'm worried that he's got some kind of infection."

"Does he need to go to the hospital?"

Emily looked away, uncertain. "Maybe. I probably would have already taken him if not for . . ."

He put his free hand on her shoulder and pulled her in for another hug. "It's okay. I'm here now. We can take him tonight if you want."

She shook her head. "In the morning. Unless the fever spikes again."

"Okay. Then let's get him home." He raised his eyes to Mikey and Liz, who were still waiting on the porch. "Guys, thanks so much for taking care of them. I'll make it up to you. I promise."

"That's what we're here for," Liz replied.

Mikey seconded the sentiment with a vigorous nod, then gestured at the old Ford pickup. "You can leave that here tonight. I'll bring it up tomorrow, first thing."

Redd tossed the keys to him, then proceeded to load little Matty into the car seat, while Emily climbed into the passenger seat and started the engine. Once the precious cargo was secure, Redd took his place behind the wheel. The interior of the Tahoe was chilly, and Redd knew from experience that they'd be more than halfway to the ranch before the engine warmed up enough to turn the heater on. Fortunately, the rig had heated seats—a luxury the old Super Duty did not possess—and he wasn't tough or proud enough to suffer for no good reason. There was something to be said for a warm backside.

As they drove away, Redd had to fight the urge to ask his wife about her encounter with the Infidels. She would tell him when she was ready. Unfortunately, he didn't really know what else to say, so the silence quickly became conspicuous.

When they were rolling back down Lausen Road, Emily finally spoke. "You're back earlier than I expected. Not that I'm complaining. Everything go okay?"

He pursed his lips, wondering how much to tell her. Compared to what she had gone through, his experiences seemed almost trivial. But he knew better than to try to hide bad news from her. "Could have gone better." He paused, took a breath, then added, "I think I'm gonna take a break from working with Gavin."

"Oh, Matty. Are you sure? I know how important it is to you. You're not doing this because . . . Don't quit because you think I need protecting."

He shook his head. "It's not that at all. I just don't think I'm cut out for law enforcement."

"Sheriff Blackwood would disagree. He'd pin a badge on you in a hot second if you let him. You know how shorthanded the department is right now."

Redd did know. Another of his side gigs was providing tactical training to Blackwood's deputies—all seven of them. With a population of about six thousand, the department should have fielded two or three times that many, but nobody seemed to want the job. Redd certainly didn't.

"You really want me working sixty hours a week, breaking up domestic disturbances and chasing meth heads?" It was a conversation they'd had before, and he was a little surprised that she would bring it up now, of all times.

"No, I don't. But I know you, Matty. You're one of the good guys. I don't think you'll truly be happy unless you're out there fighting the good fight. Protecting people. I think you could probably do a lot more good here than running off all over the world chasing Anton Gage."

That was something she had never brought up in their previous conversations, and after a moment, Redd grasped the subtext. Or thought he did.

"Do more good here." Stay home and protect your family. That's what a good husband does . . . what a good father does.

Or maybe that wasn't what she was trying to say. Emily had been nothing if not supportive of his decision to work with the fly team. Maybe it was just his own guilt talking. Regardless, the message struck a nerve. He was not going to turn into Gavin Kline.

Emily reached across the center console and laid her hand atop his on the steering wheel. "I'm not trying to talk you into doing something. I just think you could make a difference. But only if it's what you want to do."

"I'll think about it," he said, equivocating. He couldn't actually see himself in that role, but it was a career better suited to his skill set than running a cattle ranch.

So he would think about it. But only after he dealt with the Infidels.

Right now a badge would just get in the way.

EIGHT

Although he usually slept better in his own bed with Emily beside him, on this night, sleep eluded Matthew Redd. Part of it was jet lag. In the space of four days, he'd gone from Mountain daylight time to Central European summer time—eight hours ahead—and then back again just as he was starting to adjust. His body had no idea what time it was. But it was his mind, not his body, that refused to turn off. His brain kept switching channels, replaying the same old concerns, along with a new one.

Junior's sick. What if it's more than just a childhood fever? What if it's something serious?

From time to time, he heard soft whimpering over the baby monitor. When they'd gotten home, he'd asked again if they should head up to the children's hospital in Helena, but Emily had assured him it wasn't that serious. Yet.

It was the *yet* that scared him.

Hired killers and bad biker dudes he could handle, but he was powerless against whatever microscopic villains now menaced his infant son.

He gave up on trying to sleep at 4 a.m., which was when he usually got up anyway, and began his daily routine, doing some light calisthenics as he waited on the Mr. Coffee to finish brewing. Ordinarily he would savor that first mug while reading through the daily intel report from Kline's office, outlining the current state of the pursuit of Anton Gage, but today he took the mug with him out onto the porch and sat with the old Bible he'd inherited from J. B.

Since returning to Montana, he had embraced reading Scripture and even tried his hardest to put it into practice. Simple teachings such as loving thy neighbor, not committing adultery, telling the truth, and not stealing made perfect sense to him. In fact, those were all principles that Jim Bob had taught him growing up. He could see why the old man had so naturally fallen into the Word and become a man of God before his death. It was, more or less, the way he was living his life already. All that really changed was the reason for doing so.

Other biblical teachings, though, Redd struggled with. Chief among them, honoring thy father and mother, one of the Ten Commandments—and one that his father-in-law, who still preached every Sunday, had told Redd was important.

Though his mother was a drug addict who had overdosed, leaving him alone in the world at a young age, Redd held no ill feeling toward her. In fact, though he rarely spoke about her, the truth was, he missed her dearly. Then there was Jim Bob. Redd had never known a better man. Maybe his father-in-law, but either way, J. B. was in the top two. No, the struggle stemmed from Redd's complicated relationship with his biological father—which, over the past twenty-four hours, had hit yet another snag.

Finishing up a chapter in the book of Proverbs, Redd closed the worn, leather-bound Bible and set it aside. The air was chilly, but the early morning sky was clear, revealing a sight hidden from the city dwellers of the world—the starry expanse of the heavens in all its glory—and for a few minutes, he was able to put his cares aside and simply appreciate what he had. Emily. Junior. The ranch. Good friends. Those were the things that mattered.

A meteor left a long green streak in the sky to the northeast, but Redd didn't make a wish. He went back inside, refilled his mug, and then headed out to the barn to get a head start on the day's chores.

Compared to ranching, being a Marine Raider had been a walk in the park. It wasn't just the long hours of physical exertion—bucking hay, stretching barbed wire, wrangling stubborn yearlings. Running a ranch, even a relatively small operation like the one he'd inherited from J. B., meant proficiency across a spectrum of disciplines.

A cowboy had to be the veterinary equivalent of a Navy corpsman, monitoring the health of the herd, diagnosing and treating a variety of issues, and when necessary, putting a sick or critically injured animal down. During calving season, there were any number of medical interventions that might be necessary, from reaching into a pregnant heifer to turn a breech calf to performing an emergency cesarean section.

He also had to be a mechanical engineer, maintaining old—sometimes ancient—equipment because there was almost never enough money in the budget to replace anything. He had to manage both stock and the rangeland where they foraged and, like a savvy stockbroker, had to know when to buy and when to sell. The latter piece was something he had not really grasped while growing up and learning the ropes from J. B. But as frustrating as the work could be, and as different as it was from what he had done in the corps, Redd enjoyed the challenges—mental and physical—and was committed to making a go of the ranch.

Redd allowed his stock to roam free, no matter the time of year. The barn simply wasn't big enough to hold them all, and cattle preferred to roam. There was little chance of the animals freezing when winter arrived. They stayed together as a herd, and their collective body heat kept the cold at bay. Even in summer, though, they rarely strayed too far from the barn, where fresh hay was always available. On this morning, however, most of the herd had evidently found something else to keep them interested out on the range the previous day and had not made their way back before dark. So he saddled up Remington, the old quarter horse who had spent more time on the ranch than he had, and rode out into the predawn twilight to track the rest of the herd down.

The trail was easy to follow as it meandered up and down the rolling hills behind the house. Redd heard the animals before he saw them, their lowing carried on the breeze that rolled down from the mountains to the east. After about half an hour of riding, he finally caught sight of the herd, gathered together in a draw at the base of the slope, where the terrain sheltered them from the wind. Redd reined Remington to a halt and did a quick head count, confirming that none had strayed, then turned the horse around and headed home. Later, he would go back out for a closer look, but it was too dark to worry about that right now.

Besides, he had other business to attend to.

✖   ✖   ✖

Emily was up and cooking breakfast when he came back inside after tending to Remington. Redd did not fail to notice that she was dressed for work.

"How's Junior doing?" he asked as he poured a fresh mug of coffee.

She didn't look up from the pan of eggs she was scrambling with a spatula. "Better. I think we're past the worst of it."

"You don't want to take him to the hospital? Just in case?"

She shook her head. "No, I think he'll be okay. I just wish I knew what caused the fever in the first place."

"You're going in to work?"

Now she did look up, and there was a suspicious glint in her eyes. "Yes, Matthew. That's what you do when you have a job."

She only called him Matthew when she was irritated with him. "I just thought with Junior's fever, you could use family sick leave or something."

She frowned, but only a little. "Well, I could. But he's doing better. And honestly, the reason I'm going in is because I'm needed there. Dr. Bennett has been working double shifts all week."

Redd knew better than to challenge her once her mind was made up, but he was still troubled by the idea of letting her out of his sight. "I'll drive you in."

She managed a faint smile. "I appreciate it, but you really don't have to do that. I'm sure you've got a lot of work to do here."

"Nothing that can't wait. Besides, I thought I could spend the day with little man."

"He'll be fine at day care. He loves spending time with Chelsea." Chelsea was the caregiver at the clinic's day care center. "And if his fever comes back, I can be right there."

Now it was Redd's turn to frown. "I just don't like the idea of you both being . . . exposed."

She cocked her head to the side. "Exposed?"

"After what happened. With those bikers."

She shook her head. "The clinic is a safe place. There are cops and deputies in and out of there all day. And you know, that was probably just a random thing. When those guys get cranked up, they aren't exactly thinking straight. It was scary, but it's over. I'm sure it wasn't anything personal."

That's where you're wrong. It is personal, Redd told himself, though he hoped he was wrong. Deep down, he knew he wasn't.

And it isn't over.

The words were in Redd's mouth, but he couldn't bring himself to say them aloud. Instead, after taking a sip of his coffee, he said, "You're probably right."

NINE

After presenting her credentials to the corrections officer at the front desk and then securing them in a lockbox along with her service weapon, Special Agent Stephanie Treadway made her way to the visitation room of FCI Danbury—the low-security federal penitentiary that had in times past housed such famous personages as hotelier Leona Helmsley, the legendary Queen of Mean; Sun Myung Moon, founder of the Unification Church; and Grammy Award–winning singer Lauryn Hill. The prison was perhaps best known as the place where inmate 11187-424—Piper Kerman—spent most of her thirteen-month imprisonment, a journey she chronicled in the bestselling memoir *Orange Is the New Black*.

The inmate Treadway had come to visit would not be remembered as noteworthy in any way. In fact, outside of a select few senior officials in the FBI and US Marshals, nobody even knew that former Executive Assistant Director of Intelligence Rachel Culp was actually a prisoner there.

Culp—who was officially known as Jennifer Cleary by everyone in the prison system—was the sole occupant of the visitation room, aside from a pair of bored-looking corrections officers who stood near the exits. Clad in a standard-issue khaki prison uniform, she cut quite a different figure from the woman who had once risen almost to the top of the FBI leadership. Her blonde hair, which she had previously worn in a professional bob, was longer and somehow blonder—no doubt the result of a prison dye job. A onetime CrossFit trainer, Culp had been lean and fit to begin with, and she still was, but whereas her physique had previously been attractive, she now merely looked hard.

Back when Kline's subunit had been working out of the FBI annex, Rachel Culp probably wouldn't have given Stephanie Treadway the time of day. In fact, the first and only time their paths crossed had been when Treadway put the bracelets on Culp after her failed attempt to kill Matthew Redd and frame Kline as the mole inside the bureau.

Treadway crossed the room and took a seat opposite Culp. "You've come a long way, baby."

Culp did not look up but in a low voice hissed, "Are you trying to get me killed?"

Treadway smiled without humor. "Trying? No, that would definitely fall under the heading of serendipity."

As far as Treadway and many of her fellow FBI agents were concerned, Rachel Culp deserved the death penalty. She had personally carried out the murder of FBI Special Agent Kevin Dudek and was complicit in the deaths of dozens of others, including the Marine Raiders unit that had been sent to take down Willow. But the suits at DOJ had determined that Culp's knowledge of Anton Gage's operation and her testimony against him were more valuable than actual justice and had offered her a plea deal, wherein she would serve no more than ten years in federal prison, after which she would be eligible for protection and relocation under the federal Witness Security Program. In fact, she was already receiving a degree of protection, which was why she was serving her time under an alias.

Culp raised her eyes, which were narrowed into slits, and scowled at Treadway. "Why are you here? I've already told you everything."

"Have you though?" Treadway wagged her head. "You're a smart woman, Rachel—"

"Call me Jennifer," Culp snapped.

"Too smart to show all your cards," Treadway went on without missing a beat. "I have trouble believing you didn't hold something back for a rainy day."

"Does the AG's office even know you're here?" Culp said. "I'll bet they don't. And I'll bet they'd be pissed to learn that you're interfering in their investigation."

Culp was not wrong. When Kline had met with Treadway the previous day and asked her to pay Culp a visit on the down-low, she had raised a similar objection. That was when Kline had read her in on the disastrous operation in Majorca and what it portended. Kline's orders had been straightforward.

"Get Culp to talk, whatever it takes."

Treadway made a humming sound. "Could be. Are you going to tell them?"

Culp's answer was another scowl. The last thing Culp wanted was to draw attention to herself. As the lead witness against Anton Gage, she had a great big target on her back, especially while she was enjoying the hospitality of the federal prison system. The only way to stay safe was to disappear completely into her new identity.

"Thought so." Treadway leaned forward, squaring her shoulders. "There's another mole in the bureau. I want a name."

Culp's expression softened. "What makes you think there's a mole?"

Treadway held the other woman's gaze. Culp seemed genuinely surprised by the assertion. Treadway considered herself a pretty good judge of character, but Culp was a proven world-class liar. It was possible, likely even, that the woman was just trying to determine how much Treadway already knew.

"Who's the mole?"

Culp shook her head. "I don't know of anyone else."

"You must have an idea."

"Tell me why you think there's another mole, and maybe I can give you a name."

Treadway considered the request for a moment, then decided to play ball. "We've been hunting Gage for months, but he's always two steps ahead of us. The only way that's possible is if he's getting inside information."

Culp nodded slowly. "Okay. Well, it wouldn't surprise me to learn that there's another double agent in the bureau. But there's another possibility that I don't think you've considered."

"And that is?"

Culp lowered her voice almost to a whisper. "I don't think you truly appreciate just how much power and influence the Twelve really have. They're kingmakers. The real power behind the throne. They don't have to infiltrate government agencies because they own the politicians who appoint the directors of those agencies."

"So what are you saying? The president is the mole?"

"Not necessarily the president. And not a mole exactly. More like an asset. Somebody who owes somebody a favor or someone's golf buddy. They might be leaking information without even realizing it."

Treadway thought about this, then shook her head. "This is different. They're getting operational details. Stuff that we're keeping in-house until the last minute." Against her better judgment, she added, "We thought we had Gage in Majorca, but when we tried to roll him up, we discovered that he was using a body double. He knew we were coming and set us up to look like idiots."

A wry smile touched Culp's lips, evidently savoring the thought of her former coworkers' embarrassment, but then her expression became serious again. "How did you know he would be in Majorca?"

"There was activity in one of his foreign bank accounts. A transfer of funds to a bank in Palma."

"And you don't think he knew that you were monitoring those accounts?"

Treadway shook her head. "These were the accounts in the Cayman Islands. The ones he didn't think we knew about. And he was desperate. He's been on the run for a long time now."

Culp smiled again. "Anton may be desperate, but he isn't stupid. There's no mole. He was testing the waters. He made that transfer to see if anyone was paying attention. And when you tipped your hand, he got his answer."

The obviousness of it hit Treadway like a slap. Gage had set a trap for them, but not the one Kline suspected.

Kline wanted to believe there was a mole because that was the answer that would take the heat off Matthew Redd for charging in like the cowboy he was, when in reality, it was Redd's headstrong insubordination that had played right into Gage's hands. Her boss had a blind spot where Redd was concerned. She'd seen it firsthand.

On more than one occasion.

Treadway tried to hide her reaction behind a mask of skepticism. "Seems like he went to an awful lot of trouble just to see if we were paying attention."

Culp shrugged. "Don't underestimate him. He's playing the long game—3D chess. Kline is still playing tic-tac-toe. Whatever it is that Anton really wants, you're not going to see it until he already has it." She pushed away from the table. "I think we're done here. Don't come back."

✖   ✖   ✖

Treadway thought about Culp's parting shot during the forty-minute drive to Westchester County Airport and all throughout the hour-long flight back to Reagan National Airport in DC. The more she thought about it, the greater her sense of foreboding.

Why had Gage chosen this moment to test them? Was he planning something? Another nightmare scheme to reshape the world into a quasi utopia where he and the rest of the Twelve would rule as godlike kings?

If so, it was all the more imperative that they find him and bring him down. And yet they were no closer now than they had been at the start.

Kline wasn't going to be happy to hear that.

She was surprised to find him waiting for her outside the security entrance to terminal 2.

"Boss? You didn't have to come all the way out here to . . ." She trailed off when she saw that he wasn't smiling. "What's wrong?"

Without answering, he took her elbow, steering her away from the flow of arriving passengers leaving the secure area and into the seating area of a nearby Starbucks. Only when they were seated did he speak. "What did you say to her?" he whispered.

"I leaned on her, like you said. She doesn't think there's a mole." She paused. "Are you sure you want to talk about this here?"

"That's all you said?"

"I can give you the play-by-play if you want." She frowned, trying to divine his intention. "What's going on, boss? Did she go to the AG or something?"

Kline pursed his lips together for a moment. "About half an hour after you left, inmate Jennifer Cleary hanged herself in her cell with her bra."

Treadway's mouth dropped open. "Hanged? She's dead?"

"So as you can imagine, the warden and the board of parole are very curious about the substance of your conversation. I'm sure the attorney general will also want to know when he finds out that his star witness against Gage is dead."

Treadway felt her guts twist. She wanted to throw up. "They Epsteined her," she managed to croak.

Kline sighed. "The official report is going to say suicide," he said. "But yeah, it's looking like it."

She managed to raise her eyes to meet his. "We did this. Don't you see? This is what Gage wanted all along. He set the trap in Majorca to make us think that there was a mole in the bureau because he knew we would go to the one person who could tell us if it was true. And I led them right to her."

"You can't know that."

She studied his face. "You know I'm right. They were watching you. Watching *us*. And when you sent me to Danbury, they knew there could only be one reason."

"Whatever it is that Anton really wants, you're not going to see it until he already has it."

"Playing 3D chess," she murmured, shaking her head. "Boss, I think we're in real trouble here. I mean, we're . . . we're fighting ghosts."

Kline paused a moment, thinking. After a beat, he finally said, "You know what? You're right. We are fighting ghosts." Then he smiled. "We need an equalizer."

"Like what?" Treadway asked, confused.

"We need a ghost of our own."

"Boss?"

"Pack your bags," Kline said. "I need a favor."

TEN

MONTANA

Redd was working in the barn when he heard a vehicle rolling up the drive. He was relieved to see that it was just Mikey Derhammer returning J. B.'s old pickup as promised. When Redd came out to meet him, Mikey held out a large paper coffee cup.

"Hit the Coffee Stop on my way out," Mikey explained. "Thought you could use a little pick-me-up."

"You thought right," Redd replied, taking the cup from his friend. "Thanks, man."

Mikey nodded.

Although he'd already downed most of the pot of coffee he'd brewed before sunrise, Redd was still feeling the effects of jet lag and a sleepless night. He popped the lid off and took a cautious sip.

Making coffee was part of his morning ritual, so he almost never had occasion to buy a cup. When he did, it was always straight up—no cream, no sugar, and definitely not one of the elaborate concoctions that seemed more like a liquid dessert than something to start the day. Mikey had at least gotten that part right. The cup appeared to contain nothing more than black coffee, and although it had cooled a little during the drive, it tasted strong enough to strip paint off a wall.

"What is this?"

Mikey grinned. "It's called a 'black eye.' Coffee with two shots of espresso."

Redd downed the rest of the drink in a series of quick gulps, then gestured to the truck. "Hop in. I'll take you back into town."

Mikey waited until they were on the highway, heading south toward Wellington, to raise the topic that had clearly been on his mind. "So what's your plan?"

Redd gave him a sidelong glance. "Plan?"

"I know you, brother. What happened to Em . . . it's gotta be eating at you. If that was Liz and Luke, I know I'd want to even the score. I get it."

Redd returned his eyes to the road, saying nothing.

"Just be careful, okay? Don't do anything stupid."

"Wouldn't dream of it," Redd replied.

"Uh-huh." Mikey smiled. "Just remember what's really important, man. Emily and little Matty need you. They need you a lot more than they need you getting even with those two-wheel thugs."

"I appreciate your concern, but—"

"I wasn't finished," Mikey shot back. "I had to say all that. Liz made me." He smiled. "But because I know you, I know that chances are pretty good you're going to do something, and when you do, I got your back. Just promise me that you won't make a move on a whole gang of bikers without calling me first, okay?"

Redd wished he could be more forthcoming with his old friend, but the less Mikey knew about the situation, the better. For everyone.

"If it makes you feel any better, once I drop you off, I'm going to pay a visit to Sheriff Blackwood."

"It doesn't," Mikey said. "Make me feel better, I mean. I told you

Blackwood sounded kind of spooked by all this. I don't think he'll be much help."

Redd felt a twinge of irritation. "Agreed." He sighed. "Emily wants me to let it go. Pretend nothing happened."

"I think it might be best if you did. Sometimes you just gotta let it go."

Redd wanted to say, *And what if I can't? What if they keep coming? Because that's what they're going to do, Mikey.*

Redd believed that. He could feel it in his bones.

But his friend would never understand. Nobody would. Those around him, no matter how well-intentioned they were, inhabited a world where violence was just something you heard about on the news. That was the kind of world Redd would have preferred to live in, a world where Em and Junior would always be safe. But it was already too late for that.

He couldn't tell Mikey that, any more than he could tell Emily, so he just shrugged. "Maybe. I guess we'll see."

"Guess so. But like I said, don't do anything by yourself. Call me first, and I'll be there."

Redd nodded to his friend.

✖ ✖ ✖

After dropping Mikey off, Redd drove to Roy's Thriftway, where he picked up a clamshell container of frosted cupcakes, and then to the courthouse, where he placed the cupcakes on Maggie Albright's desk as if offering a tribute.

Maggie put her hands on her ample hips in a look of mock disapproval. "Are you trying to fatten me up like one of your heifers, Matthew Redd?"

Redd grinned. "Maggie, you're perfect just the way you are. And if Em knew I was bringing you sweets, she'd probably have a conniption, so let's just keep it between the two of us."

"Uh-huh." She regarded him suspiciously. "I suppose you want to talk to Stuart."

"You suppose correctly."

"He figured you'd be stopping by. Go on in."

Redd flashed his best smile as he stepped around the desk and strode toward the private office of Sheriff Stuart W. Blackwood. As soon as he stepped through the door, the smile evaporated like morning mist. "Morning, Sheriff."

Blackwood, seated behind his uncluttered desk, raised his eyes to Redd. "Matthew. Come on in."

The sheriff was not the same man Redd had met fifteen months earlier, not the same man who had delivered the awful news of J. B.'s death. That Stuart Blackwood had been a man standing on the edge of oblivion. Friendless, haunted by personal demons, tempted every day by the bottle, and worst of all, in Anton Gage's pocket. He had not actually committed any criminal acts, only looked the other way as Gage's son, Wyatt, slowly took over the town. Yet at his core, he was a good man and had redeemed himself by helping Redd deal with Gage's hit team. He'd caught a bullet for his trouble—a flesh wound that Emily had patched up.

Subsequently, the sheriff had found the motivation to reengage with life. He'd lost twenty pounds—though judging by the paunch that still strained the lower buttons of his uniform blouse, he could probably stand to lose twenty more. His bushy mustache—steel gray like his hair—still drooped down to either side of his mouth, but now it was combed and waxed, making him look a little like an older Wyatt Earp. The greatest change, however, was his general demeanor. Despite his workload, managing an underfunded, undermanned rural law enforcement agency, the new Sheriff Blackwood was known to smile on occasion.

He was not smiling today.

"I guess I know why you're here," Blackwood began.

"That's good," Redd fired back. "That means we can skip ahead to the part where you tell me what you're going to do about it."

Under his mustache, Blackwood's lips turned down. "What would you like me to do about it?"

Redd was momentarily dumbfounded. He had expected Blackwood to at least tell him that the deputies were doing their best, running down leads, or something like that. Something to placate him. But Blackwood's question sounded like an admission of defeat. Redd recalled the word Mikey had used to describe the sheriff's mood.

He is spooked, Redd thought.

He took a deep breath to keep his rising ire in check. "How about you do your job. Get these animals off the streets."

Blackwood folded his hands on the desk. "What do you know about these biker gangs?"

Redd's knowledge of outlaw bikers was limited to occasional sightings of Hells Angels cruising down the California freeways and what Rob Davis had told him. He'd also seen them portrayed in movies and television shows, but he assumed those depictions were of questionable veracity. "I know they're a public menace," he replied guardedly.

"That's putting it mildly. I dealt with them a few times when I was on the job in Chicago, and I can tell you this: We made arrests from time to time. Mostly possession. Weapons charges. Small potatoes. Sent a few of 'em away for a couple years at Stateville, but these guys treat hard time like a badge of honor. We never—not once—made a serious charge stick. Murder. Assault. Rape. They walked every time. And do you want to know why?"

Redd had a pretty good idea, but he kept his silence.

"Because of fear. These guys don't think twice about intimidating witnesses. Or jurors. Or cops and judges for that matter."

"You make them sound like the mafia," Redd muttered.

"They are like the mafia. Or maybe they're worse, because the mafia at least occasionally know how to be subtle."

"Are you telling me the almighty Chicago PD can't protect their witnesses long enough to bring a bunch of Mad Max rejects to trial?"

Blackwood shook his head with a sigh. "They may look rough—and honestly, most're rougher than they look—but they aren't stupid. Leastwise not the guys at the top. A lot of them are former military—"

"You're joking," Redd cut in but then recalled that even the corps attracted its share of dirtbags and psychopaths.

But Blackwood wasn't. "I talked to a guy . . . ATF agent who went deep under with one of the clubs. Got his full patch. That's an almost-impossible thing to do, by the way. These bikers can sniff out a narc from a mile away. And they've got all kinds of loyalty tests. Things a cop just can't do. But you know what he told me? After a couple years of riding with the guys, he felt more camaraderie with them than he did his fellow ATF agents. He said it reminded him of when he was in the Army Rangers."

"Sounds like Stockholm syndrome to me."

"Maybe so," Blackwood conceded. "The point I'm trying to make is that there's more to these bikers than just the outlaw image. They've got lawyers and private detectives . . . Pains me to say it, but they've got dirty cops on their payroll. Their internal loyalty is absolute, and their ability to find and intimidate—or kill—anyone who poses a threat is absolute."

As he listened, Redd's righteous indignation waned. He had not really expected Blackwood to provide him with any kind of satisfying legal resolution. No, he'd known from the start that he was going to have to take care of business himself. Talking to Blackwood was just a formality. But the sheriff was, without realizing it, providing Redd with valuable intelligence about his enemy.

Don't underestimate them. Check.

Redd waited a moment as if to let Blackwood's admonition sink in. "Can I read the report Em gave you?"

Blackwood shifted in his chair and returned a wary glance. "What do you want with it?"

"I just want to know what actually happened. And I'd rather not ask Em about it. She'd probably try to play it down anyway."

Blackwood stared back at him as if trying to determine the net value of sharing the report with Redd. Finally he leaned forward and put his hands on the keyboard of his computer. "I suppose it's a matter of public record," he rumbled as he entered a series of keystrokes. A moment later, he rose from behind the desk and went over to the printer-copier unit in the corner of the room to retrieve a freshly printed page, which he handed over.

Redd took it and scanned the copy for a moment. The formal legalese of the report conveyed none of the terror that he imagined Emily must have felt as the gang closed in on her, beating their fists against the Tahoe. In fact, Emily's name only appeared in the report at the top, where she was identified and afterward always referred to as "WITNESS." There were, however, a few important new details. Emily had provided physical descriptions of several of the bikers, especially one.

WITNESS described man as white male approx. 6'10" height, 300 lbs. Long red hair and full beard, and said, "Reminded me of an old Norse berserker."

Should be easy to pick that guy out of a crowd, Redd thought.

There was one other detail Redd noticed. "She said their jackets had different cities. Milwaukee. Missoula. Helena."

Blackwood nodded. "The Infidels have dozens of chapters. Maybe as many as a hundred. Mostly in the Midwest and Northeast. Two or three times a year, they come together for an organized ride, which is basically just a big party, though they probably also do a lot of illegal stuff. Moving and selling guns and narcotics. My guess is that they were just passing through on a ride. I have no idea why they decided to bother your wife, but I'm sure it was just a random thing. They'll have moved on by now."

"The members of the chapters live in those cities? Helena? Missoula?"

"That's right. The individual chapters may only have a handful of members, especially out here in the boonies. In bigger cities, like Chicago and Detroit, they might have multiple chapters." Blackwood's eyes narrowed suspiciously. "Matthew, if you're thinking about trying to . . . I don't know, take matters into your own hands . . . just put that thought out of your head. That's a fight you can't win. And you've got a family to think of."

Redd inclined his head as if ceding the point, then folded the police report. "Thanks for this."

"Matthew," Blackwood said, his tone harsh, scolding. "I'm serious. Do not pursue this. You do not want to go to war with these guys."

War? If they want a war, I'll give them one.

But Redd didn't say this out loud. He didn't say anything. He just stood and left Blackwood's office without another word.

✖ ✖ ✖

The little run-down house on Apple Street looked even worse in daylight. As he cruised past without stopping, Redd could not help but think back to the last time he'd been here: the confrontation with the two bikers that had ended with him delivering an ultimatum right out of the Wild West.

"Leave town by sunup, or pay the price."

He hadn't used those exact words, but the message had been received loud and clear. There had been too much going on in the days following to verify that the bikers had shuttered their whorehouse–slash–illicit pharmacy, but judging by the sheets of plywood nailed over the windows and the tattered foreclosure notice and No Trespassing sign stapled to the door, the place had been abandoned.

Redd wasn't surprised, though he was a little disappointed. If the Infidels had moved back into town, it would have made tracking them down a whole lot easier. Now he would have to do some legwork.

He vividly recalled the embroidered patches sewn onto the black leather vest one of the bikers had worn. The modified Jolly Roger design, the gothic lettering with the name of the motorcycle club, and the slightly smaller rocker underneath that indicated the biker's affiliation with the Bozeman chapter.

The sheriff had inadvertently answered a question that had been troubling Redd almost from the moment he'd learned of what the Infidels had done to Emily, namely how the bikers had identified him and subsequently Emily as someone important to him. With lawyers and private investigators at their beck and call, it would have been no great feat to figure out who had given the two club members a beatdown. The only real mystery was why they had waited so long to come for him.

Redd took the next right, then turned left onto the highway, heading south. As he did, he took out his phone and called Emily's cell. He did not expect her to answer. Odds were good she was with a patient, but to his pleasant surprise, she picked up on the second ring.

"Hey, Matty," she said, sounding only a little stressed.

"Hey. Just calling to check in." Since this was not something he usually did, he added, "Junior doing okay?"

"Last I checked."

"That's good. I'm heading to Boze to pick up some A-D. Anything on the shopping list that I should pick up while I'm there?"

Redd unconsciously held his breath as he waited for her answer. In fact, they had an ample supply of the injectable vitamin A and D supplement solution for their stock, and even if they didn't, he could have picked some up at Hohman's feed and supply just as easily.

But evidently Emily saw no reason to challenge the pretext, thus sparing Redd the need to create some flimsy justification for making an unnecessary trip into Bozeman. "Can't think of anything at the moment," she said. "Drive safe."

"I will. Kiss Junior for me. I love you."

"Love you, too."

He hung up the phone and steeled himself for what would come next. It was time to meet some bikers.

ELEVEN

The Harley-Davidson dealership was located just off the interstate, near the airport exit. Redd had passed by dozens of times without giving it much thought. He'd never imagined he'd have a reason to go inside. But with no idea where to begin looking for the Infidels, it seemed as likely a starting point as any.

He had tried googling them. The search yielded a Wikipedia page detailing their history, enumerating the various crimes and acts of violence to which members of the club had been linked, and even identifying several cities where they had established chapters, but no information was given about the location of any of their clubhouses. Unlike the Hells Angels, the Infidels did not have an official website.

Next he searched for biker bars in the Bozeman area, but that too had yielded nothing meaningful. Like some old Prohibition-era speakeasy, it seemed the biker subculture was open only to those who were already in the know.

The only lead he had was that the Infidels exclusively rode hogs.

The two-story warehouse building would not have looked out of place in any industrial park. Redd half expected to walk into a grungy shop with greasy biker dudes in leathers, tinkering with their rides or otherwise just hanging out, but the interior of the dealership looked more like a high-end, motorcycle-themed tourist attraction.

A trio of oversize mock oilcans sporting the Harley-Davidson shield logo greeted him as he stepped through the glass entrance door. Memorabilia of all kinds adorned the walls—posters and photographs of Harleys cruising down scenic highways, vintage signs, maps, and even, because it was Montana, a mounted bison head—along with every imaginable motorcycle accessory—windshields, handlebars, light kits. Hanging from the vaulted ceiling above the showroom was an enormous American flag. But all of these were mere accents. The star attractions were arranged in orderly ranks on the polished concrete showroom floor—at least twenty gleaming Harley-Davidson motorcycles, resting on kickstands with their front wheels canted to the left, the handlebars looking like open arms, extending a silent invitation to climb on and run wild.

Redd, who had ridden dirt bikes as a teenager, had always preferred four wheels to two, but as he gazed appreciatively at the massive metal steeds, breathing in the distinctive machine smell—grease and oil, tire cleaner and wax polish—he thought he understood, maybe for the first time, some of the appeal of the biker lifestyle.

But cruising the highway with the wind on your face and 100 hp between your legs was one thing. Hanging out with cranked-up reprobates, running drugs, guns, and girls, and tormenting the innocent . . . the appeal of *that* was something Redd would never understand.

He had not been in the showroom thirty seconds when a sales representative came over to greet him. The man was of average height and build, about the same age as Redd, with a conservative hairstyle and a neatly trimmed beard. He wore a black polo shirt adorned with the orange Harley-Davidson logo and pressed khakis and carried a tablet computer in his right hand.

"Hi, there. I'm Scott, the sales manager." Scott's fingers hovered over the screen of the tablet, ready to enter Redd's vital information. "And you are?"

"Just looking," Redd replied, dodging the question.

Scott flashed a perfunctory smile and inclined his head. "By all means. Feel free to look around. If you have any questions, I'll be right over there." He pointed to the sales counter, which was positioned against the same wall that sported the bison head, and then moved off without another word.

Redd was pleasantly surprised that the sales manager had given up so easily. He had no patience for the hard sell. Then it occurred to him that he neither looked nor smelled like the upscale establishment's usual clientele. Scott had clearly decided that Redd was just window-shopping and not worth the effort.

That realization was quickly followed by another.

What am I even doing here?

He had entertained a vague notion of staking out the dealership until one of the Infidels paid a visit, then tailing him back to their clubhouse. He now saw how foolish that expectation had been. The outlaw bikers were about as likely to patronize the dealership as he was.

Redd was beginning to see that his failure to develop a plan had been a plan to fail. Despite what Emily and Sheriff Blackwood might have believed, Redd was no cop. He didn't have a beat cop's instincts, did not possess the keen wits of a detective. No, Redd's training was much different. Back in the Marines, he was given a target to hit—and he'd hit it with everything he had. It's what he wanted to do with the Infidels, but first he needed a target.

After pondering his limited options, he decided to throw caution to the wind. He headed over to the sales desk and settled onto one of the shop stools arranged on the customer side. "Actually, Scott, there is something you might be able to help me with."

The sales manager tried to hide his look of surprise and displeasure behind a thin smile. "Sure thing. What can I do for you?"

"I'm trying to find the Infidels."

Scott started visibly, his smile sagging. "Can't help you with that."

"Look, here's the thing. My sister . . . she's just sixteen . . . took up with one of them. I'm trying to find her so I can drag her back to the farm before she ends up hooked on drugs or pregnant or . . . well, I don't want to think about what else might happen to her." Redd was actually impressed with his improvisation. He wasn't a good liar, nor did he believe in being dishonest. Jim Bob had raised him to believe that, at the end of the day, a man's word is all he's got. But if he told the truth and word got back to the Infidels that he'd gone looking for whoever scared his wife, it could put Emily back in danger. And he wasn't willing to risk that.

Scott shrugged. "Sorry. Can't help you. Try the police."

"I'd like to avoid that if I can. I mean, if Jenny got arrested or put in juvie or something, it would break Ma's heart."

Scott sighed. "Look, mister. It's not that I don't want to help. I just don't know anything about the Infidels or any of the one-percenters."

This was a term Redd had encountered in the Wikipedia article. *One-percenters* was a catchall term adopted by the unruliest motorcycle clubs. The story went that, after a press release by the American Motorcyclist Association stated that 99 percent of motorcycle riders were upstanding, law-abiding citizens, the outlaw motorcycle clubs began proudly identifying themselves as part of the one percent who preferred to raise hell.

"Those guys don't come around here," Scott went on. "So you see, I just can't help you."

"You must have some idea where they hang out. A bar? Something like that?"

"I really don't," Scott insisted. Then, dropping his voice a little as if to confide a secret, he went on. "Look, I'm sorry your sister took up with them, but even if you could find her . . ." He shook his head. "You don't want to mess with those guys. Hopefully, your sis will come to her senses and leave of her own free will before they mess her up too bad. If they let her. That's about the best you can hope for."

Redd's crestfallen expression was no improvisation.

But then Scott seemed to have a change of heart. "I probably shouldn't tell you this . . ."

"I didn't hear it from you," Redd prompted.

Scott glanced around as if to make sure that nobody was around to overhear. "The guy who does our custom builds runs with them."

Redd was taken aback. "You actually hired one of those maniacs?" This reaction was also genuine.

"Hey, what he does in his spare time is his own business. And he's a heckuva good bike builder. He's never been in any trouble that I know about." Scott's shoulders came up in a shrug. "They aren't all criminals, you know."

Redd dismissed the observation. "Give me a name."

Scott shifted his weight from side to side. "I won't do that. But I will tell you this. He's not here. He called in a few days ago and said he was going out of town for a while. He does that a few times a year. Usually when the club makes a run."

"A run?"

"An organized ride. It's one of their big get-togethers. What I'm trying to tell you is that you're not going to find them or your sister hereabouts."

Redd leaned closer. "Where are they going?"

"North. That's all I know." Scott shook his head again. "I've probably said too much already."

Redd thought about pressing harder, demanding a name, but there was real fear behind Scott's eyes. "All right," he mumbled, turning away and heading for the exit.

Back in the truck, he mentally reviewed what Scott had told him. It wasn't much, but it was more than he had when he'd gone in.

The Infidels were on a run.

That explained why the riders who had attacked Emily represented several different chapters of the club. The timing of it did not feel like a coincidence. The entire club, or at least a significant portion of them in the region, had assembled, and the feud with Redd was evidently at the top of their agenda.

Or is it?

It had been two days since the attack on Emily, and Redd hadn't seen anything from them yet. Was it possible that he'd misjudged the entire situation and maybe things weren't as dire as he feared?

No, he told himself. *They're coming.* Of that, he was sure.

But where were they?

North.

That could mean Canada, but Redd had a feeling they hadn't gone quite that far.

He took out his phone, intending to launch a Google search, but saw that he had missed a call. He didn't recognize the number, but the prefix indicated that the call had come from Wellington. The caller had left a voice mail message, which he played.

"Mr. Redd, this is Mandy Danes from the county assessor's office." Redd did not recognize the name or the slightly husky female voice, but he groaned a little when the agency was named. "We need to speak with you concerning your tax liability. It's rather urgent. Please get back to me as soon as possible so we can schedule a meeting." Mandy then supplied a phone number, the same one from which the call had originated, and after one more admonition to "call as soon as you get this," hung up.

Redd had a pretty good idea what the call was about. When he'd come back to the Thompson Ranch, he'd learned that J. B. had accumulated a considerable tax debt. The county was planning to seize the property and auction it off to pay down what was owed. It had later emerged that Wyatt Gage was pressuring the former assessor, Randall Shaw, to take the ranch because he wanted the land for his own uses. Wyatt's subsequent death and the revelation of Shaw's corruption had not erased the debt Redd had inherited, but he had been able to strike a gentleman's deal with the interim assessor, establishing a payment plan that barely covered the interest but at least served as a good faith effort on Redd's part, allowing him to keep the ranch.

No doubt the new assessor, who had taken the job after a special election following Shaw's ouster, wanted to revisit the terms of Redd's agreement. That might have met the definition of *urgent* for a politician, but it was pretty far down the list for Redd, especially with everything else going on in his life.

He deleted the message and resumed his search, opening Google and typing in *motorcycle shops in Helena*. He was surprised how many businesses popped up, but with no other leads to follow, he decided it was time to start checking them off one by one.

Throwing his truck into drive, Redd stepped on the gas and left the Harley dealership behind.

TWELVE

Montana's state capital, Helena, was actually closer to the Thompson Ranch by about fifteen miles than Bozeman, but the latter city was half-again as big, with all the amenities that came with a larger and rapidly expanding population. Bozeman was a little big city while Helena was more like a big small town, which was why Redd rarely had cause to travel there. Helena's closer proximity to Redd's home, however, made it a much likelier choice for the Infidels to establish a base of operations from which to prosecute their war with Redd. Additionally, Emily had reported a Helena patch among the pack that had waylaid her.

There were no Harley dealers in Helena, so Redd focused on motorcycle repair shops. Maybe the Infidels didn't buy their hogs retail, but they would need to get them serviced from time to time. The mechanics might know something about the social habits of their clientele, and with a little gentle persuasion, Redd felt certain they could be compelled to share it. He figured he'd start with the same ruse that had worked with Scott the sales manager and adjust as needed.

The first few on the list were reputable establishments with polished websites and glowing customer reviews. Redd skipped over those. The Infidels would no doubt take their business somewhere the general public was less likely to visit. That brought him to Jimmy J's Motorcycle Repair. The only information the listing provided was a phone number and a street address in the industrial area out by the regional airport. No website, no reviews, not even a Facebook page.

Exactly the kind of low-key operation that might cater to outlaw bikers.

As he drove past the turnoff to the ranch, fully ninety minutes after leaving the Harley-Davidson dealership, Redd felt a twinge of guilt. It was already past noon, and there was work he ought to be doing. Some of it could be put off another day or two, but some really couldn't. He knew that he'd be better able to focus on his responsibilities once he dealt with the problem of the Infidels, but there was no telling how long that might take. Today he hoped for nothing more than to identify the Infidels' base of operations, but putting an end to the threat they posed was going to take time. The thing about life, and especially ranch life, was that you couldn't just put it on pause. He would have to find a way to juggle the cares of everyday life with the looming showdown, all the while remaining vigilant.

Half an hour later, he pulled into the parking lot of a large warehouse that had been subdivided into four commercial storefronts with roll-up doors large enough to accommodate RVs and tractor trucks. Tucked in between a glazier and a used auto parts shop was Jimmy J's Motorcycle Repair. Unlike the neighboring businesses, Jimmy J's doors were rolled down and a sign on the adjacent entry door read Closed. Redd parked directly in front of the latter and got out for a closer look.

In addition to the Closed sign, a piece of paper with the message *Closed until further notice* was taped on the door's glass pane. Looking past it, Redd could see a small service lobby inside, with freestanding shelf units stocked with motor oil and various accessories. It was all very neat and utilitarian, except for the back wall, which featured an elaborate mural that looked like it might have been album art for a death metal band. From what Redd could tell, it was a likeness of the grim reaper sitting astride a big hog, wearing a leather motorcycle jacket and a *Stahlhelm*-style motorcycle helmet. There was an Iron Cross emblazoned on the helmet, and a familiar diamond-shaped patch on the rider's shoulder—the quasi-official emblem of the one-percenters.

Was Jimmy J an outlaw biker? Was he perhaps even an Infidel? If so, it might explain why his shop was closed indefinitely.

Sales manager Scott's revelation that one of the Infidels worked at the dealership had been a real eye-opener for Redd. Until that moment, he had assumed that the bikers got all their income from illicit enterprises. It had not occurred to him that they might have day jobs. It was hard to imagine big, burly dudes with shaggy hair and beards as professionals or working in retail stores, but he supposed there were plenty of other jobs where regular grooming standards did not apply, not to mention those services that would dovetail nicely with the biker lifestyle, such as custom bike builders and mechanics.

But regardless of Jimmy J's affiliation with the Infidels, his shop looked to be a dead end. As he headed back to his truck, Redd checked his phone for the next shop on the list. He was dismayed to discover that he had missed another call from the county assessor's office. There was also another voice mail, but Redd didn't play it.

He thumbed back to the home screen, then brought up the page with his search results.

"Looking for Jimmy?"

Redd looked up from his phone and spotted the source of the voice—a man standing just outside the open roll-up to the glass vendor.

"Yeah," Redd replied and then, improvising again, added, "He was supposed to get me a new carburetor for my ride."

He didn't know if motorcycles still had carburetors; it was just the first thing that popped into his head. Evidently it sufficed because the man accepted it with a nod. "Yeah, he's out riding with his boys. Don't know when he'll be back."

Redd gave the man an appraising glance. He looked like the average run-of-the-mill Montanan—midthirties, white, with brown hair and a full but neatly trimmed beard, a flannel shirt, Wranglers, and a trucker cap with the NASCAR logo on it. Yet there was nothing judgmental in his tone when he referred to his neighbor and the biker gang he rode with.

"I figured," Redd said. "Guess I'll have to wait. Don't suppose you know where they went?"

The man shrugged. "Who knows with those guys. Someone up at the Buffalo Jump might know."

Redd was familiar with the term *buffalo jump* from his high school state history lessons. As far back as prehistoric times, Plains Indians had hunted bison in a unique and rather brutal way by stampeding the animals and chasing them over cliffs where the beasts fell to their death. The practice was even mentioned in the journals of Lewis and Clark. But Redd didn't think that was what the man was referring to.

"I'll try that," he said. "Thanks."

✳ ✳ ✳

The Buffalo Jump Roadhouse was a squalid cinder-block structure located just off the highway about five miles west of the town line. Even before he turned in to the parking lot, Redd knew that he had found the place. Lined up in orderly rows outside the establishment were more than two dozen huge motorcycles.

The hogs outside the Buffalo Jump bore as much resemblance to the bikes Redd had seen in the Harley-Davidson showroom as a junkyard dog did to a finalist at the Westminster Kennel Club show. Some looked intentionally brutish. Most just looked beat-up and worn-out, but they were all big.

Unbidden, an image of those machines swarming around Emily's Tahoe flashed through Redd's mind and, with it, a surge of anger.

He hadn't really thought through what he would do if he found the Infidels' hangout. Had this been an FBI operation with the fly team, he probably would have kept right on driving, at least far enough to be out of the direct line of sight of anyone coming or going from the tavern, and established an overwatch position to surveil the establishment. From there, he would gather photographic evidence, identify the bikers if possible, and when they finally left, trail them to their clubhouse or private residence.

But Redd wasn't thinking tactically. He wasn't thinking at all.

Without really knowing what he was doing, he had parked the truck and was striding purposefully toward the entrance. The pounding bass of an old-school heavy metal song reverberated across the parking lot, keeping time with Redd's rage-fueled pulse.

The obligatory *No Minors Permitted* sign was posted on one of the red plywood double doors. On the other was a crudely written sign declaring: *NO PATCHES ALLOWED—STRICTLY ENFORCED.* Had Redd not earlier taken a deep dive into outlaw biker culture, the significance of this might have escaped him. "No patches" meant that members of motorcycle clubs were not permitted to display their affiliation, thus ensuring that rivalries between competing gangs did not flash-ignite barroom brawls or worse. It also meant that he would not be able to immediately identify the bar's patrons as Infidels. Nevertheless, he grasped the pull handle, which appeared to have been made from lengths of inch-and-a-half pipe, with elbow joints and flanges screwed into the painted plywood, and yanked the door open.

A miasma of cigarette smoke, stale beer, and body odor poured out, along with the unsuppressed fury of the music. Through the haze, Redd could see a few illuminated beer advertisements on the walls, but the rest of the interior was too dimly lit for him to make out much else. He squeezed his eyes shut for a moment, then blinked several times, trying to hasten the adjustment of his eyes to the lower light level inside the building.

Abruptly the music stopped, plunging the still-dark room into almost-total silence and leaving Redd feeling both deaf and blind. The suddenness of the change was ominous. Redd was tempted to turn around and head back into the light, but he knew that would be a mistake. He was committed now, as surely as if he'd just stepped out into a minefield. The only way through was forward.

Distinct figures began to emerge from the gloom, gathered around tables, leaning over the long bar that ran the length of the room to Redd's left, or hunched over one of two pool tables that dominated the center of the space. As the gloom receded, his estimate of their number increased almost exponentially, two or three becoming ten, fifteen, twenty-five. Strangely, none of the figures moved. Their unnatural stillness reminded Redd of the mannequins that had populated mock towns built to assess the damage caused by early atomic weapons during the Cold War. But these were statues of flesh and blood, and their immobility was by choice. They were, one and all, staring at Redd with varying degrees of astonishment.

A voice—a man's—broke the silence. "Lose your herd, cowboy?"

The speaker had a flat affect, as if he couldn't be bothered to inject enthusiasm into his speech, even when being sarcastic. Nevertheless, the observation unleashed a torrent of laughter from the rest of the onlookers.

Redd did not respond but continued scanning the room. He was now able to make out more details—not just facial characteristics, build, and hair color, but clothing styles and tattoos. Most of the men looked exactly as Redd would have expected, with long, unkempt hair and shaggy beards, though they ranged in size from hulking brutes to scrawny beanpoles. Some wore T-shirts and jeans. Only a few wore leather, and from what Redd could see, none displayed the distinctive patch of the Infidels Motorcycle Club. Evidently the no-patches rule was being honored by the clientele. While the majority looked tougher than a three-dollar steak, several of them had gone soft in the middle, with prodigious beer guts sagging out ahead of them. Redd counted only about half a dozen women, though in truth, he was having trouble telling the difference, and not just because a lot of the guys had long hair.

His visual sweep came to an abrupt stop when he beheld one distinctive figure who was not laughing with the others but was instead regarding Redd with a knowing smirk—a sure sign that he was the source of the witty remark. It was not the smirk, however, that commanded Redd's attention, but rather the man's physical appearance.

Tall—at least six-ten, but possibly taller—with the physique of a D lineman, the man had a halo of reddish-blond hair and a bushy copper beard that hung halfway to his chest.

The description from the police report came back to Redd. Emily's words.

"Reminded me of an old Norse berserker."

This was the man who had led the assault on Emily and little Matty. Redd was sure of it.

He had found the Infidels.

THIRTEEN

A host of conflicting priorities fought for primacy in Redd's mind. The impulse to charge the Berserker and pummel him into oblivion was almost overwhelming. But he also knew how that would end.

The Berserker wasn't alone.

If it had just been a question of brawling, Redd might not have hesitated. In some ways, fighting multiple opponents was easier than one-on-one combat. Groups of attackers tended to hold back, waiting for someone else to make a move, especially when their lone opponent was on his feet and unpredictable. But these outlaw bikers were almost certainly armed. Chains, blades, improvised cudgels, and probably handguns—those things changed the calculation. Redd had only his old Case folding knife. His Ruger Vaquero revolver was locked in the gun safe bolted to the floor under the driver's seat of the pickup, but even if he'd thought to bring the .44 Magnum handgun with him, it would not have significantly changed the odds he was now facing.

You got what you came here for, that reasonable part of him said. *Positive identification. Now break contact before this gets out of control.*

But doing that might be interpreted as weakness, and just the perception of weakness would invite swift escalation of this conflict. Besides, there was a good chance they knew exactly who he was and why he had come into their midst. It was already too late to walk away.

Plus, Redd didn't care.

"What's the matter, cowboy?" the Berserker asked in that same atonal voice. "Cat got your tongue?"

Another wave of collective laughter rolled through the room.

Trying to keep his anger in check, Redd waited until it petered out to break his silence. "I'm looking for the Infidels."

The Berserker's eyebrows arched in a look of mock surprise. "Infidels? You mean like al Qaeda or something? You want them, maybe you should try looking in Iraq or someplace like that."

This comment also produced laughter from the onlookers. Whether because they'd all had too much to drink or were just that dim-witted, the bikers appeared to have an exceptionally low threshold for humor. The man's exaggerated mispronunciation of the names—*AL KAY duh. I-RACK*—seemed deliberate, as if he was trying to sound ignorant.

"You must be the funny one," Redd remarked, keeping his tone equally neutral.

The laughter fell off immediately. Redd felt the eyes of everyone in the room upon him, all of them waiting to see what would happen next.

They want a fight, he realized.

He recalled J. B.'s advice: *"Don't you ever throw the first punch, but make sure you throw the last one."*

"You know what I think is funny," Redd went on. "That word, *infidel.* See, you've got it wrong. It's actually what al Qaeda calls us. And by *us,* I mean Americans. To them, we're the infidels, the unbelievers, because we're not Muslims. Most of us, anyway."

From the corner of his eye, Redd could see some of the bikers looking at each other in consternation. They had expected fireworks, and instead,

Redd was lecturing them on religion. Even the Berserker's smirk had slipped a couple notches as he continued to regard Redd with increasing bemusement.

"But that's not the funny part," Redd said. "The funny part is that word: *infidel*. It doesn't actually mean 'unbeliever.' What it really means is 'one without faith.' I think about that a lot because I was in the Marine Corps, and our motto is *semper fidelis*. Always faithful.

"Faith in your cause . . . your nation . . . your brothers. Faith in what's right. It's the kind of faith that separates real men from, well . . ." He paused and made a sweeping gesture with his hand.

It took a moment for the barb to sink in, but when it finally did, the transformation was instantaneous. The Berserker's steel-blue eyes seemed to flash red, and then he was moving, arrowing across the room toward Redd like a heat-seeking missile.

Redd braced himself to meet the charge. He had intentionally provoked the big man, just as a matador might taunt a bull. Fury had a way of clouding a person's judgment, and that would give Redd a significant advantage against an opponent who was bigger and probably stronger. It was a calculated risk, but if he could defeat the Berserker in single combat—David against the Infidels' Goliath—it would, at the very least, shake the enemy's morale.

"Baby Boy!"

The utterance was barely louder than the conversational tone Redd had been using, but it had the effect of stopping the Berserker in his tracks. Like a guard dog hitting the end of his chain, the big man fumed and glowered, his fingers clawing the air in front of him, but his booted feet seemed to be rooted to the floor.

"That's enough, Baby Boy. Stand down."

Baby Boy?

The command seemed to be coming from somewhere near the bar, but Redd did not dare break eye contact with the Berserker.

"Turn me loose, Johnny!" the Berserker screamed. "Let me finish him!"

"I said, stand down."

The Berserker hissed through his teeth but made no further move toward Redd.

With the immediate threat on pause, Redd risked glancing over in the direction from which the voice had come. There were more than a dozen men there, along with three or four women, but only one man was staring back at him. He looked older than all the others, late fifties, maybe even sixties, though it was hard to say. He had a shaved head and the skin of his scalp and face had the texture of old leather, creased and worn, weathered by the sun. His salt-and-pepper beard was full, but not as unkempt as many of the others. But it was his eyes that conveyed a sense of real age—not measured in years, but in experience. He was, Redd decided, much more of a threat than the Berserker.

Redd turned back to the Berserker. "You're not the first big guy I've met who's running on a short leash, Baby Boy. Is that your nickname or something?"

The big man bared his teeth in a fierce grin. "That's right."

"Is that supposed to be ironic?"

"I don't know what that means."

The last giant Redd fought, a man named Shevchenko, had been surprisingly well educated. While this clown was a touch larger, he wasn't nearly as smart as he thought he was. Redd wasn't sure if that was a good thing or a bad thing, and he wasn't in the mood to explain the concept.

The big man went on. "I got the name when I ate a baby boy." He licked his lips in exaggerated fashion while the rest of the tavern's patrons exploded with laughter. There was just one holdout, the dark-eyed graybeard.

Redd turned and stared at the older man for a long moment. "Johnny, is it?"

"Angry Johnny," the woman sitting beside him chimed in. "Like in the song."

Redd glanced at her, really looking for the first time. She had short, spiky, bleached-out hair, wore too much makeup, and looked almost painfully thin—likely a result of prolonged amphetamine abuse. Steel hoops and studs adorned various parts of her visible anatomy, along with several colorful tattoos. In spite of all that, Redd thought she had probably once been an attractive woman before the biker lifestyle consumed her like cancer.

"I guess I don't know that song," he muttered. "So you're holding his leash?" He thrust his chin toward the Berserker—Baby Boy.

Angry Johnny gave an indifferent shrug. "Me? I'm just a guy having a drink." He gestured at a half-full pitcher on the table before him. "Why don't you join me?"

Redd shook his head. "I don't think so."

He thought about editorializing. *I don't drink with scum*, or something to that effect, but decided against it. Despite his nickname, Redd got the impression that schoolyard insults would probably roll off Angry Johnny like water off a duck's back.

"Are you sure?" Johnny asked with obvious insincerity. "You know, beer is made from grain, so sharing a drink . . . why, that would be almost like breaking bread together. In some cultures, even sworn enemies can put aside their differences while breaking bread."

"Is that what we are? Sworn enemies?"

Johnny did not answer with words. Instead, he raised his glass as if toasting Redd, then drained it in a long swallow. When he was done, he slammed the glass down on the table. The violence of the action startled the woman.

"Johnny!" she murmured. "You scared the crap outta me."

He ignored her, keeping his gaze fixed on Redd. "What's your business with the Infidels?"

"It's my business," Redd replied. "And theirs. So unless you speak for them . . ." He gave a meaningful shrug.

Johnny leaned forward as if ready to confide a secret. "You know what I think? I think you're in over your head. You walk in here all full of fire and righteous indignation, spoiling for a fight. But you don't know the first thing about the Infidels."

Redd again resisted the temptation to taunt and instead went with "Why don't you enlighten me?"

Angry Johnny smiled but there was no humor. "You talk about fidelity. You know what fidelity really is? It's misplaced loyalty. You took an oath to defend a piece of paper full of obsolete ideas about morality and flat-out lies. To defend a government that is rotten to the core.

"But you're wrong about one thing. The Infidels *are* faithful. To each other. Without question or hesitation. If someone raises a hand against one of us or disrespects the colors . . ." He paused, letting the statement of charges sink in. "Well, that's an insult to all of us. And we're obliged to make a reply."

"*Us?*" Redd echoed. "So you do speak for them."

Angry Johnny smiled again. "I don't know what you expected to accomplish here today . . . Matthew Redd."

Redd's blood went cold at the sound of his own name.

So they do know who I am.

"You were a walking dead man from the moment you laid a hand on our brothers." The biker spoke with the dispassion of someone remarking on the weather. "If I were you, I'd go home, spend what time you've got left with your family. Make love to that pretty wife of yours one last time. We'll be coming for you soon enough."

There it is.

With an effort, Redd kept his temper in check. He took a breath, let it out. "I told your *brothers*—" he spat the word contemptuously—"what would happen if they came looking for payback." He broke eye contact with Angry Johnny and let his gaze wander about the room, looking at each and every one of the bikers in turn, then came back to the older biker. "You don't need to come looking for me. I'll be coming for you."

He spun on his heel and marched for the exit. A pair of bikers had positioned themselves between him and the door, but rather than challenge him, they stepped aside, letting him go.

Turning his back on a roomful of outlaw bikers, and especially on the ridiculously named Baby Boy, was risky, but Redd didn't think they would take any action against him. If that had been their plan, Angry Johnny would not have bothered engaging in conversation. No, the Infidels had a plan, and it didn't include a brawl on the floor of their latest watering hole.

After the gloomy interior of the roadhouse, the first step out into daylight was blinding, but Redd did not break stride. He felt an overpowering urge to keep moving, to get home as quickly as possible, in order to begin preparing for what would come next. It might have been a tactical mistake to confront the Infidels as he had, but on balance, he did not regret having done so. Now that war had been openly declared, he had a feeling things would move quickly.

Then he saw something that did cause him to falter.

Two men . . . two *bikers* . . . were walking across the parking lot, heading directly toward him.

That wasn't what brought Redd up short. What stopped him was the fact that both men were carrying unsheathed knives.

"So that's how it's going to be," he muttered. "Fine. This, I can deal with."

FOURTEEN

The bikers had also stopped short upon seeing Redd. He thought they actually looked a little surprised. Maybe they'd been planning to ambush him, and he'd come out before they were completely ready. Whatever the explanation, after a quick exchange of glances, their faces hardened, and they started toward Redd.

Both looked younger than the rest of the Buffalo Jump's current clientele, and fitter, with none of the middle-aged flab evident in so many of the others. Neither was as tall as Redd, and while both had the kind of bulging muscles that could only be earned with plenty of time in the gym, they were definitely not in Redd's weight class.

Not even close.

Evidently they reckoned that their blades gave them the advantage. That and the perception of numerical superiority.

Two-to-one odds didn't bother Redd much, but the knives demanded at least a modicum of respect. They were big, fixed-blade commando-style weapons—eight-inch-long black powder-coated blades with blood grooves and serrations on the spine. People who didn't know anything about edged weapons would have called them "Rambo knives." Redd just thought of them as cheap junk, mass-produced in China using inferior steel, sold for ten bucks at truck stops.

But even cheap junk could do damage.

Redd had learned advanced knife-fighting techniques in the corps, but of all the lessons taught, the most important one was to avoid getting in a knife fight if at all possible.

Too late for that.

His training had mostly focused on how to use the legendary USMC KA-BAR knife to best effect, but it had also included techniques for disarming a foe with a knife. The problem was, all of them involved closing with the enemy—entering the reach of the knife blade—in order to trap the opponent's wrist or otherwise render him incapable of continuing the fight.

"If someone comes at you with a knife," his instructor had told him, "you're probably going to get cut. Your wisest course of action is to put some distance between you and them and then shoot them."

It was that almost-visceral fear of being slashed, of possibly losing fingers or feeling the point of a blade pierce the body, that made even battle-hardened leathernecks terrified of the prospect of getting in a knife fight. But Redd knew he could not afford to be paralyzed, or even slowed, by any instinctive wariness of injury.

He let the pair move in closer. The one on Redd's left carried his knife low, employing the forward or "hammer" grip, with fingers and thumb closed around the hilt and the blade at the top of the hand. It was the most basic grip style, the foundation upon which the Marine training was built, but it also had limitations Redd would have to exploit if he was going to end the fight quickly. The guy on the right seemed less confident, shifting his thumb around from the flat of the blade to the spine and back again.

Redd guessed the guy on the left would make the first move and let him get close enough to try. But when the biker's arm started to rise in preparation for a slash, Redd shifted right, dropped into a fighting stance, and delivered a forward kick aimed at the chest of the second biker.

The kick landed solidly, the heel of Redd's boot driving into the man's sternum with enough force to break ribs. The man's arms flew into the air, windmilling as he stumbled backward, waging a losing battle to stay on his feet. When he finally crashed down, flat on his back on the gravel lot, the knife fell from his uncertain grip.

Well, that was easy.

Redd's focus on the less-confident biker had given his buddy an opening, or at least it must have seemed that way to him. He changed what was supposed to be a slash into a stabbing lunge, aiming the tip of his blade at Redd's throat.

Redd, however, had been expecting him to try something like that, so as soon as his kick landed, he brought the foot back to the ground, shifted his weight onto it, and pivoted away from the thrust. As the blade pierced the air where he'd been standing only a moment before, Redd pivoted back, stepping inside the man's reach to seize his outstretched wrist. With hardly any effort at all, Redd turned the man's wrist, which not only loosened his hold on the knife but brought him to his knees with an agonized cry.

Redd booted the knife away, then let go of the biker's wrist and took a step back. After a quick check to confirm that the man he'd kicked still posed no threat—he was, in fact, curled into a fetal ball—Redd faced the biker he had just disarmed, who was still on his knees. "Go tell Angry Johnny that he should fight his own battles."

The biker, who was hugging his injured arm to his chest, did not meet Redd's gaze. Instead, he got to his feet and backed away, giving Redd plenty of room as he moved over to check on his buddy. With a little coaxing, the man Redd had kicked was able to stand and, leaning on his friend's shoulder, made his way toward the roadhouse's entrance.

Redd stood his ground, staying ready just in case either man decided to make another attempt, but the fight seemed to have gone out of both. They disappeared inside without looking back.

If that's the best they can do, Redd thought, *I've got nothing to worry about.*

Then he thought about the Berserker—Baby Boy—and revised that opinion. The Infidels would almost certainly come at him again, with greater numbers and deadlier weapons. He was frankly surprised that Angry Johnny had chosen to simply let him walk out of the roadhouse and half expected the gang to come charging out to deal with Redd's latest attack on their so-called honor.

Bring it on, he thought, but then another voice entered his mental conversation. J. B.'s voice. J. B.'s words.

"Don't. Be. Stupid."

Stupid was coming here in the first place. *Stupid* was walking into the lion's den armed with nothing but righteous indignation. If the old man had still been around, he would have slapped Redd upside the head for doing something so blame-fool stupid, and Redd would have deserved it.

The fact that he was still standing owed more to luck than anything else, and luck had a way of running out right when you needed it the most. It was time to go.

But as he started for his pickup, something about it looked wrong. It took a moment for him to realize what it was.

His truck looked to be six inches lower than he remembered.

With a growing sense of dread, knowing what he would find when he reached it, he resumed moving across the parking lot.

Sure enough, the old F-250 was sitting on six flats. Even from a distance, Redd could see long slashes in the tire sidewalls.

The two bikers hadn't been waiting to ambush him. He had caught them on their way back from vandalizing the truck.

You've got to be kidding me.

Dread gave way to white-hot rage. It wasn't so much anger at the act of wanton destruction as it was at the cowardly way in which it had been done.

Redd turned and started back across the parking lot. He hadn't gone halfway when the music resumed playing, the bass beat so loud that the plywood doors were visibly vibrating like the skin of a drum. Braving the sonic assault, Redd grasped the door handle and yanked hard.

The door didn't budge. The Infidels had locked him out.

Another wave of anger surged through Redd. "Cowards!"

His shout was swallowed up by the din of earsplitting heavy metal.

He gave another hard pull on the door handle, this time with both hands. His biceps bulged with the effort, straining the fabric of his shirt-sleeves, until the screws affixing the handle to the door tore free in an eruption of splinters. The door, however, remained firmly shut.

With another howl of frustration, Redd launched a kick at the door. His boot toe left a discernible mark on the plywood but otherwise accomplished nothing.

"Cowards!" he shouted, kicking the door again and again. "Come out here and face me!"

He might as well have been kicking an anvil and shouting into the wind.

Relenting, he took a step back, then turned to look once more out across the parking lot. "Okay," he muttered. "If that's how you want to do this."

He stalked over to the nearest row of motorcycles, planted his bootheel against the gas tank cover of the first, and shoved hard. The bike was a lot heavier than he expected, especially canted over a few degrees onto its kickstand, but Redd could squat four hundred pounds without breaking a sweat. It took a little doing, but once the hog started moving, there was nothing to stop it from going all the way over. It crashed onto the gravel with a resounding crunch, barely missing the next bike in line. That machine's reprieve was brief as Redd moved to it and toppled it over as well.

As satisfying as it was to vent some of his anger, Redd was really hoping to draw the Infidels out. When he had knocked over half a dozen motor-cycles with no apparent reaction from the outlaws inside the roadhouse, his anger deserted him and he slunk back across the parking lot to the incapacitated Ford.

For several minutes, all he could think about was how much it would cost to replace six tires. It was money he didn't have.

But that didn't change what was. With a resigned sigh, he took out his phone and called Mikey.

✖ ✖ ✖

To his credit, Mikey did not ask for details over the phone. His friend needed assistance, and that was explanation enough for him to head out in Elijah Lawrence's Freightliner rollback flatbed recovery truck.

As the truck pulled into the gravel parking lot of the Buffalo Jump forty-five minutes later, Redd watched Mikey's eyes widen when he looked at the twisted heap of metal where the bikes had all been tipped over; then a quick smile formed on his face as he shook his head. Redd could tell that he'd probably have to explain some of what happened, later.

Mikey spent a couple more minutes maneuvering the big wrecker into place, lining up the rollback deck with the front end of Redd's truck, then got out and went over to the open driver's side door of the pickup, where Redd had spent the better part of the last hour waiting for assistance. Mikey made a point of kneeling down to inspect one of the slashed tires before speaking.

"So, uh, did you do *that*," he said, thumbing toward the pile of Harleys, "because they did *this*?" He nodded toward the slashed tires in front of him. "Or was it the other way around?"

Redd hopped out of the truck and folded his arms across his chest. "They messed with my rig, then hid inside. Guess I just lost my temper for a second."

Mikey turned to take one last look at the bikes. One, a fully blacked-out Street Glide, was flipped completely upside down and had a boot-size dent in the back fender next to a smashed taillight. "I'll say." He suppressed a laugh. "Same ol' Matty."

Redd grunted but never took his eyes off the front door of the bar.

"Got all six of 'em, did they?"

"Yeah," Redd muttered.

"Don't imagine you've got comprehensive coverage on this old wreck."

"Nope. Just liability."

Mikey nodded slowly. "Well, that's gonna set you back a bit. I might be able to hook you up with some used tires, but it could take a couple days to scrounge 'em up."

"I'd appreciate that." Redd wasn't sure he could even afford six used tires right now, but that wasn't Mikey's problem.

"You're lucky your tires was all that got slashed." Mikey waved a hand in the direction of the parked motorcycles. "You got a death wish I don't know about?"

Redd rolled his eyes.

"Seriously though, bro. Do you go looking for trouble, or does it just find you on its own?"

"Bit of both, I guess."

Mikey stood up and brushed off his dark jeans. "Any point in telling you to call me the next time, or you just gonna take on the whole gang of bikers by yourself *again*?"

"Might not be a next time, Mikey," Redd said, not yet ready to tell his friend about Angry Johnny's warning.

"Oh, there will be a next time. I know you better than just about anybody, so I know any attempt to talk you out of whatever you're thinking will be about as useless as these slashed tires here. Like I said, call me first next time. Deal?"

Redd nodded.

Mikey circled back to the cab of the recovery truck, where he reached inside and threw a switch. The flatbed deck began rolling back, slowly tilting down to form a ramp that met the ground just a few feet from the front end of Redd's pickup.

When the deck's automatic cycle was complete, Mikey returned to Redd. "Keys?"

Redd handed his key ring over, whereupon Mikey slid behind the wheel of the Ford and started it up. After letting it idle for a few seconds, he shifted into low gear and, with a light touch on the gas pedal, advanced the vehicle up the ramp. At such low speed, the flat tires didn't cause much of a problem. When the pickup was completely on the ramp, Mikey set the brake and shut it off, then hopped out and went to work tying the vehicle down with ratchet straps.

A few minutes later, they were on the road, heading back to Wellington.

"So you going to tell me why they slashed your tires?" Mikey asked. "Or just make me wonder?"

Redd sighed. "It's not that simple."

He gave a quick summary of his initial encounter with the outlaw bikers, then explained how their harassment of Emily and little Matty was just the opening salvo in the Infidels' vendetta.

"You make it sound like something out of the Wild West," Mikey remarked.

"Yeah."

"We've got to call someone."

It wasn't lost on Redd that his friend included himself in his newfound problem. When he first came back to Montana, he'd had nobody. Now he had Emily *and* Mikey, the two people who meant everything to him in his youth, back at his side. He wasn't convinced he deserved it, but Redd was thankful—he just didn't know how to say it.

"Who? The police? You talked to Blackwood. You know what that accomplished. No one is willing to stand up to these guys."

"Well . . ." Mikey shook his head. "There's gotta be someone."

"I have a plan" was all Redd offered.

"Uh-huh. And getting your tires slashed, that part of your clever plan?" Mikey sighed. "I know you don't want to hear it, but you could have gotten yourself killed back there."

"You're right."

"So you do know how crazy that was?"

Redd shook his head. "No, I mean you're right. I don't want to hear it."

"Matt, c'mon. That lone-wolf stuff is going to get you killed. I mean, if that whole gang of bikers came out, you wouldn't stand—"

"I know, Mikey . . . I know."

What were you thinking? Redd asked himself. Truth was, Mikey was right, and deep down, he knew it. He had walked face-first into a bar full of bikers and tried to pick a fight with all of them. It was stupid. *No,* he corrected himself, *it was dangerous.*

"What do you need from me, bro? How can I help?"

Redd didn't want to involve anyone—especially Mikey—in whatever he was mixed up in. He was playing a dangerous game, and he knew it.

"Right now I just need to know that Em and Junior are safe. These bikers, they've got it in for me. Scaring Emily was just the beginning. They're going to come looking for me at the ranch, and that's where I'll make my stand."

Mikey nodded, not saying anything.

"The thing is," Redd went on, "there's no way to know when they're going to make their move. So I need to put Em and Junior someplace where the Infidels won't be able to find them."

"You don't even have to ask. They can stay with us long as you need."

"Thanks, Mikey. These guys aren't as tough as they want people to think they are. They get what they want by terrorizing people, but that's just basic bullying behavior. If I stand up to them . . . bloody their nose, so to speak . . . that will be the end of it." He said this with more confidence than he felt. Something told him it would take a lot more than a figurative bloody nose to break the Infidels' spirit, but he was in it to win it at this point.

Mike gave another heavy sigh. "You better be careful, man. I'll make sure Em and the baby are safe, but you better watch your back. I got a bad feeling about all of this."

"Yeah. Me too."

"Yep," Mikey agreed. "Plus, you gotta tell Emily."

Suddenly the bikers weren't Redd's biggest problem anymore.

FIFTEEN

Gavin Kline was just preparing to head out the door when the call he'd been dreading finally lit up his phone. He picked up the handset like it was a stick of old dynamite and cautiously held it to his ear. "This is Kline."

The caller—the director of the FBI—did not bother to identify himself. "Gavin, I need you in my office."

"I'll be right over," Kline replied, trying to keep the dread out of his voice. Because of the lengths taken to protect her identity, news of the death of former EAD Rachel Culp was slow in making its way up the chain of command, but the reckoning was inevitable. Her assassination, mere minutes after being interviewed by Stephanie Treadway, on Kline's orders, was bad enough, but coming as it did on the heels of the failed operation in Majorca had Kline wondering if he should start cleaning out his desk. Now it seemed he was about to find out.

He was surprised to find that the director was not alone. There were two other men in the office, sitting in a pair of chairs positioned in front of the director's desk. Kline recognized one of them—Dan Jackson, assistant director in charge of the white-collar crime section of the Criminal Investigative Division. The other man was fiftyish, wearing a tailored suit and a two-hundred-dollar haircut.

"Gavin." The director did not stand. "You already know AD Jackson. This is Tim Sterling from the CFTC."

Kline interpreted the tone of the introduction as a positive sign. He could think of no good reason why the director would want someone from the Commodity Futures Trading Commission on hand to witness the sacking of his executive assistant director of intelligence, which meant this had to be about something else.

Sterling stood and extended a hand to Kline. As he shook it, Kline did not fail to note that the man wore a signet ring with a distinctive coat of arms—three open books superimposed with the letters *VERITAS*. He was a Harvard man, same as the director.

With the pleasantries out of the way, the director got right to business. "Tim, can you tell Gavin what you just told me?"

"Of course." Sterling shifted so that he was facing Kline. "How much do you know about derivatives trading?"

Kline gave an equivocal shrug. "Not a lot. It's sort of gambling that the price of something will go up, right?"

"That's a simplified explanation, but generally correct. In derivatives trading, the value of the investment is derived—thus the name—from the performance of the underlying entity, rather than its actual value. The goal isn't to buy low, sell high, but rather to accurately predict how stocks or commodity values will change over time, up or down. One way this might happen is with a commodity futures contract, where a trader buys a specific quantity of something at a set price, with a scheduled delivery date. The trader doesn't actually take delivery. The contract is sold off, either to another trader or to someone else who actually wants the commodity, and the original buyer pockets the difference."

Kline thought his explanation was more succinct but kept that opinion to himself.

"Our job at the CFTC is to monitor trades looking for potential fraud or insider trading. When there's a statistically significant change in the volume of trades in any category, we start looking for an artificial trigger event."

"I take it something like that has happened?" Kline ventured.

Sterling nodded. "In the last two days, we've seen an unusual increase in the purchase of grain futures contracts—specifically wheat and corn. Interest in those commodities hasn't been this high since those fires in Montana last year wiped out a good chunk of the year's harvest."

Kline stiffened. Those fires had been the result of Anton Gage attempting to destroy all evidence of his plot to create GMO crops that would induce mass sterility in the developing world. Sterling now had his full attention. "And you suspect insider trading?"

"At this point, it's too soon to draw any conclusions. Markets often behave . . . erratically. We take note of suspicious anomalies, and if we determine there's reason to investigate, we do so, but more often than not, there is no one single cause."

"Can't you just follow the money? I mean, these trades aren't secret."

"Unfortunately, it's not as simple as that. Trades are happening all the time, so determining who is acting on insider information and who is simply jumping on the bandwagon is almost impossible."

"That's not to say we won't investigate," Jackson interjected, "if we find evidence of fraud or market manipulation."

"Of course." Kline paused a beat. "So what kind of inside information might we be talking about when it comes to grain markets?"

Sterling was ready with an answer. "It could be that someone got ahold of a leaked crop yield forecast report or a scientific study predicting a below-average harvest or some sort of crop disease. Any supply disruption would cause a price increase, so the people holding futures contracts with locked-in pricing would be able to sell them for a significant profit."

"Could a supply disruption be engineered?"

Jackson and Sterling exchanged a glance, suggesting that it was not the first time the topic had been discussed. "It's something to be concerned about," Jackson said. "Especially given the suddenness of this development."

"That's why I decided to read you in," the director said. "While Dan chases the money, I want you to work the other side of this. If there's a threat to the food supply . . . or even the possibility of a threat, we need to know."

Kline nodded. "Will do."

The director stood. "Thanks for bringing this to my attention, gentlemen." He shook Sterling's hand, then Jackson's, but conspicuously did not extend a hand to Kline. Kline interpreted this as an indication that he should remain after the others had departed.

Here it comes, Kline thought. But if the director was going to ask for his resignation, why had he included him in the meeting with Sterling and Jackson and directed him to look into a possible threat to the food supply?

When the office door was closed again, the director sank into his chair and stared up at Kline. "Well, what do you think?"

"I think it's definitely worth looking into" was Kline's guarded reply.

The director's gaze sharpened. "If that's the best answer you can give me, then maybe my trust in you is misplaced."

"Sir?"

"You don't think the timing of this news warrants more than just 'worth looking into'?" The director affected a falsetto when mimicking Kline's response. "First Anton Gage hoodwinks you in Spain. Then someone ices Rachel Culp, despite our best efforts to protect her. And now someone is betting big on grain futures. Do I need to spell this out for you?"

Kline was only momentarily taken aback by the director's forthrightness. In his years at the bureau, he had grown accustomed to overly cautious bureaucrats in the top slot. "No, sir. I agree with you. We might have stopped Gage's plan to sterilize the developing world with GMO grains, but that can't be the only weapon in his arsenal. If there's anyone who's in a position to sabotage the food supply, it's Gage. With his expertise, there's no telling what he might be cooking up next."

The director stabbed out one finger toward Kline. "*That* is what scares the hell out of me. Something tells me we're way behind the curve on this. So I don't want you to just 'look into' this. I want you to pull out all the stops. Find Gage. Stop him from doing whatever it is he's planning to do. I won't have the next 9/11 on my watch."

Even though a lifetime had passed since Gavin Kline traded his Marine Corps cammies for an FBI shield, he reflexively came to attention. "Yes, sir." Then, relaxing just a little, he added, "When you say pull out all the stops . . ."

"Interpret it however you want. All I care about is results."

Kline hid his smile. The director had just written him a blank check.

SIXTEEN

MONTANA

As he passed what little remained of the afternoon trying to make a dent in the chores he'd been neglecting, Redd thought long and hard about how he was going to broach the subject with Emily when she returned home from her shift.

He left off his labors when he heard the Tahoe coming up the drive and went out to meet her. Her forehead was creased with worry lines, and for a moment, Redd thought that news of his encounter with the Infidels must have reached her through the gossip grapevine—Mikey told Liz, Liz told Em. But when she saw him and managed a wan smile, he realized something else was troubling her.

"Hey, babe," he said, embracing her. "Rough day?"

She reached up on tiptoes to give him a quick kiss before answering. "No worse than usual. But Junior's fever is back."

Suddenly his war with the Infidels seemed less urgent. "Do we need to take him up to the children's hospital?"

She nodded. "I think we should." Her eyes darted past him. "Where's the truck?"

So she hasn't heard yet. Redd wasn't sure if that would make it easier or harder to explain.

"It's with Mikey," he said truthfully, if not quite honestly.

She rolled her eyes. "It's just one thing after another, isn't it?"

✖ ✖ ✖

It was a two-hour drive to Missoula. Plenty of time for Redd to reveal the truth about what lay behind Emily's encounter with the Infidels and what they might expect moving forward. But somehow the timing just didn't feel right.

One crisis at a time, he told himself, and right now little Matty's health was the top priority.

When they arrived at the hospital, he held the infant while Emily took the lead in getting them checked in at the emergency room. The whole process seemed needlessly tedious to Redd, but Emily knew exactly what to say to keep things moving along. Within fifteen minutes of walking through the door, they were transferred to one of the ER beds, where a nurse took Junior's vitals, noting the fever, and let them know that the doctor would be with them soon.

Soon proved to be another fifteen minutes, which felt like an eternity to Redd. At least little Matty was finally resting. Emily cradled him to her chest, rocking slowly on the edge of the thin portable bed frame that sat in the center of the tiny room. When the doctor—a soft-spoken and too-young man of East Asian extraction—came in, Emily took charge again, summarizing the history of the illness and the steps she had taken to combat it. The doctor nodded approvingly, then began his examination. After several minutes of probing, palpating, and listening to body sounds with a stethoscope in between cries from the now-awake baby, the doctor began talking about possible causes of the fever.

"When was he last vaccinated?"

"He got his four-month vaccinations two weeks ago," Emily replied. She was fast at work trying to get Junior back to sleep, and after crying himself to the point of exhaustion during his exam, little man was just starting to crash back out. "That was actually my first thought when he spiked the fever, but a reaction like that usually happens within hours, not several days."

The doctor gave an equivocal shrug. "I've seen delayed reactions from time to time. A week after. Sometimes more. Usually it's just a rash, but a late fever isn't impossible. We'll do some blood work, take a look at his white cell counts, but my guess is this is just a delayed reaction to his shots."

Redd could tell by Emily's expression that she did not accept this explanation, but she voiced no objection.

"I'd like to put in an IV line," the doctor went on. "We'll give him some fluids, and we'll be ready to go if we need to start him on any therapies."

"Are you going to admit him?" Emily asked.

"Let's see what the blood work says." The doctor seemed to realize that this answer fell short of reassuring, so he added, "He's a strong, healthy kiddo. He's going to be fine. If this is what I think it is, the fever should go away on its own pretty soon."

After the doctor left, Redd asked, "You don't think it's a delayed reaction to vaccines, do you?"

Emily shook her head. "The kind of reaction he's talking about usually occurs with measles and chicken pox vaccines. But Junior won't get those shots until his six-month checkup." She then managed a thin smile. "The blood work will tell us what's wrong with him."

Redd could only nod helplessly.

Not long after that, a different nurse came in and, after chatting with Emily for a minute or two, began prepping Matty for his IV.

"So where should we put this?" the nurse asked.

Redd thought it might be a rhetorical question but then heard Emily answer, "Let's try the foot first."

"Sounds good."

Redd was not the least bit squeamish about blood or needles. He had been stuck more times than he could count and had in turn stuck his buddies during routine combat lifesaver courses while in the Marines, but when it came to little Matty, Redd found that he couldn't bear to watch. He looked away, wincing when the baby began crying—whether from pain or simply from being manhandled, it was hard to say.

Over the cries, he heard the nurse give a thoughtful hum. "Has he had a blood draw recently?"

"No." Emily's tone was full of fresh concern. "When did that happen?"

Despite himself, Redd looked and saw the two women examining the baby's right heel. The nurse had not actually put the catheter in yet but had only prepped the injection site with an iodine swab. He moved closer to see what the two women were looking at and saw a tiny dark spot amid the yellow-stained area of little Matty's skin.

"What is that?" he asked. "Did something bite him?"

Emily shook her head. "It's a needle mark. But we didn't have any lab work done when I took him to Bozeman."

She brought her face closer to Matty's foot, scrutinizing every millimeter of his skin, then did the same to his left foot. "There's another one here, but it's almost completely healed."

Redd struggled to process what he was hearing. "I don't understand. You said he didn't have any blood drawn. So why are there needle marks?"

When Emily raised her eyes to meet his stare, he saw barely restrained rage in them—the rage of a mother whose child is threatened. "It must have happened while he was at day care." She said it quietly, and the utterance was all the more ominous for it.

"You mean . . ." Redd didn't really know what she meant. "Did someone treat him without your permission?"

Emily shook her head slowly. "I don't think it was a treatment." She drew in a sharp breath, then turned to the nurse. "Let's get that IV line in. We need that blood work. Stat."

SEVENTEEN

Rather than wait on the results to come back from the lab, the ER doctor ordered a cocktail of medications to be added to Matty's IV drip as a precautionary measure. Acetaminophen for the fever, an antihistamine in case the fever was an allergic reaction, and an antibiotic since fever usually indicated infection. Even without knowing what, if anything, had been injected into Matty's veins, the doctor explained, the meds in the IV wouldn't hurt and might help.

Redd was barely paying attention. A single thought rang in his head like an alarm bell.

Someone hurt Junior.

He figured Emily was thinking the same thing, but she was staying focused on the immediate concern—little Matty's health. Speculating about the identity of the perpetrator could wait until the health crisis was past.

Redd didn't have that luxury. Also, he had a pretty good idea who was behind it.

"I'll be right back," he told Emily when the doctor had left them alone again.

"Where are you going?"

"To call Blackwood. He needs to start investigating this right now."

She stared back at him. "What good will that do?"

Her response left him momentarily dumbfounded. "We need to know who did this, Em. We need to know what they injected into him."

Her eyes darted from side to side as she parsed his reply. "It has to be an accident. A med error. That's the only possible explanation."

"I don't think it was an accident. I think someone intentionally hurt our son."

"Who would want to do that?"

"That's a good question. Is there anyone at the clinic you've had problems with? Or anyone acting differently?"

She shook her head. "No. And if someone had a problem with me, I'd like to think they'd bring it to me face-to-face. I can't believe anyone would take it out on a baby."

"Someone did." He knew he should tell her about what was really going on with the Infidels, but somehow it still didn't feel like the right moment. "That's why we need to turn this over to Blackwood. If it wasn't someone on the clinic staff, maybe one of them saw something. Someone hanging around the day care who wasn't supposed to be there."

Emily pursed her lips together as if she found the thought of investigating her coworkers distasteful, but then she nodded. "I guess you're right."

Redd gave her a quick hug and a peck on the cheek, then headed out to the waiting room to find a quiet place to make the call. But when he brought up the number for the Stillwater County Sheriff's Department, he hesitated. Blackwood was probably already gone for the day, and if he called now, the best he could hope for was that a deputy might conduct a cursory interview of whoever happened to be at the clinic, which, given the late hour, wouldn't include anyone in the day care facility. The deputy could presumably visit them at home, but with the department's resources already stretched thin, the best chance of starting a meaningful investigation would be to wait until morning.

Besides, if someone from the Infidels was behind this latest attack on Redd's family, then going through official channels would probably be a dead end. When the time came to deal with the outlaw bikers, it would be better if there wasn't an established record of involving law enforcement so things couldn't be tied back to him. On the other hand, it was clear that the Infidels had unexpected resources at their disposal. Not only had they tracked Redd down, and subsequently Emily and Junior, but they had arranged for someone to surreptitiously dose Matty with some unknown agent—not something lethal, but definitely something that would add to the stress Redd was already dealing with. It was a multipronged attack designed to keep him off-balance, and so far, it was working.

Redd realized now that confronting the Infidels at the Buffalo Jump had been a strategic error. At the time, he had considered the bikers to be merely brutes and had believed, perhaps incorrectly, that standing up to them, refusing to show fear or weakness, might at least slow their campaign of harassment. Clearly he had underestimated them. Now he needed to find a way to level the playing field.

Instead of hitting Send on the sheriff's number, he scrolled up to another name in the contact list—Duke Blanton, Esq.

Farley "Duke" Blanton was Wellington's top attorney. In point of fact, he was Wellington's only attorney and as such was something of an institution in the town. He specialized in real estate law and estate management, claiming that was where the money was. When Stillwater County citizens needed legal representation for anything more serious than writing out their last will and testament, they took their business to Helena or Bozeman. Blanton had handled J. B.'s estate, which was how Redd, who had an almost-instinctive dislike for lawyers, happened to have his contact information.

Blanton wasn't in his office, not that Redd expected him to be. When the voice mail greeting recorded by Blanton's secretary finished, he left a short message asking for an appointment first thing in the morning, then pocketed the phone and headed back to the examination room.

"What did he say?" Emily asked as soon as he stepped into the private area.

"No one available tonight," he said. It was probably true. "I'll try again first thing tomorrow morning."

She nodded. "The doctor wants to admit Junior. He's doing better already, but they want to keep an eye on him for the next twenty-four hours, just in case."

Redd felt a little of the emotional burden slip off his shoulders, but his relief was blunted by the knowledge that, even with Emily's medical insurance plan, an overnight stay in the hospital would cost them dearly. He felt guilty for even thinking it, but unfortunately it was something he couldn't ignore.

"I'm glad he's doing better." Redd didn't know what else to say.

"I'm going to call in and take tomorrow off," she went on. "Obviously he's not going back to the day care at the clinic."

"Obviously."

"We'll have to figure something out. In a pinch, I'm sure Mom and Dad could watch him, but that's only a temporary fix. He's more than a handful now."

Redd just nodded.

She looked at him for a long moment. "There's no sense in both of us staying. I'm okay here if you want to head home. That way, you can take care of things at the ranch, then come back and pick us up tomorrow afternoon."

It was a perfectly reasonable suggestion, but Redd felt another twinge of guilt as he considered it. Wasn't his place here, with his sick child? "I'll get Mikey to come out and feed the stock," he said. "Everything else can wait."

But Emily shook her head. "We already owe Liz and Mikey way too much. We'll be fine here."

Redd frowned, but part of him knew she was right. If he left now, he'd be able to get a few hours of sleep before the crack of dawn brought a whole new day's worth of work. Doing so would also give him a chance to take care of some other business.

And if things got ugly, the way he thought they might, he couldn't think of a safer place to stash Em and Matty.

He let his frown transform into a resigned smile. "Okay. If you think that's best."

EIGHTEEN

They rolled across the open plain like a peal of thunder. Forty bikes, riding two abreast down the empty highway, like a procession of demons bringing hell to earth. The noise of their passage was audible for several miles, though aside from the riders themselves, the only ears to hear belonged to the beasts of the field. A large herd of bison milling near the highway's edge became increasingly agitated as the bikes drew near and began stamping at the ground with their forehooves.

From her vantage on the rear seat of the lead motorcycle, the woman known to the riders as Bobbie-Sue watched as the herd began peeling away from the three-strand barbed-wire fence that separated the animals from the highway. They moved grudgingly at first, but as the noise intensified, so did their reaction. If not for the deafening roar of the motorcycle beneath her, and those behind, she might have been able to hear the thunder of their hoofbeats.

Bobbie-Sue—her real name was Susanna Decatur, but no one had called her that in a long time—was not so jaded by the biker lifestyle that she'd lost appreciation for natural wonders like the bison herd. She knew that, once upon a time, the mighty animals had numbered into the tens of millions, with herds so vast they seemed to go on forever, and that they had been driven to the brink of extinction during the westward expansion. While the herds that still roamed the wilds of Montana were only a shadow of what once had been, she felt privileged to bear witness to their continued existence. Bobbie-Sue had always liked wild things.

She unconsciously tightened her hold on Angry Johnny's waist, felt him tense in her arms, an unspoken signal for her to relax. He didn't like it when she squeezed him while he was riding. He would, no doubt, remind her of this fact later.

Like many of the women who were drawn to the lifestyle, she liked strong men, and none of the men she'd ridden with were as strong as Angry Johnny. It wasn't physical strength, though he certainly possessed that. No, it was his strength of purpose that she found so appealing. Most of the bikers wanted nothing more than to ride and party. Everything else they did served only to facilitate those ambitions. Johnny was different. Johnny could be wild when he wanted to, but he was smart. That was why he was the club's national president, and it was why she was with him.

After passing the bison herd, they continued another mile or so down the highway before turning off onto a side road blocked by a heavy iron gate. As soon as Johnny's bike made the turn, the gate swung open as if by remote control, clearing the way for the pack to continue. In the failing light of near dusk, Bobbie-Sue could just make out the figure of a man—the prospect Johnny had left behind to guard their temporary camp.

"Prospects" were prospective members of the club. When someone wanted to join the Infidels, he started out as a "hang-around," frequenting club gatherings, doing favors for club members, and generally dipping his toe in the waters of the outlaw motorcycle lifestyle. If the club members decided he was worthy of inclusion, he became a prospect. During this probationary period, he paid membership dues and was allowed to ride with the club, wearing just the lower rocker patch, the one identifying his home chapter, while earning his way to full membership by performing various menial tasks for the fully patched members—anything from guard duty to making beer runs—and occasionally carrying out various minor criminal actions such as transporting drugs or guns. Like fraternity pledges, prospects were often subjected to humiliating treatment by the members as a way of making sure they were tough enough to wear the Infidels patch and the highly prized top rocker. The hazing period was also a way of testing to make sure that a prospect wasn't a narc.

Johnny continued leading the way, following the road for another half mile until the old warehouse came into view. Bobbie-Sue had no idea how Johnny had learned of the abandoned facility, but it had quickly become an important hub for club operations.

As he entered the big parking lot outside the warehouse, Johnny raised a hand high and made a circling gesture, directing the riders to arrange their bikes in a large ring. He then demonstrated the approximate dimensions of the circle by making a sweeping turn around the lot, stopping near the entrance. He revved the throttle three times, then shut off the engine, though he left his headlight on with the wheel turned so that it was shining into the circle. All the other bikers did the same, and in the space of about thirty seconds, the thunderous noise ceased completely.

Johnny brought down the kickstand but remained astride his bike, gazing out across the circle like some ancient war leader surveying the army he was about to lead into battle. Bobbie-Sue remained where she was, waiting for Johnny to tell her when to dismount. After a long pause, Baby Boy, who'd been riding right behind them, came up to consult with Johnny.

Bobbie-Sue's ears were ringing from the prolonged sonic assault, so she didn't hear what Johnny told Baby Boy, but the exchange was brief. Baby Boy stepped away, then turned and shouted out across the circle, "Colors on!"

Almost as one, the assembled bikers dismounted and began retrieving their cuts—leather and denim vests or jackets with the sleeves cut off, adorned with the club patches—from panniers and cargo boxes mounted to their bikes. Bobbie-Sue's cut was stashed in Johnny's cargo trunk, but it didn't sport the Infidels patch. Women were not eligible for membership in the club. Bobbie-Sue's cut just had rockers that read *Property of Angry Johnny*. But Johnny had not dismounted to get his own cut, so Bobbie-Sue stayed put.

It had been at Johnny's earlier direction that they had removed their vests and ridden "sixty-six"—club code for traveling incognito—to the Buffalo Jump, a watering hole with a strict no-patches policy. Bobbie-Sue had been curious about his reasons for doing this. The Infidels were a proud bunch and wanted the world to know who they were, and there were plenty of other places where they could drink without having to hide who they were. But it wasn't her place to question him. It wasn't anyone's. Johnny was the president.

His word was law.

Once attired in their official regalia, the bikers stood by their rides, waiting for further instructions. They did not have to wait long.

Baby Boy bellowed out two names. "Prospects Dunk and Joey. Front and center!"

Because prospects rode at the back of the pack, sucking up everyone else's exhaust, the two riders who had been called out were right in front of Angry Johnny's bike, with only Baby Boy between them.

Dunk and Joey were prospects from the Milwaukee and Bozeman chapters respectively. They had been given a special assignment back at the roadhouse, one they had completed, though not entirely to Johnny's satisfaction. When they had come back inside after getting manhandled by the cowboy, Johnny hadn't said a word to them, but Bobbie-Sue could tell he was furious.

Now it seemed the two prospects were going to face the consequences of their failure.

As the two men hurried toward Johnny, she expected Baby Boy to give them a beatdown. As the club's national sergeant at arms, matters of internal discipline were usually his responsibility, but the big man stepped aside, gesturing for the two prospects to report to Angry Johnny. Both men paled visibly when they grasped what was expected of them and shuffled forward, keeping their eyes averted as they took their place in front of the club president. Bobbie-Sue thought they looked like they were about to wet themselves or vomit. Maybe even both.

Johnny stared at them for several long moments. When he finally spoke, his voice was low and unnaturally calm. "What did I tell you to do?"

Dunk and Joey—both with visible bruises from their encounter with the cowboy—looked at each other, maybe trying to decide who should answer; then both started to speak at the same time.

"You told us . . . ," Joey started but then stopped as Dunk took over.

"You said to slash the cowboy's tires."

"What else did I tell you?"

"To leave him alone. But, Johnny, he surprised us. What were we supposed—?"

Johnny's open hand came up, cutting Dunk off midexcuse. "What you were supposed to do was leave him alone. You almost ruined everything."

"Come on, Johnny," Joey broke in. "We said we was sorry. And we didn't even lay a finger on him."

"You know, if you had . . . if you'd cut him . . . even if you'd killed him, I could probably forgive that. But you let him walk all over you." Johnny shook his head. "I'm starting to wonder if you guys have got what it takes to be Infidels."

Dunk looked like he was going to protest but then thought better of it. Joey just stared at the ground.

"Baby Boy, what do you think?" Johnny said. "Are these the sort of guys we want wearing our colors?"

The big man gave an exaggerated shrug. "They're pretty pathetic."

Bobbie-Sue watched as Johnny let his gaze roam the assembly. "Does anyone here think differently?"

All around the circle, bikers shook their heads. A few verbalized variations on Baby Boy's assessment.

Johnny raised his hands in a "what can I do?" gesture but then cocked his head to the side as if struck by inspiration. "You know what? I think there is a way you could prove yourselves. Show us you've got what it takes."

The prospects looked up hopefully. "Just name it," Dunk said enthusiastically.

"You still got your blades?"

Both men drew their commando knives, holding them up as if presenting them for inspection.

Johnny nodded. "Here's the thing. You screwed up, and I can't just let that slide. So only one of you is going to get to stick around with us. The other one is going to have to pay the price. I'll leave it up to you two to work it out."

Bobbie-Sue thought the judgment was overly harsh. Prospects screwed up all the time but were rarely kicked out of the club. "Always an Infidel" was part of the club motto and applied even to prospects. To get kicked out, you had to violate one of the club's bylaws, like stealing from a brother or messing with another's ol' lady.

Still, it was Angry Johnny's call, and nobody would dispute it.

"Johnny," Dunk started, "c'mon, man. We already said we were sorry. Can't we just—?"

"Do you think this is a game?" Johnny paused a beat, letting the question sink in. "It's not a game. It's a war. We. Are. At. War." Another pause as he turned his attention to the rest of the bikers. "We are at war with a corrupt society that wants to shove us into a box. Make us conform. Make us weak. It's a society of weaklings who have created laws and power structures to keep the strong from rising up and fighting back, but we . . . We. Will. Not. Be. Kept. Down."

Some of the riders shifted uncomfortably, but Bobbie-Sue could tell that Johnny's familiar rhetoric was striking the right chord with most. She felt the seductive appeal of his words too. He often opined on how modern society had subverted the natural order of things, empowering the shrewd but weak, enslaving the strong and noble.

But how did that justify setting two brothers—even prospects—against each other?

"We are Infidels," Johnny continued. "We reject their corrupt order.

We spit in its face. But make no mistake. It's a war, and in a war, only the strong survive."

As if on cue, Baby Boy thrust his fist skyward. "Infidels!"

Several of the bikers immediately followed suit, and then all of them were shouting, pumping their fists in the air.

Baby Boy's shout rose above the din. "What are we?"

The answer was unanimous. "Infidels!"

"What are we?" he cried again.

The answering cry was thunderous. Baby Boy repeated the call-and-response a third, final time, leaving no question that Johnny's power over the club was absolute. None of the riders would question his decision to make Dunk and Joey fight to the death.

Bobbie-Sue wondered if any of them, like her, secretly felt betrayed.

Neither prospect moved for several seconds. Both men looked at each other, their faces quickly changing from confusion to realization. Then, before Bobbie-Sue could look away, the fighting started.

NINETEEN

Anton Gage set out from Calgary hours before dawn, allowing the Tesla Model 3's full self-driving package to do most of the work. With more than four hours of driving just to reach the Roosville border crossing and most of it in the dark, it would have been foolish to trust his own fallible reflexes and limited endurance to keep the car on the road and avoid unexpected obstacles, like deer and elk trying to get from one side of the Kootenay Highway to the other. Not that he would have ever chosen to drive himself when there was another option.

His only regret was that he had to make the trip in a Tesla. As if Elon needed any more of his money.

It was at times like this that he most missed his former life. Fifteen months ago, when he'd been at the top of his game, not to mention on top of the world, he'd had access to the best toys, many of which weren't yet commercially available, like his Rivian R1T electric truck or his Lilium all-electric airplane. Now he was reduced to traveling by commercial air and riding in something as plebian as a Tesla.

At least it's green, he thought ruefully. And the Model 3 was fast and quiet, the auto-drive a technological godsend, allowing him to relax in the plush driver's seat and simply enjoy the ride. Once the sun came up, the view through the windshield was magical.

Fields of grass. Evergreen-covered hills. Best of all, hardly any people.

All of the earth's problems traced back to that single variable. Population. A handful of neoliberal economists had largely tricked the world into believing that infinite growth was not only possible but desirable. Not just economic growth, but population, too. After all, more people meant a larger marketplace for goods and more people to create them. Natural resources were not a hard and fast limit to growth, or so they proclaimed, because technological innovations would always find a workaround.

Gage knew better. There was no such thing as unlimited growth. Human populations could only grow at the expense of other creatures in the biosphere, and at some point, if it continued, the global population crash would wipe out everyone and everything. It would take bold action to prevent the apocalypse, the kind of bold action that some would call villainy, but Gage knew that future generations would name him a hero.

It was almost eight o'clock when he rolled up on the border checkpoint. He flexed his idle muscles, at least to the extent his seated position would allow, then reached over to the passenger seat and donned a ball cap with the logo of the Chicago Cubs. After checking the placement of the hat in the rearview mirror, he placed his hands on the steering wheel, taking full control of the vehicle.

The outpost on the Canadian side looked deserted, but as he passed it by without stopping, he saw a blue-uniformed border services agent watching from behind the window of the checkpoint. There was no requirement to stop upon leaving the country, so Gage did not, but he did slow as he approached the actual border and the checkpoint on the American side.

By contrast with its neighbor to the north, the American border patrol station looked ready to repel a small invasion. Three green-uniformed agents were standing outside the guardhouse, two of them armed with assault rifles—Gage didn't know or care enough about weapons to identify them as anything else—and he could see at least two more inside. A security gate blocked the way and the approach to it was lined with barricades to both control traffic and prevent anyone from attempting to turn around once in the queue. Gage knew that the barricades also concealed sophisticated detection equipment—supersensitive microphones that could detect the number of heartbeats inside a vehicle, chemical sniffers, and null wave emitters that could "see" through the exterior wall of the car, looking for hidden compartments that might conceal contraband or even human cargo.

At a signal from one of the agents, Gage stopped the car. The agent then gestured for him to roll down his window for an ID check.

This was the moment of truth. Days of painstaking preparation and long hours traveling circuitous routes had brought him here, to a threshold that had to be crossed and a test that had to be passed. If he failed, if the measures he had taken to ensure safe travel proved insufficient, his mission to save the world would die an ignominious death, and he would likely spend the rest of his life in a federal supermax prison. Provided the Twelve did not send someone to silence him in custody.

He hit the button to roll down the window and smiled at the border official. The man stood slightly to one side, giving the discreet camera mounted above the door of the guardhouse an unobstructed view of Gage's face. It took only a fraction of a second for the device to scan his features. It would take longer for the data to be uploaded to the Department of Homeland Security's facial recognition database for comparison to known persons of interest.

"Passport, please," the agent said.

Gage handed over a blue American passport book, issued to one Steve Jennings. The passport was a masterful forgery, but a forgery nonetheless. The man who had provided it had assured Gage that it would stand up to scrutiny. For what Gage was paying him, it was doubtful he would have admitted to anything less. It had passed muster upon entry to Canada, but no doubt the American customs agents were better trained at detecting counterfeit versions of documents issued by their own government.

The agent took the passport, flipped it open, and studied the photograph inside, comparing it to Gage's own face. "Would you remove your hat, please?"

Hiding his trepidation, Gage complied with the request, removing the Cubs cap. He did not toss it aside but held it in his right hand, careful to keep the underside of the bill hidden, as he stared up at the agent with just a hint of annoyance.

The forger who had provided him with the fake passport had advised him not to be too obsequious at the border checkpoint. "If you're all smiles and 'Yes, sir. Whatever you say, sir,' they'll get suspicious. Real Americans are rude and don't mind letting you know. They think the borders are there to keep the wrong people out, not them."

Gage had not shared the fact that he was an American citizen—a *real* American—but he took the point to heart.

The steps he had taken to change his appearance ought to have been sufficient to distinguish him from the photographs that no doubt adorned wanted posters hanging in the security office. Those measures, however, would not fool facial recognition software. That was why he had been wearing the hat, which contained several infrared LEDs that shone down on his face with invisible light.

The technology, developed in Hong Kong in 2018, was designed to confound FRS, making him appear like an entirely different person to the multispectral camera eye. It was still experimental, and by no means guaranteed to work, which was why Gage had elected to enter the United States here, out in the middle of nowhere, rather than tempt fate by flying directly into an international airport, where his picture might be taken and scanned dozens of times from many different angles. Here, with just one or two cameras, he hoped to slip through the American border net. But without the hat, he was completely exposed. If the agent moved from where he was standing, giving the camera another look at him, there was a good chance alarm bells would start ringing in the Hoover Building.

"What's your business in the United States?" the agent asked.

"Going home. I live in Laramie. I was just in Calgary on business."

"What kind of business is that?"

"Agricultural equipment. I'm a sales rep for John Deere."

The agent made a humming sound as if he found this explanation suspicious, then took a step back. "Pop the trunk, please."

Gage fought the impulse to comply immediately. There was nothing of interest in the trunk and the sooner the inspection was finished, the sooner he'd be on his way.

Real Americans are rude, he reminded himself.

"You gotta be kidding me. Is this really necessary?"

The agent's expression hardened. Behind him, the men with assault rifles watched the exchange intently. "Pop the trunk," he said again, this time omitting the *please.* Then he added, "Maybe we should do a strip search while we're at it."

Gage did not have to feign displeasure at this prospect. Was this just routine harassment? Border guards exerting their authority to alleviate boredom? Or had something aroused their suspicion?

"Fine." He defiantly jammed the cap back on his head, then stabbed a finger at the trunk release.

The agent moved to the rear of the Tesla, where, hidden from Gage's view, he rooted around for several minutes. Then, without any further rancor, he returned Gage's fake passport to him. "Welcome home, Mr. Jennings. You can pull through. Have a nice day."

Gage nodded his thanks and, when the barrier lifted, drove through. On the roadside, a large, ornate sign declared *Welcome to Montana,* and Gage couldn't help but crack a smile.

Welcome home, indeed.

TWENTY

Duke Blanton called Redd at eight o'clock sharp the next morning. "Matthew," boomed the attorney. Blanton was a little hard of hearing and had difficulty regulating his volume. "I was wondering when I'd hear from you."

Redd wondered what Blanton meant by that, then decided that, small-town gossip being what it was, someone had probably told him about Emily's encounter with the outlaw bikers. "Good morning, Duke. Think you can squeeze me in this morning?"

"When can you get here? There's no time to waste."

Redd took Blanton's eagerness as a good sign. It suggested that he had some ideas about how best to proceed. "I can be there in thirty minutes. Forty-five if I clean up first."

"Why don't you do that? Can't hurt to show up looking presentable."

Redd had no idea what that meant, but after ending the call, he finished mucking out Remington's stall and then headed inside to take a shower.

The call from Blanton had not been his first of the day. Emily had called at 6 a.m. to let him know that Junior's fever had broken and that he seemed to be fully recovered. Slightly more concerning was the news that his white blood cell count was high, indicating a systemic infection.

"That's just his immune system doing its job," Emily explained quickly as if sensing that the news might have alarmed her husband. "Same with the fever. I think the antibiotics knocked it out, but he probably would have gotten better on his own." Almost as an afterthought, she added, "As long as nobody gave him another dose of whatever it was."

"On that subject," Redd said, "any idea what it was?"

"No. It's possible to test for certain substances like drugs or toxic metals, but you have to have an idea what you're looking for because each one is a different test. Since he's getting better, it's not as important to have all the answers."

Redd wasn't sure he agreed but understood that it was probably a sound decision, medically speaking. "When can he come home?"

"As soon as you can pick us up," she answered. "But since you've probably still got some work to do, how about we shoot for noon."

He would have to leave before ten to get there by lunchtime. Under any other circumstances, Redd would have dropped everything and started for Missoula that minute. Today, four hours didn't seem like nearly enough time to get done everything he had to do.

"Noon it is," he said, trying to sound upbeat. "Guess I'd better get cracking."

"Get to it, cowboy," she replied cheerfully. "Love you."

"I love you."

Now he hoped he would be able to finish up with Blanton in time to make it to Missoula by lunchtime.

✳ ✳ ✳

Forty-five minutes later, wearing a clean pair of Wranglers and a pressed chambray work shirt, Redd stepped into the lobby of Blanton's law office on Broadway, just a few blocks west of the courthouse. The decor was unchanged from his last visit. An interior decorator would probably call it "rustic chic" or something like that—Redd just thought of it as typical Montanan. Trophies of both the brass cup and stuffed and mounted fish and game varieties adorned the walls, along with a smattering of patriotic photographs and artifacts. The elderly receptionist greeted him as she always did—like a long-lost son coming home—and then ushered him into the lawyer's private office.

Duke Blanton, a big, ruddy-faced bear of a man, was on his feet and moving across the room to greet Redd. After pumping Redd's hand vigorously, the lawyer gestured to a chair.

"Let's get to it, shall we?" he said, circling back to his own plush chair beside a round end table that held a lamp as well as a framed picture of the lawyer's beloved dog, Rubble. "I wish you'd come to me sooner with this. I can understand you wanting to handle it on your own. You're Jim Bob's son, after all. That's why I didn't reach out to you. But your window of opportunity here is closing fast. Frankly, it may already be too late, but we'll cross that bridge if we come to it."

The rush of words left Redd momentarily foundering. He finally raised his hands. "Slow down, Duke. I haven't even told you why I'm here."

"Oh, I know why you're here."

"You do? I'm not sure what all you've heard, but I can tell you there's more to it than that."

"Always is." Blanton waved his hand dismissively. "Always is. But I'm pretty sure we can get you an extension. You've made a good faith effort to stay current on your payment plan, and that will go a long way with Judge Hackett. Honestly, there was no reason for Yearsley to go after you like this."

"Yearsley?" The name rang a bell for Redd, but he couldn't place it. Certainly not in the context of what had brought him to Blanton's doorstep. And why was Blanton talking about a payment plan?

"I think it's his way of trying to impress the voters. Show them that, unlike Randall Shaw, he doesn't play favorites. He's dead wrong if he thinks putting the little guys out on the street just because they're struggling is going to win him any votes in the general election."

When Blanton mentioned Randall Shaw, the lights finally came on for Redd. He shook his head. "Duke, I'm not here about the back taxes on the ranch."

Blanton blinked at him in astonishment. "You're not?"

"No. I've got something else going on right now."

The lawyer crossed his arms over his prodigious belly. "Whatever it is, it's not as important as this."

Redd waved the comment away. "Trust me, it is. And until I get it settled, I can't deal with any of that other stuff."

"Matthew, I don't think you're reading the situation clearly. If we don't fix this—today—you and your family will be out on your ear by month's end."

The pronouncement felt like hyperbole. "I'm sure we can work something out."

"That's what I'm trying to tell you." Exasperation sent Blanton's volume up several more decibels. His already-rosy face seemed to burn with righteous fury.

"Okay, slow down a minute. This is all news to me. I haven't actually talked to anyone at the assessor's office. They've left a couple messages, but I haven't gotten back to them yet. What have you heard?"

The explanation did nothing to soothe Blanton. "Haven't gotten back . . ." He shook his head, incredulous. "Craig Yearsley is filing the papers today. If you don't pay the remaining tax liability, with penalties and interest, by the end of the month, Thompson Ranch will be auctioned off."

Cold adrenaline pulsed through Redd, leaving him feeling both numb and faintly sick. "No," he mumbled. "That can't be right. I made a deal with them."

"You made a handshake deal with the acting assessor. Craig Yearsley has decided not to honor that agreement. And I'm afraid he's within his rights to do so."

Redd didn't know what to say. When he'd taken possession of the ranch, he'd been shocked to learn that J. B. owed $27,000 in back taxes. In the last fifteen months, the payments he had made to the county had barely touched the principal.

Where am I going to get that kind of money?

That was, he realized, the wrong question. Quite simply, there was no way he could scrounge, beg, borrow, or even steal that much. The only way to keep from losing the ranch was to go to the county assessor and beg for mercy.

"I'll talk to him," Redd said finally. "Convince him to let me keep making payments."

Blanton nodded. "Yes. That's a good first step. I'll call and let him know we're on our way."

As Blanton reached for the phone, Redd shot a glance at his watch. It was almost nine. He would have to leave for Missoula soon.

And I haven't even gotten around to the real reason I'm here.

The sound of a ringback tone issued from the speakerphone on Blanton's desk, then was replaced by a grim female voice. "Stillwater County Assessor's Office, how can I be of assistance?"

"How do you do?" Blanton said, affecting a tone of practiced bonhomie. "This is Duke Blanton. I was just calling to let Mr. Yearsley know that I'm on my way over with a client. We'd like just a few minutes of his time."

"I'll check with him. Who's the client?"

"Matthew Redd."

"Hold please."

"Just tell him we're on—"

Muzak, sounding harsh and tinny as it blared from the speaker, filled the office. Blanton frowned in annoyance and settled back in his chair. The instrumental selection played on for nearly a full minute before abruptly ending. "Mr. Blanton? Thanks for holding. I'm sorry, but Mr. Yearsley is unavailable to take your meeting."

"Unavailable? Now see here—"

A dial tone signaled the termination of the call.

Blanton stared at the phone, his eyes beginning to bulge. "The nerve."

It was a surprisingly terse comment for the normally loquacious lawyer. Evidently the brush-off had left him almost speechless. After a few seconds to regain his composure, he leaned over and dialed the number again.

"Stillwater County Assessor's Office, how can I be of assistance?"

"It's Duke Blanton. I think we must have gotten cut off before. I'd like to make an appointment to see Mr. Yearsley."

"If this is regarding Matthew Redd, I'm sorry to say that Mr. Yearsley has asked me to decline your request."

"Decline? That's nonsense. Why?"

"You'll have to ask Mr. Yearsley."

"I intend to do exactly that," Blanton roared. "That's why I need an appointment with the man."

"I'm sorry but Mr. Yearsley isn't available right now."

The tone sounded again, cutting Blanton off before he could press his case. This time he just shook his head. "I really have no idea what's going on here," he said. "If I didn't know better, I'd say this is personal."

He cocked his head to the side and stared at Redd for a moment. "Is it?"

"I can't see how," Redd replied. Yet even as he said it, he remembered what Emily had said the previous night.

"It's just one thing after another, isn't it?"

But what if it wasn't? What if this was just one more spearpoint in the Infidels' multipronged attack? First their harassment of Emily on the road to Bozeman. Then injecting Junior with something to make him sick.

No, he thought. *I've got the order wrong. Junior got sick first.*

And now this.

Personal? Maybe it was.

"Well, I'm going to pin him down and find out. If he's trying to settle some kind of grudge, that's an abuse of power. We'll sue him nine ways to Sunday. First though, I'll draw up a request for an injunction and send it over to Judge Hackett. Try to buy us some time."

Redd was only half-listening. "Duke, I appreciate you taking the lead on this. I really didn't even know that this was going to be a problem until I walked in here. But I actually wanted to talk to you about something else."

"Hmm? What's that?"

"What do you know about outlaw biker gangs?"

TWENTY-ONE

Blanton's frown deepened as he listened to Redd recount his dealings with the Infidels, from that first fateful encounter fifteen months earlier to his speculation that they were responsible for the present storm of troubles. Blanton did not interrupt or ask for clarification, but when Redd finished, the attorney leaned forward and fixed Redd with a hard stare.

"You need to take this to the sheriff's department."

Redd shook his head. "Blackwood knows about what happened to Emily. He doesn't know why, and he doesn't know that they're gunning for me. But I can tell you this: he's afraid of these guys. And for good reason. Those bikers have zero respect for the badge."

"That doesn't matter," Blanton replied flatly. "They might not play by the rules, but you have to. Look, Matthew, I know you think that you're going to have to take care of this on your own. Maybe you're right. I hope there's a better answer, but you've got a right to defend yourself. But this isn't the Wild West anymore. When the dust settles, the law is going to ask for an accounting, and if it looks like you went chasing after vigilante justice, you could wind up facing charges. If, God forbid, you kill someone, you could be looking at capital murder. The only way to get out ahead of something like that is by showing that you tried going the legal route first."

Redd frowned. "Okay, maybe you're right about that, but it's not why I'm here."

"If you're looking to form a posse, I'm afraid you've come to the wrong place."

"Not a posse exactly, but I was hoping that you could help me get an edge on them."

"An edge?"

"Blackwood told me that these guys are connected. They've got their own lawyers and private investigators . . . They've even got crooked cops looking out for them. And they've got the money to make things happen. What do you want to bet that they bribed the assessor and turned him against me?"

"That's a pretty serious accusation," Blanton countered. "And if you're going to make it, you'll need real evidence."

"That's what I mean. I need someone to find the evidence. To follow the money trail."

Blanton considered this for a long, silent moment. "This is a little outside my wheelhouse, but I can refer you to a colleague in Bozeman who specializes in criminal law. I'll warn you, though, it won't be cheap. And right now I think there are better ways for you to spend your money. Like saving your ranch, for starters."

"If I don't deal with this problem now, saving the ranch will be the least of my worries."

"It's your decision. But I insist that you call the sheriff before we proceed."

Though he remained skeptical about the good it would do, Redd saw Blanton's point. He took out his phone and made the call.

"Matthew," Blackwood barked as soon as the connection was made. "Where are you?"

It was not the greeting Redd had expected, but he saw no reason not to answer truthfully. "I'm with Duke Blanton. Listen, we need to talk."

"No kidding. Stay put. I'll be there in fifteen minutes."

Blackwood hung up before Redd could say another word. Redd raised his eyes to Blanton. "He's coming here."

Blanton nodded. "That's probably for the best. That way I can be present and act as your legal counsel."

Redd checked his watch again. "I really need to get on the road. Em is expecting me in Missoula by noon."

"You may want to let her know you'll be running a little late." Blanton regarded Redd thoughtfully for a moment. "How much have you told her?"

Redd flushed guiltily. He had played out that conversation in his head many times over the last twenty-four hours, and in that time, things had only gotten worse. "None of it. I was going to tell her last night, but then Junior got sick and we had to take him to the children's hospital. It wasn't the right moment."

"It never is. You know what they say about fish and bad news. Smells worse the longer you wait. That goes for this tax problem, too. You might think you're protecting her by keeping this all to yourself, but she's your partner now. What affects you affects her."

"You're right," Redd admitted. "I'll tell her this afternoon."

"Good. See, you're already making better decisions." Blanton clapped his hands together. "How 'bout a cup of coffee while we wait for the sheriff?"

Redd nodded. "I could go for that."

Blanton relayed the request to his receptionist over the intercom, then leaned back in his chair. "I'll get to work on filing for that injunction, but that will probably only buy you another thirty days. I'll push for ninety, but don't hold your breath. And something tells me your pleas for mercy are going to fall on deaf ears at the assessor's office. So you'd better start thinking about how you're going to come up with the money to settle your liability."

"What if we can prove that Yearsley is colluding with the Infidels?"

"That would change things, but proving it will be tough. These bikers probably operate on a cash-only basis, so if they did bribe him, it will be hard to trace it back to them."

"What if we get him to admit to it?"

Blanton's gaze narrowed. "And why would he do that? I hope you're not thinking about trying to coerce the information out of him."

Redd flashed a tight smile. "Wouldn't dream of it."

"I'm serious, Matthew. You cannot go cowboy on this. You'll lose everything if you do."

I might lose everything if I don't, Redd thought.

✖   ✖   ✖

Sheriff Blackwood somehow managed to turn fifteen minutes into nine, arriving at Blanton's office before Redd and Blanton finished their coffee. He wore a harried expression as he entered and sank into the remaining guest chair. He held his Stetson in his right hand and a sheaf of papers held together with a black binder clip in his left, and as soon as he was seated, he tossed the latter over to Redd.

"Matthew James Redd," he rumbled, "you've been served."

"Served?" For a moment, Redd thought the sheriff was joking, but a glance down at the top sheet in the bundle was enough to confirm that it was a formal court document, summoning him to appear before the Lewis and Clark County Justice Court. He did not recognize the plaintiff's name. The next page was a letter demanding payment for repairs to a motorcycle, owned by the plaintiff, in the amount of $625 plus tax. Below that was another summons, this one with a different name and a different but similar dollar amount. "What the—?"

"You just couldn't leave it alone, could you?" Blackwood said, wagging his head.

"Let me see that." Blanton was on his feet, reaching over to pluck the papers from Redd's hands. He scanned them with the brevity of experience, then turned his gaze back on Redd. "What's this about, Matthew?"

Redd, still reeling from this latest development, was slow to answer, so Blackwood jumped in. "I'll tell you what it's about, Counselor. Your client drove up to a dive bar in Helena and proceeded to vandalize the establishment, then smashed up several motorcycles belonging to the patrons."

Redd finally found his voice. "You're right. I did. But you left out the part where they slashed all the tires on my truck."

"Matthew," Blanton barked. "Not another word." He glowered at Redd for a moment, his eyes saying what he could not put into words in front of the sheriff. Redd had told the lawyer about the confrontation at the Buffalo Jump but had glossed over what had happened in the parking lot.

Blanton turned to Blackwood. "Is that correct? Did they vandalize Matthew's truck?"

"How should I know?" the sheriff replied irritably. "It's outside my jurisdiction. But the counsel for the plaintiffs told me that there's security video footage of Matthew ripping off the handle to the front door and then trashing those bikes."

"Counsel for the plaintiffs?" Blanton raised an eyebrow. "These are small claims court filings. What do they need counsel for?"

Blackwood shrugged.

"I'd like to have a talk with this lawyer," Blanton went on. "Did you get his name?"

"He's a she," Blackwood replied. "Angela Townsend. She's a partner at a firm up in Helena. I've got her card in my office. I'll forward her contact information."

"It strikes me as curious that these fellows are asking for damages but haven't included a police report."

Blackwood shrugged again. "You'll have to take that up with them. I get the impression that they aren't keen on involving the police."

"Imagine that." Blanton shifted his focus to Redd. "Matthew, did you file a police report concerning the damage to your truck?"

Redd shook his head. "I figured it wouldn't do any good."

"Even so, it's important to do this the right way. Establish a paper trail. We're going to countersue, of course." He dropped back into his chair.

"Sheriff, there's more going on here than you realize. This legal action is part of a broader campaign of harassment aimed at my client, and I'm afraid it's likely to escalate."

Blackwood's gaze narrowed. He sat up a little straighter, then looked over at Redd. "Why do I get the feeling that you haven't been completely forthcoming with me?"

Redd glanced at Blanton and, after an answering nod, faced the sheriff and told the story again.

Like Blanton before, Blackwood did not interrupt, but he made no effort to hide his growing displeasure. When Redd finished, the sheriff shook his head. "Boy, when you step in it, you jump in with both feet, don't you?"

"I didn't ask for this fight," Redd protested. "They threw the first punch and didn't like it when I punched back. Now they aren't giving me the choice of walking away."

Blanton weighed in. "Sheriff, it's clear that my client is being targeted, and we demand that you take action. You can start by investigating the assault on his child at the medical clinic day care facility."

Blackwood frowned. "I'll need a statement from the doctor who treated him to the effect that he was dosed with something. Without that, there's really no proof that a crime has even taken place, much less that it somehow connects to these bikers. Frankly, it doesn't seem like their style."

"I'll have the doctor call you," Redd said, barely keeping his temper in check. He had hoped the report of a threat against little Matty would motivate Blackwood to action, but evidently the sheriff was still playing it safe.

"As for the rest of it . . ." Blackwood let out a long sigh. "You're absolutely right about one thing. This is only going to get worse. As they see it, you've committed the worst kind of insult, and honor demands revenge."

"Honor? You're kidding, right?"

"Their version of it."

"Sheriff," Blanton interjected, "regardless of whatever justification they may have, if the threat of violence against Matthew and his family is credible, then you have to do something."

Blackwood wrung his hands. "What can I do? I barely have enough deputies to cover things on a good day."

"Call in the highway patrol," Blanton suggested. "Since these bikers are operating across county lines, I'd say that's the logical thing to do."

"MHP is spread thinner than we are," Blackwood countered. Then he softened a little. "I'll . . . I'll see to it that there's a deputy close to your place at all times. Maybe the presence of a patrol car will be enough to keep them from bothering you. But you've got to promise to call me immediately if there's any more trouble. No more taking things into your own hands."

"I have a right to defend myself and my family," Redd protested. "If they come after us, I'm not going to just hide under a table and wait for you to come save us."

"I understand that." Blackwood looked like he wanted to say more, but Blanton rose to his feet and gestured to the door.

"Thank you for coming over, Sheriff. I understand that this puts you in an awkward situation, but we all want the same thing. Now if you'll excuse us, I'd like to have a private word with my client."

Blackwood seemed to welcome the dismissal. He got to his feet and jammed his Stetson onto his head. He looked down at Redd as if he was trying to think of something else to say, but in the end, he settled for a half nod before striding out of the office.

When he was gone, Blanton leaned on his desktop with both hands. "Well, at least we're getting somewhere."

"We are?" wondered a dubious Redd. "Seems to me like things have only gotten worse. Now they're suing me. They've got me on video trashing those bikes. How am I supposed to fight that?"

The attorney tapped the sheaf of court papers on his desk. "Believe it or not, this may be a good thing. I'll talk to this lawyer, Angela Townsend. It may be that she and I can negotiate some other outcome to all of this. One that lets everyone walk away without losing face."

"Walk away?"

"Yes, Matthew. I think a peaceable end to this feud would be best for all concerned. Especially for the safety of your family. Wouldn't you agree that's the most important thing?"

Redd frowned but did not contest the assertion.

"Meanwhile," Blanton continued, "I'll give my colleague in Bozeman a call. Maybe we can find something to give us a little leverage at the negotiating table."

"I'm grateful," Redd said.

"I wonder if you'll still be when you get my bill." Blanton quickly cracked a grin. "Don't worry. We'll figure something out when the time comes. For now, just focus on taking care of your family."

Sensing that the conversation was at an end, and well aware of the fact that he needed to get on the road, Redd excused himself and hurried out to the Tahoe. It was only then, sitting alone, that he felt the weight of the burden sitting squarely on his shoulders.

He mentally ticked off the items: New tires for the truck. Junior's hospital bills. The civil suit for damages to the bikers' motorcycles. Blanton's bill. And topping it all off, a whopping $27,000 tax liability due in less than two weeks.

Talk about the last straw. Where am I gonna get that kind of money?

An old aphorism popped into his head, one he'd heard from his father-in-law. Something about the Lord never giving you more than you can carry.

Well, Redd thought, *he must think I'm Superman.*

TWENTY-TWO

Following the directions on a crude, hand-drawn map, Bobbie-Sue navigated the pickup—a 2006 Dodge Ram, red except for one rear fender that was primer gray and waiting for a coat of paint that would likely never be applied—through downtown Wellington and into the parking lot of the Stillwater County Health Center.

She was comfortable behind the wheel of the big truck, which belonged to Angry Johnny, and had driven it out from Milwaukee, trailing behind the pack as a support vehicle. But driving on the open road was a lot easier than negotiating the cramped parking lot of what passed for the small town's hospital. She wasn't sure whether to park and go find help or pull up to the entrance, off-load her charge, and then go look for a parking spot.

She glanced over her shoulder to the rear seating area, where Dunk lay, huddled under a blanket and shivering uncontrollably despite the fact that she'd run the heater on full blast. Going to the entrance was probably the smarter thing to do, but Johnny had told her not to leave Dunk alone under any circumstances, and she was more afraid of making Johnny, well, *angry* than she was of making Dunk wait a few more minutes to get medical care.

He had not punished her for speaking out the previous evening, but that did not make her feel any safer. After the knife fight, after Dunk had killed Joey, Johnny had seemed almost maniacally remorseless. It was a side of him she had never seen before, and it scared her. He was, she realized, capable of doing almost anything, and she was not about to draw attention to herself.

He'd stayed up late, conferring with all the club officers in private, while she had gone to their tent and pretended to sleep until, what seemed like hours later, she finally relaxed enough to crash out. She didn't know what time Johnny had finally come in or if he had forgone sleep altogether, which was entirely possible. Johnny tended to use a lot more crank during club events and sometimes went for days without sleep. It had still been dark out when he'd roused her and told her to take Dunk to the clinic in Wellington.

Although he'd won the fight with Joey, Dunk wasn't doing well. Joey had managed to stab him in the stomach, twisting the blade on its way in. One of the brothers with some basic first aid training had stanched the bleeding with pressure bandages, but in the hours that followed, his condition had worsened. He had spiked a high fever, a sure sign that infection had set in. As a rule, the Infidels rarely sought formal treatment at a hospital or urgent care facility, where their answers to medical questions might prove incriminating, so Dunk's condition had to be dire for Johnny to send him out for professional help. Judging by his pallor and the sick smell coming off him, Bobbie-Sue thought it might already be too late for Dunk.

She wondered why Johnny had directed her to Wellington when Helena was only a few miles farther away and would almost certainly have better facilities, but she knew better than to question his decision.

"What should I tell them when they ask what happened?" she had asked.

"Tell them he's your boyfriend. You were camping. He was cutting something with his knife but tripped and fell on it."

Bobbie-Sue didn't think the doctors would buy that story. It was more likely that they would accuse her of stabbing him and call the police. If that happened . . . she didn't know what she would do. The more she thought about it, the more she wondered if the universe was trying to tell her something.

She decided to trust her first impulse and pulled up to the urgent care entrance. She left the truck idling there and went inside. There were only a couple people in the waiting room, and neither of them looked in desperate need of medical attention. Bobbie-Sue walked past and went to the reception desk. The older heavyset woman seated behind the desk regarded Bobbie-Sue with an unashamedly judgmental eye but managed a passable smile as she asked, "What can I do for you, hon?"

"My boyfriend is real sick," Bobbie-Sue said. "I don't think he can walk. Is there someone who can help me get him inside?"

"Oh, dear." Now the woman's concern seemed genuine. She swiveled her chair around until she was facing the large open area behind the desk, which had several empty beds with privacy curtains. "Colt, hon, there's a lady here who could use those muscles of yours."

A young good-looking man who had been hidden behind a desk at the back of the treatment area rose to his feet and began striding toward the reception desk. The receptionist had not been exaggerating with her comment about his muscles. His biceps, clearly the result of plenty of time at the gym, strained the fabric of his dark-blue T-shirt, which was emblazoned with a stylized Maltese cross and the words *Stillwater County Volunteer Fire Department*. She surmised that he must be a paramedic or emergency medical technician, lending his expertise to the little Podunk town's sad excuse for a hospital.

As soon as he saw Bobbie-Sue, he flashed her a nakedly flirtatious smile. He was, she thought, very handsome, though a little too clean-cut and conservative for her tastes. Still, she could not help but feel pleased that a stranger found her attractive.

Or maybe he's just really friendly, she told herself.

"What can I help with?" Colt asked.

Bobbie-Sue was momentarily tongue-tied, but the receptionist supplied the answer. "Her boyfriend is outside. Can't make it in under his own power."

Colt flashed another smile Bobbie-Sue's way, evidently only slightly put off by the fact that she had a boyfriend. "Well, let's go see what we can do."

He grabbed a wheelchair from one corner of the room and rolled it toward the front door. Bobbie-Sue hurried over to open it for him, then went directly to the rear door of the Ram. When she opened it, the smell hit her like a physical blow. Colt noticed it as well, and his demeanor immediately became serious. He quickly donned a pair of black nitrile gloves and an M95 respirator, then moved in closer.

"I need some room," he said. "Can you hold the chair?"

She stepped out of the way, allowing him to climb inside the cab. He peeled back the blanket and did a quick visual inspection, taking note of the bandage on Dunk's hand and the bulkier one around his middle. "What happened to him?"

"He got stabbed." The words were out before she could stop them, but she quickly amended, "It was an accident. He tripped and fell on a knife."

Colt shot her a questioning look but didn't press the issue. "When did this happen?"

"Last night. We're camping. It didn't seem that serious, but when I woke up, he was like *this*."

"Well," Colt said gravely as he looked Dunk over, "it's definitely pretty serious. You should have called 911."

Bobbie-Sue didn't know how to respond to the criticism, so she held her tongue as Colt manhandled Dunk out of the cab and into the waiting wheelchair.

Once inside the clinic, Colt rolled Dunk right into the treatment area, parking the chair beside one of the beds. "Jackie!" he called out. "I need help with a patient transfer here. Doris, page Dr. Willers."

A woman in dark-blue scrubs, middle-aged and a little on the heavy side—"pleasantly plump" as Bobbie-Sue's mother would say—emerged from the back of the room and joined Colt at the wheelchair. Working together, they lifted Dunk's still-shivering form onto the bed and began assessing his condition. Colt wrapped a blood pressure cuff around Dunk's arm, while the woman—Jackie—took his temperature.

Meanwhile, Doris the receptionist picked up her telephone handset and used it to send an announcement, which blared from overhead speakers. "Dr. Willers, please come to UC. Dr. Willers, to UC, please."

Bobbie-Sue might have been a ghost for all that anyone paid attention to her. She stood by, letting the medical people do their thing, but caught snatches of their conversation. She heard "infected" and "septic." She also heard "stabbed" and "sheriff."

Panic quickened her pulse. She had been afraid that something like this might happen. What would she say if the police got involved? Should she stick to the story Johnny had supplied? Would they believe it?

Maybe I should just leave. Run away.

Johnny would be mad at her if she did that, but if the police questioned her, demanded better answers that she couldn't give, wouldn't that be even worse?

What if I just tell them the truth?

The answer to that was easy. Johnny would probably kill her. She understood now that he was capable of it.

But what if I don't go back?

In all the years she had been riding with the Infidels, the idea of leaving had never occurred to her. "Always an Infidel" meant just that. Quitting the club—whether you were patched or property—was almost impossible.

But as unthinkable as the prospect ought to have been, the question stayed in her head.

What if I don't go back?

An older man wearing a long white lab coat entered the treatment area through an interior door. Bobbie-Sue guessed this was the doctor that had been paged. She had already forgotten his name.

The doctor came over and spoke to Colt and Jackie. His voice was low and soft, and Bobbie-Sue couldn't make out his side of the conversation, but Colt's voice was easier to distinguish. "Penetration with a foreign object . . . Looks like he might have a perforated bowel."

The doctor mumbled something incomprehensible. Colt glanced over at Bobbie-Sue and nodded. "I'll talk to her."

Bobbie-Sue felt another wave of panic, but then Colt was speaking to her. "I need some more information, Miss . . . I don't think I caught your name."

She answered without thinking. "Bobbie-Sue."

"Bobbie-Sue. You said he's your boyfriend? What's his name?"

"Dunk."

Colt raised an eyebrow at the odd nickname. "Last name?"

Bobbie-Sue stared blankly at the medic. She didn't know Dunk's real name, didn't know anything about him. "We . . . uh, just met. I don't really . . ."

Colt nodded. "It's okay. It happens. Do you know if he has any allergies?"

Bobbie-Sue gave a helpless shrug.

Colt regarded her for a moment. "You don't really know this guy, do you?"

This is it, she thought. If she answered truthfully, it would be a first step into unknown territory. There would be no going back. And yet the idea of remaining where she was, of being Johnny's property, no longer seemed quite as desirable as it once had. Or as inevitable.

She shook her head.

"That's what I thought." Colt looked back over his shoulder. "Jackie, check him for a wallet. We'll need to find someone to authorize treatment."

Jackie had no difficulty finding Dunk's wallet, which was attached to a chain hooked to his belt. "Patient's name is Duncan Simmons. He's from Milwaukee." She detached the wallet from the chain and brought it over to Doris at the reception desk. The older woman seemed to know what was expected of her without being told.

Colt now addressed Bobbie-Sue again, speaking almost in a whisper. "Did he try to hurt you? Is that how this happened?"

The question surprised her, and she again answered truthfully without thinking. "No. That's not what happened."

Colt nodded as if he didn't quite believe her. "Well, I don't know what *did* happen, but I do know that we're going to have to call the sheriff in to investigate this, and he's going to ask some hard questions. Questions that maybe you don't want to answer. If I'm reading the situation right, that is."

Bobbie-Sue stared back, dumbly. Why was he telling her this?

"What I'm saying," Colt went on, "is if you were to leave right now . . . Well, it might be a while before anyone from the sheriff's office gets back to us."

Now she understood. Clearly Colt believed that she was the victim, that she had injured Dunk in an act of self-defense, and he was now giving her a chance to slip away in order to avoid being questioned.

"Just something to think about," he went on. "If you're going to stay, you'll have to wait over there." He gestured to the lobby beyond Doris's desk.

As he started to turn away, Bobbie-Sue found her voice. "What's gonna happen to him?"

"It looks like he might have a punctured intestine. The wound leaked bacteria into his abdominal cavity and turned septic. He's going to need surgery to repair the injury and a lot of antibiotics to stop the infection. We aren't really equipped for that kind of operation here, so we'll probably transport him on to Bozeman."

"But he's going to be okay?"

"Honestly? I don't know." He reached out awkwardly and patted her shoulder. "But you don't have to worry about that now . . . if you know what I mean."

Then he turned and went back to Dunk's bed.

Bobbie-Sue's mind raced to process everything Colt had said. What if Dunk died? What if the sheriff questioned her?

What would Johnny want her to do?

What if I don't go back?

She was still trying to figure it out as she walked past the reception desk, heading for the exit.

"You doin' okay, hon?" Doris asked.

"Gotta park the truck," she mumbled. "Be right back."

The worst part was that she didn't even know if that was true. Or what she'd do next.

TWENTY-THREE

Redd started feeling better once he was on the highway, heading north. The golden fields dotted with early snow, herds of cattle and bison roaming, evergreen forests melting into the mountains, and above it all, a sky that went on forever . . . drinking in the sprawling landscape was a tonic for the soul, and Redd couldn't get enough of it.

Call it Big Sky therapy, he thought. *At least no one can take that away from me.*

He got a call from Mikey Derhammer as he was nearing Helena. He activated the hands-free mode and answered. "What's up?"

"I have some good news."

About time, Redd thought to himself.

"Well, I think it's good news."

Perfect.

"A dealer friend in Bozeman can set me up with six brand-new Pathfinder ATs for seven fifty."

Redd groaned. While $750 for six heavy-duty truck tires was actually an unbeatable price—a full two hundred dollars less than he expected to pay—it was still a lot more than he could afford.

"But the good news," Mikey went on, "is that we can put you on an installment plan."

Redd had lived most of his life being almost terminally averse to buying anything on credit, and despite the fact that he had inherited a whopper of a debt load, he had done his level best to resist the temptation to go deeper into debt to stay afloat. Emily had told him that he was being hopelessly old-fashioned in his thinking. She was probably right, but J. B. had drilled into his head that the first thing to do when you're in a hole is stop digging.

One thing was certain, though: he needed a functioning truck.

"Are you sure Elijah will go for that?" Redd's relationship with his father-in-law was considerably better now than it had been in the past, but this felt an awful lot like asking a relative for money, and that was something Redd wanted to avoid at all costs.

"Dude, how do you think we stay in business? If the old man didn't extend credit, we wouldn't have any customers at all."

Redd nodded unconsciously. "Then I guess that is good news."

"Sweet. I'll drive down and pick up the tires this afternoon. Should have it ready for you by this evening. How's little man doing?"

The abrupt shift in topic caught Redd off guard. Evidently Emily had spoken with Liz about the baby's illness, and Liz had told Mikey. The question was, how much had Emily told them?

"He's doing a lot better. I'm on my way to pick them up now."

"Glad to hear that. I'll let you know when I have the tires, man."

"Thanks, Mikey. I appreciate it."

"No problem."

After ending the call, Redd decided to try to keep a positive mindset. Mikey did bring *some* good news, even if it meant shelling out cash he didn't have. Redd told himself he'd make it work. After all, solutions to real-life problems were rarely perfect, and sometimes you had to accept the little victories and focus on the important things.

✖ ✖ ✖

He reached the hospital just a few minutes after noon. Emily was waiting for him in the vestibule with Junior in her arms. She looked tired and a little rumpled but greeted him with a relieved smile and a kiss. The baby squealed with delight when he saw Redd.

"How's he doing?" Redd had asked the same question twenty minutes earlier when he'd called with his ETA, but it seemed like the right thing to say.

"Hundred percent better. Whatever was in his system, it's gone now."

"Let's make sure it stays that way."

"What did the sheriff say?"

The question caught him by surprise. How did she know about Blackwood's visit? Then he remembered he'd told her he would call the sheriff first thing in the morning. "He's going to need the ER doc to send him a full report of the incident so he can open an investigation."

"I'll give him a call." She let the subject hang while she put the baby in his car seat but picked it up again as soon as they were on the road. "I still can't believe that someone did this to him on purpose. I mean, why would they do that?"

Redd winced, then took a deep breath. "Em, there's something I need to tell you . . ."

✖ ✖ ✖

Although this latest retelling of the story should have been easier, his recollection of events sharpening in his mind's eye, Redd struggled to find the right words. It didn't help that Emily remained inscrutably silent throughout, not once asking for clarification or expressing dismay, shock, or outrage. Throughout the telling, she regarded him with a stony gaze, and Redd, who had faced off against gun-wielding terrorists, mercenary shooters, and outlaw bikers, felt uncharacteristically apprehensive. Because he was driving, he could not look at her the whole time, but even when his attention was on the road, he could feel her eyes on him. As he brought his summation to a close by expressing his belief that their son's fever and the situation with the assessor's office were part of the Infidels' campaign of harassment, he braced himself for her reaction.

Although they'd had their share of disagreements in the past, none had approached the level of what Redd would call a fight. There had been long silences, unspoken requests for time and space apart, but those always ended with one of them making a conciliatory gesture. Voices were rarely raised. They did not shout at each other, did not slam doors or stomp off muttering curses. But all of those incidents could be chalked up to miscommunication and the unintentional thoughtlessness that occurs when two fiercely independent souls join their lives together.

This was something different.

If those other disagreements were storms, then this had the potential to become a category 5 hurricane.

"So," he finished, "that's the situation."

When she didn't respond after a long moment, he added, "I'm sorry. I didn't mean for any of this—"

"Why didn't you tell me sooner?" There was nothing acrimonious in the question. She seemed genuinely curious.

It was a good question, and he didn't have a good answer. He kept his attention on the road, hiding the fact that he didn't want to look her in the eye. "I guess I thought I could handle it. Then things started happening so fast I didn't know how to tell you."

"This wasn't just your problem to handle, Matty. We're a team, remember?"

"Em, it wasn't like that—"

She raised a hand. "Just stop." She took a breath. "If six years of practicing emergency medicine has taught me anything, it's that you have to prioritize treatment. We'll talk about what you should have done later. Right now we need to talk about what we're going to do to start fixing all this."

He nodded, grateful for the reprieve. "I've already talked to Mikey. You and Junior can stay with them until—"

"Excuse me?" This time there was a sharp edge in her tone. "I know you're still new to this, but that's not how talking about things works. You don't get to just decide what I'm going to do."

He shook his head. "Em, this is one of those times when you need to trust me."

"I do trust you, Matty. You want us to be safe. I get that. But we're talking about our home. *Our* home." She gestured her hand between the two of them. "We can guard it and keep our son safe together."

"Everything they're doing is just to keep me off-balance. Eventually they're going to come after me, and when they do . . . let's just say I'm going to have enough to worry about without having to also be worried about you and Junior being safe."

"So you're just going to go all *High Noon* on them? One man against an army of outlaw gunslingers?"

Redd shrugged. It sounded stupid when she said it out loud, but he didn't see another way. "I have to do this, Em."

"You *don't* have to. That's the point, Matthew. You don't have to take this on all by yourself. In case it slipped your mind, I can hold my own in a fight."

He shook his head. "No. I couldn't live with myself if you got hurt. And somebody has to be there for Junior if . . ." He hesitated. "If something bad happens."

"Don't you dare bring our son into this, Matthew Redd. Not now."

Using his full name represented a serious escalation. "Look, I know what I'm doing. I can handle this. These guys think they're a lot tougher than they really are."

"Fine. But don't go it alone. Please?"

Redd took his eyes off the road long enough to look over at her. She was pleading, genuine concern flooding her face. He didn't even feel he deserved her worries at the moment and wished he knew how to express his feelings better. He wanted to tell her how sorry he was for everything, how much he loved her and Junior.

Instead, he said, "I can't ask Mikey. Blackwood won't help. He's terrified of these bikers, and even if he wasn't, he doesn't have enough manpower to make a difference."

"Then call Gavin. Ask him to help."

Redd scoffed. She might as well have thrown a bucket of ice water at him. The idea of asking Kline for help was anathema under the best of circumstances, but approaching him now, after he'd effectively fired Redd from the fly team, made it an especially odious proposition.

Through clenched teeth, Redd muttered, "That ain't going to happen. I'd rather die first than call him and beg for help. No way."

"One, that's not funny. And two, this goes way beyond your personal beef with him. The Infidels are criminals. I'm sure the bureau is already aware of their activities. If anyone has the muscle to stand against them, it's the Feds. And Gavin has a personal stake in this. They've targeted your son. His grandson. You may not ever accept him as a father, but that doesn't change his relationship to Junior."

"Wanna bet?"

"You know I'm right. So help me, Matty Redd, if you get yourself killed because you were too proud to ask the one man who could actually help you win this fight, then you'll have no one to blame but yourself." She paused a beat, then added, "The man I fell in love with is smarter than that."

Redd glowered but he had no rejoinder. She was right—she usually was—but that didn't make the pill any easier to swallow. As he turned the problem over in his head, he saw a way out of the corner she'd backed him into.

"Okay," he said finally. "You're right. It's stupid not to make use of every resource. But I'd feel a lot better if you and Junior went somewhere safe. If not with Mikey and Liz, then stay with your mom and dad."

Emily frowned. "I don't want to loop in my parents, Matty. They're old, and honestly, this is the last thing they need. I'm worried about them as it is. I don't want them pulled into anything dangerous."

Redd actually agreed and was happy she made that call herself without him bringing it up. Beyond the fact that his in-laws had only recently expressed their approval of Emily marrying him, feelings he didn't want them to second-guess, he felt guilty enough involving Mikey. He didn't want to involve any more innocent people. But since Mikey was already involved . . .

"Then Mikey and Liz's house it is."

"I'll consider it." The allowance surprised Redd, but she quickly added, "But only after you call in the cavalry."

Redd smiled at her choice of metaphor. He couldn't quite bring himself to see Gavin Kline astride a horse, saber raised to the sky, charging into battle.

"I'll make a call," he promised.

But it won't be to Kline.

TWENTY-FOUR

When it became apparent that nobody at the Helena law office was in any hurry to take his call, Duke Blanton reviewed the notes he'd written on a yellow legal pad, which summarized the information he'd gleaned from a stack of printouts that now occupied a corner of his desk. The pages, which had been sent to him as email attachments, contained the results of background checks conducted by a Bozeman-based private investigator, targeting the men named in the civil suits filed against Matthew Redd. Blanton was old-fashioned, preferring to read from paper rather than a computer screen and taking meticulous notes as he read. It had taken him a couple hours to sort through the volume of material, but the effort had been worthwhile. Those men, known members of the Infidels Motorcycle Club, had extensive criminal records—more arrests than convictions, but still enough to give him some leverage.

The on-hold music stopped abruptly, and a woman's voice issued from the speakerphone. "This is Angela Townsend."

"Ms. Townsend, Duke Blanton here. I'm representing Mr. Matthew Redd, whom I believe you are familiar with."

"That's right. Mr. Redd is the respondent in a legal action being pursued by several of my clients. But I'm guessing you don't need me to tell you that."

Her voice was husky and her manner professional, if a little clipped. Not rude exactly, but just a little condescending.

"No, it's all here," Blanton replied smoothly. "Ms. Townsend . . . May I call you Angie?"

"I'd rather you didn't."

Blanton chuckled. "Well, that's fine. Ms. Townsend, I'm calling in the hope that we can find an equitable solution to this little matter."

"I'm sure my clients would appreciate that. Just have Mr. Redd remit payment for the damages, and we can end it right now."

Blanton chuckled again, this time without humor. "Now, Ms. Townsend, it sounds like maybe you and I aren't on the same page, so let me just catch you up. Mr. Redd won't be paying a dime to your clients. Quite the opposite, actually. We're planning to countersue for damages to his vehicle—"

"Good luck proving that," Townsend snapped. "We've got video of Mr. Redd's actions. What have you got?"

"Oh, I think I can make a pretty convincing case. Six slashed tires. Mr. Redd's description of the two men he saw, with knives, walking away from the truck. I am especially looking forward to questioning your clients under oath."

Townsend was silent for a long moment. "All right, Mr. Blanton—"

"Call me Duke."

She ignored the interjection. "I'm listening. What are you offering?"

"Offering? Well now, that's an interesting way to put it. As I'm sure you already know, your clients are not the most savory folks to walk God's green earth."

"They have the same legal rights as anyone else."

The statement was not completely accurate. Two of the men identified as plaintiffs had criminal records for a variety of offenses, including domestic violence, and were on parole, which placed restrictions on their freedom of movement and their right to own and use firearms, among other things. Blanton decided not to play that card just yet.

"I'm sure they do," he said. "I'm sure they do. And one of those rights is the right to face their accuser."

"I think you're confused, Mr. Blanton. Mr. Redd is the accused."

"In addition to our countersuit," Blanton went on, "I'm advising my client to file a police report with the Lewis and Clark County Sheriff's Department. Between the damage done to his truck and the attempted assault, I think there's a good chance that charges will be filed. By the way, I do appreciate you providing me with the names of the suspects. It would have been almost impossible to identify them otherwise."

"My clients had no involvement with Mr. Redd. They were inside the establishment minding their own business when the alleged action occurred. And, I might add, when Mr. Redd trashed their motorcycles."

Blanton thought Angela Townsend was starting to sound just a little bit rattled. Clearly she had not anticipated that Redd would seek legal redress.

"Could be," Blanton replied. "Could be. But I'm sure that once the detectives get involved, the truth will come out. Your clients may not have been directly involved in the *crimes*—" he stressed the word, pausing a beat to let it soak in—"perpetrated against Mr. Redd, but I'm certain they have a pretty good idea who was."

"You're bluffing."

Blanton laughed again. "Well, maybe so and then again maybe not."

"Then I'll ask again: what are you offering?"

Blanton leaned forward in his chair as if Townsend were sitting across the desktop. "Let me speak plainly, Ms. Townsend. I don't know if your clients have been forthcoming with you, but here's the situation. The Infidels Motorcycle Club and Matthew Redd have an ongoing difference of opinion regarding something that happened over a year ago. It's a situation that I can only describe as a feud. Like something out of the Wild West."

He paused to see if she would comment. She did not.

"Matthew Redd is a proud man, and my guess is the same could be said for your clients. They don't know how to back down from a fight. But unless they do exactly that, this fight is going to get bloody. And I am not employing hyperbole, Ms. Townsend."

There was a long sigh over the line. "Mr. Blanton, I don't know if what you are saying is true. My clients don't share that kind of information with me. But I can only advise them. I can't compel them to take or eschew action."

"Ms. Townsend, I'm trying to keep this whole thing from blowing up. Nobody wins unless everybody walks away. Tell your clients that enough is enough. They've made their point. Counted coup. Satisfied honor."

"Can you guarantee that Mr. Redd will abide by these terms?"

"Mr. Redd will do whatever it takes to keep his family safe. If that means swallowing his pride, he'll do it." Blanton wasn't completely certain of his answer, but he reckoned himself a pretty fair judge of character.

Townsend sighed again. "I can't make any promises, but I will pass this along."

"That's all I'm asking."

After the call was over, Blanton sat back in his chair and allowed himself a satisfied smile. He was eager to call Redd, to let him know about the conversation with Angela Townsend, but decided to hold off. Better to wait and see if she could rein in the Infidels.

It felt good to be using his legal skills—his *mind*—for something meaningful. He had always been content to limit his scope of practice to things like estate planning and bankruptcies—the kind of stuff that almost nobody dreamed of doing when they went to law school—but it was, even he had to admit, boring as all get-out.

He couldn't recall the last time doing his job had left him feeling so exhilarated. So alive. Smiling, he leaned back and kicked his feet up onto his desk and interlocked his fingers behind his head.

I could definitely get used to this, he thought. *Maybe I'll even expand my practice.*

For a moment, he dreamed of getting his son, Tyler, involved in that idea. Tyler was a lawyer too, and if Duke was honest, a far better one than him. They didn't talk often—heck, he wasn't even sure when they'd seen each other last—but he loved the idea of building something together.

Maybe, he told himself.

But first, he had to get Redd on board and convince him to walk away from the Infidels. And that, Blanton knew, would be easier said than done.

TWENTY-FIVE

Redd had interpreted Emily's concession to "consider it" as an agreement to take refuge with the Derhammers. Emily, however, did not see it that way and explained this to Redd when he drove past the turnoff to the ranch. After a very brief and mostly one-sided discussion, Redd turned around and headed home.

In some respects, he was glad that she had been so insistent. After spending so much time on the road—chasing the Infidels, running back and forth from the hospital in Missoula—it felt good to be in his own house, surrounded by the familiar. Unfortunately, he didn't have the luxury of remaining there to enjoy it.

"I need to go deal with this tax thing," he told Emily once she and Junior were settled in, and even though he knew what her answer would be, he added, "I'd really feel better if you and Matty weren't here alone."

"We'll be fine," she insisted. Then she softened a little. "If it will make you feel better, leave the shotgun where I can grab it."

"Is that supposed to be a joke?"

"I never joke about home defense." She quirked a smile. "We'll be fine, really. Go take care of your business."

Redd didn't think she was taking the threat seriously enough but decided not to press the matter. His instincts told him that the Infidels would make their move soon, but he could tell he wasn't going to convince her to leave and that any attempt to do so would be a waste of time that they really didn't have. So after making sure the shotgun *was* readily accessible, he climbed back into the Tahoe and headed into town.

As he rolled down the drive, he scanned the vegetation on either side of the road, looking for motorcycles and men in black leather lurking in the brush, ready to ambush him, and wondering if it would happen like that or if the Infidels had something else in store for him. Once he reached the highway, he placed the call he'd promised Emily he would make.

He half expected it to go to voice mail, but after a couple rings, Rob Davis's voice—friendly but a little wary—filled the Tahoe's interior. "Redd, good to hear from you. What's happening?"

"Oh, you know how it is," Redd hedged. "How are things there? Are you still on the bench, or did Kline tell you not to talk to me about it?"

"Ah, *well*..." The way Davis drew out the word was answer enough.

"Say no more," Redd said, letting the other man off the hook. "I understand. Actually, that wasn't why I called."

"I'm listening."

"So this is just between us, right?"

"You, me, and the NSA," Davis said with a chuckle.

Redd had mentally rehearsed how he was going to approach his request, but the words he had carefully chosen now deserted him. He was overcome with anxiety and self-doubt.

What will I do if he says no?

"Do you remember ... umm ... that thing I was ... dealing with? Just before I left?"

"The OMG?" The humor was gone from Davis's voice in an instant, the wariness doubling. "Still having a problem with them?"

"You could say that."

"I told you not to mess with them, Redd."

"They didn't give me a choice." This part—the justification—came a little easier. "It's their code or something. I disrespected them and they aren't going to let it go."

Davis muttered a curse under his breath. "What are you going to do about it?"

"Whatever I have to," Redd answered honestly.

There was a long sigh on the other end of the phone before Davis finally said, "You can't take them on alone. You'll need help—trust me on that."

Here it is, Redd thought.

"I know. You're right. That's kind of why I'm calling . . ."

Evidently sensing the difficulty Redd was having, Davis jumped in. "It's okay; I get it. You don't even have to ask. But you need to tell me everything."

Redd gave a quick rundown of the situation. When he was done, Davis asked the important question.

"So what's your plan?"

Redd had thought about this a lot. "Sooner or later, they're going to come after me. I figure in the next few days. I don't get to choose the time, but I can choose the place. My place. I want to have a warm reception ready for them. But I'm just one man, and I have no idea how many of them will be coming. I need some backup."

"All right," Davis said. "I think I know how we can help. I might have an idea."

"*We?*" Redd asked.

"Me and the rest of the tac team. I mean, I need to talk to them first, but they'll be in. Think you can hold out a little while longer? Forty-eight hours, max?"

"Like I said, that's not going to be up to me, but I'll do what I can to stay off their radar until I hear back from you. I really appreciate this, Rob."

"I know you'd do the same for any of us. Stay strong, brother. Help is on the way."

✖ ✖ ✖

Redd's feeling that his luck might finally be changing was short-lived. When he walked through the door of the county assessor's office, the receptionist's chilly demeanor was indication enough that his visit was not unexpected. It had been more than a year since his last in-person visit, but he recalled the woman being pleasant and personable, greeting him warmly.

Today she did not even attempt to fake a smile. "Can I help you, sir?"

"I need to talk to your boss."

The receptionist made a face like she'd just bitten into a lemon. "Mr. Yearsley isn't available to speak with you, Mr. Redd."

After the response Blanton had received when calling on Redd's behalf, this brush-off was not unexpected. Redd crossed his arms over his chest. "I'll wait."

She shook her head. "He's not going to talk to you."

Despite his determination to stay calm, Redd felt heat rising in his cheeks. "He's trying to take my ranch away from me. The least he can do is tell me why to my face."

The woman shifted in her chair as if she found this confrontation physically uncomfortable. "Mr. Redd, you need to leave. I've been instructed to tell you that if you remain on the premises, we'll call the sheriff and have you arrested for trespassing."

"Trespassing? I'm just trying to discuss my taxes with the tax collector. How is that trespassing?"

"Mr. Redd . . ."

Redd threw his hands up. "This is ridiculous."

He looked past her, staring into the open office plan work area and locating a line of closed doors labeled with brass nameplates. Even from across the room, he had no trouble making out the one with Yearsley's name on it. As he started for it, the receptionist jumped to her feet and scurried back several steps as if he were advancing on her.

"Mr. Redd," she gasped, "I'm calling the sheriff."

"Call him," Redd snarled, even as he reached the door to Yearsley's office. "Better tell him to bring all the backup he's got." He did not bother to knock but grasped the knob and turned.

If it's locked, I'm kicking it down.

It wasn't. The door swung open to reveal a plain office, tastefully decorated. A man seated behind a large oak desk—Yearsley, Redd presumed—looked up in shock, frozen in the act of reaching for the ringing telephone on his desk.

The assessor was slightly built with thinning black hair. He was a young man, probably no older than Redd himself, but his bitter expression gave him the appearance of premature age.

Redd marched forward. "I'm here to talk about my tax bill."

Yearsley jolted in his chair as if he'd just received an electric shock. He placed his hands on the desktop, palms down, as if bracing himself in the face of Redd's wrath. "You can't be here. We're calling the sheriff."

The oft-repeated threat was not lost on Redd. Blackwood's office in another wing of the courthouse was only a few minutes' walk away, and despite their friendship, Redd knew the sheriff would not hesitate to drag him away in handcuffs. That meant he didn't have much time to get the assessor to admit the truth.

Well, I tried being diplomatic.

Abandoning his original plan to plead for reinstatement of the payment plan, Redd took the nuclear option. "How much did they pay you?"

This accusation seemed to take the wind out of Yearsley's sails. "Excuse me?"

"How much did those maniacs pay you to take my ranch?"

"What on earth are you talking about?" Yearsley's confusion about the question seemed genuine.

"I had a deal to pay off my tax bill. Then you decided to pull the rug out, and the only reason I can think of for you to do that is they got to you." He searched the other man's face for some hint of guilt. "Or maybe they threatened you. Is that what happened?"

The look of bewilderment on Yearsley's face only deepened. "You're crazy." The assertion seemed to buttress the man's courage. "Saving your ranch just became the least of your worries. You're going to jail for this. I'll make sure of it."

"Go for it," Redd spat. "You're taking away my ranch, leaving me nothing to lose. A warm bed and three free meals don't sound that bad." It was a lie, of course, but judging by Yearsley's fear-induced wide-eyed stare, it was working. "But you're not really going to do that, are you? No, because if you press charges, the truth will come out. Now what are you hiding?"

"Hiding? What truth?" Yearsley's voice went up an octave. "The truth is that you can't pay your taxes, so we're seizing your ranch and selling it to settle your debts. That's the only truth that matters. And you coming in here and threatening me is only making your situation worse."

"Threatening you? Oh, I haven't even started threatening you yet."

"Matthew!" a voice barked from behind him. Blackwood's voice. "Stand down. *Now.*"

Redd shot an involuntary glance over his shoulder and saw the sheriff standing in the office doorway. His right hand was resting on the butt of his service weapon.

Yearsley shrank back into a corner as if terrified for his life. "Arrest him, Sheriff."

"For what?" Redd demanded. "I've got a right to ask you why you're taking away my ranch. Unless there's some reason you don't want me to know."

"I already told you why. Unpaid taxes. There's nothing more to it."

"I've been making payments. Honoring the agreement I made with this office." Redd was explaining this more for Blackwood's benefit than Yearsley's. "You changed the terms of our deal without even letting me know."

"We called you," Yearsley protested.

"To let me know you were already planning to seize my property." Redd turned to Blackwood. "I think the timing is very interesting, don't you?"

Blackwood squinted back at him. "I'm afraid I don't follow."

"Isn't it obvious? The Infidels. They're coming after me on all fronts. They got to him." He jerked a thumb toward the assessor. "Either paid him off or threatened him."

Blackwood and Yearsley both spoke at the same time, saying much the same thing. Redd only paid attention to the sheriff's response. "That's a pretty serious accusation to make, Matthew."

"I'd like to hear him deny it," Redd said.

"Of course I deny it" was Yearsley's strident reply. "Nobody's bribed me or threatened me. I'm just doing the job the people of this county elected me to do."

As much as Redd wanted to believe otherwise, he sensed the assessor was telling the truth. He faced the man again. "Then tell me why. The real reason. It's not just about the taxes. Why refuse to meet with me?"

"Frankly, I was scared that something like this would happen. And I was right. Once a bully, always a bully."

The accusation blindsided Redd, leaving him momentarily speechless. *Bully? Where did that come from?*

Seizing the moment, Yearsley turned to Blackwood. "I want him arrested, Sheriff."

Blackwood conspicuously moved his hand away from his still-holstered weapon. "I'm not going to do that, Mr. Yearsley." Then, in a lower voice, he added, "Matthew, it's time to go."

"That's unacceptable," Yearsley cried, stamping his foot like a child throwing a tantrum. "I demand that you arrest him!"

"For what?" Blackwood asked, echoing Redd's own question.

Yearsley spluttered, incredulous. "Take your pick. Trespassing. Intimidation."

The sheriff crossed his arms over his chest. "This is a public facility, Mr. Yearsley, so by definition, Mr. Redd has as much right to be here as you do."

"He can't just barge into my office and threaten me."

"He threatened you? What did he say?"

Yearsley's mouth opened and closed several times, working like a fish's. Finally he managed to say, "The threat was implied. I mean, look at him."

Blackwood did, giving Redd a sidelong glance, then shrugged, unconvinced. He looked to Yearsley again. "Did you refuse to meet with him?"

"I did. Because I knew something like this would happen."

"Mr. Yearsley, you're a public servant. If you're unwilling to explain your decisions to your constituents because you're afraid of what the consequences may be, then maybe you should consider a different line of work."

Yearsley recoiled. "How dare you lecture me—"

"You know," Blackwood went on, talking over the other man, "it strikes me that this is about more than just back taxes. Lots of folks are behind, what with the economy the way it is, but you aren't going after all of them. I think Mr. Redd has a right to ask why you've singled him out."

Yearsley's mouth closed and he folded his arms over his chest, unconsciously mirroring Blackwood. "Everything I've done is entirely in accordance with the statutes and policies of Stillwater County."

"Well now, that doesn't sound like an answer, Mr. Yearsley." Blackwood turned back to Redd. "Matthew, come with me."

"Not until he tells me why he's doing this."

"Matthew!" Blackwood barked. "You can either walk out of here, or I can drag you. Your choice."

Redd almost dared Blackwood to try, but the sheriff's calm intercession had already cooled some of his fervor. With a final contemptuous glance in Yearsley's direction, he stalked out of the office.

Blackwood didn't say a word as he marched Redd through the courthouse. When they were out on the street, the only thing he said was "Call me when you've cooled down a bit."

Still fuming, Redd debated how best to carry out that directive. His first impulse was to head to Spady's, the preferred watering hole of most of Wellington's residents, and drown his sorrows in a pint or two of Mountain Man Scotch Ale, but two things stopped him.

The first was the fact that he needed to keep his wits about him while the threat posed by the Infidels remained extant. The second was the certain knowledge that, while alcohol might give momentary respite from a problem, it didn't do anything to solve it and most of the time just made things worse.

Instead, he got back in the Tahoe and headed home.

TWENTY-SIX

Dmitri Georgiev had no earthly idea where he was.

He was fairly certain that he was still in the Northern Hemisphere, but that was more a matter of statistical probability than logical deduction. He had a starting point—a mostly abandoned warehouse in Brooklyn, New York—and a rough time frame of no more than twenty-four hours, but probably less. After a short drive in a van with blacked-out windows, he had been taken to a nondescript aircraft hangar, where he was escorted aboard an executive jet—a Gulfstream V if he was not mistaken; Dmitri paid attention to things like that. The plane had taken off and flown for a long interval—exactly how long, he couldn't say, but long enough for the flight attendant to provide two gourmet meals and for him to catch several hours of sleep in one of the luxurious reclining seats. He figured eight hours flight time, but it might have been as much as ten.

Based on that estimation and his knowledge of the jet's range and speed, he might be anywhere in North America, Europe, or possibly somewhere along the Mediterranean rim. Yet it was possible—probable, even—that the jet and the tour bus with blacked-out windows that had picked him up from another nondescript hangar building shortly after landing had spent much of that time going around in circles to prevent him from knowing or guessing his final destination.

Dmitri didn't really care what that destination was, but he was encouraged by the fact that his mysterious new employer had put so much effort into concealing it from him. It meant that, when the job was done, not only would he get what he was owed, he'd also live to spend it.

When his employer of several years had been forced to close up shop over a year ago, he'd been unable to find legitimate work. Although a skilled coder, his immigration status—he was a Bulgarian residing in the United States on an expired work visa—had limited his prospects. He had become, in the modern parlance, a black hat. A hired gun for the digital age, carrying out various illegal activities ranging from cyber-espionage to malware and sabotage on behalf of clients who would do anything it took to get ahead of a competitor. As such, he was accustomed to dealing with dangerous men. The risk of betrayal went with the territory. He had safeguards in place to protect his life in the event that someone tried to double-cross him after a job, but these were mostly of a punitive nature—a threat of malicious action to be carried out if any harm should befall him or if final payment was not made. Safeguards, however, were not guarantees. While there were ways to minimize the risk, every job was a gamble with his life.

He had learned of this job the usual way, through an anonymous post on a subreddit he moderated. There had been precious little information about the nature of the job, but the money was too good to pass up, and when the initial deposit—a number with a lot of zeroes after it—showed up in his Cayman Islands bank account, he decided to take a chance. He'd certainly done more, and faced greater risk, for less. With the final payout from this job, he would be set for years.

After two hours of more or less nonstop driving on what he assumed was open road, the bus slowed, made a turn, and then stopped. The driver—a man as nondescript as the hangars—got off, and another man took his place. The newcomer was anything but nondescript, and for the first time since arriving at the Brooklyn warehouse, Dmitri felt a little uneasy.

The driver was a big man, thick-bodied with beefy arms covered in an intaglio of mostly gruesome tattoos. He had long hair and an unkempt beard and stank of stale tobacco smoke. He was the sort of man Dmitri usually went out of his way to avoid. Two more men fitting a similar description boarded after the driver, both of them conspicuously armed with holstered handguns. Dmitri couldn't help but think of them as thugs—hired muscle. One of them regarded Dmitri with a slightly contemptuous glance before settling into an empty seat in the front.

They drove on for at least another hour; then the bus slowed and turned onto a rough road where it continued for fifteen or twenty minutes before finally coming to a stop. One of the thugs rose and debarked, and then after a brief delay, the other one called out to Dmitri. "Hey. Let's go."

The man spoke in English. Though his brevity made it difficult to detect an accent, Dmitri guessed American. After a surreptitious stretch to reawaken muscles that had been dormant too long, the black hat made his way down the aisle and stepped out into daylight.

It took a few seconds for his eyes to adjust to the relative brilliance, but when they did, Dmitri was no closer to identifying his whereabouts.

The bus had pulled into a small fenced area with a single dilapidated building and not much else. The building looked like a double-wide mobile home gone completely to seed. There were no other vehicles. Outside the fence was nothing but open rangeland and endless sky.

Two more armed thugs emerged from the building. After quickly conferring with the two new arrivals, the latter boarded the bus, after which the driver made a wide U-turn and steered through the still-open gate. Dmitri glimpsed a sign hanging from the gate, with black-and-red letters that said Warning and Restricted Area. There was more, but Dmitri's eyes were drawn to the last line, written in red: "Use of deadly force authorized."

One of the thugs who had ridden in with Dmitri walked over to close the gate. The other gestured to the building. "Inside."

Dmitri quickly discovered that the building's ramshackle exterior was camouflage. Just beyond the doorway was a small entry foyer and a heavy steel door, which opened into a long, sterile hallway. They passed several closed doors and one that opened into what looked like a combination dining room and recreation area. The room was unoccupied, but the smell of recently cooked food hung in the air. Evidently noticing Dmitri's curious appraisal of the space, his escort grunted, "You'll get the tour later, after you meet the boss."

There was an open freight elevator at the end of the hall. The building was a single-story structure, which could only mean that the elevator went down into a basement.

Although he didn't think of himself as claustrophobic, Dmitri did not like the idea of going into basements or caves or really anyplace where many thousands of tons of earth were between him and daylight.

The thug stepped into the car, then turned to face the control panel. That was when he realized Dmitri hadn't followed him in.

"Dude. C'mon. I don't got all day."

The request was so unexpectedly benign that Dmitri couldn't help but laugh nervously as he stepped into the elevator. The thug manually closed an accordion-style safety gate inside the car, then turned a key on the otherwise-blank control panel. The lift car shuddered and then slowly dropped into the shaft.

While it was hard to guess the depth of the shaft, Dmitri was certain they had descended at least two or three stories. This was no simple basement, but something else. Finally, after almost a minute, an opening rose into view outside the safety gate.

The hallway beyond the opening reminded Dmitri of the interior of a ship or submarine. He'd never actually been on any sort of oceangoing vessel, but he'd seen them in movies and TV shows, and this place looked similar. There were exposed pipes and conduits suspended from the ceiling overhead and running along blandly painted metal walls. Farther along, he saw what appeared to be an enormous vault door, presently open, leading deeper into the facility.

"This is as far as I go, dude." The thug gestured toward the vault. "The boss is in there."

With another nervous laugh, Dmitri ventured into the atrium and stepped around the vault door. Just beyond was a narrow passage a few yards long, which led onto what appeared to be a short wooden bridge connecting to another chamber. The height and depth of the gap was concealed in shadow. Dmitri could not fathom the reason for the gap, or for an open traverse to cross it, but gamely stepped onto the bridge. As he did, he could hear the sound of voices up ahead.

One of the voices was oddly familiar.

The chamber on the far side of the bridge was cramped and claustrophobic, the walls lined with racks of blade servers. When he realized just how much computing power he was looking at, Dmitri completely forgot about being underground. He also forgot that he was not alone.

"Ah, Dmitri. You made it."

The Bulgarian turned to look at the three figures who were hunched over a computer workstation on the desk that ran the length of one wall. The voice was the familiar one he had heard earlier, but he did not recognize the man who had addressed him.

Except there was something about his face . . . no . . . his smile.

"Mr. . . . Gage?"

The smile broadened. "In the flesh, Dmitri."

"I heard . . ."

Dmitri had actually heard a lot of things about his former employer—that he was on the run and living as a fugitive, that he'd been arrested and spirited off to Gitmo or some other black site, that he was dead. When the Gage Food Trust had abruptly ceased operations under a cloud of suspicion and seemingly without any warning, the upper-echelon employees—Dmitri among them—had scattered like rats abandoning a sinking ship. Many of them were foreign nationals, men and women who had learned their respective skill sets in the former Eastern Bloc nations but had been unable to leverage those abilities into a sustainable career in their home countries. Anton Gage had provided them with an opportunity to do just that, but when his biotech empire had cratered, so too had their prospects. Dmitri had maintained contact with a few, but none had been able to explain what had happened at the end.

"Never mind what you've heard," Gage said. "To borrow a line from the great Mark Twain, rumors of my demise have been greatly exaggerated. There will be plenty of time to catch you up on everything that's happened, but right now we've got a deadline to beat, and you're the man to help me do it."

"Deadline? I don't understand, Mr. Gage. What is it you want me to do?"

"The same thing you did for me before. What you're best at."

"You want me to program drones again?" Dmitri's career with the Gage Food Trust had begun with simple coding, but he had quickly distinguished himself by writing algorithms for Gage's fleet of autonomous aerial vehicles. The drones, which carried out a variety of tasks—from monitoring crop health to spreading plant-based organic fertilizer and pesticides—had to be able to cover a great deal of ground in the most efficient way possible, while monitoring battery life, adjusting for wind conditions and the changing weight of the craft as the payload was gradually dispersed, and generally dealing with a variety of unpredictable variables. His solution, achieved through countless hours of trial and error, had been nothing less than a miracle of artificial intelligence.

Gage nodded vigorously. "I need your algorithm, Dmitri."

"I don't understand," Dmitri said in what was already feeling like a tired refrain. "You have it."

"If only that were true. I no longer have access to the GFT mainframe. We'll have to rebuild it all from scratch, I'm afraid. Or rather, you'll have to. The good news is, I'll pay you a boatload of money to do it." His radiant smile slipped just a little. "And the bad news is that I need you to do it in three days. Less, if possible. Can you do that for me, Dmitri?"

"Three days?" Dmitri was incredulous. It had taken months to develop and refine the original version, and he'd had a team of coders working under him, each one focused on a particular set of operations.

Still, they'd been working in the dark, breaking new ground. That had been the really hard part. He now knew what worked and what didn't, what shortcuts could be taken, what pieces of code he could borrow from other applications.

Three days? It wasn't impossible.

And for a boatload of money, he could dare the impossible.

"Why the rush?" he asked.

Gage waved a dismissive hand. "Nothing that need concern you. Suffice it to say, there will be a . . ." He hesitated, searching for the right word. "A confluence of events, which will peak in the next three days. That's our optimal window for success."

"It's not a lot of time."

"Then you'd better get started." Gage clapped him on the shoulder. "Don't worry, Dmitri. You won't be the only one around here with his nose to the grindstone. There are a lot of moving pieces that will have to synchronize. I'll give you whatever support I can, limited access to the Internet, provided you can utilize a secure VPN."

"Can I bring in the old team?"

Gage winced. "That's . . . not something I'm comfortable with. You saw the lengths I had to go to in order to bring you here discreetly."

"Yes, I was wondering about that." Dmitri had assumed the purpose of the elaborate travel plan was to ensure the anonymity of his employer, but that clearly wasn't the reason. "Why go to so much trouble?"

"I had to make sure that your movements weren't being tracked by the authorities. Perhaps you've heard: I'm presently a wanted man. It will all get cleared up soon enough, but at the moment, I can't reveal my whereabouts. And I won't do anything that might jeopardize this endeavor. It's very important to me."

Dmitri rocked his head from side to side, slipping back into an old habit. In Bulgaria, one shook their head to signify agreement and nodded to indicate a "no." It was a habit that confused most outsiders, sending the opposite of its intended message, and so he usually made an effort to conform to the more universally accepted versions of the gestures. "Very well. I will do my best. What are the parameters?"

"Four thousand autonomous units. Spreaders. We need to deploy them to cover approximately forty-four million acres."

Dmitri gawped in disbelief. "Forty-four million?"

At its peak, the Gage Food Trust had covered more than a million acres, spread across several different countries. In Montana, where Dmitri had done most of his work, Gage had owned less than two hundred thousand acres.

He did some quick mental math. "Allowing time for battery changes, reloading, and movement to and from the field, a single unit can cover only about two hundred acres in a twenty-four-hour period. Even running around the clock, it would take at least two months to cover that large an area. And that's only if you have a network of charging stations strategically deployed to optimize movement to the objective."

Gage did not seem particularly put off by this revelation. "I've got other people working on the logistics. Just give me the algorithm. That's the key to everything."

Dmitri blew out his breath. Gage was asking him to do the impossible. And promising him untold riches if he could do it.

"How can I say no?"

TWENTY-SEVEN

Emily met Redd on the porch, greeting him with a hug and a kiss. "Junior's down for a nap," she said, lingering in his embrace. "Went right out as soon as I laid him down."

Redd sensed an unspoken invitation in her comments. Nap time for Junior meant alone time for the two of them, something that had become increasingly rare given their respective schedules and the responsibilities of parenthood. But as tempting as the thought was—and it was infinitely more tempting than boozing it up with strangers at Spady's—it was an offer he had to refuse for much the same reasons.

He managed a smile. "How often does that happen?"

"Right? I think he missed the familiarity of the nursery." She gazed up at him for a moment, her brows furrowing as she read the worry in his forehead. "I guess it didn't go well?"

"That's putting it mildly." He shook his head. "I don't want to talk about it right now."

"Matty, you don't have to carry this all on your own. We're partners, remember? We're in this together. No matter what."

"Yeah," he muttered, trying to conceal the fact that her admonition had almost brought him to tears. "But it's nice to be reminded once in a while." He sighed. "That guy, Yearsley, the assessor . . . he's a real piece of work. Tried to have me arrested just for wanting to talk to him."

Emily leaned back, looking Redd in the eyes. "I hope that's *all* you did."

"It's not all I wanted to do, but I was the very definition of restraint."

She arched a skeptical eyebrow. "Uh-huh."

"Seriously. I don't think I even raised my voice. Fat lot of good it did. He's not going to budge on this." He shook his head. "You know, when I confronted him about being involved somehow with the Infidels, he looked at me like I had two heads. I don't think they're the reason he's doing this."

"Then why? Is it a political thing?"

"No idea. Honestly, I'm a little worried, Em." His throat tightened again, but he forced the words out. "I don't want to lose the ranch, but I don't know how I'm going to save it."

She hugged him again, pressing her head against his chest. "We'll find a way, baby. Together."

Redd wished he could share her optimism, but J. B. had raised him to be a pragmatist.

J. B.'s the reason I'm in this fix.

The thought landed in his head like a crow on roadkill, and he was quick to shoo it away. It was true that J. B., through no fault of his own, had neglected his affairs toward the end of his life. But if Redd had been there when J. B. needed him, maybe he wouldn't have fallen behind on his tax payments.

Maybe he'd still be alive.

That too was an unwanted thought, one that held on a little more tenaciously.

Enough with the pity party. If J. B. were here, he'd set me straight and say, "Don't. Be. Stupid."

"Yeah," he said equivocally. "Well, one problem at a time."

She nodded and then let go, stepping back. "Speaking of which, did you call Gavin?"

He bobbed his head in something that wasn't quite a nod. "The cavalry is on the way," he said, recalling her words. "Could take a day or two, so until they get here, it might be best for us to go off the grid."

She cocked her head to the side, regarding him with suspicion.

"Hey," he said, trying to head off her protest. "You promised, remember?"

"I promised nothing. I said I'd consider staying with Liz and Mikey until this blows over, and that's exactly what I'm going to do. Consider it." Before he could offer a challenge, she went on. "Oh, by the way, Liz called. We're going over there for dinner tonight. And Mikey says the pickup is ready."

Redd grunted an acknowledgment. Somehow getting the truck back didn't seem that important under the circumstances.

"It'll be good to have two cars again, won't it?" Emily prompted.

"Is that your way of saying you want to go back to work?"

"Well, as you just pointed out, we could really use the money right now." Then she hastily added, "But I'm not taking Junior back to the day care. You don't have to worry about that."

With Emily running point on all that, allowing him to focus on more immediate threats, the day care situation had been pretty far down the list of things Redd was worried about, but it did remind him that he had not followed up with Blackwood on the investigation into what had happened to his baby. He also owed the sheriff an apology. And a thank-you.

"That's good," he murmured, taking out his phone.

Before he could bring up Blackwood in his contact list, however, Emily looked past him. "Someone's coming."

Redd was instantly on guard. "Get inside," he said, even as he placed his hands on her shoulders and maneuvered her toward the front door.

Once she was safely over the threshold, he risked a look back at the driveway. Sure enough, a maroon sedan was rolling toward the house, the crunch of its tires on the gravel growing louder with its approach.

Redd hurried inside the house and grabbed the shotgun off the wall rack near the mantel, then went to the gun safe, where the rest of his arsenal was stored. He quickly punched in the combination and opened the door, removing the holstered Ruger Vaquero .44 Magnum and the lever action Henry .45-70 rifle, along with two boxes of shells—one for the shotgun and one for the rifle.

"I only see one person," Emily remarked, sounding more curious than alarmed.

Redd looked up and saw her standing at the window in the front room, peering out at the approaching car, which was pulling up alongside the parked Tahoe.

"It's Gavin!" she cried, evincing both relief and surprise. "Wow, how did he get here so fast?"

Redd frowned. "That's a good question. I didn't call him."

Emily wheeled on him, eyes blazing an accusation. "You said—"

"I said help was on the way. I called Rob Davis from the fly team. Gavin was never going to help. He's a bureaucrat. He would have just given me the runaround . . ." He let his voice trail off, wondering if that was the reason for Kline's sudden appearance. Had Kline found out somehow? Had Davis been compelled to reveal Redd's request?

But that didn't make any sense. It had only been an hour or so since they'd spoken—not nearly enough time for Kline to fly cross-country.

No, Kline was here for something else, and it probably wasn't good.

He faced Emily again. Judging by her defiant stance, hands on hips, and the thrust of her jaw, she was not impressed by his clever ruse to avoid reaching out to Kline. "I don't want his help, Em. I don't want him to know about any of this."

She sighed but relented just a little. "Fine." And then, "I'm going to check on Junior."

He turned, set the guns on the coffee table, and went out to meet his visitor.

Kline was already on his way up to the front porch. When he spied Redd, he broke into a big smile. "Matt, sorry to drop in unannounced, but what I've got to tell you is best said face-to-face."

Redd stopped on the bottom step and folded his arms across his chest. "You really didn't need to go to the trouble. I would have been fine with you just putting my final check in the mail."

Kline's smile slipped. "Don't be so dramatic. That's not why I'm here."

"Well, whatever you've got to say, say it. I've kind of got my hands full here."

Kline glanced past him to the house. "Can we at least go in and sit down like civilized people?"

"That wouldn't be my first choice."

Kline sighed. "Do we really have to keep doing this, Matty?"

"You know, I really hate you calling me that."

"Sorry. Matt. Do we really have to keep doing this?"

"What do you want, Gavin?"

"I want you. I need you back on the team, I mean."

Despite his antipathy for Kline, Redd's curiosity got the better of him. "Just like that? I thought I was suspended indefinitely. Now you come out here in person to ask me back. What's changed?"

As he spoke, Redd was reminded of Gavin's last visit. He'd come unexpectedly then too, braving a snowstorm late at night to tell Redd about the fly team and offer him a spot on it.

"Gage is what's changed. We've got intel that he's planning something big. Targeting the food supply again. And soon. The director has written me a blank check. Whatever it takes, we have to stop Gage. This time for good. I thought you might want to be a part of it."

When Redd did not answer, Kline went on. "You were right. It was stupid of me to put you on the team and then tie your hands. Tell you not to do what you're best at. This time, the gloves are off. No holds barred. No more bureaucratic nonsense. Whatever it takes," he repeated. "You in?"

Redd weighed the offer carefully. His first impulse was to refuse out of hand. There were plenty of people who could go after Anton Gage, but Redd was the only person standing between his loved ones and the Infidels.

On the other hand, there was no reason he couldn't make his return to the team conditional. With the FBI backing him up, the threat from the outlaw motorcycle gang could be dealt with in short order. Instead of helping him unofficially, Davis and the rest of the team could hunt the Infidels with an official sanction. And even if they couldn't get the go-ahead to take the bikers down, at the very least, Kline could arrange for round-the-clock protection for Emily and Junior while the search for Gage was ongoing.

So why am I not all over this? he wondered.

Kline must have mistaken Redd's silence for resentment because he hurriedly added, "Look I know you're upset about the way I handled things. You've got every right to be. I screwed up. I had hoped that this might make up for it."

Redd shook his head. "Thanks for thinking of me, but I'm going to have to pass."

Kline cocked his head to the side. "Matty . . ." He caught himself. "Matt, did you hear me? This isn't just about hunting Gage now. It's about stopping him. Saving lives. The clock is ticking. This is what you were born to do."

Redd shook his head again. "Can't do it. I'm dealing with something here right now. You'll have to save the world without me this time, Gavin."

"Whatever it is, it can't be more important than the millions that will suffer and die if Gage succeeds."

Kline's comment touched a raw nerve. "Is that how you did it?" Redd snapped. "Is that how you justified abandoning your own son? Ignore one life to save a thousand?"

"Matt—"

"There's always going to be some bogeyman out there trying to kill everyone. If not Gage, then someone else. But this—" he made a sweeping gesture, indicating the ranch—"this is what's important to me now. My family. My ranch. Being with them. Time is something you don't get back. I'm not going to make that mistake."

"Like I did?" Kline shot back. "That's what you mean, right? Can't you see I'm trying to make up for it? You're right. There are plenty of door kickers out there who can do this. But I wanted you. I thought we could do this one thing together."

The impassioned plea almost brought Redd up short.

Almost.

"Well, I appreciate the thought, but right now my wife and son need me more than you do."

Kline started to answer, but just then Emily stepped out onto the porch with a gurgling little Matty in her arms. "Hi, Gavin," she said, her calm voice immediately lowering the temperature of the air between the two men. "Would you like to say hi to your grandson?"

Redd shot a frown in Emily's direction, but when he saw how the offer discomfited Kline, his annoyance evaporated. However, as Emily held the baby out, a change came over the man's face. His lips turned up in a smile, his eyes coming alight with fascination. He reached out, hesitantly at first, then eagerly took Junior into his arms. He gazed into the child's eyes, scrunching up his face in a playful expression.

"Look at you," he cooed, letting Junior grasp one of his fingers. "How'd you get so big?"

With her hands now free, Emily wrapped an arm around Redd's waist in a side hug. She didn't say anything to him. She didn't need to. The unspoken message came through loud and clear: *Just give him a chance, Matty.*

Redd, who was already struggling to maintain his hostility toward Kline, just sighed.

After only a few seconds of playing with little Matty, Kline began looking uncomfortable again. It was, Redd realized, quite possibly the first time the man had ever held an infant. Redd's mother hadn't given Kline the chance to hold him when he'd been Junior's age.

Maybe if she had . . .

Redd shook his head, refusing to let his thoughts go down that road.

Emily came to Kline's rescue, taking the baby back into her arms. "It's good to see you again, Gavin. Are you staying in town?"

"I'm flying out tomorrow," Kline said, letting his gaze float from Redd to Emily and back again. "I'm staying at the Holiday Inn near the airport. Matt, if you change your mind—"

"I won't."

"Or if you just want to talk, maybe grab a beer together . . ." Kline let the invitation remain unfinished and turned to Emily. "Thanks for letting me hold him."

Emily answered with a smile and an encouraging nod.

Kline awkwardly turned away, went back to his car, and without looking back, started the engine and drove off.

"So if you didn't call him," Emily said, "why did he come?"

"Why else? He wants me to come work for him."

"And you told him no?"

Redd looked at her, incredulous. "Of course I did. This is where I belong."

She stared up into his eyes. "Are you sure? Because I don't want you staying here out of some sense of obligation. You didn't ask for this life and—"

Redd gently placed a finger to her lips, silencing her. "I didn't ask for it, but I'm glad I got it anyway. I love you and little man."

She lightly kissed his finger, then moved it away. "I'm not talking about us, Matty. I'm talking about this place. The ranch. Montana. I can see what a struggle it's been for you. Trying to take on everything. And now, with this tax thing and these bikers . . . maybe God is telling us something. Maybe it's time for us to think about getting out of here."

Redd shook his head. "I can't ask you to leave. Your family is here. Our friends—"

"I left before, Matty. Believe it or not, sometimes I feel a little trapped out here, too."

Redd was silent for a long moment. Was this the answer to all their problems? A way out of the mess they'd somehow landed in? A way to get out from under all the debt and start making a better life for Junior?

If so, why did it feel like the wrong answer?

Finally he said, "I don't think I want to give this up."

She slid her arm around his waist again. "Just tell me that you're staying because it's what you want. You're not doing this for me or Jim Bob or anyone else. And not because you're too stubborn to call it quits."

He laughed despite himself. "Well, maybe a little."

"Uh-huh."

"I'll think about it."

She tightened her hold on him in a gentle squeeze and then let go. "We should clean up. I told Liz and Mikey we'd be over around five."

TWENTY-EIGHT

Dinner at the Derhammers was a spaghetti bake that utilized some of the ground venison Mikey had stored in the freezer, with sautéed string beans and a loaf of seasoned focaccia that Liz had made using her bread machine. Not surprisingly, there was very little conversation at the table. They were all too busy enjoying the repast.

"Liz, you've outdone yourself yet again," Emily remarked as Liz scooped a second portion onto Redd's plate.

Liz smiled. "I'm just happy we got to use up some of that deer meat from the freezer. Plus you know we love having you guys over." Nodding to Mikey and then Redd, she added, "You two better keep eating, or we're going to have more leftovers than we know what to do with."

After everything that had happened in the last two days, the meal felt like an escape from reality for Redd. With their busy schedules, he and Emily rarely had the time or energy to devote to meal planning and preparation. More often than not, supper was a one-dish affair, chili or stew made in the Instant Pot. Redd was fine with that. The primary purpose of food was fuel, after all. That had been drilled into his head in boot camp.

"Just throw it down your neck," the drill sergeants had advised. *"You can taste it later."*

The idea of enjoying food at leisure was almost a foreign concept to him.

After clearing away the dishes—a job that Mikey took upon himself without any prompting—Liz suggested they retire to the living room to catch up and hang out.

At first, conversation was light. Liz and Emily did most of the talking. Mikey jumped in with a sarcastic quip or a bad pun now and again, and Redd was content to merely nod his head at appropriate intervals. It wasn't long, however, before the subject of Junior's mysterious illness came up.

"Was it just some kind of bug or something?" Liz asked. It was a reasonable question. Luke, only a few years older than Matty, might also be at risk.

"Actually," Emily said, a little hesitant, "it looks like somebody may have intentionally made him sick."

Liz was aghast. "*What?* You're kidding me. Who would do that to a baby?"

"We don't know yet," Emily answered honestly.

"But I plan to find out," Redd added.

Mikey gazed at his friend over the top of a steaming mug of decaf coffee. "You think maybe those bikers had something to do with it?"

Redd nodded and said simply, "Wouldn't surprise me." In fact, he was almost certain the bikers were behind it but wanted to be careful what he said in front of Liz.

"Bikers?" Liz glanced at Emily. "The same ones that attacked you?"

"It's one possibility," Emily said. "It will be up to Sheriff Blackwood to get at the truth." Her eyes conspicuously flicked to Redd as she said this. "But until he does, Junior's not going back to the clinic day care."

Liz shook her head. "It's crazy that they can get away with this stuff."

Redd thought that was an appropriate time to nod.

"What I don't understand," she went on, "is why they've decided to give you a hard time." Redd, Emily, and Mikey exchanged a glance. Liz did not fail to notice. "Why do I suddenly feel like the only person in the room who doesn't know what's going on?"

Mikey, who had the most to lose by keeping secrets from his wife, jumped in. "Matt got into a tussle with a couple of them a while back. Apparently they aren't exactly the type to forgive and forget."

"So they're coming after Emily and Junior?" As she spoke, Liz's eyes fell on Redd. "Why?"

"Revenge, I guess."

"Well, they already scared your wife half to death; what more could they want?"

"They'd like to kill me."

Liz stared at him for a long moment. "You're serious?"

Realizing that his simple answer had done nothing to defuse the rising tension in the room, Redd asserted, "I've got it under control."

Emily made a noise that might have been a choked cough or a laugh. Redd couldn't tell which.

"I'm in touch with some guys I served with." It was almost the truth. "They're coming out in a couple days to provide some backup. If those bikers try anything, they'll regret it."

Liz frowned, then turned to her husband.

Mikey shrugged and took another sip of his Colombia roast. "He's got a right to defend himself."

To Redd's surprise, Emily came to his defense as well. "Matty didn't ask for this fight. He's doing what he can. And . . ." She glanced over at him and nodded. "He knows what he's doing."

Liz wagged her head. "I'm just having trouble . . ." She took a deep breath. "So these friends of yours will be here in a couple days. What if the bikers come after you before they get here? Tomorrow? Or tonight? Are you going to take them on all by yourself?"

That was a question Redd had been wrestling with. He did not have a good answer. "I'll do what I have to."

"Matt," Liz protested, "you can't go lone wolf on this. I mean, there could be a couple dozen bikers here. You're a big guy, but you can't fight that many men by yourself. You just can't."

"He won't be standing alone," Emily said, her tone sharper than usual.

Liz sighed. "You're as bad as he is."

Mikey leaned forward. "Liz is right. You guys can't go home. Not until Matt's friends get here. You're staying with us."

Liz nodded vigorously in agreement. "Absolutely."

Emily frowned. "There's no need for you guys to put yourselves out like that. We'll make our own arrangements."

Liz raised both hands, palms out. "Stop right there. Not another word. You're staying here and that's final."

Redd hid his smile. He hadn't been looking forward to trying to convince Emily to absent herself from their home, at least until Rob Davis and the rest of the team showed up, but now it seemed his friends had done the heavy lifting for him. "Thanks," he said, speaking out before Emily could raise further protest. "We really appreciate it. I'll have to go over there in the morning, of course, to do the chores, but at least I won't have to stay up all night keeping watch."

"Well, I can't promise you'll get an amazing night's sleep on the sofa bed," Mikey said. "And your back probably won't thank us come morning."

"Your sofa bed won't even make the top ten list of worst places I've had to spend the night," Redd assured him. "Really, thank you both."

"That's what friends are for."

Emily also managed a smile, but Redd could tell that she was still a little bothered at the thought of imposing on the hospitality of their friends. He decided a change of subject was in order. "Hey, I've been meaning to ask you something. Do you know the county assessor? Craig Yearsley?"

Mikey screwed up his face in thought, then shook his head. "I remember seeing his name on campaign signs."

Liz let out a laugh. "I swear, men have memories like goldfish, Michael Derhammer. We went to school with Craig Yearsley."

This revelation came as a surprise to everyone else seated around the coffee table.

"We did?" Emily asked before either Mikey or Redd could frame the question.

Redd searched his memory, trying to recall the name or, failing that, a face that might have been a younger version of the man who was presently trying to ruin his life, but nothing came to mind.

Liz rolled her eyes, then rose from the couch and walked over to the bookshelf, which was mostly packed with hardcover editions of various thriller and mystery novels. Bypassing the top half of their collection, Liz selected a considerably thinner volume from the bottom shelf. Even from across the room, Redd could see the bold letter *S* on the cover and the stylized roaring grizzly bear mascot of Stillwater High School.

Enrollment at Stillwater High had historically hovered around two hundred students at any given time, so it didn't take long for Liz to flip through the yearbook and find what she was looking for. "Here he is," she announced, setting the open book on the table. "He was in my graduating class."

Liz had been a year behind the others, which at least partially explained why Redd did not remember Yearsley. At different grade levels, they likely had not shared any classes. He leaned forward to look at Yearsley's picture and saw about what he expected—a younger version of the assessor, with more hair, a severe case of adolescent acne, and an only slightly less angry expression.

Redd shook his head. "I don't remember him at all."

"I kinda do," Mikey said, though it almost sounded like a question.

"He wasn't exactly Mr. Popular," Liz said. "Mostly kept to himself. He was smart, though. Got an academic scholarship to UM. I didn't know he'd come back to Wellington until I saw that he was running for assessor. I'm not surprised he got into politics though."

Redd, recalling what Yearsley had said about him, hesitantly asked, "Did he get bullied?"

"Oh yeah. Relentlessly."

"That's a shame," Emily said. "Kids are so cruel."

"It was mostly the jocks that picked on him. To impress the mean girls.

The usual stuff. Humiliation mostly, but sometimes they got physical. I think I remember him getting beat up once junior year or so."

Redd did not think often of his high school days, but when he did, he recalled good things—his friendship with Mikey, his romance with Emily, playing football. He also remembered how all of that had come to a screeching halt when J. B. had injured himself and Redd had been obliged to drop out in order to keep the ranch afloat. Was it possible that, among the many moments that had failed to make an impression in his long-term memory, he had done something hurtful to Craig Yearsley?

"Did I ever . . . ?" He trailed off, embarrassed that he even had to ask.

Liz recoiled as if the very idea was ludicrous. "Oh, I'm sure you never did. That's not like you at all."

Emily, evidently reading her husband's mind, quickly added, "No, Matty. You were never a bully. Not to him or anyone else. What I remember most about you is that you stood up to bullies. It's one of the reasons I fell in love with you."

"Why do you ask?" Mikey said.

"Ah, he's giving me a hard time about some unpaid taxes. J. B. got a little behind on them. I had an arrangement with the county to take care of it, but now this guy is giving me grief."

"And you think it might be because of something that happened in high school?" Mikey asked.

Redd returned a helpless shrug. "I don't know why he's doing it, but it kind of feels personal."

"Maybe it's guilt by association," Liz ventured. "You were a star athlete, so he associates you with the jocks who bullied him."

"Yeah, maybe." Redd wasn't entirely sure of that but realized it might provide him with a solution to one of his problems. If Yearsley's beef with him was personal, if he had done something to the other man when they were both in school, whether directly or by failing to protect him from the other jocks, then that might be resolved with a sincere apology.

If he accepts it.

TWENTY-NINE

The bison herd was still there, grazing near the roadside, and this time they did not even raise their heads as Bobbie-Sue drove past. Evidently the pickup's muffled engine wasn't loud enough to disturb them.

She wished she could be so indifferent to the world around her.

As she approached the turnoff to the old warehouse, she considered turning around or maybe just driving on, taking her chances. Going as far as the gas left in the tank would take her. But of course, that was an impossible fantasy. She didn't have any money, didn't have a mobile phone with which to call for help. And even if she did, who would she call? Where could she go that they wouldn't find her?

Property of Angry Johnny.

That was what she was. That was the choice she'd made. Maybe she hadn't understood what it would really mean back then, but it was a choice she couldn't easily undo.

Once an Infidel . . .

She made the turn, slowing as she approached the gate. As before, a prospect was there to open it. Recognizing Johnny's truck, he didn't even bother to stop her, just waved as she rolled past.

As she entered the parking lot where Dunk and Joey had fought to the death the previous night, Bobbie-Sue felt her heart begin racing. Up until this moment, she had believed she could go through with it. That she could go back to Johnny, tell him what had happened—how she had abandoned Dunk at the hospital and run away—and face his wrath for having failed to strictly follow his orders. But now? Now that she was just moments away from actually doing it, it was no longer merely a mental exercise.

Would he punish her? Almost certainly.

Would he kill her?

Until yesterday, she would not have thought so, but now? Now that she had seen his true nature, there was just no telling.

Nevertheless, she had to do this. If she was to have any chance of ever getting free, she would have to go back to him.

There were only about a dozen bikes in the lot, all lined up in two rows. Evidently the others were out conducting club business or maybe just partying somewhere. As she drove past them, she looked for Johnny's bike but didn't see it. For a fleeting moment, she found a measure of relief in knowing that the expected confrontation would be postponed, but then another thought occurred to her.

Maybe he's out looking for me.

The thought sent a fresh wave of panic washing over her, and it was all she could do to park the pickup without crashing it into one of the other support vehicles.

She sat in the truck for a while, dreading the thought of going in, hanging out with the brothers and their ol' ladies, all the while knowing what awaited her when Johnny returned, but staying outside would only draw more attention to her. Mustering what little courage she had left, she got out.

A whiff of tobacco reached her nostrils as soon as she opened the door. Following her nose, she found a group of riders seated on lawn chairs arranged in a loose circle on the side of the warehouse. Baby Boy was among their number. He sat with his arms folded over his chest. His eyes were unnaturally wide and his teeth were bared in a manic grin. With his red hair and beard wreathing his head like a crown of fire, in that moment, Bobbie-Sue thought he looked like the devil.

"Bobbie-Sue!" he called out to her. "You found your way back to us. I thought maybe you got lost."

"Uh . . . no, Baby Boy. I didn't. Get lost, I mean."

She could tell that her nervous quaver did not escape his notice.

"Hey, I'm just messing with you. Relax." He gestured to one of the riders who was holding a cigarette. "Let her have a drag, man."

Bobbie-Sue desperately wanted a toke, just one to calm her nerves, but knew that was a really bad idea. She'd quit smoking months ago and didn't trust herself enough to start the habit back up. Then again, if she was too nervous when Johnny asked her what had happened, she might not be able to keep her story straight.

The old antidrug slogan from her childhood came back to her. *Just say no.*

That was what she was going to have to do. Like her life depended on it, because just maybe, it did.

"I'm all right," she said, trying to smile. "Maybe later. Where's Johnny?"

Baby Boy made a dismissive gesture. "He's taking care of some club business. I don't know when he'll be back."

Club business, she knew, usually involved one of the club's money-making enterprises, and when Johnny got directly involved, it meant big money. She knew that the decision to make Montana the destination for the big run wasn't just about getting even with the cowboy for disrespecting the colors. He had another reason for coming here, something bigger than guns or narcotics. She wished she knew what it was but didn't dare ask. The club's women did not question the men. Not if they wanted to keep all their teeth.

"How's the prospect doing?" Baby Boy asked.

It took her a moment to realize what he was talking about. "Dunk?"

She shook her head. "Not good. He might not make it. I think they took him up to Helena."

The big man gave her a sidelong look. "You think? You didn't stay with him?"

Here it comes, Bobbie-Sue thought. She took a breath. "I couldn't. I told them what Johnny told me to say, but they were going to call the cops anyway. Dunk is out cold, so he couldn't answer their questions, and I was . . . I was afraid they'd trip me up. Know I was lying. You know how the cops are. I got out of there as soon as I could."

Baby Boy did not react the way she expected. Only at the end did his eyes narrow into an appraising stare. "So where were you this whole time?"

She had expected this question, had rehearsed her answer, but even so, she had to fight through another surge of fear. "I was afraid they might have seen me leave in the truck. I didn't want to lead the cops back here, so I drove around all day until I was sure they weren't following me."

"That was smart." Baby Boy broke into a big, fierce grin. "Johnny's right. You aren't as dumb as you look."

She laughed along with everyone else. Left-handed compliments were about as close as men like Johnny and Baby Boy ever got to showing appreciation to a woman. But when she realized that Baby Boy had accepted her explanation, had even praised her actions, her fear turned to hope.

I might just survive this, she thought.

"Sure you don't want a drag?" Baby Boy asked again.

She shook her head. "I'm good."

"Okay. You might want to get some rest then. Johnny says tomorrow is going to be an important day, so we're probably gonna be up all night."

Unlike ordinary people who liked to get a good night's sleep before a big day, Angry Johnny preferred to get wired on crank, party all night, and hit the ground running at daybreak. Bobbie-Sue was used to this habit, used to the mercurial moods and sadistic predilections that rose to the surface when the amphetamines hit his bloodstream. She was more interested in what tomorrow would bring.

"What's so important about it?" She had to be careful here. A little bit of curiosity was to be expected, but if she pressed too hard, Baby Boy might wonder why, and then she'd be in serious trouble.

But Baby Boy was too lost in the possibilities to care. With an almost-beatific smile, he crowed, "Tomorrow it all comes together."

THIRTY

Mikey had not been wrong about the sofa bed's comfort level, but Redd had nonetheless gotten six hours of decent sleep—the best he'd had since returning from Spain. He'd finally been able to let his mind stand down from the state of heightened awareness that had kept him poised for battle, even when resting. He arose at 4 a.m. feeling refreshed, kissed a still-sleeping Emily on the forehead, peeked in on Junior to make sure he was sleeping soundly, and then stole from the house without rousing anyone. Once he was in the pickup and rolling down the highway toward the ranch, with his Ruger unholstered and resting on the seat beside him, he was back on high-alert status.

There was no indication that anyone had visited the ranch during their nightlong absence, but Redd kept his head on a swivel as he rolled up the drive, went inside the house, and brewed a pot of coffee. With the revolver on his hip and one ear cocked and listening for the roar of motorcycle engines, he headed out to the barn and started saddling Remington.

A few hours later, with his outriding done, as he was busting open a bale of alfalfa, his phone started vibrating with an incoming call. With more than half a dozen cows and yearling steers lowing loudly and nuzzling at him, demanding to be fed, there was no way he was going to stop to check the caller ID, never mind answering. Nevertheless, the call concerned him.

It might just be Emily calling to say good morning. If so, she wouldn't mind waiting five or ten minutes for him to finish what he was doing.

But what if it was something else? What if she was calling to warn him that the Infidels had found her?

He knew he was letting his imagination run away from him. Emily was fine. Everyone was fine. If there was really a problem, the caller would try again.

Don't be paranoid, he told himself. *That's what they want.*

Even so, he attacked the bale with a sense of urgency, breaking off handfuls and tossing them out for the cattle. Finally, with the last of the grass scattered on the ground and the herd munching noisily, he stripped off his work gloves and checked his phone.

There were two messages on the screen. The first read: "1 missed call from Duke." The second: "1 new voice mail."

Redd sucked in a breath. A call from his lawyer might or might not be good news, but his thoughts immediately turned to worst-case scenarios. Had his imprudent visit to Craig Yearsley generated more negative consequences? Were the Infidels lobbing more legal action at him?

He hit Play on the voice mail and held the phone to his ear.

"Matthew, Duke Blanton here. Listen, I'm on my way up to Helena to meet with Ms. Townsend, the lady lawyer representing those bikers who are suing you." Blanton spoke fluidly, as if he'd rehearsed this message. "Now, I don't like to make promises I might not be able to keep, but I think we might be able to hash this out and find some kind of outcome that we can all agree on. Not just for what you did to their motorcycles, but all of it. The first step is getting them to agree to a . . . well, a cease-fire, if you will. I'll call you again when I've got something more, but I just wanted to let you know that things might be looking up. Take care."

Redd replayed the message, parsing Blanton's statement. His initial reaction bordered on outrage. He wasn't interested in making peace with the Infidels. The situation was way past the point where things could be "hashed out." There was no outcome where everyone could walk away happy. They had threatened his wife and child, destroyed his property, even attacked him. How could he ever make peace with men like that? But after just a moment's consideration, he realized how foolish that attitude was.

He suddenly remembered a sermon his father-in-law had preached a few weeks ago about turning the other cheek. Redd didn't always go to church, with chores around the ranch and all. Emily, on the other hand, was faithful in attending each Sunday morning service. She liked when Redd went with her, but while she encouraged him to grow closer to the Lord, she never pressured him. It had taken him a while to realize that Emily didn't want him just going through the motions for her. She wanted any change to be inspired by his own understandings and convictions. He appreciated that, and when he was at church, he really listened. He even found comfort in most biblical teachings. But this particular sermon had stuck with him because of how hard he found the concept of putting it into action—much like the difficulty he had honoring his biological father.

On a normal day, he was all for turning the other cheek. But not with the Infidels or anyone else threatening his family. Still, given a choice between a truce that protected his loved ones from further harm at the expense of his pride or an endlessly escalating war of recriminations that might eventually cost him his life or, worse, hurt the people he was trying to protect . . . well, it really wasn't a choice at all.

Of course, all of that was predicated on convincing the Infidels to set aside their grievances as well. Redd didn't think that was very likely, but if anyone could do it, it was Duke Blanton.

He thought about calling back and giving Blanton the go-ahead but decided it was unnecessary. He put the phone away and went back to work.

With all that had been going on in his life—the abortive deployment to Majorca, the hunt for the Infidels, Matty's hospitalization—he'd seriously neglected the ranch. Fortunately, things had not completely fallen apart. The cattle were all in relatively good health, though it had taken him a while to track them all down. In the process, he'd discovered a couple sections of fence that had been knocked down and would need to be repaired. He had also identified a couple acres of pasturage that might benefit from a program of seeding. If he could increase the amount of available forage, he might even be able to add another twenty or thirty head.

He tried not to dwell on the fact that in a couple weeks he might not have a ranch anymore.

When Blanton called again, just after noon, Redd was ready to talk. "Duke," he said before the other man could identify himself. "Tell me you have some good news."

Blanton's voice boomed from the little speaker. "Well, that depends on you, Matthew. And on whether you're willing to come to the table, so to speak." Despite the evasive answer, the lawyer's chuckle indicated that he thought the meeting had gone well.

"Whether you're willing to come to the table . . ."

Redd knew Blanton had been speaking figuratively, but an image popped into his head—Angry Johnny and Baby Boy sitting opposite him in a conference room, like diplomats from warring nations trying to hammer out a peace treaty.

What would the Infidels want in exchange for a permanent end to hostilities? An apology?

Redd couldn't see himself doing that. Everything he had done had been done in self-defense. Well, except for trashing their bikes. But even that was in response to their slashing his tires.

Would they demand money?

Not a chance.

Even if he had the money to pay them off, he never would, for the same reason that the American government had a policy of refusing to negotiate with terrorists. To do so would only invite further extortion.

So what does that leave?

Blanton was talking again. "Why don't you come by my office this afternoon . . . No, scratch that. Meet me for lunch at Spady's. My treat. I won't call it a celebration just yet, but I'm hopeful. I'm just leaving Helena now . . . Let's say forty-five minutes?"

Redd shook his head ruefully. At this rate, he was never going to get caught up on his chores. But he owed it to himself and his loved ones to at least hear Blanton's proposal. "I'll be there," he promised and ended the call.

✖   ✖   ✖

Located on the northern outskirts of town, Spady's was something of an institution in Wellington. Once a watering hole for weary ranch hands at the end of the workday, it had in recent years undergone a sort of gentrification, transforming into a bigger, family-friendly establishment, and in the process, lost a lot of its old charm. The place still had the best burgers in town, but now they came on a china plate instead of in a paper-lined wicker basket and cost more than twice what they had when Redd left for boot camp.

Spady's didn't get much of a lunch rush—family-friendly though it was, business really didn't pick up until happy hour—so there were only a handful of vehicles in the lot. None of them was Blanton's black Escalade. Figuring that the lawyer was probably just running late, Redd parked and headed inside.

He didn't recognize any of the staff on duty. For a few months after his return to town, he'd been eighty-sixed as a result of a parking lot confrontation with one of Anton Gage's mad dog bodyguards. A subsequent change of management had restored his privileges, but eating out was a luxury that Redd and Emily rarely indulged.

When the hostess approached, he said, "I'm supposed to meet Duke Blanton here. Did he reserve a table?"

The young woman made a show of checking the tablet computer at her station before shaking her head. "No, I'm sorry. People don't usually call ahead for lunch since we're never that busy. I can seat you if you want to wait for him."

Redd shot a look at his watch. Blanton was now officially late, but only by a few minutes. He loathed the idea of sitting alone at a table, fending off repeated visits from a too-eager server trying to get him to order a drink or appetizer "while you wait."

"Thanks, I'll just wait here."

Sitting on the banquette in the foyer, he watched the parking lot. Five minutes ticked by. Ten. At fifteen, he decided to call Blanton for an ETA. The call rang several times, then went to voice mail. With a frown, Redd tried calling Blanton's office, but the lawyer's receptionist had no information about his whereabouts. Redd asked her to have Blanton give him a call if he checked in, then hung up and went back to waiting.

It wasn't the fact of Blanton's tardiness that raised Redd's level of concern; it was his failure to communicate. Mobile coverage was pretty good on the main highways, so if something had gone wrong on the road—a flat tire, construction delays, a wreck—Blanton should have let someone know.

Unless, of course, he was unable to do so.

At the thirty-minute mark, he tried Blanton's mobile number again, this time leaving a voice mail message to the effect that he was going to head home to get some more work done, and to give him a call to reschedule. After finishing the message, he placed another call.

"Sheriff's department, what do you need?"

"Maggie, it's Matthew Redd."

"Hi there, hon. You want to talk to Stuart?"

"Not right now. Listen, have there been any reports of traffic accidents on the highway between here and Helena?"

"Not that I've heard. Nothing on our side of the line anyways." She paused a moment, then asked, "Why? Have you heard something?"

"I was supposed to meet Duke for lunch at Spady's, but he's a no-show. He was coming from Helena, and I was worried that something might have happened."

He expected her to dismiss his concern with some platitude—*"Oh, you know Duke. He probably stopped for gas and ended up talking someone's ear off"*—and probably would have taken a measure of comfort from it. Instead, when she responded, it was with unexpected concern. "Well, that doesn't sound good. I'll put the word out to our patrols and MHP and have them keep an eye out. I'll call you back if we find something."

"I'll do the same if he calls me. Thanks, Maggie. Appreciate it."

"Anything for you, hon. And hey, just an FYI, but I think it might be a good idea for you to come by and have a talk with Stuart soon. I don't know what happened with you and him yesterday, but it curdled his cream, I can tell you that."

Redd grimaced. "Yeah, I was out of line. I'll try to stop by this afternoon and make it right. Once I get things sorted with Duke."

"Okay, hon. We'll see you then."

Redd couldn't shake the feeling that something bad had happened, that the lawyer wasn't just broken down along the roadside but wrecked in a ditch. Injured and unconscious. Or worse.

He considered whether to keep going north past the ranch toward Helena to look for Blanton but decided he had already done what he could. The sheriff's deputies and highway patrolmen had far more resources available for the search. And besides, Blanton probably *was* talking someone's ear off at a gas station or coffee shop.

As he reached the turn onto the rutted double-track driveway up to the ranch, he saw something that sent a spike of cold adrenaline through his body. He slammed on the brakes, skidding to a halt beside a vehicle that was parked just beyond the turnoff—a black Cadillac Escalade.

Duke Blanton's Escalade.

Redd came out of his truck with the Ruger in hand, staying low, his head turning back and forth searching for any indication of hostiles lurking in the woods to either side of the driveway. The fact that he saw none did not ease his anxiety.

The Escalade had tinted windows, so Redd wasn't able to see inside until he came around the front end of the big SUV and could look through the windshield. When he did, he saw that the front seats appeared to be empty.

Redd could not conceive of any good reason for Blanton to have parked his rig and abandoned it, but he could think of a lot of *bad* reasons for it to be there. He carefully walked all the way around the vehicle, peeking in the windows, before returning to the driver's door. With his right hand aiming the revolver forward, he tried the latch with his left. The door opened.

He stepped back, returning his free hand to the pistol, ready to fire, but there was no need. The front seats were unoccupied. A pinging tone began to sound, indicating that the key fob was still within the vehicle's interior.

Redd figured that if Duke had hopped out of his Escalade without grabbing his keys, it probably meant he had left in a hurry.

Was he running from someone?

After another quick check of his six, Redd leaned inside and plucked the keys out, silencing the alarm. Behind the driver's seat, the two captain's chairs in the middle row and the bench seat in the back were likewise empty. There was something in the air, however, an unpleasant odor— stale cigarette smoke, maybe—that intensified his uneasiness.

Redd had never seen Blanton with a cigarette and was pretty sure the man was a nonsmoker.

Something isn't right here, that's for sure.

He turned away, scanning the surrounding area again, looking both for Blanton and for any signs of trouble as he made his way to the rear of the vehicle. Without looking down, he thumbed the button on the key fob to open the rear cargo door. The taillights flashed as the latch disengaged and the automatic hydraulic mechanism activated. The door slowly began to rise.

A second later, Duke Blanton's bloodied body flopped out onto the ground at Redd's feet.

THIRTY-ONE

Redd looked down at the badly beaten body before him. There was no question that he was dead. Blanton was all but unrecognizable. While there was no sign of bullet or stab wounds, stamped into the bloody fabric of his clothes were several dirty boot prints.

Red cringed.

He was stomped to death.

The extent of Blanton's injuries suggested that his killers had continued to ravage his body long after his life force had been extinguished.

Redd had seen more than his share of death. He had even braced himself against the possibility that Duke might have met with foul play. Nevertheless, the savagery of his murder unsettled him to a degree he would not have thought possible. Which was, no doubt, exactly the point.

He could not completely shut off the anger and guilt that surged through him. Anger at the Infidels for having taken a good man before his time and for the brutality of the act. Guilt for having put Blanton in harm's way. But neither emotion would help him do what now needed to be done, so he bottled the feelings up and put them aside. Now wasn't the time to process and reflect on Duke's death. That would come later.

If Redd could survive what he knew was coming.

Steeling himself, he tore his gaze away from the bloody spectacle and made another visual sweep of the area. He expected to find a horde of outlaw bikers charging toward him, hoping to catch him paralyzed with horror at the discovery, but there was no sign of the enemy. He was still alone. But were they watching?

I would be, he thought.

Staging Blanton's body as they had was classic psychological warfare. For maximum effect, the enemy should have launched their attack immediately upon Redd's discovery. Either they had a poor grasp of tactics . . .

Or they've got something worse planned for me.

Maintaining a one-handed grip on the Ruger, he ducked down in the space between his truck and the Escalade and took out his phone. As he waited for the call to go through, he murmured, "C'mon, pick up. Pick up."

The ringtone stopped with the establishment of a connection and Redd held his breath in anticipation of the familiar voice mail greeting. Instead, he heard Emily say, "Hey, babe. I've only got a sec. What's up?"

"Em, listen. It's happening. *Now.* They've killed Duke and I think they're coming for me next, but they might try to come after you or Junior." He kept his voice even so as not to scare his wife any more than necessary. "You'll probably be safe there at the clinic, but whatever you do, don't leave. I'm going to call Blackwood and have him send deputies to protect you. Where's little man? Is he with Liz?"

"Matty, stop!" The command cracked in his ear like the snap of a whip. "Where are *you?*"

"At the ranch. I found Duke's rig here. They stomped him to death, Em. He never had a chance."

"Have you called 911?"

"Not yet. I just found him."

"Don't try to take them on by yourself. Get out of there. Right now. Please."

Redd unconsciously shook his head. "I'll be fine. I can handle things here, but I need to know that you and Junior are safe."

"Matty, do not—"

Crack!

A single gunshot erupted in the near distance, interrupting Emily. Before she could ask what was going on, he said, "Gotta go, Em. I love you."

Ending the call, Redd dialed the sheriff's department directly. He'd been shot at enough times to know that he wasn't the target of whoever was firing, but that didn't mean he was in the clear. When Maggie answered, he said, "It's Redd. Let me talk to the sheriff. *Quick.*"

A moment later, Blackwood's voice came on the line. "Matthew, I'm glad you called. I understand that you're upset—"

Redd cut him off. "The Infidels killed Duke Blanton. I need you—"

"Wait. Hold on. Duke's *dead*?" Blackwood gasped. "Where are you?"

"That doesn't matter. You have to protect Emily and my son. She's at the clinic. I don't know where the baby is . . . He might be with Liz Derhammer at her home. I'm not sure. Emily will know. You have to get there, just in case they go after her instead of me."

"Matthew, slow down. I need to understand what's—"

Crack!

Another gunshot rang out, this time closer, and Redd hung up the phone, cutting the sheriff off midsentence, then held down the Power button until the phone shut off completely. If the Infidels were lurking somewhere ahead, waiting to ambush him, he did not want the distraction of an incoming call that he had no intention of answering.

Moving quickly, he walked in a crouch to the front end of the pickup and peered around, scanning the trees again. He was anticipating an attack, but nothing happened.

What are you waiting for?

He wanted to shout the challenge aloud but knew better. The time for bravado was past. To survive this, he would have to fight smart.

Redd knew there had to be an observer out there somewhere, hidden in the trees and keeping watch on the Escalade, reporting Redd's arrival to the others. If the trap was not to be sprung here, that could only mean they were waiting for him at the house.

As if to confirm this suspicion, the sound of a third gunshot split the air. Before the echoes of the report had passed, though, a different but equally familiar sound followed—the shrieked lowing of a heifer in distress.

They're shooting my stock.

Redd's vision momentarily clouded with barely contained rage, and it was all he could do to keep from getting back in the pickup and charging up the drive to stop the killers from wreaking further harm.

There was another shot, and more animal cries followed.

Redd bit down hard on his anger. There was nothing he could do for the cattle. Taking the bait, rushing headlong into battle wouldn't save the animals but only get him killed as well.

"Don't. Be. Stupid."

He scuttled back to the rear of the vehicles, then made a fast dash into the woods at the roadside, counting silently as he ran. When he got to five, he threw himself flat and rolled to the right, seeking cover behind the trunk of a denuded maple, then bounded up again, running deeper into the woods along a slightly different vector.

After three such movements, he stopped and waited, looking and listening for any sign of a nearby enemy presence. He was now far enough into the woods that any observer would have been hard-pressed to locate him. With the trees hiding his movements, he got slowly to his feet and began walking, stepping heel to toe in a rolling gait to minimize sound.

There were more reports in the distance, coming at random intervals. The cries from frightened and presumably wounded cattle were less frequent. Redd hoped the creatures were scattering, seeking safety elsewhere.

The drive up to the house was only about a quarter of a mile, but the uneven terrain through which he now moved slowed him down, as did the need for stealth. It took him almost five minutes to reach the creek that served as a natural boundary to the ranch property. Had he been driving,

Redd would have had to cross a decades-old beam bridge to reach the gate leading onto the ranch. But because he was moving cross-country, he simply slid down the bank and splashed across the stream.

Fed by snowmelt from up on the mountain, the water was knee-high in the middle and bitterly cold, especially as it poured into Redd's boots. Thankfully, the current was not strong enough to unbalance him, and he made his way across without falling. Once on the other side, he paused just long enough to remove and empty his boots, then scrambled up the bank and resumed making his way toward the ranch.

A few yards from the creek, he encountered another obstacle—the three-strand barbed wire fence that served mostly to prevent the herd from tumbling down into the creek. The gap between the strands was wide enough for someone to slip through without injury if they were careful. Redd didn't have time to be careful. One of the barbs caught his back, tearing his shirt and the skin underneath. He barely felt it.

Beyond the fence, the trees thinned. While this meant less concealment for his approach, it also gave him a better view of what was going on near the house. Crouching behind a pine bough at the tree line, he easily spotted six hostile targets. That they were Infidels was not in question. Even from a hundred or more yards, he could see the distinctive Jolly Roger logo of the club on their black sleeveless jackets. He also had no difficulty picking out one familiar figure—a head taller than the rest, the redheaded Berserker was impossible to miss.

A cold spike of rage slipped through Redd's reserve as he imagined Baby Boy driving his booted foot into Duke Blanton's defenseless body.

The six bikers were clustered together in a group near the fence that separated the house and parking area from the pasture. At least three, but probably all, were armed with handguns, which they were presently aiming out into the fenced pasture. Three shapeless brown masses lay out there, motionless.

Cattle, Redd thought, *senselessly gunned down.*

As anger filled his body, Redd calculated the odds of taking out all six of the bikers. He would have to get a lot closer to ensure that each round from the Ruger found its mark, but his chances of crossing fifty-plus yards of mostly open ground without being seen were virtually nil.

He continued his visual sweep of the area and spotted three more Infidels—two on the front porch of the house and another just stepping out of the barn.

Remington!

Redd's heart skipped a beat. Had one of the shots he'd heard felled the dependable old horse?

He pushed the thought away. Remington was either alive or dead; there was nothing he could do about it.

With the total count of enemy now at nine, the odds were decidedly not in his favor. A frontal assault was out of the question. It was simple math. Even if he could get closer without being detected, six bullets—even .44 Magnum rounds—could not kill nine men, especially if some or all of those men were shooting back.

No, if he was going to defeat his enemy, he would need a different set of tactics.

And more guns.

He slipped back into the woods and began moving parallel to the tree line, following the curve where the trees wrapped around behind the house and putting more distance between himself and the Infidels. The nine men in the front were hidden from view, but there was another biker lurking on the back porch, idly smoking a cigarette.

Like the rest of the house, the porch was a simple affair, constructed of partially finished logs, with upright posts supporting a gabled roof that extended out from the house a few feet, covering the deck—which was just big enough for a small patio table—and the steps down to the backyard.

The mere fact of the man's presence indicated that the Infidels had anticipated Redd might try to sneak in the house from the back. Did that mean there were others lurking nearby? Or even inside the house?

He knelt there, watching the man on the porch, searching for other watchful eyes. The lone biker looked bored and inattentive. It might have been a ruse to draw Redd in, but after two minutes—in which the man stubbed out the cigarette on the porch and then proceeded to urinate off the top step—Redd decided he was overestimating the Infidels' battlefield savvy. The biker's complacency was genuine.

Redd continued moving parallel to the house, coming up along the southeast corner. After checking to make sure that he was not in the line of sight from either the man in the back or the main group in the front, he broke from cover and crept to the corner. He paused there only a moment before edging around the corner and sidling along the rear of the house.

For a few seconds, Redd was completely exposed to view. The biker had finished his business and taken a seat at the patio table, facing the steps. If he happened to glance to the left, or even if his peripheral vision was above average, Redd would be caught. After a moment, however, he was in the man's blind spot where he would only be detected if the biker turned around and looked in his direction.

It took Redd only about fifteen seconds to reach the edge of the porch deck, where he ducked down just long enough to mentally rehearse what he would have to do next.

It was time to take out the biker on the porch.

THIRTY-TWO

Emily stared at the phone in her hands and breathed a rare curse.

She thought about calling her husband back, then thought better of it. He was unlikely to answer now, and if he was doing what she thought he was doing, calling might actually put him in danger. She then considered dialing 911, alerting the sheriff's department that her husband was about to get himself killed—

Stop it. Don't even think things like that.

But Matthew had probably already made that call. Hadn't he promised to have deputies sent to protect her and Junior?

Was she actually in danger? Was the baby?

Now she knew whom to call. Nodding, she opened her contact list and quick-dialed Mikey Derhammer.

"Hey, Emily," he answered. "What's up?"

"Mikey, I don't have a lot of time to explain, so please just listen. Matthew just called me and it sounds like things are heating up with those bikers."

"Oh no. Is he okay? Are you?"

"I don't know." It was the truth. "There's a chance—a small one, I think, but a chance—that they might know about you guys. Might know that Liz is watching Junior. If so, someone should be there with them."

There was a rustling sound over the line, as of someone moving or shuffling papers. "I'll head home right now."

She allowed herself an audible sigh of relief. "Thanks."

"Do the police know what's going on?"

"I'm honestly not sure." Emily was talking fast, words rattling out of her mouth before her brain could process. She took a breath to calm her nerves a bit. "I think Matty might have called the sheriff, but I'm not a hundred percent sure."

"Okay. Where is Matt now? Does he need any help?"

"He's at home." She quickly recounted what Matthew had told her, which didn't take long.

Mikey was incredulous. "They *killed* Duke?"

"Yeah."

Miley exhaled slowly, a *whoosh* sound filling the speaker. "And Matt's taking them on all by himself?"

"I hope not. Like I said, I think—I hope—he was calling the sheriff." *For whatever that's worth,* but she didn't say this last part out loud.

"Maybe I should . . . you know, go out there?"

Despite everything, Emily smiled at the suggestion, and not just because the idea of Mikey charging into battle alongside her husband was amusingly absurd. Mikey didn't have Matthew's background. He could shoot and had a freezer full of elk steaks every year to prove it, but killing an animal wasn't the same as taking a human life.

And elk didn't shoot back.

Still, Emily's smile was one of admiration. Mikey's willingness to put himself in harm's way for Matthew was just one of the many reasons why he was such a good friend.

"I think you can do the most good at home right now," she said. "Keeping your family and little Matty safe."

"If you think that's best," Mikey said, sounding not at all convinced. "I gotta tell you, though, I don't like the idea of Matt going it alone against those guys."

"Me either, Mikey."

"There's got to be someone else we can call."

Suddenly an idea occurred to her. "Actually, there is! Mikey, I'm so sorry to ask, but I need one more favor."

"Name it."

She told him her plan, knowing full well that if her husband knew what she was thinking, he would flip his lid.

"All right. Done." Mikey paused a beat, then said, "Wait, what about you?"

She recalled Matthew's urgent exhortation for her to remain at the clinic.

"I need to know that you and Junior are safe."

That works both ways, Matty.

"Emily," Mikey repeated, "what about you?"

"I'm going to find my husband."

THIRTY-THREE

Matthew Redd knew a lot of ways to kill a man. The Marines had done a good job training him to be an elite predator when necessary, and all of them required the balancing of three factors—speed, stealth, and neatness. Any gain in one area was offset by the sacrifice of at least one other. Using suppressed weapons gave a shooter a stealth advantage, but at the cost of muzzle velocity—a round from a silenced 9-mil wasn't as lethal as a .44 Magnum round from a hand cannon like the Vaquero. So to ensure that a target stayed down, it was standard practice in many special operations teams to use the Mozambique Drill—two shots to the chest, one to the head—before moving on to the next target.

Redd knew he had to take the biker down fast and quiet, so shooting him was out of the question. That it would be a messy kill was a foregone conclusion.

In a movie, the steely-eyed killer would just grasp his would-be victim's head and give it a hard twist, breaking the neck and causing instant death.

In the real world, such a move was all but impossible, especially when attempted on a full-grown adult.

Never mind that a broken neck did not always cause instantaneous death.

In the seconds before making his move, Redd visualized a solution that he thought had a decent chance of being effective, if somewhat less than elegant.

He rose up, slowly at first to make sure that the biker wasn't looking and then quickly, reaching up to grab the rail, even as he flexed his legs and propelled himself up and over. The movement did not go unnoticed, but in the fraction of a second it took for the biker to turn and realize what was happening, Redd was on him.

Throwing a lightning-quick jab at the man's throat, Redd delivered a blow just hard enough to ensure he wouldn't be able to yell for help. Then, grabbing the biker around the back of his neck, Redd spun around, driving the man downward and slamming his head into the very railing he'd vaulted over seconds ago. There was a hollow *thunk* sound, followed by silence.

It wasn't a technical move taught in a dojo anywhere, but it got the job done.

Satisfied that the most immediate threat was neutralized, Redd crouched down and listened for any sounds that might indicate his presence had been detected. After a silent ten count, he quickly searched the biker's limp body, appropriating his gun—a short-barreled Smith & Wesson .38 revolver—and his knife—a decent Buck hunting knife with a six-inch fixed blade in a leather sheath. He jammed the gun into his back pocket and slipped the knife into his belt, and then, after one more check to make sure he remained undetected, he moved to the back door and tried the handle.

The door was unlocked. Redd had left the house locked up tight, so the unlocked door could only mean that the Infidels had broken in and might be waiting inside.

The time for stealth, he decided, was done. Now speed was of the essence. He had to clear the house and reach the gun safe before the men outside could react. Although he didn't know how many hostiles might be lurking inside, Redd had one thing going for him.

This was his home, and he knew it like the back of his hand.

He cocked the Ruger, then threw the door open and flowed into the kitchen. He immediately saw that the door to the refrigerator was open and, a moment later, realized that a figure with a shaved head and a black leather motorcycle jacket was standing before it, rummaging through the contents in search of something appetizing. The man, average in height but with a few extra pounds on his frame, turned. His eyes widened when he saw Redd, and in the split second it took his brain to register the threat, Redd made his move.

Without hesitation, Redd fired the Ruger once, a center-mass shot that sprayed the interior of the refrigerator with blood and tissue, then thumbed the hammer back and kept moving.

Two down.

Three quick steps brought him to the front room, where two Infidels were in the process of rising from their seats on the couch in order to investigate the report. Redd acquired, sighted, and fired two times in as many seconds, dropping both men with devastating head shots before they could unholster their weapons.

Four down, Redd noted.

The standard operating procedure for clearing a structure held by hostile forces required a visual inspection of every room, including closets, but now that the enemy was alerted to his presence, there simply wasn't time. Rearming was now the priority. And if one or more of the bikers were hanging out in one of the bedrooms or using the bathroom, Redd would still be able to cover them from the front room.

He crossed to where his gun safe now lay toppled over on its back. There were fresh gouges in the front where someone had tried unsuccessfully to jam a pry bar or a tire iron into the door seam. Redd was grateful that J. B. had not skimped when making the grudging decision to buy the Old Glory gun safe.

He held off on punching in the combination and instead rolled across the fallen safe and took cover behind it, facing the front door, which he now saw hung ajar. A moment later, one of the bikers he'd seen out front stormed in, brandishing a pistol and searching for a target. Redd held off just a beat, letting the man advance into the room, clearing the way for his buddy to follow, then fired the Ruger twice again. The second man staggered back through the open door, collapsing on the threshold.

Six down.

Redd figured it would take Baby Boy and the other guys out by the fence at least thirty seconds to make their way up to the house, if they were stupid enough to come charging in like the last two. That was plenty of time for him to open the safe and rearm, but he wasn't about to lower his guard. Holstering the Ruger, which had just one round left in the cylinder, he took out the .38 he'd acquired from the biker on the back porch and aimed it one-handed at the front door while he punched in the combination.

As soon as he had the door open, he swapped the little revolver for the shotgun, then grabbed the small case that contained the Ruger's speed loader and thirty rounds in a foam range block, arranged into five loads that matched the configuration of the revolver's cylinder.

With both shotgun and case in hand, he moved over to stand beside the front window, edging carefully around the hanging drapes to get a look outside. As expected, the bikers in the front had crouched down, finding what cover they could in the mostly open ground between the house and the barn.

One of them must have spotted him because a moment later, a shot was fired into the front window. Redd pulled back reflexively just as several more shots struck the pane, completely shattering it. The rounds zipped through the house's interior, burrowing into the rear wall, filling the air with swirls of smoke and dust. Pictures and hunting trophies, many of which had been hanging since before Redd's childhood, were blown apart, showering the floor with debris. More shots struck the exterior wall, and while the pistol rounds lacked the velocity to completely penetrate through the thick old logs, Redd could feel the transfer of kinetic energy as the bullets punched into them. He did not allow himself to think about the material damage. Irreplaceable though some of those things were, they were only things. Right now all that mattered was staying alive and winning the fight.

They're firing blind. Not very tactical.

Since he couldn't safely return fire, Redd took a moment to reload the Ruger. He flipped open the cylinder and shook out the spent brass, catching the unfired round as it fell and dropping it onto the range block when he removed the speed loader. It took only a second to snap the speed loader around one of the prearranged loads and then another to match the bullets with the holes in the cylinder and release them.

If the Infidels had any grasp of combat tactics, the fusillade of incoming fire at the front would have served as a distraction to allow a flanking move, probably one or two shooters trying to come in through the back door. To defend against this possibility, Redd holstered the loaded Ruger and low-crawled back over to the gun safe where he could cover both the front and rear of the house with the shotgun.

No sooner had he settled in than the shooting abruptly ceased. Redd kept watch on both avenues of approach, letting his gaze switch back and forth as if watching a tennis rally. His ears were ringing from the thunderous reports of the Vaquero, so there wasn't much chance of hearing footsteps, but in his mind's eye, he could see them making their approach. Judging by their actions up to this point, he guessed they would come in through the back door, so he kept the shotgun aimed that way, though it would take only a moment to shift the weapon to meet an encroachment at the front.

A noise, like the sharp crunch of glass breaking, reached through his dulled auditory senses. Though he couldn't quite fix the location, he thought it had come from the front porch. He immediately swung the barrel of the shotgun toward the front door, but in the instant that he did, a distinctive smell joined the miasma of woodsmoke and burnt gunpowder—the smell of gasoline. A moment later, tongues of orange fire began licking at the drapes.

The analytical part of Redd's brain understood the significance of this. The Infidels had just lobbed Molotov cocktails at the house. They were trying to flush him out with fire, and in fact, this had probably been their plan all along. How else to explain the fact that they had improvised fire-bombs readily at hand.

The other part of his brain, the emotional part, was stunned with disbelief.

They're burning my house down.

THIRTY-FOUR

For a fleeting second, Redd thought about how he might save the cabin. There was a small fire extinguisher in the kitchen . . . But no, it wasn't designed to put out anything bigger than a stovetop grease fire. The blaze on the front porch was already far too big for the little dry-chemical cannister to make a difference. The garden hose outside might be able to douse the flames, provided he could get to it before the fire spread much further . . . but *could* he get to it? There were still at least six or seven Infidels outside, maybe more, just waiting for him to poke his head out so they could blow it off.

He would have to deal with them first, and quickly.

Opening the gun safe once more, he grabbed the Henry rifle, stuffed it into the leather scabbard he usually hung from the pommel of Remington's saddle, and then jammed in as many boxes of cartridges and double-aught buck shells as the leather pouch would hold. He probably wouldn't get a chance to reload, hoped it wouldn't even be necessary, but if it proved so, he wanted to be ready.

The flames had already spread across the front porch to block his exit, so with the rifle scabbard slung across his back, Redd quickly moved toward the kitchen with the shotgun held at the high ready. He didn't see anyone moving outside but felt certain that some if not most of the bikers were lurking there, just out of the direct line of sight of the door, waiting for him to come running out.

Staying low, he approached the doorway at an angle, changing his line of sight by a few degrees until he glimpsed a shoulder clad in black leather, just visible above the porch deck. He eased back, switched the shotgun for the Ruger, then edged sideways again until the biker's shoulder was once more in view. Drawing back the hammer with his thumb, he extended the weapon in a two-handed grip, aiming at a point just above the man's shoulder, and then leaned a little farther out, pulling the trigger as soon as the biker's head appeared above the front sight.

He didn't wait to see the impact, didn't need to, but pulled back as soon as the hammer fell.

A volley of answering fire sizzled in the air above and around Redd, forcing him to pull back even farther. Behind him, the living room was filling with smoke. Through it, he could see the dull orange firelight spreading out in every direction.

The realization that he would not be able to save the house twisted his gut. He had failed to save his home, failed the sacred trust J. B. had bequeathed him.

It's just a thing, he told himself. *You've got bigger problems right now.* "Don't. Be. Stupid."

He realized now that the Infidels had been better tacticians than he'd given them credit for. He had not anticipated the possibility of fire, had thought that merely capturing the house would give him the advantage. Now he was trapped, and the flames were spreading fast, driving him right toward the waiting Infidels.

He weighed his chances of surviving a mad dash through the gauntlet waiting just beyond the back door. How many were there? Five? Six? If he ran fast enough, got between them, they wouldn't be able to fire without hitting each other.

He shook his head. That plan was suicide. He might get one or two more of them, but the others would cut him down, and that would be the end of that.

So what did that leave?

He knew the answer, and as much as he dreaded it, he knew he had to act *now*.

Drawing in and holding a breath, he pivoted toward the living room and charged headlong toward the flames.

The heat soared with each step forward. A stray thought about whether the fire was hot enough to cook off the ammunition he was carrying shot through his head, but it was too late to worry about that now. He had too much momentum to stop even if he wanted to. Charging full speed, he aimed himself at the front window, closed his eyes, and leaped through.

There was a moment of pure hell as he flew through the air, into the heart of the blaze. Even with his eyes closed, Redd could see the heat, like a piece of red-hot steel taken from a blacksmith's forge. He imagined it blistering the exposed skin of his face and hands, singeing his hair and beard. His feet struck something solid—the front porch deck—and he let his momentum carry him forward.

A second too late, he remembered the waist-high rail that bordered the porch. He slammed into it, the collision pitching his upper body forward. He might have flipped over the rail completely, but the charred wood snapped apart under his weight, sending him careening forward off the porch.

The brief fall brought instant relief from the heat, but before he could even open his eyes, the ground came up to meet him. He crashed onto his stomach, the impact forcibly expelling the breath he'd been holding, and slid forward through what felt like a bed of coals.

Shaking off the impact, Redd bounded up and tried to put some distance between himself and the source of the pain that was lighting up his nervous system. Somewhere along the way, he finally opened his eyes, which were stinging from exposure to smoke and heat, and as he did, some part of him sounded a warning.

They're still here. Head on a swivel.

The warning came a fraction of a second too late. Even as he was raising the Ruger, starting to turn and search for a target, a blow from out of nowhere slammed into the left side of his head.

A flash of light erupted in his eyes and a ringing filled his head that had nothing to do with the deafening reports from the Ruger. He reeled sideways, his sense of equilibrium at odds with the message filtering through to his eyes. His overriding concern, however, was to identify the source of the assault, neutralize it before—

Redd caught a glimpse of the hulking red-haired Berserker just as another sledgehammer fist drove into his gut, right below the sternum. The punch lifted him off his feet, hurling him backward to land in the pile of red embers that had, just moments before, been the front porch of his home.

The heat shocked him into action even though the punch had driven the wind from his lungs, but as he started to rise, a massive hand seized his wrist, pulling him to his feet and in the same motion tearing the Ruger from his grasp. Reacting too late, Redd's empty hand closed into an impotent fist. He wrenched himself sideways, trying to tear free of the grip, but to no avail. Baby Boy was as immovable as granite. He lifted Redd's trapped wrist up, pulling him off his feet.

The unexpected move hyperextended Redd's arm and sent a jolt of pain through his shoulder. Gritting his teeth against the sensation, Redd threw his free hand up and caught hold of the man's wrist, lifting himself a little higher to ease the stress on his shoulder, and then drew up his knees and kicked out, driving his bootheels into Baby Boy's ribs.

It was like kicking a tree trunk.

The Berserker threw his head back and uttered a sound that was somewhere between a laugh and a howl, then met Redd's gaze. "That all you got?" Another laugh. "Huh?"

The biker flung his arm out, as if Redd's body was a whip he was trying to crack. When his arm was fully extended, he let go, and Redd went flying.

Despite the torrent of brutality he had just endured, Redd recovered quickly. Fueled by adrenaline, he twisted in midair, tucking into a roll that allowed him to come up on his feet in a fighting stance.

Baby Boy faced Redd, still laughing, and as he stalked forward, screamed, "I knew you'd choose the fire!" He snorted. "I could tell that about you." He raised a finger and tapped it beside his right eye. "I could see it, man. You're strong. You're not afraid of anything. That's why it has to be you and me. I'm gonna eat your heart, Redd. Gonna take your power." He punctuated the last by thumping a fist against his chest.

This dude is nuts.

Redd had no idea what the biker was talking about but was grateful for the brief respite. While Baby Boy was wasting his breath spouting quasi-spiritual nonsense, Redd was getting his breath back, along with his wits.

Fight smart, not hard, he told himself. *What are my advantages here?*

The shotgun and the scabbard with the rifle were gone—lost, he presumed, in the tumble from the porch or one of the subsequent falls. He reached behind his back, searching for the sheathed knife he'd slipped into his belt, but it was gone, too.

So, gonna have to do this the old-fashioned way.

Baby Boy was immensely strong, maybe even stronger than Redd—possibly even stronger than the Ukrainian mountain of a man he'd fought a year prior—and to all appearances, possessed an insane kind of fearlessness. That might give him an edge in a fight, even against someone of equal strength, but it would also make him overconfident and therefore vulnerable.

In a battle between two opponents of similar size and strength, skill was usually the determining factor. Redd had received extensive training in hand-to-hand combat and had sparred and grappled with the very best. His instincts told him that the Berserker probably had a lot of real-world brawling experience and probably favored striking—punches and kicks—over grappling. While one good punch could end a fight, in a match between a striker and a grappler, the odds favored the latter. Redd's formal training in both styles of combat would give him an edge, but luck would play a role as well.

Rather than charge the big man, Redd chose to back away, turning slightly so that each step took him farther from the fire. He wanted the Berserker to make the next move, to commit to an attack and perhaps reveal a weakness. Baby Boy tracked his movements, adjusting with each step, but did not quicken his pace.

"C'mon, tough guy," Redd goaded. "Or are you all talk?"

Baby Boy laughed again. "Waiting for you, man. Waiting to see what you got!"

"Fine by me." Redd bent his knees, bent forward at the waist to lower his center of gravity, and raised his hands, keeping them open, his palms facing his opponent, then took a step forward. He was still hoping to draw Baby Boy into making the first move, but failing that, he was determined to get the big man on the ground, where his prowess with Brazilian jujitsu could be used to best effect. When Baby Boy didn't take the bait, Redd went for it.

As he closed to within Baby Boy's reach, he ducked even lower, throwing his left arm up to sweep his opponent's arm out of the way, clearing a path to the real objective, Baby Boy's right leg. Once in close, he dropped to his knee and shot his right hand between the big man's legs, curling around the right thigh and driving in with his shoulder in an attempt to knock the biker off his feet. When Baby Boy did not immediately fall, Redd lifted the leg off the ground while simultaneously reaching around to plant his left hand behind Baby Boy's left knee, forcing the joint to buckle under the big man's weight. Redd felt the biker starting to topple, but then something crashed into the back of his head.

One good punch . . .

The blow sent him to the edge of consciousness, his vision tunneling, his arms and legs momentarily going limp. As he and Baby Boy fell together in a tangle of limbs, Redd's window of opportunity to turn the takedown into a submission hold quickly closed. He felt the biker wriggling out from under him, then felt more sledgehammer blows on his exposed back.

The strikes were painful, far more so than any punches he could remember taking, but luckily only a few struck near his head, and those were glancing blows. A second strike like the first would probably have ended the fight permanently, but despite the punishment, Redd's grasp on consciousness returned quickly, and he pushed away, rolling twice to escape the relentless pounding.

Baby Boy's laughter followed him. "You can do better, Redd! Aren't you some kind of super soldier? Captain America? Show me what you got!"

Redd shut his ears to the taunts, resisting the temptation to respond in kind. The words would have been wasted anyway. Whatever it was that fueled the Berserker's fighting machine, it wasn't unbridled anger.

Once clear, he pushed up onto hands and knees, breathing heavily as he watched the biker resume his advance. He hoped he looked worse than he felt, more vulnerable.

You're getting beat up, Redd told himself. *End this.*

"Come get it," he shouted back at Baby Boy.

This time the Berserker obliged him. He got to within arm's reach, approaching from Redd's left side, then drew back one booted foot and lashed out with a kick.

Redd waited until the last possible instant, until the steel-toed boot was only a whisper away from impact, to make his move. He pressed up, arching his back so that instead of driving into his ribs, the toe of the boot slid under his torso, and only the instep made contact. The blow hurt, but not as much as Baby Boy intended. And in his tumult of emotions, Redd barely felt it at all. As soon as the foot was under him, he curled his left arm around Baby Boy's ankle, trapping it, and then spun away at a ninety-degree angle, twisting the foot hard.

Baby Boy let out a howl of pain as he tried, unsuccessfully, to pull free. Unbalanced, he toppled forward.

With the giant finally on the ground, Redd slid up the length of the Berserker's body and snaked his left arm around the man's throat. Baby Boy immediately realized what Redd was trying to do and reached up with both hands to peel Redd's arm away, but even as he did, Redd brought his right forearm across the back of the biker's neck, locking his left hand around his right elbow and grasping his left biceps with his right hand. The configuration completed a triangle that closed tight around Baby Boy's neck, cutting off the flow of blood to the big man's brain.

Redd felt the Berserker's fingers gouging into the flesh of his forearm, surely drawing blood. He gritted his teeth against the pain, knowing that he only had to endure it a few more seconds.

Evidently recognizing that he would not be able to pry Redd loose, Baby Boy did what few men in his position could have done. Overcoming the animal instinct to keep clawing at the choke hold, he let go and used his mighty arms to push himself off the ground, then rolled over, sandwiching Redd between himself and the ground. As soon as he did, Redd wrapped his legs around his opponent's legs and locked his ankles together, immobilizing Baby Boy and depriving him of the leverage he would need to smash Redd into the ground and break loose.

Realizing that Redd had outmaneuvered him, Baby Boy resorted to thrashing, flinging desperate punches over his shoulder. Redd had anticipated this too and had lowered his head against his right forearm, which not only removed it from the reach of the biker's punches but also increased the pressure on Baby Boy's neck. After an initial flurry, the punches weakened, then stopped.

Suddenly a supernova of pain exploded at Redd's right elbow. His arm, now nerveless, flopped away, breaking the deadly triangle. He made a futile attempt to regain his hold, but Baby Boy was already being pulled out of his grasp.

Another blow from out of nowhere slammed into his right shoulder, followed by another that caught him in the ribs on his left side. Only then did he catch a glimpse of the three figures, lashing out at him with their feet. In the corner of his eye, he saw a fourth man pulling the Berserker away, trying to rouse him. The surviving Infidels had regrouped and rallied to support their defeated leader.

The kicks came in so fast and hard that by the time Redd realized what was happening, his ability to mount any kind of counterattack was already severely compromised. The steel-toed boots had struck nerves and traumatized muscles, leaving him all but paralyzed. His only defense was to curl into a fetal ball, protecting his vital organs with his arms and legs, but doing so left his back exposed, a vulnerability his attackers did not fail to exploit.

The kicks landed with the fury of a hailstorm. Pain bloomed at the small of his back as boots struck near his kidneys. He tried to roll over onto his back, but all that did was present his head and arms for punishment. His vision flashed white, then went dark, the noise of the impacts reduced to barely audible thuds amid the ringing in his ears. An image of Duke Blanton's savaged body appeared in the darkness of his mind, a harbinger of what awaited him.

This is it, he realized. *This is how I die.*

I'm sorry, Em. I'm so sorry . . .

THIRTY-FIVE

A loud noise rose above the insistent pounding of boots striking his body, but it was just a single pebble thrown into the ocean of sensations overloading Redd's nervous system. Then the sound came again, and a strange thing happened. The rain of blows against his body ceased as suddenly as if someone had thrown a switch.

Some primal part of his brain warned that this might be a trick, a deception designed to get him to relax his defensive posture, opening himself up to further abuse, but curiosity overcame this protective instinct. Cautiously he raised his head and opened his eyes.

For a moment, all he could see was stars—phosphenes resulting from the beating—but as the effect faded and the darkness receded, he discerned that his attackers were gone.

No, that wasn't quite true. One of them was still with him, stretched out on the ground beside him, unmoving. But the others, including Baby Boy, had fled.

The question of where they had gone was answered a moment later when a new sound filled his head—the tumult of several motorcycle engines roaring to life. The noise rose and fell as the riders revved their engines, and then four bikes shot out of the barn, tearing away toward the drive. Despite his lingering disorientation, Redd was able to make out the flaming red hair of the Berserker.

The loud noise sounded again, and this time Redd recognized it for what it was—the report of a small handgun. He thought he saw one of the bikers wince, but whether this was a reflex or because the shot had found its mark, he could not say. A moment later, the bikes were gone, the roar of their engines diminishing in the distance.

Redd felt a hand on his shoulder, heard a familiar whispered voice, almost a sob. "Matty! Don't move. I'm here. Just stay still for a second while I—"

"Em?"

He blinked as her face appeared above him. Tears streamed down her cheeks, her forehead creased with concern. He tried to smile, to reassure her, and then willed his body to uncurl so that he could reach out to her.

"Don't try to move," she cautioned. Her hands flew gently over his body, and Redd realized she was assessing his injuries. "Help is on the way."

"I'll be okay," he assured her. He felt her weight as she leaned over and hugged his battered body. Tears dripped on his exposed skin.

Over her shoulder, Redd saw her Tahoe, parked only a few yards away. There were no other vehicles around, nor any other people, which meant she had come alone. He realized that she had killed one of the bikers stomping him and scared the rest away.

She must have left as soon as I called her, he thought.

Ignoring her advice, he put out his hands, levering himself into a sitting position.

"Matty, don't," Emily said, sitting up to meet his eyes.

"I'm okay, Em," he said, but his voice betrayed him. The words came out in a wheezing groan. Then as his brain finally caught up, he added, "You shouldn't be here."

"Oh, Matty." She gave an exasperated laugh and put her arms around him, holding without squeezing. "I'm going to pretend you didn't say that."

He returned the embrace, though his arms still felt weak and barely responsive. "They burned our house down."

"I know, baby. It doesn't matter. As long as we're safe." She let go, held him at arm's length, then shook her head. "You're a mess. Can you walk?"

He didn't actually know, but he wasn't about to admit it. "Help me up."

Cautiously she took his extended hand, steadying him as he hauled himself to his feet. It was beyond agonizing, but he gritted his teeth and fought through it.

A memory of boot camp fluttered through his head, a drill sergeant's monotonal recitation of Chesty Puller's axiom: *"Pain is weakness leaving the body!"*

I must have been a lot weaker than I realized.

Once on his feet, he felt the full radiant energy of the fire. The cabin was engulfed in flames, well beyond saving. A column of gray smoke rose skyward, surrounded by bright-red embers, some of which were falling back to earth, alighting on the ground, scorching the grass where they landed. He watched the fire fall for a minute, then saw a few embers drifting toward the barn.

"Remington!" he gasped, and before Emily could even try to stop him, he was moving, shambling toward the barn. After the first uncertain steps, the aching in his extremities receded a little, and he was actually able to run.

To his immense relief, he heard the horse's anxious nickering even before he reached the stall. He quickly opened the door and then stood back, urging the animal to come out. After stamping his hooves in the hay a few times, Remington obliged. Redd shooed him toward the door out to the pasture where he would be safe in the event that the fire spread to the barn.

Seconds later, Emily joined him. "The fire department is on the way. We need to get you to the hospital though, just in case. I'll drive."

He stared at her blankly for a moment, wondering again why she thought he needed medical attention. "I'm okay."

"You're not, Matty. You look like hell. And I saw what they were doing to you. You could have internal injuries. We need to get you checked out."

He shook his head and immediately regretted it as his skull began throbbing. "There's no time, Em. This isn't over. I *have* to go after them."

"Are you insane?" She reached out to him, gripped his bicep. "You're in no shape to go anywhere."

She's not wrong.

"Maybe not, but I have to do this. If they get away, they'll just keep coming back. This has to end. *Now.*"

"And what are you going to do? You can't take them on all by yourself. They almost killed you."

He couldn't disagree. If she hadn't shown up when she did . . .

"After this, they'll probably make a run for it. Hide out somewhere. I just need to know where they are. After that . . ." He winced as he took a painful breath. "After that, I'll let the police take care of it."

"Let them take care of it now! Blackwood is probably on his way out here already. He's going to want to talk to you, Matty." She glanced down at the motionless form of the Infidel she'd killed in order to save her husband. Her hands shook; so did her voice. "He's gonna want to talk to both of us."

"That's why I've gotta go right now. If I wait around for him to figure out what happened here, we'll lose the trail."

She pursed her lips together. "How are you going to track them?"

This was something he'd only partially thought through. "They've got a lawyer up in Helena." He searched his memory until the name appeared. "Angela Townsend."

"Outlaw bikers have lawyers?"

"Yeah. Hard to believe, right? Duke was on his way back from meeting with her when they . . ." He let the sentence go unfinished. "He was trying to negotiate a truce."

"You think the meeting was a setup?"

"I'm not sure. I can't believe any lawyer, even one working for the Infidels, would be a party to cold-blooded murder. My guess is that she was probably negotiating in good faith. They killed Duke to send a message to me. No truce. I'm hoping that when she hears what they did to Duke, she'll rethink her obligation to her clients and give up their location."

Emily regarded him with a skeptical gaze. "Getting a lawyer to turn on her client sounds like wishful thinking to me."

"I can be very persuasive." He looked over her shoulder. In the distance, the wail of sirens was just barely audible but growing louder. "I gotta go, Em."

"I'm coming with you."

"Em . . ."

"You're in no shape to drive, much less defend yourself if you run into any trouble." Before he could protest, she pointed a finger at him. "Don't even think of arguing with me, Matthew Redd." She gestured to the passenger side of the Tahoe. "Get in."

I love this woman, Redd thought and then did what she told him.

THIRTY-SIX

Rebuilding the algorithm from scratch had proven far easier than Dmitri Georgiev had originally anticipated, which was a good thing since, following their initial meeting, Anton Gage had been conspicuously absent from the underground facility. Evidently the rest of the project was demanding his employer's full attention, which made Dmitri think that maybe, just maybe, if things didn't go off according to Gage's timeline, it would not be because he had failed to deliver the drone control AI program ahead of the deadline.

He'd been lucky to find huge sections of code available in other applications, which were easily enough modified to fit his purposes. That had not been true when he and his team had been developing the original algorithm. What a difference a couple years could make.

Since his arrival, he had not returned to the surface. The underground level had a small bathroom, and one of the other systems engineers had brought food to him, so there had been no reason to leave his workstation for more than a few minutes at a time. Just long enough to stretch his legs every couple hours. But after more than eighteen hours of nearly nonstop work, he was ready for a break, so he logged off and headed back to the elevator.

There was an old telephone handset mounted to the wall next to the outside safety cage door, a phone that connected only to a similar unit on the surface. Dmitri only needed to pick it up to summon the elevator, but he verbalized his request anyway. "I want to come up."

"Be right down," answered a gravelly voice that might have been the same man who had dropped him off the previous day.

After about thirty seconds, he heard the sound of the elevator machinery whirring to life and could see movement inside the shaft as the lift car descended to his level. When the accordion gate slid aside to reveal the operator, Dmitri saw that it was not the same man as before but definitely one of his ilk. This man had the same disheveled appearance—tattoos, an unruly beard—and stank of body odor and cigarettes.

Despite that first impression, the man seemed friendly enough, acknowledging Dmitri with a nod. "Coming up for air?" he asked.

Dmitri laughed politely. "Yes. Is long time to be underground. I am starting to forget what the sun and sky look like."

This was just banter. When he was fully involved in his work, like he was now, he might go days without stepping outside. Even now, he had no plans to go much beyond the little rec room he'd seen the previous day. With luck, he'd find an empty couch where he could stretch out and grab a quick power nap. Half an hour was usually enough to recharge his batteries.

The elevator operator also chuckled. "Man, I tell you. They all talk about how big the sky is here . . . I mean, it's on their friggin' license plates. But it's the same sky everywhere you go. Am I right?"

Dmitri had suspected that he was in the American West, but the offhand statement seemed like confirmation that he was back in Montana. That wasn't a surprise really. The Gage Food Trust facility in Montana had been the organization's flagship operation, and despite the abruptness with which it had been shut down, it only stood to reason that Gage still had resources in place, just awaiting his return.

Was the trust preparing to resume large-scale agricultural experiments? Was that why Gage needed a new drone fleet?

Dmitri shook his head, recalling the parameters Gage had given him. Forty-four million acres—that was almost half of the state, and much of the land was open range.

What are you up to, Anton? Dmitri wondered, not for the first time.

Anton Gage was a great man, with global ambitions, so whatever it was, it would probably make history.

The recreation–cum–dining room was not empty, as he had hoped. Two men, one of them a senior systems engineer Dmitri had seen working below, occupied one of the tables, drinking coffee and eating oversize muffins. There was, however, an empty couch in the back of the room, and Dmitri went directly to it, sprawled out upon it, and flung one arm over his eyes to block out some of the light.

He was just starting to drift off when a boisterous utterance brought him back to wakefulness. He raised his arm, casting an irritated glare toward the source of the disruption, which proved to be one of the thugs. The man was standing in front of the coffee urn, complaining about the quality of the brew. The two men at the table stared at their muffins, refusing to engage. After a few seconds, the thug seemed to get the hint and stalked out of the room, leaving his unused coffee mug on the counter. Dmitri covered his eyes again.

"Can you believe those guys?" muttered one of the men at the table.

"Yeah, they're something else," the other replied. "I don't know where Mr. Gage found them."

"Prison, probably."

They both laughed.

"They're hard workers though," the same man continued. "Gotta give 'em that. They just keep going and going. Like big, ugly Energizer Bunnies."

"You would too if you were snorting what they're snorting."

"What do you mean?"

"Meth."

243

"You're kidding."

"Nope. You can see it in their eyes. They're all completely wired."

"Huh. Well, I guess if it helps them stay awake. Especially the guys driving the trucks." The man laughed. "Maybe I should get some. Might help us make the deadline."

"Stick to Red Bull," the other man advised. "Meth will mess you up."

Despite hearing the siren song of sleep, Dmitri could not help but follow the conversation with great interest. He had not really paid attention to the thuggish men working for Gage, but now that his attention was drawn to it, he recalled noticing some of them displaying the telltale signs of amphetamine abuse.

But why was Anton Gage hiring men like that to work for him?

Probably, he realized, *for the same reason that he hired me using an anonymous post on Reddit and not through conventional channels.*

Did that mean Gage was doing something illegal?

Dmitri understood that men like Gage had little regard for laws and could usually use their money and influence to get whatever they needed, regardless of legalities. And yet there had been rumors that Gage had been a fugitive and that the sudden closure of the Gage Food Trust had been due to some kind of illegal activity. Was this project a similarly illicit endeavor?

No doubt Gage's promise of "a boatload of money" had been intended to buy his discretion, but that money would do him no good if he wound up in prison.

What are you up to, Anton? he wondered again.

He gave up on the idea of sleep but remained where he was, eyes covered, pondering how best to root out the truth about Gage's new secret project. When the two men at the table finally left, Dmitri got up and, after splashing some water on his face, hurried to join them on the elevator ride back down to the sublevel.

As the car descended, he turned to the engineer he'd recognized from earlier. "I need to talk to Mr. Gage. Do you know how I can reach him?"

The man regarded him warily. "Is it urgent? Mr. Gage is super busy."

"Trust me. If he wants to make his deadline, he'll need to give me five minutes."

The man shrugged. "I'll pass it along."

Dmitri accepted this with a nod and, as soon as the ride down ended, went to his workstation. He did not, however, dive back into the search for preexisting strings of code he could cannibalize. Instead, he began reviewing his work in progress, looking for vulnerabilities. He'd barely gotten started when the man he'd spoken with on the elevator approached him.

"Mr. Gage can give you two minutes," he said, then gestured for Dmitri to follow.

Dmitri expected to be ushered into Gage's presence, but the man did not even lead him out of the little control room. Instead, he stopped at a wall-mounted phone, remarkably like the one used to call the elevator, only this handset was red instead of black. The man handed the receiver to Dmitri and then went back to work.

Dmitri held the phone to his ear. "Mr. Gage?"

"Dmitri. What do you need?" There was none of Gage's earlier enthusiasm in the terse question.

"Mr. Gage, I realize that I did not ask you about the payload specifications."

"I told you. Spreaders. Just like the ones we used to use. Only better."

"I understand that, but I need to know what they will be spreading."

Dmitri thought he could hear Gage grumbling in irritation over the line. "It's a proprietary formulation."

"Yes, but is it a liquid? A solid? I need to know the mass and density of the payload in order to set the operating range and power regulation."

This was not strictly true. One feature of the original algorithm he had written was a smart sensor system that could automatically adjust for differing payloads without any additional inputs. If Gage challenged him on this matter, he was prepared to point out that meeting the deadline meant cutting a few corners, and the smart sensors would be one of them.

Gage, however, did not raise the question. "It's a liquid solution. Mostly water."

That told Dmitri nothing useful. "Mr. Gage, in order for these drones to do what you're asking, I need to know everything. What may seem like a minor difference in specific gravity can translate into as much as a kilogram per liter."

This was another slight exaggeration, but Gage did not challenge the assertion. Instead, he sighed. "All right. I'll have the specifications sent to you. Is there anything else?"

"Not at the moment."

There was a click from the handset.

Dmitri breathed a sigh of relief. His ploy had worked, though whether the knowledge would be worth the risk he'd taken remained to be seen. Really, what cause did he have for concern? If Gage was telling the truth—if the payload his drones would be delivering was only an experimental growth serum or a genetically engineered pesticide—then he was worried about nothing.

But if that was all it was, why hire the thugs? Why all the secrecy?

And why does he need to cover more than forty million acres?

True to his word, the specifications of Gage's proprietary formula were waiting for him in an old-fashioned IRC chat message on his computer. He opened it and perused the information.

The first ingredient, deionized water, comprised nearly 90 percent of the product. The second ingredient, something called *Puccinia graminis Ug99 GFT-MOD 008 (spores)*, made up another 9 percent, and the remaining list of chemical components, all in trace amounts, accounted for the rest.

Dmitri was no scientist, but in the course of his work, he had developed a working knowledge of several scientific fields, including both chemistry and biology. He also recognized the notation indicating a genetically modified organism developed by the Gage Food Trust.

Puccinia graminis Ug99.

He had no clue what it was, but spreading it over millions of acres of the American heartland appeared to be Gage's sole purpose in mobilizing the drone fleet.

As much as he wanted to run a search on the organism, Dmitri stifled the impulse. The information Gage had forwarded to him included specific gravity notations, which would allow him to calculate mass per liter. That was all the information he needed to do what he'd told Gage he was going to do.

Gage had allowed him limited Internet access for his code search, but Dmitri was certain that his activity was being monitored. If Gage's project was harmless or even beneficent, then there was nothing to be gained by digging for more information.

On the other hand, if Gage was doing something potentially harmful, his curiosity might just get him killed.

THIRTY-SEVEN

During the drive up to Helena, Redd and Emily discussed how best to approach Angela Townsend. Redd favored the shock value of a direct confrontation, while Emily preferred a more diplomatic approach.

"In fact, maybe you should let me go in first," she suggested. "You look like you just arrived from a war zone."

"I did," he pointed out. But she wasn't wrong. He actually felt much worse than he looked, though this was only because most of his injuries were covered by his clothes, which were stained with soot and blood. He had a feeling that under his shirt, his body was just one big bruise. The fistful of ibuprofen he'd gotten from Emily's purse hadn't kicked in yet, or if it had . . . well, then he was in even worse shape than he thought.

"They're lawyers," he went on. "They're used to seeing accident victims."

Emily frowned but then nodded. "I suppose it does make the point that the Infidels are dangerous. Okay, we'll try it your way."

A Google search revealed that the offices of Lerner, King, and Townsend, attorneys-at-law, were located in a three-story complex a few blocks from the state capitol building. They parked and went in, earning more than a few astonished looks from passersby. With Emily still in her hospital scrubs, they looked more like doctor and patient than husband and wife.

The law office was decorated in faux rustic chic, more like a movie set designer's fantasy of an office in Montana than the real thing. The plush furniture in the waiting room appeared as though it had never actually been used.

"Apparently defending outlaw bikers is a lucrative field," Emily remarked. "Makes you wonder who else is on their client list."

"The bad guys always have the most money."

"Not to mention needing legal representation more than most people."

"Can I help you?" asked the sour-faced receptionist, who had evidently overheard their musings.

"I need to speak with Angela Townsend," Redd barked in his best imitation of a drill sergeant. "Now."

The man flinched a little but stood his ground. "Do you have an appointment?"

"You could say that. My attorney, Duke Blanton, was going to arrange a meeting with her clients. Maybe you know who I mean. The dirtbag bikers."

"I'm afraid I can't discuss our—"

Redd cut him off. "Unfortunately, Duke isn't going to be able to make the meeting because your boss's clients murdered him."

The man's jaw dropped, then closed. He swallowed nervously.

"So," Redd went on, "I need to speak with Angela Townsend. Now."

"She's not here," he said, his voice almost a squeak.

"Well, where is she?"

"I can't tell you—"

Redd narrowed his eyes and leaned forward, projecting menace.

"But I can call her," the receptionist went on.

"Why don't you do that?"

As the man picked up his desk phone and began dialing, Redd shot a look at Emily. When their eyes met, a hint of a smile touched her lips and she gave a barely perceptible nod.

Score one for direct confrontation, Redd thought.

"Sir?" The receptionist was holding out the handset. "I have Ms. Townsend for you."

Redd snatched the receiver from his hand and held it to his ear. "This is Redd."

The voice on the other end was husky and a little breathless. "Mr. Redd, Brandon just told me about Mr. Blanton. Is that true? He's dead?"

"*Dead* as a heart attack. Those maniacs murdered him. Right after he met with you. From where I'm standing, it sounds an awful lot like you set him up for them."

"I did no such thing. I was negotiating in good faith."

"Good faith?" Redd spat the words into the phone. "I don't think you even know what that means. Otherwise, you'd be a little pickier about your clientele."

"Everyone is entitled to legal representation," she huffed.

"I'm not interested in debating this with you. Your clients killed a man. Stomped him to death. Then they tried to do the same thing to me. Now, unless you want to be considered an accomplice to their crimes, I suggest you tell me where I can find them."

"I—it's not that simple."

"Make it simple."

There was silence on the line, long enough that Redd was just about to escalate his threats; then Townsend spoke again. "We should meet. Can you come to my house?"

Redd was incredulous. "Your house?"

"I don't feel comfortable discussing this over the phone. I'm ten minutes away, up on LeGrande Cannon Boulevard, west of town. Tell Brandon to give you the address."

She hung up before Redd could offer a definitive answer. He handed the phone back to the receptionist. "You're Brandon? She said to give me her home address."

Brandon raised a skeptical eyebrow but then nodded and bent over his desk and began writing on a Post-it note.

"We're going to her house?" Emily said. "Are you sure that's a good idea?"

"Nope," Redd admitted.

"I mean, it could be a trap, right?"

"Yep."

Redd didn't actually think that Angela Townsend was trying to set them up for an ambush. She had sounded genuinely alarmed at the news of Duke Blanton's death and had not rejected his demand for cooperation out of hand as he had expected her to. Even the fact that she wanted to meet with him privately, rather than in her office, where she might be observed by her partners and employees, seemed like a hopeful sign.

Nevertheless, he was going to keep his guard up and Emily's .38 where he could reach it in a hurry.

✖ ✖ ✖

Townsend lived in an upscale neighborhood on the northern flank of Mount Helena—a modest peak that rose about 1,300 feet above the city. The house, a sprawling two-story gabled structure, was positioned so that the front faced upslope, while the rear looked out over the road, commanding a sweeping view of the city below. One advantage of this layout was that the driveway and front door were hidden from view— nobody on the road would be able to see the Tahoe parked in front of Townsend's home.

A woman came out onto the porch to meet them. She was blonde and slender, attired in a designer T-shirt and yoga pants. Redd, who was not a good judge of women's age, thought she looked like she was in her early forties, not really old, but old enough to be worried about outward signs of aging. As she stepped out into the open, she looked around nervously as if afraid someone might be watching. When she saw Redd, she flinched as if shocked by his appearance but then shook it off and stepped down to meet them. "You must be Mr. Redd. I'm Angela Townsend."

Redd nodded. "This is my wife, Emily."

The women exchanged nods by way of a greeting, and then Townsend gestured to the door. "Won't you come inside."

Ordinarily, Redd would have stepped aside and allowed Emily to go ahead of him—growing up, J. B. had insisted on strict adherence to etiquette—but because there was a slim possibility that they might be walking into a trap, he elected to take point.

His caution proved unnecessary. There was no ambush waiting inside—just a spacious sitting room with surprisingly few places to actually sit. The interior decor was modern and minimalist, with bare hardwood floors and Scandinavian-design furnishings; it looked more like a showroom than a place where real people actually sat and talked. Townsend walked to one of the low-profile chairs, then indicated that her guests could have a seat on the matching couch.

Once they were all seated, Townsend got right to the point. "Were you telling the truth about Mr. Blanton?"

Redd nodded. "They stomped him to death."

"And the police are involved?"

Redd thought that was an odd question but didn't see any harm in answering. "I told Sheriff Blackwood about it myself."

This revelation was clearly a source of relief to the attorney. "That's good."

"What makes you say that?"

"Mr. Redd, I get the impression that you're not someone who has much respect for my profession—"

"Was it that obvious?"

She pursed her lips together in irritation, then continued. "But I take my professional obligations very seriously. That means ensuring that my clients are not subjected to harassment or any kind of extrajudicial action. However, if they are suspected of having committed a serious crime, then of course, it is my responsibility to comply with any requests made by legitimate authorities."

"So you're saying you'll tell the cops where to find them, but not me." Redd rolled his eyes. "You could have just told me this over the phone."

Townsend raised a hand. "Please, just listen."

Redd folded his arms across his chest. "Go ahead."

"I'm not trying to be coy here, Mr. Redd. The truth is, they scare the hell out of me. When I started representing them, I thought it would be easy money. I mean, I know what kind of people they are. They're criminals. Almost all of them have done time for one thing or another. But guilty or not, they still deserve legal counsel."

"And of course, they could afford you," Emily interjected with more than a trace of sarcasm. "They probably paid in cash."

"You're not wrong." Townsend sighed. "I figured since they were going to keep breaking laws anyway, I'd always have work. Mostly it was just drug charges. Occasionally assault. I never imagined that they would kill someone. I'm still a little shocked by it."

Redd almost told her to get over it but realized that she was using her confession to justify the fact that she had already decided to break attorney-client privilege. *Just let her talk,* he told himself.

"I know what kind of people they are, Mr. Redd. Believe me, I want them locked up as much as you do."

"Then tell me where to find them."

"I want to help you. Please. Just hear me out. I have to be very careful about how I do this."

"Why?" Redd asked. "You've already said that you want to cooperate. Why are you still holding back?"

"Because the Infidels are not the only party involved here."

Redd exchanged a glance with Emily. "What do you mean?"

"The place where they're staying right now belongs to another client of the firm."

"Do they know what the Infidels are doing?" Emily asked. "Are you afraid of implicating them, too?"

"I don't care about that," Redd cut in. "Just tell me where they are."

Townsend pursed her lips again, then rose to her feet. "The place doesn't have an address per se. It's out in the middle of nowhere. I'll have to show you on a map."

She turned and headed through an arched opening in the wall that separated the great room from a formal dining room, then turned right down a hallway, out of their line of sight. She returned a moment later carrying an atlas and gazetteer of Montana, which she opened and placed on the coffee table.

"It's here," she said.

Redd leaned forward and studied the location. It intersected a road—US Highway 90, which ran east to west across the state's agricultural heartland. He traced the highway with his finger and spotted a familiar name—a little farming community called Voight.

Redd's heart skipped a beat. He knew exactly where the marked place was. He'd been there before.

He looked up and fixed Angela Townsend with a laser-focused stare. "Who's your other client?"

She shook her head. "I can't tell you that. I won't."

"Is it Gage? Is it Anton Gage?"

He saw the answer in her eyes. She opened her mouth as if she was about to answer.

But before she could, a thunderclap seared through the air, and Angela Townsend's chest erupted in a spray of red.

THIRTY-EIGHT

Instinctively Redd threw his arms around Emily and pulled her to the ground, covering her with his body. As he pulled her to safety, a part of his brain was calculating trajectories, trying to pinpoint the location of the shooter.

Judging by the loudness of the report, the weapon had been fired at close range, perhaps even from inside the house. He was pretty sure the shot had come from behind Townsend—the spray of blood was consistent with an exit wound—and when it happened, she'd had her back to the rear of the house, which meant the shooter had fired from there, maybe even from the back porch, shooting through a window or patio door.

Without raising his head, he scanned the great room, looking for better cover. There wasn't much. The Scandinavian furniture barely afforded any concealment. And it definitely wouldn't stop a bullet. Nor would the interior walls, he realized.

We gotta get out of here.

Once outside, Redd knew they could find better cover or, if necessary, escape in the Tahoe. Of course, the enemy would know that as well, and there was a chance that the attack from the rear of the house was designed to flush them out the front door—a variation of the same tactic they had used against him back at the ranch. But if they were waiting out there, they were doing a much better job of hiding their presence than they had at the cabin. The great room's floor-to-ceiling windows afforded a panoramic view of Mount Helena. They also revealed a conspicuous absence of any hostiles in the front yard.

Redd put his head close to Emily's, speaking almost directly into her ear. "That shot came from the back." He drew the .38 and held it at the ready. "When I start shooting, you start running for the door."

"Matty, I'm not leaving you!"

"I'll be right behind you," he promised.

But before he could execute his plan, an enormous figure burst through the back window in an eruption of glass and billowing drapes. Though the man's face was hard to see amid the flurry, there was no mistaking the furious mane of copper hair.

Baby Boy.

Redd shifted his aim and pulled the trigger. The weapon bucked in his hands, but Baby Boy was already rolling out of the way, ducking behind the dining room table, which he promptly tipped over to create a barrier between himself and Redd.

Redd knew the .38 could punch through the tabletop, but he only had five shots left and without knowing exactly where Baby Boy was crouching, there was no guarantee that any of his shots would find their mark. He also knew that Baby Boy wouldn't stay hidden for long.

"Same plan," he whispered to Emily, thumbing back the hammer. "On three. One. Two . . ."

He felt her tensing as he counted and knew that she would go on cue, so when he got to three, there was no hesitation. He lifted off her, rolling out from behind the couch, and fired into the tabletop. At the same instant, Emily began scrambling on all fours toward the front door.

The .38 round punched a splintery hole in the exact center of the polished wood surface. Redd kept the revolver aimed at the table, finger poised on the trigger, but did not fire. Instead, he followed Emily's progress from the corner of his eye, and when she was through the door, he began creeping backward, keeping the revolver trained on the table and ready to fire.

Suddenly the table itself began to move, lifted into the air horizontally like a massive shield. Redd caught a glimpse of Baby Boy's legs and lower torso, but before he could adjust his aim, Baby Boy hurled the table across the great room, directly at Redd.

Redd tried to leap out of its way but was a half second too slow. The table crashed into him with the force of a battering ram, knocking him into the sofa, which in turn flipped over backward, spilling Redd onto the floor with the table atop him.

Unlike the great room furniture, the table was constructed of sturdy hardwood and granite and must have weighed close to two hundred pounds.

After a moment the table shifted off him, easing the pressure on his bruised body. The relief was short-lived as he saw the red-haired Berserker standing over him, teeth bared in a fierce grin, with a table leg in one hand and Redd's own Ruger .44 Magnum in the other.

Redd struggled to bring the .38 to bear, but as his arm twitched up, he saw that the gun was gone, knocked out of his grasp by the flying table.

Baby Boy flung the table aside and then, inexplicably, tossed the Ruger away as well. "How 'bout let's try this again," he said, almost crowing the words, making a "come here" gesture with his right hand. "Only this time, don't count on your old lady jumping in to save you."

Redd involuntarily glanced over at the empty doorway, hoping Emily had made it someplace safe. He wanted to shout to her, urge her to get as far away as she could, but didn't want to draw attention to her.

Instead, he managed to cough out a laugh. "Funny," he wheezed. "I think you're forgetting the part where it took six of your buddies to save you last time."

Trading taunts with an opponent was not a preferred close-combat technique for Redd, but every second spent talking was a second in which he was able to regain his wits.

Baby Boy laughed. "It's only us this time, Redd. I'm going to enjoy breaking you."

Redd wondered if that was true. Did Baby Boy come by himself? He tried to envision a scenario where the bikers had split up. Maybe Baby Boy was sent to check on Townsend after the carnage that ensued on his ranch; then again, maybe they had somehow followed him here.

Either way, I have to deal with this big dude first.

Redd planted his hands to either side and, with a focused burst of energy, brought his feet up and drove them into the Berserker's left knee.

Baby Boy must have sensed the attack was imminent because as Redd struck, the biker shifted to a ready stance, which changed his position relative to Redd just enough that Redd's heels scored only a glancing blow. Baby Boy grunted and hopped back a step but remained on his feet, uninjured. The oblique contact deprived Redd of the expected energy of a rebound so that all he could do was twist away to the side. He managed to come up on all fours and bounded to his feet, but in the time it took him to do so, Baby Boy was moving in for an attack. The Berserker cocked his right fist and punched straight out at Redd's face.

Redd threw up his left arm in a rising block that redirected the punch over his shoulder, then delivered a strong blow to Baby Boy's solar plexus. He could tell, even as the punch was thrown, that it wasn't going to do the kind of damage he needed it to. Baby Boy was as solid as a rock, and Redd's muscles were still compromised by the beating he'd taken earlier. Rather than throw good effort after bad, he pulled the punch and tried to back away before the Berserker could launch a counterattack. Once again, he was a heartbeat too slow.

Instead of drawing back his extended arm for another punch, Baby Boy swept sideways, clouting the side of Redd's head. It wasn't a particularly hard strike, but it was enough to unbalance him. As he staggered away, Redd's left ear flared hotly and a ringing noise filled his head.

Focus, he told himself. *Fight smart. You know you're better than he is. You beat him once already.*

Baby Boy was untrained, relying on his size and strength, not to mention his uncanny fearlessness, to give him the advantage in a fight. Redd had turned those imagined strengths against him during their first clash but that had been before the other Infidels had ganged up on him, trying to do to him what they had done to Duke Blanton.

They had almost succeeded.

Now Redd was the one who felt slow. He felt like he was fighting underwater. Every movement was an agonizing effort.

Baby Boy pivoted and stalked toward him, laughing maniacally as he advanced. Redd faced him, lowering into a grappler's stance, and began looking for his opening. He knew several standing takedowns but every single one would leave him open to reprisal. Ordinarily he simply took his lumps, suffering a few blows in order to wrap his foe up in an unbeatable submission hold.

But how much more punishment could he withstand?

As much as I have to, he thought and made his move.

Just as he had done before, he went low, going for the leg grab to put Baby Boy on the ground. But as he ducked inside the big man's reach, Baby Boy pivoted left, grabbed Redd's right arm and leg, and heaved him across the room.

Redd barely had time to curl into a protective ball before slamming into a wall. He hit with such force that his body smashed through the drywall, breaking through two of the studs underneath, and punched through the Sheetrock on the other side.

Redd shook off the wave of pain that shot through his body and got back to his feet just as Baby Boy charged toward him at a full run. Seeing that there was no way he would get free in time, Redd braced himself in anticipation of another pounding.

Baby Boy, however, had a different plan.

Instead of stopping once he got within striking range, the big biker lowered his shoulder and plowed straight into Redd.

It was like being hit by a freight train.

The impact smashed Redd clear of the wall, propelling him into the next room—a spacious, sparsely decorated bedroom. Baby Boy came through after him, erupting out of the shattered wall in an explosion of wood and drywall fragments.

Momentarily stunned, Redd could only watch helplessly as the giant reached down, scooped him up, and heaved him over the bed and into the opposite wall.

It wasn't lost on Redd that Baby Boy was having no issue literally toss-ing him around. He wasn't sure what the man weighed, but with all the hard labor that came with ranching, on top of grueling workouts he'd kept up from his time with the Raiders, Redd had kept his own weight just over 260 pounds. He guessed the biker was somewhere closer to 350, comprised of muscle, drugs, and bad choices.

The Sheetrock cracked under the impact but remained mostly intact, while Redd slumped down to the floor on the other side of the bed. Still chortling, Baby Boy reached down and shoved the bed—frame, box spring, and mattress—out of his way, clearing a path to Redd. When he got within a few feet, he reached out again, no doubt planning to smash Redd through another wall, but this time, Redd was ready for him, driving his fist up, directly into the other man's face.

Baby Boy's head snapped back, blood spraying from his mouth and nose. Redd took full advantage of the momentary reversal to get to his feet and then, with his back to the wall, raised his right leg and drove his heel into the biker's abdomen.

The kick sent Baby Boy staggering backward across the room until a corner of the bed caught him behind the knee and he sprawled onto his back. Redd waited until the big man was starting to rise, then charged across the room, lowering his shoulder at the last instant and plowing into Baby Boy, slamming into him like a tackle sled. The hit lifted the biker off his feet and drove him back into the bedroom door, which tore free of its hinges, sending both men spilling out into the hall. As they fell, Baby Boy wrapped his arms around Redd, lifting him off his feet, and tried to whip him around, but Redd had his arms around the biker's waist, holding on tight. Unbalanced by the attempted throw, both men crashed to the floor, demolishing a small table in the process.

With Baby Boy on the ground, Redd immediately began looking for his opening, using both his arms and his legs to trap his opponent's limbs, which would not only prevent the biker from inflicting further harm but also exhaust him. That was the plan at least, but Baby Boy showed no signs of tiring. He heaved and bucked, alternately trying to shake Redd loose and smash him into the walls and floor. After several seconds of struggling, he succeeded in freeing one arm and used it to peel Redd off him. Before Redd could regain his hold, Baby Boy lifted him off his feet and hurled him down the hall toward the great room.

Redd slammed facedown on the hardwood floor. He tried to roll over into a seated defensive position, where he could use his legs to fend off an attack, but Baby Boy was already on him. The biker came in low, dropped to his knees beside Redd, and started raining down blows with both hands.

The punches landed like lightning strikes. Under any other circumstances, he could have weathered the storm almost indefinitely, but the earlier beating had weakened him, depleted his stamina, and tenderized him like a piece of meat. He curled up, throwing his left arm up to deflect some of the punches and then reaching out with his right, trying to trap one of Baby Boy's arms. The biker swatted his hand away as if it were nothing more annoying than a mosquito.

Through the dull roar of the merciless beating, Redd heard a loud crash, accompanied by a sound like shattering glass. The sound seemed to trigger a momentary lull in the attack, and once the message filtered through the fog, Redd acted quickly, backpedaling away. As he did, he saw Baby Boy, face streaked with blood, jagged pieces of ceramic and glass littering his hair and falling off his shoulders like autumn leaves. The big man turned slowly, menacingly, to face . . .

Emily!

His wife had run back inside and smashed a table lamp over Baby

Boy's head. The blow probably would have knocked an ordinary person unconscious or even killed him, but all it did to Baby Boy was irritate him.

"Em," Redd gasped. "Run!"

Emily didn't run, but she did back up a step. "Leave him alone, you monster," she screamed. "You think I'm afraid of you?"

Baby Boy held up a finger, wagged it at her like she was a wayward child, then lunged at her.

Emily stood her ground, defiant, but she was no match for the Berserker. He backhanded her so forcefully that she flew across the room, crashing into the overturned dining table.

"No!"

The sound that tore from Redd's throat was the howl of an awakening beast. The inner voice that was, even now, warning him to fight smart, not angry, was swept away in the rush of blood and adrenaline. Before he knew what he was doing, Redd was on his feet and hurling punches at the Berserker.

Baby Boy pivoted to meet the attack but was unprepared for its ferocity. Redd's punches came in fast and hard, his right arm working like a piston, his fist a pile driver aimed squarely at Baby Boy's face. The biker tried to get his hands up to block the incoming assault, but for every punch he blocked, three more got through.

Baby Boy's face was a mask of blood. It streamed into his eyes. Crimson droplets sprayed in all directions as the rain of blows continued. Unable to mount any kind of defense, the biker fell back to the last refuge of the overwhelmed, punch-drunk fighter—he went for the clinch. Falling forward, he threw his long arms out to wrap Redd in a bear hug and buried his face in Redd's chest. Redd didn't fight the embrace. He simply changed the target of his focused fury, punching down at Baby Boy's exposed back.

Too exhausted to squeeze the life out of Redd, Baby Boy instead started shoving him back toward the dining room. The realization that Baby Boy was going to try to slam him into another wall finally filtered through Redd's black rage. He stopped punching and instead wrapped both arms around Baby Boy's torso and threw his weight sideways. Locked together, they half stumbled, half fell into the kitchen, smashing up against a cupboard.

The collision broke their mutual embrace, but Redd, still burning the rocket fuel of righteous anger, was back in the fight in an instant. He grabbed Baby Boy's leather vest and, using it like the handle of a battering ram, lifted the biker off the ground and heaved him headfirst into the stainless steel door of the dishwasher. The metal buckled under the impact, and when Baby Boy fell away, there was a bloody face print stamped in the metal. Still gripping the vest, Redd drew back and repeated the move.

This time Baby Boy managed to get one of his hands up, planting it on the dishwasher door and pushing back against Redd. The unexpected move unbalanced Redd, causing him to lose his grip on the vest and fall forward into the sink. His chest struck the granite countertop hard enough to make him gasp, but he pushed away, spinning around to face Baby Boy. The biker was already scrambling across the kitchen, presumably trying to put some distance between them.

Too late, Redd spotted the Berserker's real objective—a wooden knife block resting on the counter in one corner. Before Redd could even think about pursuing, the biker grabbed the top knife handle and drew out a long, broad-bladed chef's knife. When he turned to face Redd, his white teeth shone out of his bloody face in a fearsome grim. Then he lunged, swiping the knife before him like a scythe.

Redd had no choice but to retreat. He looked around for something . . . a frying pan, a cutting board, a cookbook . . . anything with which to parry the attack, but the counters were as empty as the void.

Then Baby Boy was directly in front of him, slashing at his face. Redd dropped into a shoulder roll, coming up on the opposite side of the kitchen, right in front of the stainless side-by-side refrigerator. The desperate maneuver only bought him a momentary reprieve. Baby Boy whirled and lunged at him, thrusting the knife out like a bayonet.

Redd sidestepped, and as he did, he yanked the freezer door open, trying to use it as an impromptu shield. Unable to halt his momentum, Baby Boy could not help but jam his blade deep into the contents of the freezer compartment, and before he could even think about withdrawing it, Redd slammed the door shut on his arm, trapping both the limb and the knife. Bracing the door with his body, Redd drove his fist into the side of Baby Boy's head, then punched again and again.

The biker howled, thrashing like a bear caught in a trap. With a titanic effort, he heaved himself against the door with such force that the entire refrigerator began to tilt forward. Redd was forced to retreat again, which allowed Baby Boy to extricate his arm and scramble out of the way of the appliance as it crashed down between them.

Baby Boy had lost his knife in the freezer, but he had found something else. His eyes were ablaze with a fury to match Redd's own. Emily had chosen his nickname well—like a Norse berserker, the hellish battle had not left him weakened but had instead awakened a primal energy. Redd's own rage boost was a mere firecracker compared to the rocket fuel that now suffused his foe.

With a bearish roar, the biker bent forward, grasping the toppled refrigerator with both hands, and drove it into Redd with such speed and ferocity that Redd didn't even have time to think about leaping out of the way.

As the refrigerator took Redd's legs out from under him, he managed to fall forward onto the back of the appliance and just barely had time to get his legs out of the way before it slammed into the cupboards beneath the counter like a wrecking ball.

The cabinet doors were smashed apart. The interior shelves and their contents were driven back into the wall. The top corner of the refrigerator struck just below the kitchen sink, the impact sending up an explosive spray of cleaning solutions and demolishing the drainpipe assembly.

Redd, who had been riding the appliance like a surfer caught in the impact zone, was pitched into the collapsing countertop. The hit left him a little stunned, but the sight of Baby Boy's massive hands reaching for him jolted him into motion. He scrambled back onto an oddly tilted section of granite countertop, narrowly evading the other man's grasp, then spun around and drove his heels at the bloodied mask of Baby Boy's face.

The kick landed solidly, driving Baby Boy back a step, but that was the extent of damage inflicted. The Berserker shook his head like a dog shaking off water, only instead of water he flung a spray of crimson droplets. Then, with another roar, he reached out, gripped the sink in both hands, and ripped it out of the broken countertop. Water supply lines tore loose from their fittings in the demolished under-sink cabinet, unleashing a steady stream of both hot and cold water that poured out from the mess and splashed onto the floor.

The basin was no lightweight aluminum insert but a heavy-duty restaurant-quality prep sink, yet Baby Boy lifted it over his head like it was a beach ball and then proceeded to hurl it at Redd.

The projectile missed Redd by scant inches and instead slammed into the wall above the stovetop with sufficient force to smash through the tile backsplash. There was a loud pop and a brilliant-blue flash from behind the range as the impact from the crashing basin tore the electrical wiring out of the wall socket, and a pall of ozone filled the air.

Redd kept scrambling across the countertop, trying to put some distance between himself and the enraged Berserker, but Baby Boy clambered over the wreckage with a speed and agility that seemed impossible for someone so big.

Redd felt something clamp down on his left ankle, and then he was yanked back, hauled in like a prize fish. Frantic, he grabbed ahold of the first thing within reach, which turned out to be the console for the electric range, and held on with all his might while kicking back with his right foot. His heel struck something solid and mashed down hard, trying to strip the hold, but Baby Boy's fingers were vise grips. The big biker kept pulling, and despite its mass, the range wasn't heavy enough to anchor Redd. With Redd still clinging to it, the oven-stove combo slid out of its niche, exposing the ruined wall behind it.

Realizing that he could not hope to break free through resistance, Redd stopped struggling and instead braced his hands against the range console and pushed away, thrusting himself toward the big man.

Fully controlled as he was by primitive instincts, Baby Boy did not immediately grasp Redd's intentions. Sensing success, he hauled Redd in closer, which was exactly what Redd was counting on. With a final push away from the stovetop, Redd whipped his body around, wrapping his free leg around Baby Boy's neck, practically sitting on the big man's shoulders. His right leg remained caught, but he was able to twist in the Berserker's grasp just enough to bring his feet together, hooking his left leg under the right, closing the scissor hold.

Baby Boy did what anyone facing a similar situation would do—he grabbed Redd's right leg with his other hand and began trying to pry them apart. Unlike most people in that situation, however, Baby Boy was actually strong enough to do it. Although he was squeezing his thighs together with every ounce of his strength, Redd felt his ankle lock separating. He heaved sideways, trying to unbalance the big man, but had already lost his hold and instead of taking Baby Boy down, he merely went sprawling, splashing down on a floor that was awash under an inch of foamy water spraying from the broken sink lines.

As he slid through a mess of spilled food from the refrigerator and other random pieces of debris, Redd knew that he would not be able to overpower his foe. Everything he tried, every blow he struck, only seemed to energize Baby Boy.

Think! he raged at himself. *Fight smart.*

He looked around for a weapon, something he could use to amplify his flagging strength . . . a bludgeon with which to beat back the relentless Berserker . . . but there was nothing of sufficient size or heft within reach. And Baby Boy was coming for him again.

Redd backpedaled away, his feet slipping uncertainly on the slick tile, then felt a solid wall behind him. There was nowhere left to go.

In desperation, he braced his back against the wall, and as Baby Boy pounced on him, Redd drove out with both feet. As before, the kick knocked the Berserker back, but this time, unbalanced and unable to find purchase on the slippery floor, Baby Boy began flailing and skating in a futile effort to stay upright. Seizing the opportunity, Redd sprang to his feet and, once more pushing off the wall, launched himself at Baby Boy, slamming into him and propelling the big man into the exposed niche where the range had been.

Baby Boy crashed into the already-damaged wall, falling in a tangle of gypsum drywall and pink Owens Corning insulation. He twisted around, groping for something to hold on to in order to pick himself up, then abruptly went rigid, his body jerking taut like an overwound guitar string. His eyes rolled back in his head and a gurgling sound slipped from between clenched teeth. The strange seizure lasted only a few seconds; then the biker went completely limp as if his very bones had dissolved.

A fresh tang of ozone in the air illuminated what had happened. Baby Boy had inadvertently grabbed the exposed wires of the oven-range's 220-volt power supply line. Because most of his body was in contact with the floor and thus grounded, Baby Boy had not merely received a nasty shock but had been fully electrocuted.

Redd guessed that the short circuit had probably tripped a breaker and that there was no longer current flowing through the wires, but he wasn't going to take the chance of going in for a closer look. He watched Baby Boy's still form from a safe distance but saw no rise and fall of the chest to indicate breathing, no stirring to wakefulness. The electrical current had stopped the Berserker's heart.

Baby Boy was stone-dead.

THIRTY-NINE

When he was certain that the Berserker would never rise again, Redd got to his feet and hurried to the great room, where he found Emily stirring. Aside from an angry welt on her cheek, she appeared uninjured, but he was nevertheless gentle as he wrapped her in his arms.

"Em," he whispered. "Thank God."

"Matty," she murmured, returning the embrace. After a moment, she let go and looked around. "Is he . . . ?"

"He's dead."

"Good." He felt her shudder in his arms and gave her a reassuring squeeze before releasing her. "Can you walk on your own? We should probably get out of here."

"I can walk." Despite this assurance, she was a bit unsteady as she rose to her feet, so he held on to her.

"I'm okay," she said after a moment, then looked around again. "Oh no!"

Emily pulled free of him and hurried over to kneel beside the bloody, unmoving form of Angela Townsend. Redd had seen the exit wound left by the .44 Magnum round, so he was surprised to hear Emily cry out, "She's still alive! Quick, help me out here."

By the time Redd reached her side, Emily already had both hands pressing down on the woman's chest, applying pressure to stanch the flow of blood. "Find me something I can use as a pressure bandage," she said. "And call 911!"

Redd grabbed a couple throw pillows off the floor and shoved them under Townsend's limp legs, then searched his pockets for his phone. Realizing that he must have lost it back at the ranch, he began searching the room for either a telephone or material for bandages. As he did, he spied the map book on the floor, still open and spattered with Townsend's blood. His gaze lingered on it only for a moment; then he moved into the shambles that was the kitchen.

He began opening cupboards and drawers and soon found a stack of neatly folded dish towels. He grabbed them all and hurried back to Emily. "Will these work?"

She nodded, folding one several times until it was a thick block of cloth and pressing it down on the chest wound. "Did you call 911?"

"Haven't found a phone yet."

"Use mine. Back pocket." She rose up a little and cocked her hip to the side to give him better access. He carefully dipped his fingers in and withdrew her iPhone, which, thankfully, had not been damaged by her fall.

Redd didn't bother keying in her passcode but used the emergency call feature to bypass the phone's security measures. A few seconds later, the voice of an emergency dispatcher sounded in his ear.

"Nine-one-one, what's your emergency?"

"Send an ambulance. A woman has been shot."

"What's your name, sir?"

"Uh . . ." Redd hesitated, not sure he wanted to reveal that information.

"Put it on speaker," Emily said without taking her eyes or her hands off Townsend.

Redd did as directed. "You're on."

"This is Dr. Emily Redd." She rattled off the address of Townsend's home, which Redd had already forgotten, then launched into a description of Townsend and her injuries.

"Emergency services are en route," the dispatcher said when she finished. "ETA, five minutes. Please stay on the line."

Emergency services, Redd thought. That didn't mean just an ambulance. The police would come too, and even though killing Baby Boy had been an act of self-defense, Redd couldn't afford to be detained while the police tried to decide whether his actions had been justified.

He reached out and thumbed the Mute button on the phone. "Em, I have to go."

"Go? Go where?"

"After them."

She shook her head. "No, Matty. That can wait."

"No. It can't—not if they're working with Gage. I'm sorry." Redd unmuted the phone, placed it on the floor beside her, and stood up.

"Matty." For the first time, she looked away from Townsend and up to Redd. He saw tears forming at the corners of her eyes. "Be careful. Please?"

He nodded, even though he didn't think he would have that luxury. He made a quick sweep of the room, realizing for the first time just how bad the damage was. His fight with Baby Boy had left the home looking like someone took a wrecking ball to it. He found Emily's .38 and the Ruger; then with both weapons tucked in his belt, Redd headed for the door.

"Wait!" Emily cried.

He stopped but didn't turn.

"Take the map."

"I don't need it. I know where they are."

"*I* don't," she said. "Take the map."

He nodded slowly in understanding. When the police arrived and questioned her, as they surely would, they would ask where he had gone. Without the map book, she would be able to answer truthfully that she did not know.

Smart.

Redd grabbed the atlas off the floor, then started for the front door again. "I love you, Matty."

This time he did turn. "I love you, Em." He was going to leave it at that but then had a sudden compulsion to add, "I'll see you soon."

Just before turning her attention back to Angela Townsend, she smiled—tears now streaming down her face—and said, "You'd better."

Once Redd was sitting down behind the wheel, the adrenaline that had sustained him through the fight with Baby Boy quickly ebbed, leaving him sore and exhausted. He thought about stopping at a convenience store to get a cup of coffee or an energy drink, but one look in the mirror told him that was a bad idea. He was covered in blood, only some of it his own, and would definitely make a lasting impression on anyone who saw him. He had to settle for rolling down the windows and letting the cool mountain air blast through the Tahoe's interior, hoping the chill would keep him from falling asleep at the wheel.

As he left Helena behind, his thoughts turned to the matter of his destination. The Infidels had established their temporary headquarters on the old Gage Food Trust compound, where Anton Gage had attempted to cultivate a genetically modified strain of wheat designed to drastically reduce world population.

To the best of Redd's knowledge, all of Gage's assets in Montana—and everywhere else—had been seized and were currently in a state of legal limbo while the search for Gage was ongoing. That a gang of outlaw bikers might want to squat on the abandoned property was not at all unusual, but the Infidels were not simply occupying the site. Angela Townsend must have secured permission for them. Whether this was from a legal representative of the Gage Food Trust or from Anton Gage himself was something Townsend would probably never be able to tell him, but the coincidence left Redd feeling uneasy.

What were the odds that a new enemy would have chosen to plant their flag on territory once claimed by an old enemy?

Redd thought about what Kline had told him. *"We've got intel that he's planning something big. Targeting the food supply again."*

If the Infidels had forged some kind of alliance with Gage, just as Gage was about to make his move, then the timing of their campaign against Redd was doubly suspicious.

But was it just a marriage of convenience? Or were the Infidels playing some greater role in Gage's plot?

He shook his head. The likelier explanation was that Gage was the one piggybacking, using the Infidels to exact his own revenge against Redd for the death of his daughter, Hannah.

An image of Hannah Gage—beautiful but psychotic—flashed in his mind's eye. Redd had not, in fact, been the one to take Hannah's life. Emily had, saving Redd's life in the process, but Gage couldn't have known that.

But the timing . . .

Redd brushed the concern away. He had to stay focused on the immediate threat. Baby Boy might be dead, but Angry Johnny and the rest of the gang were still out there, still on the warpath. There could be no peace between him and them—no truce, no cease-fire.

Will it ever end?

The Infidels could not be reasoned with, could not be negotiated with. They had proved that when they'd murdered Duke Blanton. They were no different from al Qaeda or ISIS or any of the fanatical terrorists he'd fought against overseas.

But Redd wasn't the same man now that he was then. And he wasn't overseas.

Battered, beaten, and tired beyond words, he wanted the fighting to stop. A year ago, maybe two, he would have reasoned that the Infidels, all of them, deserved to die. Now he didn't believe that was up to him. It wasn't just the teachings he'd learned on the Sundays he did make it to church that gnawed at him. It was the realization that he wanted a different life. He *had* a different life now.

I have to protect my family.

Still, he knew he couldn't fight them all. Not by himself.

For the moment, Redd decided to focus on just those bikers waiting at the GFT campus. The force that had assaulted the ranch was only a fraction of those he'd seen at the Buffalo Jump, and there was no knowing if the gathering at the roadhouse represented the club's full strength, but it was safe to assume that he would be going up against twenty or more bikers.

A frontal assault was out of the question.

There were just four rounds in the Ruger's cylinder. He'd reloaded the .38 from the box of shells and could do so again if circumstances allowed—which was doubtful. But even if he made every shot count—which was also doubtful—he'd still come up short. Just as at the ranch, he was going to have to use stealth to adjust the odds in his favor.

From that realization, a plan began to form. And Redd knew exactly what he had to do next.

FORTY

Although it meant risking exposure, Redd made a reconnaissance pass, driving by the entrance to the old Gage Food Trust campus at regular highway speed, surveying the landscape and trying to identify possible enemy positions. Unfortunately, there was not much to see.

The single-story concrete buildings were just visible from the road, but if there were any bikers hanging out in the open, they were too far away to see with the unaided eye. Redd was more interested in getting a feel for the surrounding terrain.

Less than two years ago, the fields outside the complex had been planted with endless rows of wheat, which Gage had then burned in an attempt to destroy the evidence of his scheme to cause mass sterilization. Nature had evidently reclaimed the burned fields, which now served as forage for a large herd of bison. Redd guessed there were at least two hundred animals meandering out in the open.

The mere fact of their presence was unusual. To the best of Redd's knowledge, there were hardly any truly free-roaming herds in Montana.

Wild bison could be found in Yellowstone National Park and on a couple of remote preserves, but they did not range across open land like elk or moose. Most bison in the state were semidomesticated stock animals, being raised for meat by ranchers or Native American tribes. Either a canny rancher had found a way to move his herd onto the unused rangeland or these were mavericks, a feral population thriving on its own.

Redd had already determined that the best way into the compound was by traveling overland on foot. His plan was to get within sight of the facility and then wait for nightfall—still about an hour and a half away—after which he would rely on the cover of darkness to close the remaining distance. The bison would provide some concealment during his approach, though he would have to give them plenty of room. The creatures weren't normally aggressive toward humans, but they would nevertheless react if they felt threatened. Although their bulky bodies supported by short, almost-spindly legs made them appear ponderous, even lethargic, when charging, they could quickly achieve and sustain speeds close to forty miles per hour—similar to a bull. And with an average weight of between one and two thousand pounds depending on maturity, getting hit by a charging bison was literally like getting hit by a car.

The gate at the entrance was closed, but as he cruised past, he saw movement in the guard shack, which he hoped meant that the Infidels had not yet abandoned the site. He drove past without slowing and continued on to Voight, where he turned around and headed back down the highway. About five miles west of the entrance, and a good mile beyond the bison herd, he spotted an overgrown access road leading out into the field, blocked by a simple wire fence gate. He pulled into it and after a back-and-forth shuffle to open the gate and then close it behind him, he slowly drove out into the field.

When he was sure the SUV would not be visible from the road, he parked, got out, and started walking. He kept more or less parallel to the road, moving at a casual pace but constantly checking in all directions. If it did not exactly soothe his battered muscles, the walk at least helped him stay limber and, counterintuitively, reenergized him. The quiet was a little unnerving, though. Aside from the occasional rumble of a truck on the highway, the only sound was the crunch of his boot soles on the ground— a noise that seemed ridiculously loud amid the silence of open range. Soon he began to perceive other sounds—insects buzzing and chirping, the rustle of small rodents darting about, and the faint chain-saw buzz of bellowing bison carried on the breeze.

When he spied a small cluster of grazing bison, he changed course, giving them a wide berth, and slowed his pace. He spent the next hour weaving between little groups of the shaggy beasts, watching for any signs of agitation. The farther along he went, the denser the population of animals became. To keep making forward progress, he had to risk ever-closer encounters. For the most part, the bison continued to ignore him, far more interested in their foraging than in a puny man they could demolish without a second thought. When he did get a little too close, they let him know with a snort and a bellow, to which he responded by quickly backing off. Finally, as the sun was just kissing the mountaintops to the west, he spied the rectangular outline of a man-made structure, and not long thereafter, the herd began to thin. Rather than risk being spotted by someone in the compound, he decided to hunker down and wait for the sky to darken just a little bit more.

Without the rhythmic crunch of his footsteps, the aural landscape surrounding him seemed to grow louder and more distinct, but one sound stood out among the others—the deep, resonant thump of a bass guitar amplified by a big woofer speaker.

Music. More accurately, judging by the beat, heavy metal.

No wonder the bison don't want to come any closer, Redd mused. *At least now I know somebody's home.*

When twilight deepened enough to allow the brightest stars to appear in the firmament, Redd resumed his advance, staying low to avoid creating a distinctive man-shaped silhouette. After another fifty yards, he was able to distinguish the other instruments being played, though the song was not one he recognized. He'd grown up on what was, even then, considered classic rock—Zeppelin and Skynyrd—and some country music. You couldn't live in Montana and not listen to country. Old-school Metallica was about as hard as he had ever rocked. But the heavy metal rampage was good for one thing—nobody would hear him coming.

Another fifty yards brought him close enough to see vehicles—motorcycles, but also a few cars and pickups—in a large parking lot. Farther out, the orange-yellow glow of a bonfire gave off light without providing any real illumination. The flickering flames and the faint smell of woodsmoke were an all-too-painful reminder of what the Infidels had taken from him.

Redd watched for a few minutes without moving, noting the silhouettes of several people meandering about the bonfire. The fire seemed to be a hub of activity, so Redd decided to make it the last stop on his tour of the compound.

He was just about to pick up and continue on his way when he heard a rustling sound from directly behind him. He froze. It was probably just one of the bison, looking for somewhere new to graze, but he wasn't going to bet his life on it. Moving slowly, he reached down and drew the .38 from his belt, then, lightning quick, rolled over onto his back, aiming the revolver into the darkness. It was still for a moment, but Redd waited. Then it happened.

Bathed in moonlight, the shadowy outline of a man emerged.

FORTY-ONE

"Don't shoot me, Matt," said a familiar voice.

"Gavin?" In the darkness, Redd could only just make out the shape of the man, but there was no mistaking the voice. He lowered the Smith & Wesson. "I *should* shoot you. What are you doing here?"

With the music still pulsing out at an ear-shattering decibel level, there was little risk of being overheard.

"What do you think? I'm trying to keep you from getting yourself killed."

"Well, gee, thanks. But I've been doing just fine without you."

"Oh, cut it out, Matty."

"I told you—"

"Matthew. Sorry. Old habits." Kline squatted down beside him, close enough now that Redd could make out his features. "Look, I'm not here to talk you out of this, if that's what you think. I heard what you've been going through, and believe me, I'm just as pissed off as you are. I'm here to help."

Redd shook his head. This was classic Kline—showing up at the last second like the cavalry coming over the hill, thinking that would somehow make up for squandering a lifetime's worth of opportunities to be a father.

"How did you find me?" Even as he asked the question, he knew the answer. "Emily called you."

"No," said another voice from behind Kline. "She called *me*. I called him."

"Mikey?"

The vague outline of a second man appeared beside the first. "Emily told me to pick him up and to find you. She said you'd need our help, and well, since you keep refusing to let me know before you go playing lone wolf—" Mikey shrugged—"I didn't have the chance to run anything by you. So here we are."

"I meant how did you find me out *here?*"

Kline answered that one. "When Emily mentioned that these outlaw bikers were hiding out at a place owned by Anton Gage, it wasn't too hard to put two and two together. You're lucky I could only get a late flight. I was in the security line when Mike here called me."

"Lucky?" Redd snorted.

Kline ignored the comment. "It also helped that I was able to track the GPS in your Tahoe."

"What GPS?"

Kline chuckled. "I thought you knew. Most newer cars are chipped. All it takes is a phone call and a VIN to get your location."

"Don't you need a warrant for that?"

"Only if I wanted to prosecute you for something." Kline smiled. "Once we found your rig, Mike was able to track you cross-country."

Redd glanced over at Mikey. "You tracked me?"

Mikey nodded.

"I'm impressed."

"So," Kline said, "now that we're all caught up, what's your plan?"

"Easy. I'm going to sneak in there and kill 'em all." He said it as a matter of fact, daring either man to question his determination. To his astonishment, they did not.

"We saw your place," Mikey said, as if that was all the explanation he needed. "We saw what they did. That why you're here?"

"Because they turned my home into a pile of ash and burned everything I own? No. They also sent their biggest goon to shoot their lawyer, Angela Townsend, and take me and Emily out too. If I don't kill them, they'll never stop. It's as simple as that."

Mikey let out a sigh as he nodded. "That *big* biker? The one who scared Emily to start all this mess?"

"Yeah, he came to finish the job."

"And from the looks of it," Kline shot, his eyes scanning Redd up and down, "he was almost successful. You gotta stop picking fights with guys bigger than you."

Tell me about it, Redd thought. "He's dead now."

There was a moment of silence, until Gavin finally spoke.

"I agree. We have to take them down. But we also have to be smart about this."

"*We?*"

"We're with you, Matt," Mikey said. "Like it or not, you're not going it alone this time."

"Mikey, I appreciate it, but you're not trained for this. Does Liz even know you're out here? If something happens to you—"

"I can shoot." He held out an oblong object that, even in the dark, Redd easily recognized as Mikey's Remington Model 700 hunting rifle. "I can provide covering fire from here."

Redd wasn't sure how Mikey knew about the concept of cover fire but assumed he probably read about it in one of his favorite thrillers or saw it in a movie.

"We can use him," Kline said, his reproof absolute. "And while you may think I'm just a washed-up bureaucrat, I *am* trained for this. I was a jarhead just like you. Granted, three against however many they have is not ideal, but it's a lot better than you trying to do this on your own."

Redd knew he wasn't going to talk them out of helping, and if he was being honest, he welcomed the assistance, even from Kline. But there was no way he'd admit that out loud. "Fine," he finally said after a long sigh, "but we're still going to do this my way."

"'Sneak in there and kill 'em all'?" Kline mimicked. "That's not a plan. It's a prescription for suicide. And if by some miracle we make it out alive, we'll spend the rest of our lives in prison."

Redd threw his hands up. "If this is your idea of helping—"

"Just hear me out. We can't do this like you did in the corps. Extrajudicial killing and vigilante justice is murder, no matter how much they deserve it. But if we do this right, the law will be on our side."

"So what? We try to arrest them first and kill them when they resist?"

"Not to put too fine a point on it, but yes. We get in close enough, announce ourselves, and tell them to surrender. I think we both know how that's going to go over. Once they engage, anyone still holding a weapon is a legitimate target."

Redd narrowed his eyes. "And that's not suicide?"

"Not if we choose the battlefield. We can keep them contained in between those buildings. Kind of like what King Leonidas did at the Battle of Thermopylae."

"You do remember how that ended?"

Kline shrugged. "Our odds will be better."

Redd sighed. He looked to Mikey, knowing that if they had any chance of surviving, his friend would have to do a lot more than just laying down suppressive fire. Mikey was a good shot, he knew that, but Redd also knew firsthand that killing a person wasn't the same as shooting a deer.

"You don't have to do this, Mikey. Really. You have a family, man. You don't need to be mixed up in all this stuff."

"I know" was Mikey's somber reply. "But you'd do it for me, and if a man can't fight for his friends and family, then what kind of man is he?"

Redd gripped his friend's shoulder. "I hope you still feel that way tomorrow."

✖   ✖   ✖

After sketching out the finer details of the plan, Redd and Kline headed out, circling south toward the entrance and moving to the complex under cover of darkness to reach the outermost building, which had once been the security office.

Fifteen months earlier, Redd *had* done things the Marine Corps way, smashing in doors with a splitting maul and moving room to room, engaging in close combat with Anton Gage's security force. Despite the passage of time, the battle scars were still visible. The doors he'd battered down and the windows that had been shot up had not been replaced or even boarded over. The facility was too far off the beaten path to become a haven for squatters or even schoolkids looking for a place to hang out and party, and with Gage on the run and his assets frozen, nobody cared enough to take even cursory security measures. A quick glance inside confirmed that things were pretty much unchanged since his last visit. There was no sign that the Infidels or anyone else was actively using the building. He made a rolling motion, signaling to Kline that they should keep going.

The plan did not call for them to clear all the buildings, but only to make sure that nobody would be able to come in from behind them. The next structure they approached appeared to be similarly empty, as was the next one after that. Evidently the Infidels had elected to stay in close proximity to each other rather than spreading out and occupying all the buildings on the campus.

That, Redd thought, would make things easier.

But as they moved closer to the bonfire, Redd's instincts began to tingle a warning. The music was still pumping out at jet-engine intensity, but aside from that, things were . . . quiet.

Too quiet.

There was no movement around the fire. Nobody getting up to grab another beer or relieve themselves. It was almost as if, having built the fire like a beacon to draw them in, the Infidels had slunk away into the night.

Redd paused at the edge of the old laboratory building, the bonfire just thirty yards away, pouring light past the corner. He debated whether to ease out from his place of concealment and issue the challenge that would initiate the fighting or listen to his gut and retreat to a safe distance to rethink the direct approach.

"What's wrong?" Kline whispered.

"Not sure." That was as close as he could come to putting his apprehension into words.

"If you've got a bad feeling," Kline said as if reading his mind, "listen to it."

Even in the height of that moment, it wasn't lost on Redd that Kline had once listened to his own bad gut feeling. And though he hated to admit it, it had ultimately saved his life.

Redd nodded. "Something's not right here."

"Want to pull the plug?"

Redd considered the question a second longer than he probably should have. His internal alarm was screaming at him, and the only thing preventing him from making a hasty retreat was stubbornness.

Good sense finally won out. "Yeah, let's back off."

Keeping the .38 at the high ready, he started backing away.

The music abruptly stopped.

Redd froze.

The sudden silence was eerily reminiscent of his visit to the Buffalo Jump, but this time he felt far more vulnerable.

"I think we need to go," Kline hissed. *"Now!"*

"I think you're—"

"Leaving so soon?" The sardonic voice boomed from the speakers that had just moments before been pumping out heavy metal mayhem. "Why don't you come on in? The party's just getting started."

Redd recognized the voice immediately.

Angry Johnny.

FORTY-TWO

Bright lights—high-intensity LED flashlights, Redd guessed—appeared along the roof of the laboratory building, shining down on the two men, transfixing them, blinding them.

Redd cursed his own stupidity . . . his arrogance.

He had underestimated his foe, rushed headlong into battle, trusting his own abilities and the purity of his purpose to overcome the numerical odds. He had not stopped to consider that his enemy might be smarter than he gave them credit for.

"Seriously," Johnny said with a steely edge to his electronically amplified voice. "Come to the fire. I'd hate to have to shoot you both like dogs in the street. Trust me when I say that, from up here, we won't miss."

Redd involuntarily glanced up, trying to distinguish the men behind the flashlights. He couldn't tell how many guns were aimed at them, but even one was one too many.

"When Baby Boy didn't check in, I figured I'd be seeing you," Johnny continued. "He told me he could take care of you by himself, but I had a feeling things might not go his way."

"I'm going to draw their fire," Kline whispered. "When I do, run."

"Forget it. I'm not leaving you here."

"Matty, just listen for—"

A shot rang out, the bullet raising a puff of dust not two feet from where Redd stood. He could feel particles of grit on the exposed skin of his hands.

"That's your only warning," Johnny admonished.

Redd took a step forward, his right hand raised, letting the .38 dangle by the trigger guard from his index finger. "You want to talk?" he shouted. "Why don't you come down here so we can do this man-to-man?"

"Matt!" This time Kline didn't bother trying to keep his voice low.

Johnny laughed. "You've got guts, I'll give you that. You know, I thought about offering you a chance to join us. You defeated Baby Boy, and that's a pretty impressive thing. But fundamentally, your will is too weak. Your devotion to your woman . . . to your country . . . to the values of this bloated, moribund *society* . . ." He spat the last word out like a bitter taste. "Your attachments make you weak. Vulnerable. You're not worthy to be one of us."

"Tough talk from someone who won't even look me in the eye," Redd retorted. "Come on. What are you afraid of? You wanted to talk. Let's talk about how much Anton Gage paid you to come after me."

Judging by the silence that followed, the accusation had struck a nerve. Then Angry Johnny's laughter filled the air again. "He didn't have to pay me a red cent for you. After the way you disrespected our colors, I would have paid *him* for the chance to take you out."

"So you *are* working for him."

"For. With. Take your pick. We have a mutual interest. *You.* Or more to the point, making you suffer."

Kline had fallen silent during the exchange, evidently still processing these revelations. Redd was too. Why *had* the Infidels chosen to ally with Gage? Why had they waited so long to make their move against him?

The timing . . .

Realization dawned. "He knows," Redd murmured. "He knows what Gage is up to."

"All the more reason for one of us to make it out of here," Kline said.

Redd shook his head, then shouted once more. "This is between you and me. So let's settle it that way. Just the two of us. If you're man enough, that is."

"Sorry, but that's not how this is going to go down. You're going to die. Probably right where you're standing."

"Is that your idea of making me suffer?"

"Oh, you'll suffer. You'll die knowing that you failed to protect your family. Because I am going to find them. Don't worry, though. I'm not going to kill them. Oh no. That would be such a waste. Do you have any idea how much I can get for a healthy white baby? I don't know—maybe you'll find it comforting to know that a stranger will raise your child, give him a better life than you ever could. But he'll never even know you existed. Your woman might fetch a decent price too, though after we get done with her, I don't know how much value she'll still have." Several throaty chuckles broke out, sounding somewhere behind Johnny.

Redd's pulse quickened with a flush of anger, which was no doubt exactly what Angry Johnny was hoping for. But before he could allow that impulse to become action, something slammed into him, knocking him sideways.

"Run, Matty!" Kline cried, charging out into the open and then firing his service weapon at the nearest rooftop.

Redd barely had time to register what was happening as return fire began raining down from above. Rounds split the air all around him, kicking up dust and grit on impact, but miraculously, none from the initial volley found him. The same was not true for Kline. Redd saw a spray of blood, dark in the glow of the firelight, and then Kline was stumbling . . . falling . . .

"Gavin!"

"Run!" Kline said again, but this time his weak shout was barely audible over the din.

In the instant that followed, Redd made the only decision he could. As much as he hated the idea of leaving a fallen comrade—even one with whom he had such a troubled relationship—if he stayed and died alongside Kline, the man's sacrifice would be rendered meaningless. One of them had to make it out alive, if only to let someone know that Anton Gage and the Infidels were working together and that there was a lot more to their partnership than anyone realized.

So without looking back, Redd veered off and began running full speed as bullets chased after him. Something slapped against his left thigh, and he knew he'd been hit, but he felt no pain and the limb did not fail him. When the rounds started falling ahead of him, he threw himself into a sideways combat roll and headed in a different direction. Three seconds later, he changed direction again and made a mad dash for the shadows near another building.

The flashlights followed him. Up on the roof, the Infidels were running to the northwest corner of the building in order to light up the darkness where Redd was seeking refuge. Redd, however, did not stop once he reached the shadows but instead pivoted and ran the other way, out into the open, toward the edge of the campus and the field beyond.

Mikey, he thought, *now would be a good time to start shooting!*

For all he knew, Mikey might already have started laying down suppressive fire. In the tumult, the report of the Remington would have been just one more loud noise. The flashlight beams continued to chase after him, spotlighting him out in the open, but as Redd left the gravel lanes of the compound behind and reached the scrub terrain of the rewilded fields, the intensity of enemy fire from behind fell off and then ceased altogether. In the silence that followed, Redd heard a different noise—the unmistakable, throaty roar of motorcycle engines.

A lot of them.

FORTY-THREE

The bikes swarmed out of the compound like an army of angry wasps. There were too many to count, but Redd guessed they numbered at least twenty and probably closer to thirty. Their headlights lanced through the darkness, illuminating Redd from behind and casting a bizarre shadow across the landscape. When the first of the riders ventured beyond the graded parking area, the lights seemed to jump up and down randomly as the bikes negotiated the irregular surface. Redd knew they were road bikes, built for rolling across miles of pavement, not all-terrain vehicles. Still, even traveling at the relatively slow speeds demanded by the rough terrain, he didn't figure he had very long before they would overtake him.

The good news was that while they were riding, they weren't shooting.

After running for almost a full minute, Redd wheeled around, took aim at what looked like the closest bobbing headlight, and pulled the trigger. The light stayed on, and the bike kept coming. He steadied his hand and fired the .38 again, to no better effect. The motorcycle was just out of the effective range of the revolver, and if he waited for them to get close enough that his shots would count, they'd be on him.

Boom!

Another report suddenly split the night, echoing from the compound walls, and the headlight of the bike closing in on Redd suddenly dropped over onto the ground, sliding a few yards before going still.

"Thank you, Mikey," Redd muttered, turning to resume his run.

The first shot, however, seemed to have been more a matter of luck than skill. More shots followed in quick succession, but none of them seemed to find a target. And the bikers were closing in. Fast.

And then, before he could even begin to think about how he was going to fight back, a motorcycle shot past him, about twenty yards to his right. There were two more right behind it. As soon as they were past, the three turned across his path, moving to cut him off.

Redd did the only thing he could. He veered left, trying to get around them before they closed in, but even as he did, more bikes shot past on that side. He glanced back and saw the bulk of the pack, at least a dozen bikes, riding side by side in a picket line.

Redd stopped again, turned, took aim with the .38, and fired at the centermost headlight. The light winked out. Redd couldn't tell if his bullet had done any more damage than that, so he fired again, aiming at another headlight near the middle of the picket line. He fired two more shots, then heard the hammer snap against a spent primer.

The .38 was empty.

Tossing it aside, Redd drew the Ruger. The picket line was so close now that he couldn't miss. Deafened by the din, he didn't hear a bike closing in on him from behind. As he was leveling the .44 Magnum, a length of chain struck his leg with sufficient force to knock him off his feet.

Ignoring the flare of pain where the chain had made contact, he scrambled up but spied another bike careening toward him and had to fling himself out the of the way. The bikes were all around him, circling him like Lakota and Cheyenne warriors around Custer's Seventh Cavalry. He brought the Ruger up, tried to aim, but the riders were moving too fast, their headlights flashing in every direction in a seizure-inducing shadow show.

Suddenly one of the headlights began whipping around crazily, lofting off the ground and spinning completely around as it sailed away from the rest of the pack. Redd's eyes were drawn to the movement, and as he turned toward it, another light bounced into the air, this one heading right toward him. He dove to the side, barely evading a motorcycle tumbling through the air above him. As it flew past, he glimpsed another twisting figure—a man in black leather, arms and legs flailing.

Redd's initial assumption was that two of the Infidels had inadvertently collided. He could think of no other force capable of launching one of the eight-hundred-pound motorcycles into the air. But then another rider-less bike sailed out across the circle. This time Redd could hear the solid crunch of an impact. And he could feel the ground shaking beneath him.

More bikes went flying through the air, tumbling end over end like bowling pins after a solid strike. The rest of the motorcycles broke forma-tion and wheeled toward the compound. That was when Redd heard an ominous, bone-shaking rumble growing louder by the moment.

When he'd been stationed in California, he'd experienced too many minor earthquakes to count. This was like one of those only much, much worse, because the shaking was just a precursor of something far more terrifying.

The bison are stampeding.

In the diffuse glow of scattered headlights, Redd could just make out their shaggy forms. Several had already passed him and were charging after the fleeing motorcycles, the source of their agitation. Those, Redd knew, would be the largest bulls, seeking out and pursuing the perceived threat to the herd. At six feet in height, weighing nearly a ton, and moving at close to forty miles an hour, they were an unstoppable force of nature. But they were just the vanguard. Behind them, the cows and young calves—smaller but just as motivated and far more numerous—would sweep across the landscape like a tsunami.

And Redd was in their path.

He could not hope to outrun them, and trying to dodge out of the way seemed like a similarly foolish strategy. While they would not be running shoulder to shoulder, in the darkness, they would be on him before he knew it, and even a glancing hit would knock him down to be crushed under their hooves.

He looked around, desperate to find some place to shelter from the onrushing wave, and spied the remains of one of the Infidels' motorcycles some twenty yards away. The front wheel was missing and the steering assembly was twisted, but the headlight continued to shine, its beam illuminating the dust-heavy air. The current condition of the vehicle testified to the fact that it would not offer much real protection from the charging creatures, but Redd was hoping that, now that it no longer posed any sort of threat, real or merely perceived, the stampede would go around it.

It was a slim hope, but better than nothing, so he shoved the unfired Ruger into his belt and took off in a sprint.

No sooner had he started running than a bulky form flashed across his path. Had he moved a fraction of a second sooner, the beast would have hit him head-on, but instead, Redd merely struck its heavy flank as it passed by. The impact spun him around and he went down, sliding on his face. Frantic, he didn't try to get up but monkey-crawled the last few feet to the broken motorcycle. As soon as he reached it, he ducked down behind it, wrapping his arms around the gas tank cover and hugging it to his chest.

A moment later, the thundering of hoofbeats reached a crescendo as the wave broke over him.

FORTY-FOUR

The noise and fury were like nothing Redd had dreamed possible. The closest thing he could imagine was being downrange in a mortar bombardment but with the frequency of machine-gun fire. He understood now what shell shock really meant.

Head down, he felt more than saw the movement of massive bodies around and above him. Most of the bison treated the broken motorcycle as an inert obstacle in their path. Those that could not veer around it simply leaped over it with surprising grace. One of them, however, must have either decided the bike still posed a threat or missed his cue to jump, because in the midst of the tumult, the bike took a solid blow that sent it—and Redd—spinning.

The hit nearly shook him loose. As he held on for dear life, he felt the secondary impacts of hooves glancing off his back, but once the bike stopped moving, the pounding stopped.

Another hit followed, though this one was a mere bump by comparison to the first, and amid the relentless shaking of the ground, Redd almost didn't notice it.

The vibration overwhelmed his nerves like an electrical current. The air, thick with dust and redolent with the musky smell of the bison, felt stifling. Just trying to draw a breath was almost impossible. Yet even worse than the sensory assault was the knowledge that thousand-plus-pound behemoths were leaping over him and that any one of them might, with just a slight miscalculation, stomp him into oblivion.

And then, as quickly as it had begun, the ordeal ended. Redd held on a few seconds longer before cautiously raising his head. The darkness that enveloped him was absolute.

His arms ached and it took real effort to unclench them and let go of the motorcycle. Once free of it, he rolled over onto all fours and laboriously got to his feet.

He was pleasantly surprised to find the Ruger still in his belt. He didn't know how many Infidels had survived the stampede or if any had found refuge in the campus and wondered if the four Magnum rounds would be enough.

One problem at a time.

Turning slowly, he oriented himself in the direction of the diminishing rumble of the stampede and was about to start back toward the buildings when he heard someone shouting his name.

Mikey.

Gratified to know that his friend had managed to avoid getting trampled, Redd tried to shout back, but his mouth was so thick with dust that no sound came out. He cupped a hand over his ear, trying to pinpoint his friend's location.

"Matt!"

Redd licked his lips and swallowed, trying to create some saliva to rinse away the dust, then tried again. "Over here!"

"Matt!" There was audible relief in Mikey's voice, which was getting louder by the second. "I can't believe you're alive, bro."

"Yeah" was all Redd could think to say. Some of the dust was settling, and through the gloom, Redd could see a fuzzy glow. "I see a light. Is that you?"

The light began moving back and forth, signaling. "This is me. I'm using the flashlight on my phone."

Redd smiled, then started toward the light. When they met up, Mikey threw his arms around Redd in a bear hug, and Redd, who would never consider himself much of a hugger, returned it, pounding his friend on the back. After a couple seconds, Mikey released him and stepped back, holding the light up and examining Redd. "You look awful, man. And that's really saying something, because you looked like hell before getting trampled in a stampede."

"Thanks."

Mikey pointed to Redd's thigh. Despite, or maybe because of the liberal coating of dirt, there was a conspicuous dark blotch on the denim of his Wranglers. "Is that blood?"

There was a long tear in the fabric, surrounded by a dark-red crust. Redd recalled the sting he'd felt during his flight from the compound. "Just a graze," he said. "Barely felt it."

And that was true, but only because it was hard to differentiate that one sore spot from all the others.

"When I saw the lights come on," Mikey volunteered, "I knew that something wasn't going according to plan, so I picked up and hurried over to the north side for a better angle. Good thing I did, too. Otherwise I'd have gotten stomped."

"Good thing," Redd agreed.

"I tried to pick a few of them off, but I guess it's a lot harder to hit a moving target."

"Yeah."

Mikey looked past him. "Where's Gavin?"

Redd winced. He shook his head.

Mikey looked confused. "What? He's dead?"

"I saw him go down. He drew their fire so I could make it out."

"That's . . ." He faltered. "I guess I knew it could happen, but . . . what now?"

"We keep going." He turned, looking back toward the buildings that were now visible through the settling dust.

"What do you mean?"

"This isn't over." Redd held up the Ruger. "We have to finish it."

Mikey stared at him for a moment, then nodded. "Let's do it."

✖ ✖ ✖

Redd soon had cause to reassess the question of unfinished business. The landscape was littered with shattered motorcycles and thoroughly trampled human remains, and judging by the numbers, few if any of the riders who had come out in pursuit of Redd had managed to reach the safety of the buildings. It appeared as if the rampaging bison had purposely chased down every single one of the offending motorcycles, dispatching them with ruthless efficiency. The unhorsed riders, left stunned and out in the open, had probably not been targeted by the enraged creatures but merely caught in the stampede and crushed to death.

Redd hoped to see Angry Johnny among the dead, but after checking just a couple of the bodies, he gave up on the effort. Identifying any of them would be possible only with a DNA match.

The trail of wreckage did not stop at the edge of the campus. Bodies and bikes were strewn about the gravel parking lot, which, thanks to the stampede, was now all but indistinguishable from the fields beyond. There was no sign of the herd, and Redd thought it unlikely that they would ever see them again. Stampeding animals were known to run for miles before settling down.

Still, as they neared the buildings, Redd shifted to a more alert posture, moving in a Weaver shooting stance with his body turned slightly—bladed—to reduce frontage exposure, the Ruger held in a "push-pull" grip, his right arm fully extended, pushing the gun out, and his left pulling back to create maximum stability.

"Head on a swivel," he advised, keeping his voice low. "They could be anywhere."

"Got it" was Mikey's somber reply.

As before, Redd checked each of the buildings they came to, this time ensuring that they were completely clear before moving on. Each empty structure seemed to confirm the supposition that the Infidels had either been utterly annihilated or fled their temporary camp and dispersed. Nevertheless, Redd studied the rooftop of the laboratory building from cover for several long minutes before making a quick crossing to its entrance.

"See anyone up there?"

Mikey, who had been scanning the roofline through the scope of his Remington, shook his head. "If there is, they're not peeking over the edge."

"All right, cover me from here. I'm going to move to the entrance and go in. If you see any movement, don't bother calling out. Just start shooting. I'll get the message."

"Got it."

Redd calculated the distance to the laboratory entrance, then broke from cover. As he moved, he realized that Kline's body was not where he had fallen. Redd could only assume that he had been dragged off by the stampede. It was a grim thought, but Redd took comfort in the knowledge that Kline's sacrifice had made his own survival possible.

All thoughts of Kline's fate, however, were set aside as he neared the open doorway and saw a light inside. Instead of heading in, Redd flattened himself against the wall just to the right of the entrance. He could just make out the low murmur of conversation coming from within.

Redd had cleared more buildings than he could remember, both in training and in actual combat, but had always done so as part of a team. It was the job of each shooter in an entry team to sweep in and cover a different sector of the room, trusting that his fellow assaulters would watch the others. Operating solo, Redd would have to cover every sector himself, adjusting his aim quickly to find and neutralize the targets.

Further complicating matters, the Ruger was a single-action handgun, which meant pulling the trigger only fired the weapon; it did not rotate the cylinder and recock the hammer. He would have to do that either with his thumb or his nonshooting hand.

And he only had four rounds.

Hope it's enough, he thought, then launched himself through the doorway, finger tense on the trigger, poised to kill the first man he saw.

FORTY-FIVE

Two things prevented Redd from pulling the trigger.

The first was that the first man he saw was not a man, but a woman. A woman he recognized from his visit to the Buffalo Jump—Angry Johnny's girlfriend. She was hunched over another figure sitting propped up against the back wall, evidently administering first aid to his wounds in the glow of a small electric lantern.

The identity of the injured man was the second thing that stopped Redd in his tracks.

"Gavin?" he gasped.

The subject of the biker chick's ministrations was indeed Gavin Kline, not only alive—albeit bloody—but conscious. He jolted upon seeing Redd's entry but then broke into a relieved smile.

The woman let out a squeal of dismay and threw her hands up. "Don't shoot!"

Redd had already slipped his finger out of the trigger guard but kept the Ruger trained on her. He wasn't about to trust an Infidel's surrender, even if the Infidel in question was female. J. B. had raised him to never hit a woman, and unless she was armed, he wasn't going to shoot her, but she didn't need to know that. "Where are the rest of them?" he demanded.

"Gone. They all took off."

"And you stayed behind?" Redd poured skepticism into the question.

"Matt, she's okay," Kline said. "She's a CI."

Red knew that a CI—confidential informant—was someone with knowledge of criminal activity, often someone inside a criminal enterprise, willing to provide information to law enforcement agencies, usually for dubious reasons. The fact that this woman claimed to be such an informant did not immediately earn his trust.

"So she says," he replied.

"She's working with O'Meara out of the Bozeman satellite office. I just called in and he vouched for her. And she saved me. Dragged me in here when things went sideways out there."

Redd regarded the woman a moment longer, recalling how she'd gazed adoringly at Angry Johnny and wondering what had made her go over to the other side. He lowered the Ruger and turned to Kline. Despite his injuries, he appeared lucid. The woman had evidently done a passable job of bandaging wounds to his right arm and both of his legs.

"Don't take this the wrong way," Redd said, "but how are you alive? I saw you go down. You were hit."

"I was. Several times. Fortunately, the vest stopped the ones that should have killed me. The rest are just flesh wounds."

Body armor. Of course.

"I'm still not exactly in fighting shape," Kline went on. "But help's on the way. O'Meara's working with local LEOs, putting together a task force. They should be here in an hour or so." He focused his gaze on Redd. "What happened out there? You look like hell."

"Everyone keeps telling me that," Redd sighed. He brushed Kline's concern aside and returned his attention to the woman. "What's your name?"

She swallowed nervously. "Everyone calls me Bobbie-Sue."

"Okay, Bobbie-Sue. Where did they go?"

She shook her head. "I don't know. I know there was club business somewhere around here. Maybe an hour's ride? Something that didn't have anything to do with coming after you. Johnny was planning to head there after he killed you. I think maybe that's where they're going, but he never told me exactly where."

"Johnny's still alive?"

She nodded. "He's . . ." Her eyes met his, then just as quickly looked away. "He's not right. In the head, I mean. I don't know why I didn't see it sooner."

"How many are with him?"

Bobbie-Sue shrugged. "Six, I think? And the other girls left after he did. But those were just the guys that were here with us. The rest of the club is out doing the job. He'll probably meet up with them."

"The rest? How many is that?"

"All of them. At least a hundred guys."

The answer staggered Redd. To have fought so hard, gone through so much, thinking that he had dealt the Infidels a mortal blow, only to learn that he'd done little more than kick them in the shins, felt worse than failure.

As if sensing Redd's dismay, Kline spoke up. "We'll find them, Matt. You aren't going to have to do this on your own anymore."

Bobbie-Sue spoke up again. "Did you really kill Baby Boy?"

Redd nodded.

"Good," she whispered.

Redd stared at her for a long moment. "Did Johnny ever mention the name Anton Gage?"

She shook her head. "He never talked about club business around me. Unless he needed me to do something for him."

Kline shot him a questioning glance. "You think they're working with Gage?"

"I do," Redd answered simply. "And I don't think it's a coincidence that all of this is happening here and now. Whatever Gage is planning, I think it's going to happen soon."

"Matt!" Mikey's shout postponed further discussion. "Everything okay in there?"

"Yeah, Mikey. Come on in."

Mikey stepped through the doorway a moment later, eyes going wide in surprise when he beheld Kline. Then he turned to Redd again. "I think there's a helicopter coming this way."

Kline perked up at this news. "I guess they took my request seriously. C'mon. Give me a hand up."

Redd shoved the Ruger back into his belt, then knelt down beside Kline, looping an arm around him and helping him to his feet. Mikey slung his rifle on his back and moved in from the other side, and in a matter of seconds, they were shuffling toward the exit with Bobbie-Sue right behind them.

Even before he cleared the doorway, Redd could hear the rhythmic *thump, thump, thump* of helicopter rotor blades and knew that the aircraft approaching was something much bigger than the ubiquitous Bell 206 used by most law enforcement agencies. "That's a military bird," he muttered, mostly to himself.

Kline glanced over at him. "We don't have a lot of resources in Montana. They must have partnered up with the National Guard for transport. Good thing, too. Otherwise, we'd probably be out here all night."

As they stepped into the open, they saw the running lights of the approaching helicopter moving in from the west. As it neared the airspace above the compound, the brilliant beam of a searchlight shone down, illuminating the dust motes that still floated in the air above the field where the bison had wreaked havoc upon the Infidels. The spotlight swept back and forth, revealing the extent of the damage done, before finally moving toward the compound. Redd couldn't tell if they were looking for a landing zone or checking for hostiles.

"Mikey, shine your phone light up at them," he advised. "Let them know we're friendly."

Mikey did as instructed, directing the relatively weak little LED up at the hovering aircraft and then waving it overhead. The spotlight immediately moved over them, transfixing them in the beam. Redd raised a hand in a thumbs-up gesture to indicate that the area was clear of enemy forces. It wasn't the standard signal, but he figured the crew aboard the helo would get it. As if in answer, the spotlight moved back to the open ground of what had once been a parking lot, and the helicopter moved in and touched down.

Once it was on the ground, Redd could see that it was a UH-60 Black Hawk with the olive-drab matte paint scheme used by the US military. The rear doors were open and as soon as the wheels touched down, several men wearing tactical clothes and gear, with assault rifles carried at the low ready, stepped out and quickly moved toward them. It was only when the leader of the group spoke that Redd finally recognized them.

"You were supposed to wait for us, Redd."

"Rob?" Kline gasped, correctly identifying the speaker as the acting leader of the fly team's tactical unit. "What are you doing here?"

Davis offered a sheepish grin. "Uh, Redd invited us to come out and . . . umm, conduct a wilderness training exercise."

Kline looked at Redd. "Was that before or after I reinstated you?"

Redd shrugged.

Davis regarded Redd with a raised eyebrow. "You're back on the team?"

"We'll see. Thinking about it. Kind of been busy with other stuff."

"Don't change the subject," Kline said. "You shouldn't have left me out of the loop."

Davis held his boss's gaze. "Sir, Redd's one of us. He asked for help, and I wasn't going to say no. And I wasn't going to take a chance on you saying no either."

"I wouldn't have," Kline protested.

"Like I said, I wasn't going to take that chance, sir. If you want to reprimand me for that, it's your prerogative, but I stand by my decision."

Kline appeared to consider this for a moment, then shook his head. "Reprimand? For what? I'm glad you're here, Rob."

As they were talking, a figure wearing a blue FBI windbreaker joined them. "Director Kline?"

Kline waved to the man. "I'm Kline."

"Special Agent O'Meara. Sorry we didn't get here sooner. Looks like we're late to the party."

"Actually, your timing is perfect," Kline said. "We believe there may be a connection between the activity of this biker gang and a high priority counterterrorism case I've been coordinating through DI. If our intelligence is accurate, the Infidels and a man named Gage are planning a significant act of terrorism from somewhere here in Montana."

O'Meara raised an eyebrow. "*Anton* Gage? Public enemy number one?"

"I think he's more like number four," Kline said with a wry smile. Then he was serious again. "Whatever Gage is planning, it's imminent. If we move quickly, we can not only bring him in but possibly save hundreds . . . maybe thousands of lives."

O'Meara cocked his head to the side. "Well then, why are we standing around talking about it? Let's move."

Kline looked at Redd. "Are you in?"

"Let's finish this."

Kline gave him a nod and a smile, then turned to Bobbie-Sue. "Does this Angry Johnny have a mobile phone? Do you know his number?"

She nodded.

"Then we've got him."

"What if he's tossed his phone?" Redd asked. "Or doesn't go back to Gage?"

"We'll look at his GPS activity over the last few days. That will tell us where he's been conducting this business of his." He motioned to the waiting Black Hawk. "Help me get aboard. There's no time to lose."

As they crossed the open ground, Davis leaned close to Redd. "Hey, what happened out there? It looks like the day after Armageddon."

Redd allowed himself a smile of satisfaction. "The Infidels picked a fight they couldn't win."

"With you?"

Redd shook his head. "With Montana."

FORTY-SIX

It took just twenty-five minutes for the Black Hawk to reach the Air National Guard hangar at Helena Regional Airport, where O'Meara's task force had established an ad hoc command center. Dozens of federal agents from different divisions of the Justice Department had been called in from nearby satellite offices, along with troopers from the Montana Highway Patrol, and were in the process of gearing up for the currently undefined tactical mission.

Over his strenuous objections, Kline was taken to St. Peter's hospital to have his wounds tended. He did not leave, however, before assigning Redd the role of liaison between the fly team and the task force, which effectively put him in charge, albeit as Kline's proxy.

"Matthew Redd speaks with my authority," he told O'Meara as the gurney to which he was strapped was rolled out to the waiting ambulance. "And I have been given full authority from the director himself. If you've got a problem with that, let me know now so I can give your job to someone else."

If the FBI special agent did have a problem with that, he chose to keep it to himself.

The first order of business was to obtain a FISA warrant to track the mobile phone activity of one John Owen Simpson—aka Angry Johnny.

While waiting for the warrant to come back, Redd debriefed Bobbie-Sue, hoping to learn more about the Infidels' relationship with Anton Gage.

As a woman in the male-dominated world of outlaw biker gangs, her knowledge of their activities—legal or otherwise—was limited to things overheard or inferred. She knew that the run to Montana had been organized quickly, seemingly on the spur of the moment, but that the plan to "get payback" for Redd's offenses against the club had been in the works for more than a year.

"I've never heard of that guy, Gage," she reiterated, "but I know that whatever business brought us here, it was worth a lot of money. Enough for Johnny to call in all the chapters."

Redd had learned that after an initial meeting of the entire North American membership out at the old Gage Food Trust compound—a gathering of more than two hundred Infidels—most of them had departed, following Angry Johnny to the undisclosed location. A select number had remained behind, under the leadership of Baby Boy, to carry out the campaign against Redd.

Bobbie-Sue went on to reveal how she had become disillusioned with the club following a brutal gladiatorial battle between two prospective members—the same two men who had accosted Redd in the parking lot of the Buffalo Jump—which had ended with the savage death of one man and serious injury to another.

"It wasn't right," she said, tears welling up in her eyes. "Brothers aren't supposed to ever fight brothers. It's in the bylaws."

Redd found it bitterly amusing that the woman had no problem with the gang swearing vengeance against Redd or harassing Emily and Junior on the road but was appalled at the thought of the bikers fighting among themselves. He did not, however, interrupt her story.

"So when I brought Dunk into the clinic," she went on, "I knew I had to do something. That's when I called the cops and told them what I seen."

"You called the FBI?"

"Not at first. I didn't know who to call. I didn't have a phone or anything . . . Johnny never let me have one. But I found a deputy and told him that I knew about someone who'd gotten killed. When I told him it was Infidels, he turned it over to the FBI. They came out and talked to me for hours. Said that if I cooperated and helped them arrest Johnny, they'd keep me safe."

"You're safe now," Redd assured her.

She nodded dully, then added, "They aren't all bad, you know. We had some real good times."

Redd didn't know what to say to that, so he simply said, "Sure."

✖ ✖ ✖

Once the warrant was signed, the FBI techs were quickly able to establish both the present location of Angry Johnny's phone and a record of his movements over the course of the preceding week. The latter record showed him moving between the Gage Food Trust facility, various locations in and around Helena, and a remote location near the northern boundary of the Lewis and Clark National Forest, southwest of Great Falls, where the phone had been more or less stationary for over an hour on at least five different occasions.

"That's got to be the place," Redd said, pointing to the GPS map displayed on the screen of an FBI laptop. "What's out there?"

One of the troopers from the MHP fielded the question. "A whole lot of nothing. Honestly, I'm surprised you got a ping. I didn't know there was coverage out there."

"Is it possible you're reading this wrong?" Davis asked. "Maybe this doesn't have anything to do with Gage. Maybe they've got a meth lab out there. Or a weapons cache. Something like that."

The timing . . .

Redd shook his head. "If that's all they're doing up there, they wouldn't need that much manpower. No. That's where Gage has set up shop. I'm sure of it."

Davis raised his hands in a gesture of surrender.

"Whatever it is," O'Meara intoned, "I'm sure it's not legal. Either way, we should check it out."

"There's got to be something about that location," Redd continued. "Can we find out who owns that land?"

"Hang on a sec," called out another trooper, an older man with a brushy gray mustache and sergeant's chevrons on his collar. He took out his smartphone and began tapping the screen. After a long moment, he nodded. "I thought so. That—" he pointed at the laptop display—"is the site of a United States Air Force missile alert facility. Or I should say, it was. That's one of the ones that was decommissioned back in 2008 as part of an arms reduction treaty." He paused a beat, then added, "I was stationed up at Malmstrom AFB back in the day. Missile security."

Redd stared at the satellite map on the display. "Can we zoom in on that?"

The tech maneuvered the focal point and focused in on a small complex of buildings clustered together in a section of otherwise-desolate landscape.

"A missile silo?" O'Meara asked.

"Not a silo," the MHP sergeant said. "That's the launch control facility. The silos were located ten or so miles from the MAF. Each launch base controlled ten Minuteman missiles, spread out in every direction. That way, the Russkies wouldn't have been able to knock them all out with one nuke."

"Unless they hit the launch facility," O'Meara countered.

The sergeant shook his head. "The launch control capsules are underground. They were built to survive almost anything except a direct hit. During the Cold War, there were hundreds of sites like this. Taking them all out would have been impossible."

"Could Gage be planning some kind of missile attack?" Davis asked. "I mean, I know the nukes probably aren't there anymore, but if he got his hands on some missiles, could he use the silos to launch them?"

"The decommissioned silos were capped so they can't ever be used again. And I'm sure the Air Force pulled all the hardware out. Not that it would be considered very sophisticated by today's standards."

Redd continued studying the image on the screen. "Kline's intel suggests Gage is targeting the global food supply. His specialty is genetic engineering. I don't see him launching missiles unless there's a way to use them to disperse some kind of GMO bioweapon."

"There are easier ways to do that," the MHP sergeant agreed.

"What else could you do with a decommissioned launch facility?"

"Like I said, the launch control capsule is hardened. You could hole up in there for a while, but you couldn't very well stay forever. If the hydraulics on the blast doors are disengaged from the inside, it's still possible to open the doors manually. It just takes a while. Like five hours with a hand crank. But eventually you'd get in. If someone knows you're in there, it's a lousy place to hide."

"Anything else?"

The sergeant rubbed his chin. "The launch control station is basically a communications hub. The crew is on standby to receive orders, and when they do, their job is to confirm that the orders are genuine and then launch the missiles. That's it."

"How were orders transmitted?"

"Incoming orders would come through encrypted radio transmissions. Outbound signals went out directly to the silos through buried hard lines."

Redd chewed this over. Something the other trooper had said now flashed through his mind.

Coverage.

"Could the radio equipment be used to transmit as well as receive?" Redd asked.

"I'm sure they took most of it out when they decommissioned it," the sergeant said. "But they probably left the antennas behind. I suppose if you hooked up a new transmitter . . . it'd have to be pretty powerful, but sure, you could start your own pirate radio station. I don't know who would be listening though."

Redd turned to Davis. "Gage's operations at the GFT were fully automated, with a fleet of drones to monitor crop health and do whatever else needed doing. At the end, when he wanted to destroy the evidence of what he'd been up to, he used them to set fire to the fields."

"We seized all those drones," Davis pointed out.

"He could buy more. That's not my point. The drones were all controlled from a mainframe computer, using 4G wireless broadband."

"And you think he could be using that old missile base as a control center for a new fleet of drones," Davis said, adequately summarizing exactly what Redd was thinking. "Using their antenna to transmit instructions to them. To what end? He doesn't have any cultivated cropland."

"I don't think he plans to grow anything this time. Kline said Gage wants to disrupt the food supply. Maybe he's planning to spray the crops with poison or some new genetically modified crop disease."

Davis still looked skeptical. "He'd need to spray a lot of it to make any kind of difference."

"Don't underestimate his resourcefulness," Redd said. "Or his arrogance."

Davis nodded. "Let's say you're right about this. How do we handle it?"

Redd turned to the highway patrol sergeant. "We need to know everything there is to know about this old missile base. If Gage is running his show from an underground bunker, we need to get in there before he can close that blast door."

"I'll see what I can find out," the sergeant said.

"Why not just take out the antenna?" Davis asked.

Redd had thought of that already. "We might have to do that, but only as a last resort. If the drones are already operational, we may need to use the transmitter to send out a recall code."

"That's assuming you can even get in there," O'Meara said. "Our CI says there could be more than a hundred Infidels guarding the place."

Redd shook his head. "I don't think that's why Gage partnered with them. You don't set up shop in a place like that with the expectation that the FBI is going to come knocking. He might have some of them standing guard, but I think he's got most of them doing something else."

"Like what?"

"I don't know. Logistical stuff maybe? That facility doesn't look like it was designed to house a hundred or more people. Point is, I don't think they're standing by to defend the base."

"They might be now," Davis said. "After what happened tonight."

"Maybe," Redd agreed. "Which makes it all the more imperative that we move quickly, before they can shift to a defensive footing."

"The National Guard has another helo we can use. With two birds, we can put thirty agents on the ground in half an hour."

Redd looked over at the assembly area where the agents of various law enforcement organizations—FBI, ATF, Border Patrol, and even rangers from the Bureau of Land Management and the Forest Service, along with a handful of troopers from the Montana Highway Patrol—were checking and rechecking weapons and body armor, keeping busy until the order to deploy was given. All of them were trained in the use of deadly force, but he guessed few had any real combat experience.

"They'll hear us coming from miles away," he said. "We'll lose the element of surprise, and it will almost certainly turn into a standoff. And while we're laying siege, Gage will have plenty of time to carry out his plan."

"What's the alternative?" Davis asked.

"The fly team will take point on this. We'll move to the objective overland for maximum stealth, get as close as we can before identifying ourselves and ordering them to surrender. Once we're ready to move, the helos can begin moving everyone else in. That way, if we run into trouble, the cavalry will already be on the way. If things go smoothly, they'll be able to help us secure the scene and process any prisoners."

Davis's skeptical look returned. "If you're wrong about how he's distributed his forces, we could get in over our heads in a hurry."

"If it looks that way, we'll pull back and wait for reinforcements."

Davis stared at Redd for several seconds, his lips pursed in deep thought; then he nodded. "It's a solid plan."

"Then let's get moving."

"What about me?"

The question from Mikey caught Redd doubly off guard. In the flurry of activity that had followed their arrival at the command center, he'd forgotten that Mikey was even there. He faced his friend and delivered what he thought would come as unwelcome news. "Mikey, I appreciate all you've done tonight. I owe you. For this and so much more. But this is now a law enforcement action, and you can't be a part of it."

An odd smile cracked Mikey's expression. "Sounds good. Don't get me wrong. I'll always be there when you need me, but this . . ." He made a sweeping gesture. "This is your world, not mine."

Is it? Redd almost laughed at the insight. Slipping back into the role of team leader had been effortless, like putting on a favorite pair of combat boots.

Is this my world? Am I fooling myself in thinking I'm meant to settle down and run a ranch?

He shook his head, trying to bring his focus back to the moment. "I'll have the highway patrol drive you out to pick up your vehicle and Em's Tahoe." The mere mention of Emily reminded him of something else he'd forgotten to do. "After that? Go home. Hug your family. Tomorrow, one way or another, this will all be over."

✖ ✖ ✖

Even though he wasn't required to, Redd decided to run his plan past Kline, just in case. When he called the hospital, however, he was informed that Kline was undergoing surgery under general anesthesia and would not be lucid for at least a few hours.

He hung up and made another call, one that he'd put off too long.

Emily answered on the first ring. "Hello?"

"It's me, Em."

"Matty!" There was relief and concern in that single breathed word.

"I'm okay," he said, answering the unasked question. "Mikey, too. He's on his way home. Gavin got banged up a little—" he hoped that she would not press him for more detail—"but he'll be fine. Thanks for sending them out to help. I couldn't have gotten through it without them." He paused a beat, then went on. "Where are you?"

"St. Peter's. I came with Angela Townsend."

"Is she going to make it?"

"Too soon to tell. She lost a lot of blood and had a collapsed lung. If we hadn't been there . . ." She trailed off, perhaps realizing the same thing Redd did—if they hadn't been there, Townsend probably wouldn't have been shot in the first place.

Redd decided to change the subject. "How's Junior?"

"Loving all over Liz, I'm told. We're lucky to have them in our lives, you know. Don't know what we'd do without them right now."

Redd agreed. "Yeah, we owe them big-time." Changing the subject again, he said, "I'll have someone bring the Tahoe to you. It'll probably be a couple hours. You good until then?"

"I'm good," she said, and then, "So this isn't over?"

He took a breath. "Almost. Gage is involved in this, and we're going after him."

"We?"

"The FBI. The fly team. This is it, Em. This is what we've been working toward for over a year. It ends tonight."

"Promise you'll be careful."

"I always am." The answer came easily. Too easily. So he added, "I promise."

FORTY-SEVEN

As the clock ticked over into the last twenty-four hours of Gage's time-table, getting direct access to the man was no longer an issue. If anything, Dmitri found himself wishing Gage would leave him alone. Whatever other issues had demanded Gage's attention outside the control center had evidently been resolved, allowing him to devote himself fully to tasks that could only be managed from inside the underground facility.

Gage did not openly inquire about his progress, merely lurked in the background. Dmitri was grateful that he'd been able to complete his surreptitious research into the drones' payload earlier in the day, because with a pensive Gage now looking over his shoulder, it would have been impossible to get at the truth, much less do anything about it.

Work on the algorithm was effectively done. All that remained was the somewhat-tedious process of debugging it. Doing so meant running simulations of the program and waiting for something to go wrong—an errant line of code, a data error, or worst of all, a situation that he had failed to anticipate. For better or worse, he had done his work a little too well. Thus far, the simulations had been going smoothly, and he suspected that Gage knew it. He tried not to dwell on the matter of what Gage would do with his work once he took full control and concentrated instead on the "boatload of money" he'd been promised. So consumed was he in his work, he failed to immediately grasp the presence of a visitor in the underground control room.

"Gage. We need to talk." It was the sound of the man's voice—a flat monotone that nevertheless hummed with the energy of a high-voltage line—more than what was actually said that grabbed Dmitri's attention. He looked back and saw that the new arrival was not one of the systems engineers, but rather one of the thugs. The man had a shaved head and a long gray beard that looked thick with dust. His skin was leathery from exposure to the elements, but his eyes looked hard as diamonds. Dmitri didn't think he had seen this man before.

Gage turned as well. "You're back?" There was the briefest pause. "Is it done then?"

The man's eyes flicked over to Dmitri. "Are you sure you want to talk about this in here?"

Gage glanced at Dmitri as well, then nodded in understanding. "Of course," he mumbled and strode toward the exit.

Despite his curiosity regarding the strange visit, Dmitri remained at his station, focused on the task at hand. Whatever the two men were discussing, it surely didn't involve him. He was surprised when, just a few minutes later, Gage returned alone, looking even more pensive than before.

"How close are you to done?" he demanded.

It was not the first time he had asked, but this time there was an unexpected urgency to the question. Something had changed for Gage. Something to do with the news the thug had brought him.

But what?

Dmitri's answer was the same. "Very nearly done. I am debugging now."

"So the algorithm itself is finished? We could initiate now if we wanted to?"

"Well . . . theoretically, yes. But it would be better to continue running diagnostics while we have the time. You did say three days."

This reminder of their agreement did not seem to sit well with Gage. "We may need to accelerate our timeline. Can you debug on the fly?"

"On the fly?" Dmitri wasn't sure he understood Gage's idiom.

"Fix problems as they appear. Write patches or updates as needed while the drones are operational?"

"That would . . ." Dmitri hesitated, trying to find a diplomatic way to phrase his answer. "Not be ideal."

"But you *can* do it?"

"I . . . can try. I cannot guarantee success. If the system crashes, the drones may crash too. Literally."

Gage frowned. "All right. Keep running your diagnostics. But I want to be ready to initiate at a moment's notice. Set up a master control interface at my terminal. Password secured. Can you do that?"

Dmitri was hesitant. "I can, but if something goes wrong . . ."

"If something goes wrong?" Gage barked a mirthless laugh. "That's what worries me."

FORTY-EIGHT

The whirring of the camera drone's quadrotors was only a touch louder than the hum of a mosquito's wings as it zoomed through the air, fifty feet above the flat, rocky terrain. Although small, it was by no means invisible, but in the darkness it might as well have been.

Half a kilometer away, in the back of a rented U-Haul truck, ten men were huddled around an iPad Pro, watching the feed from the drone's 4K high-definition video camera. Nine of the men wore tactical garb—camouflage-pattern ripstop fatigues, matching plate carriers, and bump helmets. The tenth also wore a plate carrier, but instead of camo, he was attired in tattered and dust-streaked Wranglers and a long-sleeved flannel shirt. His name was Matthew Redd.

As the drone cruised above the dilapidated buildings of the former Minuteman missile launch control facility, its camera relayed real-time footage of the fenced compound, lit by a single light mounted above one of the exterior doors leading into the main structure. The cone of illumination it cast revealed a handful of men idling out front. All were wearing motorcycle leathers and cut-down jackets emblazoned with the distinctive logo of the Infidels MC. All were armed with handguns.

"I guess this is the place," Rob Davis remarked as the drone finished its pass.

"They've got power," Special Agent Fleetwood observed. "Must have a generator."

"I see four tangos," Redd said, employing military shorthand for *targets*.

"Same here," Davis agreed. "Gotta figure there are more inside."

"Let's just worry about the ones outside for now," Redd advised. "Bring it around for another pass."

The display became a blur of motion as the drone turned 180 degrees, then stabilized with the compound once more centered in the frame. The bikers were congregated around the front entrance of the main building, smoking and otherwise idling the night away.

"They don't exactly appear to be on high alert," Davis said.

"Don't assume anything. And don't underestimate them. Mac, check out the south side. Switch to IR. I want to make sure there's no one lurking in the shadows."

The agent holding the iPad adjusted course, activating the drone's low-light camera as the little spy craft zoomed over the building to covertly observe the other side. The infrared display stripped away the shroud of darkness, revealing the narrow buffer zone between the building and the fence to be completely empty.

"I stand by my original statement," Davis said.

Redd nodded. "They might suspect that I made it out, but they can't be expecting us to move this quickly. I think it's safe to say we still have the element of surprise on our side."

"So how do we want to do this?"

Redd thought back to the last time he and the team had been in this situation. The villa in Majorca, waiting on a green light from Kline, thousands of miles away, hamstrung by bureaucratic red tape.

This time he was the one making the call.

There was not a doubt in his mind that Angry Johnny was inside that building. He was only slightly less certain that they would also find Anton Gage inside.

Redd had felt just as sure of himself in Majorca. He remembered all too well how that had turned out.

He pushed the thought aside. Even if Gage wasn't there, the Infidels were.

"We'll deploy from here, head south a klick or so, then come around and approach from the dark side. We'll cut the fence and then move in and secure the interior."

"They might have motion sensors or cameras along the perimeter," Davis pointed out, playing devil's advocate as was expected of the second-in-command.

"They might," Redd agreed. "We'll keep the drone on station. If they start getting squirrelly when we close in, we'll know they've made us. If so, we'll reassess. But this is still our best chance to preserve the element of surprise."

Davis nodded. "Then let's do it."

✖   ✖   ✖

They moved quickly and quietly across the flat terrain, careful not to raise dust but mindful of the need for haste. Although the objective was illuminated by artificial light, they wore night vision devices to speed them along during the movement phase of the mission. All were armed with suppressor-equipped Heckler & Koch MP5SD6s, chambered for 9 millimeter, and equipped with Aimpoint Micro T-2 reflex sights, along with whatever backup weapon they individually preferred. One man carried a shotgun, ostensibly for breaching secure doors, but if the need arose, Redd had his trusty Fiskars splitting maul, which Davis had brought to Montana.

It took about half an hour for them to make the broad flanking maneuver to approach the compound from the south side. Redd maintained an open comm line with Fleetwood, who had remained behind along with

Special Agent Jones to monitor the drone feed. During the course of their march, the number of hostiles in the open had fluctuated, briefly increasing to five, then dropping down to just two. This was a mixed blessing. Dealing with two tangos would be a lot easier than four, but they would now face even greater numbers of Infidels once they entered the structure.

Redd reminded himself of his own advice to Davis.

Worry about the outside.

"We're coming up on the fence now, Mac."

"I see you," Fleetwood replied. "No change on the inside."

Redd took this as a good sign. If there were motion sensors along the perimeter, their approach would have triggered some kind of response, like exterior lights coming on to draw attention to their presence or even an alarm.

"I'm moving to the fence," Redd said and then to his teammates added, "Cover me."

Using the wire cutters on a Leatherman multitool, Redd snipped through the chain link to form an opening big enough for a crouching man to pass through. It was a tedious, time-consuming process, but after the first few cuts, when it became evident that the intrusion had not raised any alarms, Redd relaxed a little. They would still have the element of surprise.

Once the opening was made, the fly team operators came through one at a time and lined up along the south side of the main building—half of them on the southeast corner, the other half led by Redd on the southwest.

"Mac, give me a sitrep," he murmured into his lip mic.

Fleetwood's voice came back instantly. "No change. Two subjects are about five meters from the front door. Pulling guard duty if I had to guess."

"Notify HQ that we are about to go hot and to get those birds in the air."

There was a brief pause; then Fleetwood spoke again. "The cavalry is on the way."

Redd swiveled his night vision device away from his eyes, blinking several times to help his unaided vision adjust to the darkness. Even with a building between them, the glow of the exterior light provided just enough illumination for them to advance without fear of stumbling.

"All right, Bravo team, move up to the northeast corner and hold. Alpha, on my signal we're going to come around the corner, identify ourselves, and give the order to disarm. Anyone still holding a weapon after that is to be considered a hostile target. Lethal force is authorized."

Redd heard no pushback from the team. Not that he expected it. Every single one of them knew what the Infidels had done to Redd and his family.

After a few seconds, Davis's voice came over the comms. "Bravo, set."

"Roger, Bravo," Redd answered. "Alpha, we're moving in three . . . two . . . one . . . go!"

Redd strode forward, keeping his weapon at the high ready. He did not pause at the corner but quickly came around and put the red dot of the reflex sight center mass on the closest of the two Infidels.

"Federal agents," he called out. "Drop your weapons!"

The men jolted in surprise but, instead of dropping their guns as ordered, tried to bring them to bear.

Redd tightened his finger on the trigger and sent two rounds into his designated target's chest and then put another between his eyes. The suppressor so effectively muffled the reports that the machine pistol's action sounded louder to Redd than the actual discharge, but there was no minimizing the lethal results. The biker went rigid as the first two rounds punched into his heart and then completely limp as the third drilled a neat hole above the bridge of his nose.

As the first biker puddled onto the ground, Redd swung the red dot over to the remaining target but saw that the man was already going down, felled by rounds from one or more of the agents flanking Redd. Neither of the Infidels had gotten a shot off, much less called out a warning.

Redd spoke into his lip mic. "Alpha, check the bodies and secure all weapons. Bravo, check the other buildings."

As the agents went about their respective tasks, Redd kept the business end of his MP5 aimed at the door, ready to engage if anyone ventured out. No one did.

"All clear," Davis said after completing a quick inspection of the other buildings in the compound, a task that required less than ninety seconds.

"Form up on the main entrance," Redd answered. "We're going in."

As they had rehearsed dozens . . . hundreds of times in the past, the assault teams stacked up on either side of the door. Redd took his place at the head of Alpha team, hefting his splitting maul, but then, recalling how things had gone down in Majorca, tried the doorknob instead.

Unlocked.

He slung the maul across his back and opened the door the old-fashioned way. Alpha team flowed into the room, followed by Redd and then by Bravo team.

The entry foyer was completely empty, devoid of even furniture. There was a heavy-duty steel door at the back of the room and Redd immediately advanced toward it.

Also unlocked.

At the command center in Helena, they had reviewed the basic layout of the missile alert facility, which, surprisingly, was not hard to find online. Beyond the door, Redd knew, they would be in the part of the complex dedicated to the support staff. There would be a long hallway with doors to either side—rooms where personnel bunked and lived, along with a kitchen and a dining room and recreation area—and at the end of it, the security office with an elevator that descended thirty feet to the launch control capsule. There was another door leading directly into the security office closer to the northwest corner—this had been the door used by missile crews rotating to their assignment—but it was secured behind a sheet of plywood. While the underground part of the facility was the main objective—where they expected to find Anton Gage—to reach it, they would have to clear the ground level.

How Gage and the Infidels had elected to make use of the rooms in the aboveground part of the structure was the big unknown. Those rooms might be packed with dozens of gun-toting bikers, or they might not be in use at all. The only way to know for sure was to check each one, a time-consuming and dangerous process. And odds were good that once they made contact with hostiles inside the building, they would have only minutes to reach the LCC before Gage locked himself inside.

"Here we go," he said and opened the door.

Bravo team, with Rob Davis in the lead, was the first inside. Two men hooked left into what had, during the facility's active days, been the senior airman's quarters. The other two went right, entering one of two bunk rooms.

Redd heard members of both teams calling out, almost simultaneously, "Federal agents. Drop your weapons!" followed by the faint sound of suppressed gunfire.

"Clear!" Davis called out.

"Clear!" Special Agent Bryan Tanaka echoed from the bunk room.

Redd and the rest of Alpha team moved right, past the bunk room, and continued down the hall to the next set of open doors. Redd was just reaching for the door to a second bunk room when he glimpsed movement at the far end of the hall. He quickly brought his weapon around, putting the red dot on the chest of a man wearing the distinctive regalia of the Infidels.

There was no time for the standard warning. After only a moment of confusion, the biker went for his gun, and Redd pulled the trigger.

Redd was pretty sure that at least one of the shots from the controlled pair went where he'd intended it to go, but the biker was moving and the second shot missed completely, striking the wall behind him with a sound like a hammer blow. So did the third.

Redd corrected his aim, going for a head shot, but before he could, the biker got his pistol up and fired wildly down the hall.

The unmuffled report rang in the air. Redd bit back a curse as, up and down the hall, doors swung open and armed bikers poured out.

FORTY-NINE

In that moment, Redd was reminded of the time-honored axiom of military strategy: no plan survives contact with the enemy. That they had made it as far as they had was, in hindsight, due more to luck than anything else, but that single, stray, unsuppressed report ended their run of luck with the finality of a guillotine, and in that instant, everything changed.

Redd could not think of a worse place for a gun battle than the narrow hallway. The enclosed space meant that the enemy could simply spray and pray from the relative safety of doorways, while his team, for all their superior firepower, had no clear targets. The real problem, though, was that the hallway was a "fatal funnel"—a choke point where the only way to advance would be to walk into enemy fire.

"Fall back!" Redd shouted over the din.

His admonition was unnecessary. They had trained for situations like this and knew the importance of concreted action. Those in the front—Redd foremost—laid down cover fire, emptying their magazines in several quick bursts as they backed away, while the agents bringing up the rear hastily retreated, clearing a path for the lead element bearing the brunt of the assault. In a matter of seconds, they were all back around the corner, out of the enemy's direct line of sight. As soon as the suppressive fire stopped, the counterattack began, filling the interior of the structure with smoke and noise. Chunks of wood splintered as clouds of plaster dust exploded all around them, showering the team as stray rounds ripped apart the bunker's inner walls.

The tactical retreat was only the first step in the team's react-to-contact drill. As soon as Redd was out of the line of fire, Rob Davis took a small cylindrical grenade from a pouch on his plate hanger, yanked the pin, and then shouting, "Flash-bang!" reached around the corner and flung it down the length of the hallway.

Redd lowered his head and closed his eyes a fraction of a second before an incandescent explosion shook the world. The flash-bang grenade contained all the explosive power of a lethal fragmentation grenade but none of the deadly shrapnel. Instead, the metal-oxidant shell deflagrated in a flash of light so bright as to cause both temporary blindness and disorientation. The flash, coupled with the bang of the detonation, was usually sufficient to leave the occupants of a room incapacitated long enough for a hostage rescue team to enter and disarm or kill the hostiles. Even though he was around the corner from the blast, looking away and wearing tactical earplugs to reduce hearing damage from gunfire, Redd still felt the detonation like a gut punch.

As soon as the shock wave passed, Davis and the rest of Bravo team were up and moving down the hall, hurrying to enter and clear the rooms before the men inside could regain their wits.

They were just a few steps from the first bunk room door when an Infidel, looking not nearly as stunned as he ought to, jumped out into the hall, brandishing a big revolver, and fired point-blank at Davis's chest. The shot knocked the FBI agent back a step. In the same instant, one of the other assaulters unleased a burst into the biker's chest and he went down. No sooner had this threat been neutralized than more Infidels peeked out from around other corners and rejoined the fray.

Redd quickly grasped how Davis's gambit had gone awry. Because the flash-bang had exploded in the hallway, the full intensity of its dazzling light show had been contained by the interior walls. Only those bikers who happened to be looking out a doorway at the instant of detonation would have been affected. Similarly, the sound produced by the grenade, which was only about twenty decibels louder than the report of an unsilenced pistol, was likewise muffled by the architecture.

Crouching low, with Redd and Alpha team firing high over their heads, Bravo team braved enemy fire as they dragged Davis back to the corner. Redd saw that Davis was not bleeding and, more importantly, that he was still breathing. The level III ballistic plates in his Kevlar armor had done their job and kept the bullet from penetrating.

Redd returned his attention to the battle. With the hall cleared again, there was a lull in fire. The Infidels were probably reloading, and given their mad-minute approach to shooting back, they would likely run out of ammunition completely with one or two more exchanges. The problem with simply waiting them out was that with each passing second, the window of opportunity to stop Gage from unleashing an environmental catastrophe closed a little more. That had always been Redd's worst-case scenario—winning the battle but losing the war.

He grabbed Bryan Tanaka's shoulder, pulling him close to shout in his ear. "Keep them busy!"

"What?"

Redd didn't have time to explain himself. He was already moving, retreating toward the entry foyer, his weapon up, just in case the Infidels had reopened one of the boarded-over exits in order to come at them from behind.

After the smoke and noise of the battle, emerging into the cool night was as refreshing as a plunge into the ocean, but there was no time to savor the fresh air. Redd hurried down the length of the building, aiming for the northwest corner and what had once been the security entrance to the missile alert facility.

He'd taken only a few steps in that direction when the sound of shooting from inside the building reached his ears. The walls muffled the sound a little, but Redd knew they probably wouldn't stop a bullet. As long as the battle was confined to the hallway, which ran parallel to his direction of travel, there wasn't much cause for concern, but if the assault team reached the occupied rooms, there was no telling where rounds might penetrate. Redd decided the course of wisdom was to be somewhere else when that happened.

As he neared the boarded-up entrance to the security office, he let his MP5 fall away on its sling and used his free hands to unlimber the maul. Without pausing even a moment to catch his breath, he raised the wood-splitting tool in a two-handed grip, arms fully extended over his head, and chopped down into the plywood with all his might.

The fat wedge-shaped head cleaved an eight-inch-long splintery gash in the barrier. Light from within streamed through the rent. Under normal circumstances, the noise of hacking through the plywood would have brought a swift response from someone on the other side, but with a gun battle raging inside, the crash of the maul was just one more thing going *bang*.

Redd set his feet and took another swing, followed by another. Five chops in as many seconds opened a six-inch vertical in the sheet from top to bottom. He hooked the head of the maul under the plywood and, using it like a claw hammer, pulled back. For a few seconds, the sheet refused to budge, but then with a torturous squeal, the nails holding the weathered wood affixed to the equally weathered exterior wall pulled free, and the plywood fell to the ground at Redd's feet.

The door that had originally guarded the main entrance into the building was still there, but the glass observation window that comprised its upper half was gone, probably smashed out by vandals. Redd didn't bother trying the doorknob. He simply raised the maul again and aimed his next blow at a spot just above it. The door was hinged to open outward, but that single blow from Redd's maul blasted it through the frame and knocked it several yards inside.

The crash of the heavy steel door into the hallway beyond did get the attention of the hostiles inside. A biker materialized from around the corner and unhesitatingly took aim at Redd.

There was no time to switch to his primary weapon, so Redd simply hurled the maul at the man. The tool-turned-weapon flew as sure as Thor's hammer and the heavy steel head caved in the biker's face, but in the instant it made contact, the pistol in the man's hand spurted fire. Redd felt something like a mule kick slam into his chest. He grunted as the breath was forcefully expelled from his chest. Pain flared across ribs that were already on fire from too many injuries to count, but the armor plate stopped the round. Redd stayed on his feet and, gritting his teeth, hastily drew the Ruger from his belt, even as a second biker appeared from around the corner. Redd snap fired, the bullet blasting the Infidel off his feet before he could get a shot off, and then pushed through the open door with the big revolver still at the high ready.

Multiple reports thundered out of the hallway. Less obvious but still impossible to ignore were the 9mm rounds from the assault team's weapons smashing into and through the walls much closer to where Redd stood. The security office was situated through a door to his immediate right, but with the battle raging down the hallway that led back into the personnel area, Redd was loath to divide his attention. He kept the Ruger aimed down the hallway with his right hand and reached back for the MP5 with his left. Once he had control of the machine pistol again, he stuck the Ruger—now with just three rounds remaining—back in his belt before trying the handle of the door into the security office.

Unlocked.

Here we go.

He threw the door open and flowed inside, sweeping every corner of the room with his weapon.

No targets.

He moved around the desk where US Air Force missile security officers had checked the IDs and orders of Minuteman missile crews on their way down to keep their fingers on the nuclear trigger, 24-7, for decades during the Cold War. There was another door on the other side of the counter, this one propped open, providing a straight shot to the elevator that was the only means of entrance or egress for the subterranean launch control facility.

The elevator car stood empty, the accordion gates left open by the last person to ride it up.

Redd approached cautiously, wary of any situation that looked too easy, and stepped inside. Keeping one hand on his MP5 at all times, he slid the safety gates shut and hit the button marked with a downward-pointing arrow.

The car shuddered and then began descending. Outside the security gate, the concrete walls of the shaft passed by, but after just a few seconds, an opening appeared and grew larger as the elevator dropped down to the subterranean level. Redd crouched down, aiming the suppressor end of his weapon through the diamond-shaped holes in the gate, ready to engage any target that appeared.

In that moment, the thought occurred to him that Gage might have gathered the bulk of his forces on the underground level as a last line of defense against invaders. He didn't think it likely. The Infidels aboveground had been taken by surprise. There was no reason for Gage to have more than a token force waiting below on the off chance that they might be attacked.

But it is Gage, he reminded himself. *Don't underestimate him.*

It was too late to worry about that now. He was committed. There was no turning back.

His concerns appeared unjustified as the elevator completed its downward journey. Through the double diamonds of the inner and outer accordion gates, he saw only a high-ceilinged atrium. There were a few exposed pipes and metal lockers, but otherwise the space was empty. Ten yards ahead to the left, a prodigious, floor-to-ceiling block of steel, at least two feet thick, jutted into the open.

Redd felt a mix of relief and suspicion. The blast door was open. It wasn't too late.

But why was it open? Had he guessed wrong? Was this an elaborate deception on Gage's part? A decoy to draw Redd and the FBI here, into a trap, when the real scheme was being executed somewhere else?

Maintaining constant contact with his weapon, Redd threw back first the inner, then the outer gate and stepped out into the atrium.

A strange, rhythmic slapping sound echoed in the enclosure, putting Redd back on full alert. He spied movement near the blast door and then saw the source of the noise—a pair of slow-clapping hands.

Redd put the red-dot sight on a spot just above the hands, ready to pull the trigger if the person to whom the hands belonged made the wrong move.

"Federal agent. Step out into view and keep those hands where I can see them."

The hands continued to clap as the man emerged into the open. "Baby Boy was right about you," Angry Johnny said, slowly raising his hands. "You are a worthy foe."

FIFTY

Redd's finger tightened, taking out the slack in the trigger. A twitch would put a 9-mil round in the Infidels president's heart.

But Johnny wasn't resisting. To all appearances, he was surrendering.

So what? Just do it. End him.

The thought was almost overpowering.

"Coward," Redd snarled. "Are you just going to give up?"

"Give up?" A strange smile split Angry Johnny's weathered visage. Although his outward manner seemed calm, there was a manic energy in his eyes, a barely contained frenzy. "Oh, that's not what's happening here. I'm going to kill you."

He did not say it boastfully, but matter-of-factly, as if commenting on the weather. *Looks like rain.* Then he cocked his head to the side. "Or maybe you'll kill me, if you've got the stones." He shrugged. "The fates will decide. This battle between us has always been inevitable. It's symmetry. It has to be this way."

The monologue was reminiscent of Baby Boy's psychobabble, but

Redd got the impression that Angry Johnny was stalling, trying to lull him into complacency while waiting for an opportune time to strike. *That's not going to happen.*

"The fates say that you are under arrest," Redd barked. "Are you armed?"

Johnny chuckled. "Of course I'm armed."

He rotated his right hip forward, showing a holstered pistol partially covered by the tail of his leather vest. "Not as fancy as that gat you're packing, but it will do the job." He paused a beat, then added, "In a fair fight."

"Fair?" Redd almost choked on the word. "What the hell do you know about fighting fair? Was it fair to attack my wife and child on the highway? Was it fair to send a dozen of your goons to burn my house down? Did Duke Blanton get a fair fight?"

Even as he said it, a voice in his head was shouting, *Don't engage with him. That's what he wants.*

Angry Johnny's smile broadened, as if he was tuning in to Redd's inner struggle. "You said you wanted to settle this face-to-face. Man-to-man." His voice took on a sardonic tone. "Or was that just your way of begging me not to shoot you?"

"That ship has sailed," Redd replied. "Very slowly, go to your knees and then your stomach. Do anything else, and I'll assume you're going for your weapon and react accordingly."

"Come on. We both know that's not how you want this to end. Send me to prison and you'll be looking over your shoulder for the rest of your life." He shrugged. "Which won't be very long. No, the only way this ends is with one of us dead, and you know it. But your sense of *honor*—" he spat the word out contemptuously—"won't let you just kill me."

He's stalling, Redd's inner voice shouted. *Keeping you busy while Gage is doing who knows what.*

"That's why you're hoping I'll go for the gun," Johnny droned. "Make it easy on you. Ease your conscience." He drew out the word *ease*. He shrugged again. "A fair fight. We owe each other that. We put our guns down and settle this like men."

"Like men, huh?" Redd shook his head. "You don't deserve to be treated like a man. You're an animal . . . No, you're worse than that. You're filth. I shouldn't kill you. I should flush you."

A nerve in Johnny's cheek twitched. It might have been barely suppressed rage or just the effects of methamphetamines in his system—Redd suspected the former.

"I don't owe you anything," he went on. "But you're right. I'll sleep better knowing that I gave you a chance."

Slowly, and without taking the red dot of the reflex sight off Johnny's chest, Redd moved his left hand away from the MP5, then took hold of the sling and carefully slipped it over his head. Maintaining eye contact with the other man, Redd bent his knees, lowering himself to a squat, and placed the MP5 on the concrete floor. He allowed his hand to rest on the weapon a moment after setting it down, then stood up, keeping the hand outstretched and hovering above it. Throughout, Angry Johnny remained statue-still, his stare unwavering.

"A fair fight," Redd said. "Or was that just your way of begging me not to shoot you?"

Johnny chuckled. Moving just as slowly as Redd had, he lowered his hands. With his right he drew back his vest to expose the holstered pistol. With his left, he reached across his body and, pinching the butt of the weapon between thumb and forefinger, drew it out and held it up as if presenting it to Redd for inspection.

Then, as Redd knew it would, Johnny's right hand flashed up to take hold of the pistol grip.

"Sucker," he chortled as he straight-armed the semiauto toward Redd.

Then the Infidel's eyes went wide as he saw the Ruger in Redd's hand pointing straight back at him. He jammed his finger into the trigger guard, tried to fire . . .

Redd was faster.

The report filled the atrium like a clap of thunder. A hole about the diameter of Redd's pinkie appeared between Johnny's eyes. The back of his skull, along with most of its contents, splattered across the wall behind him.

Redd kept the big revolver trained on his foe as the lifeless body sank to the floor, just in case some last vestige of primal malevolence remained inside it, but there was no need.

Angry Johnny's soul was already on its way to hell.

Something moved in the periphery of Redd's vision. He swung both his attention and the Ruger toward the motion and felt a fresh surge of adrenaline when he saw the blast door swinging shut.

FIFTY-ONE

Cursing himself for squandering precious seconds savoring his victory over Angry Johnny, Redd dove into the rapidly diminishing opening to the launch control capsule. He instantly felt his plate carrier catch on the edge of the door, arresting his forward motion, and then felt the squeeze of the doorframe pushing from the opposite side. The door was eight tons of concrete and steel, and the hydraulic motor that opened and closed it wouldn't be slowed down at all by two-hundred-odd pounds of human flesh.

Frantic, he gripped both door and frame and shoved as hard as he could, even as the pressure against his chest tightened. For a desperate half second, Redd envisioned himself squashed flatter than a bug under a flyswatter, but then, like a miracle from heaven, the shoulder straps on the plate carrier tore free and he squirted through the opening, tumbling onto the steel decking as the immense door seated into place behind him. There was a faint whine as the hydraulics struggled to finish cycling and then a protracted crunch as the plate carrier and all the attached gear were obliterated.

Redd bounded quickly to his feet, bringing the Ruger up as he glimpsed more movement directly ahead. Someone—no doubt the person who had just closed the blast door—was fleeing into the inner recesses of the capsule. Only too aware of the fact that he had sacrificed his body armor to make it inside and that he only had two shots left in the Ruger, Redd started across the bridge.

"Federal agent," he called out. "Nobody move."

In that instant, he saw five men wearing ordinary street clothes. None of them looked like Infidels and none of them were armed. Four were already in surrender pose, arms held high and reeking of fear. The fifth, however, was bent over a keyboard, frantically typing.

"Back away," Redd shouted, thrusting the Ruger at the man.

The holdout glanced up at him, a determined look on his face as he tapped one last key. Then he threw his hands up and stepped back. Redd flicked his eyes toward the screen just long enough to see a two-word message displayed there—*TERMINAL SECURED*—then brought his attention back to the man.

"What did you just do?" Even as he said it, Redd recognized him. His appearance was dramatically changed, but there was no mistaking the smug smile. "Gage! What the hell did you just do?"

"Matthew. My, my. You're looking . . . hmmm . . . not so good."

Redd rammed the Ruger forward, jamming the barrel into Gage's gut. "You're going to look a lot worse if you don't tell me what you just did."

Gage winced from the blow, but then his arrogant smile returned. "Do that again and you'll regret it."

Redd showed his disdain for the empty threat by ramming the gun forward again, doubling Gage over. As Gage slumped to the floor, Redd placed the barrel close to his eye. "One way or another, you're telling me what you're doing down here. The only question is how much pain you're going to feel first."

Gage raised his head and stared up at Redd, defiant. "Oh no," he grunted. "I disagree. The real question is whether you can keep that murderous temper of yours in check. I don't think you can. You're a brute, Redd. All muscle, no brains. And that's why I'm going to win."

"Brute, huh?" Redd whipped the barrel of the Ruger across Gage's temple. There wasn't a lot of force behind the blow, but Gage nevertheless slumped to the floor in a daze.

Redd stood quickly, sweeping the Ruger back and forth between the other men in the control room. "What's he doing down here?"

There was no resistance in the faces that stared back at him, but neither was there an outward display of willingness to cooperate. Finally one of the men squeaked, "Drone operations."

"What kind of operations? What's he doing with them?" The question elicited only a blank look, so Redd pointed the Ruger at the man's face. "Are the drones spraying something? GMOs? Poison? What and where? I need answers."

"I don't know," the man wailed. "We're just systems techs. Mr. Gage didn't tell us what the drones would be used for."

A strangled noise filled the silence that followed this admission. Redd dropped his eyes to the source and saw Gage, still on the floor, laughing through teeth clenched against the pain caused by Redd's blow.

"That's right, Matthew," he said. "I'm the only one who knows what's really happening here. And I'm the only one who can shut it down. But please, abuse me some more. Who knows? Maybe I'll change my mind and cooperate."

But then another voice spoke up. "I know what he is doing."

Redd glanced over to the man who had spoken. He was youngish, with short-cropped hair and broad Slavic cheekbones to match the Eastern European accent that colored his speech.

Gage's defiant laughter switched off, replaced by anger. "Dmitri, don't say a word."

But Dmitri would not be stopped. "It is spores of something called *Puccinia graminis*."

Redd recognized the scientific term from his last go-around with Gage. "Stem rust?"

Stem rust was a fungal disease that killed wheat crops. Modern fungicides were efficacious in preventing its spread, but there had been a time when outbreaks of rust had devastated the American wheat harvest. No doubt Gage had tinkered with the organism to make it resistant to those countermeasures.

"Dmitri—"

Redd silenced Gage's outburst with a hard kick to the man's gut.

Dmitri's shoulders twitched in a shrug of ignorance. "Genetically modified. That's all I know about it."

"Where is he deploying it?"

Dmitri swallowed nervously. "Everywhere. He has forty thousand drones to cover forty million acres."

"Forty million?" The number boggled Redd's mind. How big an area was that?

He recalled reading somewhere that Montana had over five million acres cultivated with wheat. Gage intended to destroy twenty Montanas' worth of grain.

Gage's soft laughter rose up again. "Okay, Matthew. You earned that one." He pushed himself onto all fours and stared up at Redd. "I suppose it doesn't hurt to tell you this much. Maybe knowing what you've actually lost will make my victory that much sweeter.

"Dmitri is telling the truth. Right now my drones are flying over fields all across the wheat belt. Montana, Wyoming, Nebraska, the Dakotas, Kansas, Colorado. I even sent some of them up into Canada. And yes, they are spraying spores of engineered stem rust. It's a hardy strain I stumbled across during my original research. In addition to being extremely prolific, it's also resistant to heat. It can survive in the soil even after the field is sterilized with fire and come back year after year. Not only will it remove a billion bushels from next year's global food supply, it will kill the ground itself. And there's nothing you can do to stop it."

Redd hid his dismay at the environmental apocalypse Gage was describing. "That's why you needed the Infidels. They aren't just your hired muscle. You needed them to distribute the drones."

Gage inclined his head. "I guess you're not just a brute after all. Yes, I hired them to truck the drones and base station units to a hundred and twenty central locations. If there's one thing they're good at, it's driving. They were quite eager to help out when I promised them a chance to make you suffer." He managed another smile. "Fortunately, they're better at logistics than they are at carrying out a simple assassination.

"I'm sure eventually you'll be able to hunt them all down and stop the drones, but that will take days. By then, it will be too late. So you see, it's checkmate, Matthew. You lose."

"You would condemn millions to a slow death by starvation?" Redd shook his head. "And you think *that* is saving the world."

Gage's smile hardened, then disappeared. "I *am* saving the world. Saving it from the pestilence that is humanity. We are a cancer that has grown out of control. If something isn't done, our extinction is inevitable."

"And so you and your buddies . . . the Twelve . . . you've cast yourself in the role of gods. Is that right?"

Gage flinched at Redd's mention of the Twelve, but he quickly regained his insolent demeanor. "Someone has to make the hard decisions."

"Well, this is an easy one. Shut it down."

Gage rocked back into a sitting position on the floor and crossed his arms like a petulant child. "No."

"You shut it down voluntarily, and maybe, just maybe you'll have some leverage. Refuse, and I swear, I'll personally find a deep, dark hole and throw you in it."

Gage's smirk was answer enough.

"Fine. Then I'll destroy your computer. Knock down the antenna. That's how you're controlling the drones, right?"

Redd hoped to see a hint of concern cross Gage's expression, but the smirk remained. "Why don't you tell him, Dmitri?"

"The drones are fully autonomous. The data link is only there to change their programming. If you sever the link, there will be no way to stop them."

"And I'm the only person on earth who can unlock that terminal. Oh, I'm sure you can torture the password out of me. How long do you think I can hold out? A few days?"

Redd lowered his voice to a conspiratorial whisper. "I like a challenge."

"Well, for your sake, I hope that you get it in one. You'll only get one chance. Enter the wrong password, and the lockout is permanent."

Redd glanced at Dmitri. "Is he telling the truth?"

Dmitri glanced down at Gage as if looking for approval.

"Go ahead and tell him," Gage said.

"Yes. Is true."

Gage laughed again.

Dmitri wasn't finished. "But there is admin password that also unlocks terminal."

The laughter died. "Dmitri, you son of a—"

As he spoke, Gage launched himself at the programmer, only to be snatched out of midair by Redd, who expertly redirected the man into the back wall. Gage's head smacked into the concrete with a sickening thud, and he collapsed to the floor, this time out cold.

Redd faced Dmitri. "Do it."

The other man bent over the locked terminal, arching his fingers above the keyboard, but then hesitated. He looked up at Redd. "I want immunity. And witness protection."

Redd didn't have the authority to make a deal like that but didn't see any advantage to admitting it. "You stop those drones, and the sky's the limit."

The implicit promise was good enough for Dmitri. He lowered his fingers to the keyboard and typed in a long string of characters. The *TERMINAL SECURED* message disappeared, replaced by a screen that looked a little like the interface for a flight simulation video game. It presently showed a camera-eye view of a flight over green fields sown with winter wheat.

Dmitri tapped a key, accessing a text box, and entered a command prompt.

A moment later, the view on the screen changed as the drone came around and began flying a straight line back across the field. Dmitri sat back. "Is done. I've sent recall code."

"For all of them?"

"Is universal code. I wrote the protocol into the algorithm when I realized what he was planning."

Redd let out his breath in a long sigh, watching the drone arrowing toward a black ribbon of highway and a waiting cargo truck.

Finally he turned away and went over to Gage. After checking to make sure that the man was merely unconscious and not actually dead, Redd rubbed his knuckles against Gage's sternum. The pain brought the fallen billionaire back to bleary-eyed wakefulness.

"Good news, Anton. Dmitri recalled the drones, so there won't be any need to waterboard you."

Gage grunted his displeasure. His glazed eyes moved back and forth for a moment, then seemed to focus on Redd. "Go to hell."

Redd chuckled. "The bad news, at least for you, is that there's really no reason to keep you around."

Gage glowered up at him. "So you're just going to murder me? Like you murdered Hannah? Now who's playing God?"

"I'm not going to murder you, Anton. I'm just going to arrest you. But I suspect it won't be long at all before your buddies in the Twelve take you off the board, if only to keep you from naming names. After failing not once but twice, I'm sure they'll be only too eager to cut their losses."

Gage's defiance evaporated, and Redd knew he'd found the correct pressure point.

"So if I were you," he went on, "I'd start naming names right now. While you still can."

Gage's tongue darted out, moistening his lips, as he contemplated Redd's suggestion. It took him less than thirty seconds to reach a decision.

"You should probably write this down."

FIFTY-TWO

RICHLAND, MICHIGAN
SIX WEEKS LATER

Special Agent Stephanie Treadway cupped both hands around the paper cup that still held two-thirds of the venti mocha latte she'd picked up at the local Starbucks, hoping to draw some last vestige of heat from the beverage. It was a futile effort. The coffee drink had already cooled, another victim of the freezing wasteland to which Kline had sent her.

"Pack your bags. I need a favor."

This better be worth it, she thought.

The heater in her rented Hyundai Sonata had kept the chill at bay while she'd been driving, but as soon as she'd shut the motor off, the cold had wrapped around the car, pried its way inside, and invaded her very bones. She was sorely tempted to turn the engine back on and let it idle while she waited, but the plume of warm exhaust billowing from the tailpipe—invisible under ordinary conditions where most actual humans lived—would have been a dead giveaway to her presence. The fact that she had pulled to the side on the backcountry road where, clearly, there was no good reason for anyone to park was already conspicuous enough. If the man she had been sent to find was even half of the legend Kline had made him out to be, she didn't dare do anything that might spook him.

Finding him had been no easy task. Without any official documentation to go on, besides a bare-bones file that hadn't been properly updated, not to mention the secrecy of her inquiry, Treadway had spent the last several weeks trying to locate the man Kline now needed. While tracking him down had proved challenging enough, doing so without raising any red flags had taken even longer. But here she finally was. This was her chance, and if the stories about the man were true, it might be her only shot to make contact.

She gulped down the last of the mocha, now barely lukewarm, and returned her attention to the driveway turn-in, about a hundred yards up the road from where she was parked, which fed into a complex of townhomes, one of which was believed to belong to the man she was trying to find.

Kline had called him a ghost. An operator like no other. The best of the best. It was hard to imagine someone like that choosing to up and disappear into suburban southwest Michigan, though.

Maybe his memory is being colored by nostalgia.

The problem before her now was how best to make the introduction. She could just walk up and ring the bell, but that might spook him. She could stay put and wait for him to come out, maybe to make a run to the store for a newspaper or a gallon of milk, and then approach him in a more public setting. But that would mean sitting in the cursed icebox that was her rental car for longer than she wanted. And she was more than ready to get back to DC.

Treadway was still considering her options when a new variable was suddenly thrown into the equation. Up ahead, a quartet of figures, all of them bundled up against the cold, emerged from the driveway to stand on the roadside. She grabbed the compact binoculars off the passenger seat and scrutinized them.

Three of them were children, or at least Treadway assumed them to be so, judging by their height relative to the fourth and the fact that they carried backpacks—two of which looked to be made of shiny vinyl and decorated with cartoon characters. The lone adult was bareheaded, despite the cold, which made it easy for Treadway to confirm that this was indeed the man she had been sent to find.

Her only picture of him was from early in his military service—the standard ID photo taken during boot camp, an unsmiling recruit wearing cammies, his shaved head concealed under the distinctive eight-point "cover" of the USMC. This man was older, with blond hair and a neatly trimmed, slightly reddish beard, but the steel-blue eyes were the same. She couldn't really estimate his height, but he appeared slender, even in his heavy winter coat. With his smiling face and his pastel-green Yeti travel mug in one hand, the other holding the mitten-covered hand of the smallest child, laughing at some silly joke, he looked the very picture of an ordinary suburban dad as he stood with his kids.

This is the ghost Kline sent me to find? He looks more like Mr. Mom.

The arrival of a school bus interrupted her musings and momentarily blocked her view of the family. Treadway figured she wouldn't have a better opportunity to make contact. Leaving the binoculars behind, and with the wallet containing her credentials gripped in her right hand, she got out just as the bus's flashing red lights went dark. She had only gone a few steps when, with a sibilant hiss of air brakes disengaging, the bus pulled away.

Mr. Mom was nowhere to be seen.

Treadway laughed despite herself. *Maybe he* is *a ghost after all.*

Figuring that the man had already started back up the driveway, she quickened her step to catch up to him, but when she reached the turnoff a few seconds later, she did not see his retreating back.

She shook her head, disbelieving. "Now where the heck did you—?"

"Who are you, and what are you doing here?"

Treadway barely contained a surprised yelp. She whirled around to confront the source of the voice and found herself almost nose to nose with the man, who, she now saw, no longer held his green travel mug.

"How did you—?"

He took a step forward, compelling her to back away. "I said, who are you, and what are you doing here?"

His voice was barely louder than a whisper but projected a degree of menace that made her want to clutch her service weapon. Instead, she flashed her creds. "Special Agent Treadway. FBI."

The man held her gaze, not even glancing down at her shield. "That's one question answered."

Treadway swallowed. "I'm looking for Aaron Decker." Before the man could deny anything, she quickly added, "Gavin Kline sent me."

That brought him up short, but only for a moment. "That's not who I am anymore."

Treadway heard the double meaning in his refusal. He wasn't Aaron Decker anymore—that man was officially deceased—but more importantly, he was disavowing the person Aaron Decker had been.

He sidestepped around her and started up the driveway.

Kline had warned her to expect resistance. "Think about it, Aaron. Would Kline really have sent me if it were just any old job?"

He took another step, then stopped. He didn't look back, but he didn't keep walking.

Treadway seized the moment. "Look, I don't know your story, but I know Kline. Whatever . . . arrangement . . . he made with you so that you can be here, have this life . . . he wouldn't ask you to risk all of this and get back in the game if it wasn't important. And believe me when I say it is."

Decker stared at her for several long seconds. "What does Gavin want from me?"

She took a burner phone from her coat pocket and tossed it to him. For a fleeting moment, she thought he was going to let it fall to the ground, but at the last instant, he plucked it out of the air. "For now? Just be ready. Oh, and when that phone rings? Answer it."

Decker sighed, then nodded as he shoved the phone into his pocket.

EPILOGUE

A fierce wind was blowing down from the mountains, the chill air reminding Redd that winter was just around the corner. The intermittent gusts rocked the truck as he rolled down the highway toward Wellington, and a band of dark clouds loomed to the north. Patches of snow already covered the ground, and given that it was Montana, Redd figured the odds were good that more was on the way.

He hoped it was not an omen of what lay ahead.

The storm that had descended on him and his young family had, to all appearances, blown itself out. Anton Gage was in custody, held at an undisclosed location where he was cooperating with Gavin Kline and a select investigative task force—which included the agents assigned to the fly team, all of whom had survived the assault on the old missile facility with nothing more than scrapes and bruises—to track, isolate, and ultimately arrest the eleven remaining members of the mysterious Twelve. Because they were high-profile international figures, men of great wealth and outsize influence, bringing them down would be a dangerous undertaking and require precise planning and timing on the order of a lunar landing.

Kline had urged Redd to join the effort, to see final justice against those who had taken so much from him, but Redd had demurred. His part in that great effort was done. The scales of justice required balance. Punishing the wrongdoers was only the beginning of restoring what had been lost. Balance also required healing. Rebuilding.

That was a lesson the Infidels had taught him in spades. The senior leaders of the organization were dead, and nearly all the rest—the men who had driven Gage's drones to far-flung parts of the wheat belt—were either in custody facing conspiracy and terrorism charges or fugitives on the run. The club's chapter houses were shuttered, their assets seized, and those who had knowingly facilitated their criminal endeavors—lawyers like Angela Townsend, who was still recovering from her wounds, private investigators, even active police officers in cities across the Midwest—were either also in custody or under investigation.

That investigation had yielded surprising results close to home. Colton Manners, a twentysomething EMT who worked alongside Emily at the clinic in Wellington, had been identified as an Infidels "hang-around"—a potential recruit who was expected to perform various tasks, many of them illegal, for the club in order to prove his loyalty. Colton's task, which he confessed to Sheriff Blackwood, had been to inject little Matty Redd with a small quantity of human blood—just enough to trigger an immune response and keep Redd and Emily off-balance while the bikers initiated their campaign of harassment and revenge. Colton's cooperation, which included pleading guilty to assault and conspiracy charges, had been contingent on an immediate transfer to a high-security prison facility. Colton, it seemed, feared reprisal from the parents, though from which he feared it more, he did not say. Though Junior would require a few more tests to ensure the injections had no lasting implications, for their part, Redd and Emily were happy to know that little Matty was safe again and that his routine had quickly returned to a semblance of normal.

Not all of the storm damage could be so easily undone.

Several hundred acres of prime agricultural real estate had been exposed to Kline's GMO stem rust before the recall of the drones. Agents from the Department of Agriculture and the Environmental Protection Agency had moved quickly to isolate the affected areas in order to prevent the organism from spreading, but whether it would ever be safe to grow crops on the land again remained in doubt. Although Gage's mad scheme had been thwarted, it had left scars that would never completely heal.

Redd woke up to one of those scars every morning when he stepped outside and beheld the charred remains of the cabin.

Although Mikey and Liz had volunteered their sofa bed "for as long as you need it," Redd and Emily had agreed that the only way to move on was to move back to the ranch. The plan had been to convert a corner of the barn, which had escaped fire damage, into temporary living quarters, but when Elijah Lawrence learned of their intent, he had put his foot down.

"My grandson will not be raised in a barn," he declared and a few hours later had delivered a twenty-two-foot travel trailer to the ranch. After a bit of MacGyvering, he and Redd had the trailer hooked up to the well and the electrical grid.

"All the comforts of home," Elijah pronounced when the interior lights came on. "And you won't have to wake up to the smell of horse crap."

To call the old trailer, which had been sitting idle behind the body shop for as long as Emily could remember, *run-down* would have been charitable, but once the windows were opened, replacing musty air with fresh, both Redd and Emily agreed that it would do until they could rebuild their home.

There was just that one dark cloud on their horizon—one final storm that might blow all their dreams away.

Redd glanced down at the cashier's check on the seat beside him. Twenty-five thousand dollars, the first payout from the insurance company.

The fact that he had the check less than two months after submitting the claim was nothing short of miraculous. The miracle would not have been possible if not for the tireless efforts of Tyler Blanton—Duke's son, who had followed in his old man's footsteps and become a lawyer, specializing in real estate law. Although still mourning his father's brutal murder, Tyler had jumped in to continue representing Duke's clients, especially Redd, tenaciously following up on the insurance claim so that it would not get bogged down in the inertia of corporate bureaucracy.

Twenty-five thousand dollars wasn't a lot in the scheme of things, but it was enough, when combined with the last of their savings, to take care of the one obstacle that stood in the way of rebuilding.

The wind chased him all the way into Wellington, intermittently blasting him broadside as he drove through town to the courthouse. Tyler had delivered the check late Friday afternoon, obliging Redd to wait until Monday morning to visit the office of County Assessor Craig Yearsley.

The deadline for paying off the outstanding property tax liability had come and gone. There had been no subsequent notifications from the county regarding the status of the property. Tyler had assured him that the wheels of bureaucracy turned slowly, but Redd worried that Yearsley's irrational personal animus toward him might grease those wheels, accelerating the machinery of government to ramming speed.

He sat in the truck for several minutes, taking deep breaths to work up the courage for this encounter. Facing off against Baby Boy and Angry Johnny had seemed easy by comparison because he'd known going in that he had the skill and strength, not to mention the inner fortitude, to win. The assessor was a different kind of foe, and this fight—if that was even the right word for it—could not be won through reliance on self. He was not David facing Goliath, but Daniel stepping into the lion's den.

He only wished he possessed a tenth of Daniel's faith.

Realizing that procrastination was doing him no favors, he scooped up the check, stuffed it in his coat pocket, and headed into the courthouse. He made it through the door to the assessor's office, but when he met the surprised stare of the receptionist, his courage deserted him.

The woman regarded him with stony indifference for several long seconds. Behind her, the everyday business of the office had come to a complete halt. Every eye in the room was on Redd, watching him with the same morbid curiosity of people driving past a car accident. Redd half expected the receptionist to reach for the phone and call the sheriff to have him escorted out of the building. Instead, she simply crossed her arms over her chest. "What can I do for you today, Mr. Redd?"

Redd shambled forward, waving the check like a flag of truce. "I'm here to settle my account. And . . . uh, I'm sorry about what happened last time I was here. I was way out of line. I'd like to apologize to Mr. Yearsley . . . if he'll listen."

The woman appeared completely unmoved by the apology. She sniffed imperiously, then stood without speaking and walked over to Yearsley's office. She disappeared inside, leaving Redd to wither under the scrutiny of her office mates.

The wait was interminable. Under his coat, Redd could feel beads of perspiration rolling down his spine. It was nearly ten minutes before the receptionist emerged from the office, conspicuously alone, holding a single sheet of paper.

Redd felt his heart stutter to a full stop as the woman strode toward him and placed the printout on the counter in front of him. "Good day, Mr. Redd," she said, then snatched a mug off her desk and retreated to a different corner of the office.

Redd lowered his eyes to the paper, expecting the word *eviction* or *seizure* or something like that to leap out at him. But the page was simply the same tax statement he'd been getting from the county ever since taking possession of Thompson Ranch, albeit with one conspicuous difference. At the bottom, next to the words *Balance due*, there were just three digits instead of the seven he had grown accustomed to seeing.

Balance due: $0.00

Uncertain of what this portended, he scanned up a few lines to check the account history and saw that a payment in excess of twenty-seven thousand dollars had been posted to the account more than three weeks prior.

This is some kind of sick joke, he thought. *Yearsley twisting the knife.*

He read it again, trying to spot the trick, but the bottom line remained the same.

Balance due: $0.00

He looked up, searching until he found the receptionist standing near the back of the open office, sipping from her mug as she watched him.

"Excuse me," he called out, waving the paper. "I have some questions about this."

She frowned but crossed back to her desk and set down the mug. "Yes?"

He strove for a grateful smile. "I was wondering if you could explain this to me."

"What's to explain? You're paid up. It's pretty straightforward."

"I didn't make a payment."

She shrugged.

"Did someone else make this payment?" Even as this possibility flitted through his head, his brain began spinning with possibilities. It couldn't have been anyone local. Not Mikey or Emily's parents. His friends and family might have wanted to help, but none of them had that kind of money to throw around. Who did that leave?

Kline.

The thought put the squeeze on his nascent relief.

If he thinks he can buy my love . . .

"There's really nothing more I can tell you," the still-frowning receptionist said. "Good day."

✼　✼　✼

Redd began the drive back to the ranch fuming.

Kline. It's got to be Kline.

On some level, he knew that anger was the wrong emotion to be feeling. He ought to have been fall-down-on-his-knees grateful. But instead, all he could think was that Kline—or if not Kline, then someone else—had judged him incapable of solving his own problems and taken away his chance to prove that he was the equal of any challenge.

He resolved to give Kline a great big piece of his mind as soon as he got back.

Gradually, however, as he drove into the teeth of the wind, his ardor cooled and the true significance of what had happened finally settled in.

The ranch was his again, free and clear. No more struggling just to pay the interest on his debts. Now, instead of depleting every last reserve just to hang on to the property, he would be able to make a proper start on the rebuild, maybe even have it livable by the time Junior was ready to walk. Possibilities that had once been little more than crazy notions now swirled through his head.

When he finally reached the turnoff to the drive, he was only slightly annoyed with his biological father's alleged meddling, though he resisted the temptation to accept that maybe he had earned it. After all, he had saved the world from Anton Gage. Twice.

A few grainy snowflakes swirled around him as he moved from the truck to the trailer, where Emily sat curled up on the couch that folded out into a bed, drinking coffee with Rubble snuggled around her feet. "Forgive me if I don't jump up to give you a hug," she said with a wry smile. "But someone else has dibs on my feet."

Rubble had been Duke's dog. Blanton, a widower, had left everything to Tyler, but while the younger Blanton was more than willing to take over his father's law practice, he was less enthusiastic about giving up his condo in Bozeman. Nor did he have the time and space to bring a dog into his life, so when he had broached the idea of rehoming the "puppy" with Redd and Emily, it had seemed like an obvious solution. Although he wouldn't have said it aloud, Redd still felt guilty about Duke's death. The least he could do was take in the man's little dog.

Except Rubble wasn't a little dog. He was 130 pounds of purebred rottweiler, and at just thirteen months of age, he was sure to keep growing.

From their first meeting, however, it was obvious that Rubble belonged in their family. He immediately took to Redd, demonstrating both loyalty and obedience, as well as an innate protectiveness for little Matty. Emily had taken little convincing, agreeing that it would be good to have a big dog as added security. Her only concern was that, if the puppy grew to his full potential, there wouldn't be room enough for all of them in the trailer.

Fortunately, Redd knew, that was no longer going to be a problem.

"Well, how did it go?" Emily prompted. "Judging by that smile, I'm thinking we're safe?"

"Better than safe," he said. "Somebody paid it off."

Her eyebrows came together in a bemused frown. "I don't follow."

"When I got there, the bill had already been paid. Somebody—Kline, I'm guessing—paid the whole thing." Just saying it out loud brought back some of his earlier irritation.

Emily wormed out from under Rubble and got to her feet to face her husband. "The taxes are paid and we still have the insurance money?"

He nodded.

She let out a squeal of joy and threw her arms around him, squeezing tight. Thankfully, his bruises were mostly healed. "That's fantastic," she said into his chest, then drew back to look him in the eyes. "Gavin paid it off?"

"I don't know who else it could be. I guess he couldn't pass up a chance to play the savior."

"Matthew Redd." She punched him in the chest, not hard, but not exactly playfully, her voice taking on a sternness that he knew brooked no argument. "You are going to call him right now and thank him. Do you hear me?"

He managed a chuckle. "Maybe in a little bit. First, I want to show you something. Outside."

She glanced over to the playpen, where little Matty was fast asleep, then pulled on her boots and coat. When Redd opened the door, Rubble shot past him like he'd been fired from a cannon and began leaping playfully and catching snowflakes out of the air. Redd noticed, with just a hint of dismay, that while the wind had fallen off, the dark clouds were now over-head and there was already a dusting of powder on the ground.

"All right," Emily said. "What have you got to show me?"

He pointed to the mess of charred timbers—all that remained of the old cabin. "This way."

As they trod across the fresh snow, he explained his vision for the future of the ranch. The old cabin had been a total loss. While that remained an emotional gut punch—especially for Redd, who, unlike Emily, had no other repository for family memories—it also represented a clean slate upon which to build their life together.

For his part, Redd would have been happy to build back J. B.'s cabin exactly the way it had always been. After several generations of hard ranching, he felt he owed it to his adoptive father to preserve the Thompson legacy.

Emily, however, wanted a new, updated design—a home built for a family, not a bunch of ranch hands. In the end, Redd decided it wasn't an argument worth winning. J. B. himself would have agreed that she was better equipped to lead the charge on the rebuild and that Redd ought to occupy himself with more important things, like chores. There was plenty of work to be done, and the truth was, Redd didn't really care whether the master bedroom was upstairs or down or if they had their own bathroom. Besides, with that first insurance check already spoken for, their discussions about what the new house should look like had a fantastic quality about them.

But now that the looming tax problem had been resolved, the idea of having their dream house no longer felt quite so much like a dream.

He began walking her through the vision in his head, and despite the cold swirling around them, her smile was radiant. Only once did it falter.

"You're kidding," she said, looking him dead in the eye.

"Do I ever kid?"

"Matty, we're not having trapdoors and bulletproof glass. No."

Redd shook his head. He didn't need to remind her of what they had come through, what they had barely survived. "Don't think of it as a 'panic room.'" He was already regretting the use of the term. "It's just somewhere secure for you and little Matty to go, where I know you'll be safe if something ever happens." He nodded to the spot he had earlier indicated. "That's the perfect place for it. We've got the room."

Through the thick snowflakes, Redd watched his wife rest her hands on her hips and stare him down. A gust of wind kicked fresh powder around her, but she didn't so much as flinch.

"That," Emily said, nodding to the area where Redd had pointed, "is where the mudroom is going. So you can put your dirty clothes straight into the wash when you come in, instead of traipsing through the house smelling like cattle. I think that's a much better use of the space, don't you?"

Redd sighed. She always was stubborn. Tugging on the zipper of his coat, he said, "You've got to work with me here, Em. It's important for me to know that you and little Matty will always be safe. Give me something."

"I did," Emily shot back, chinning off in the direction of the barn. "Him."

As if on cue, Rubble let out a loud bark.

Redd turned to see what the dog was barking at and laughed as Rubble rolled on his back in the snow. A liberal coating of powder clung to the dog's dark hide, making him look more like a polar bear than a rottie.

Abruptly he stiffened, then got to his feet and began nosing at something under the snow.

"Did you find something, boy?"

A moment later, Rubble trotted over to them and dropped something at his feet. Redd bent down, patted the dog on the head, and retrieved what he quickly realized was a large black leather glove.

It wasn't his. It could only have been left behind by one of the Infidels.

"This . . ." He held it up for Emily to see. "This is why you need to take me seriously about this. We survived last time. Barely. What happens next time?"

Under her hood, Emily's expression softened. She reached up and put her arms around his neck. "Matty, they're not coming back. You won, baby. We won. Just relax."

He wanted to believe her. It was true that the Infidels had been defeated . . . in theory. But years of fighting terrorists abroad had taught Redd that, like weeds, enemies never truly went away. Someone was always there to pick up the torch and carry on.

And the Infidels weren't the only enemies he had made.

Regardless of how hard he tried, he couldn't get over the nagging feeling that somehow, in some way, there was another threat out there lurking, waiting to strike.

Wrapping his arms around Emily's waist, Redd pulled her into his chest, nuzzled under her hood, and kissed her cheek. He felt her shiver in his arms and rubbed her back to warm her.

"Maybe you're right," he finally said, sounding more confident than he felt. Truth was, he really did think they needed more security. Maybe a panic room was a little much, but there were other options. There had to be a middle ground between building a bunker and simply trusting your fate to a dog.

"I know we've been through a lot," Emily said, "but it's over. Now we can get onto rebuilding and being a family again. C'mon, let's go inside."

Redd didn't fight her as she pulled him back toward the trailer. As they walked, he felt his mood lighten.

Maybe she's right, he told himself. *Maybe . . .*

When they reached the stairs, Emily stopped abruptly and turned around.

"What?" Redd asked, alarmed by the suddenness of her movement.

"Kiss me, Matty." A playful grin spread across her face, and he didn't need any more convincing than that. Redd leaned forward and kissed his wife.

"See," Emily said, "everything is perfect. It might not be forever, but it is for now. And if things ever take a turn, we'll deal with it. *Together.* But until then, relax. Deal?"

Redd sighed. After a moment, he finally said, "Deal."

Her grin spreading into a magnificent smile—the kind that made Redd blush and fall in love with her all over again—Emily opened the door and stepped inside. Hesitating, Redd turned around. Using his hand to shield his eyes from the sun, he scanned the horizon. He wasn't sure, exactly, what he was looking for, but he didn't notice anything out of place.

Relax, he told himself.

But try as he might, Redd couldn't shake the feeling that something else was lurking right around the corner. The Infidels were gone, Gage was neutralized . . . but the remaining members of the Twelve were still out there. Men hell-bent on reshaping the world, with unimaginable resources at their disposal. Men Redd had thwarted and embarrassed not once, but *twice*.

And now he knew their names.

Silencing him was no longer just a business decision; it was personal.

They'd be coming for him.

And they would be out for blood.

Acknowledgments

Let me start by thanking my Lord and Savior Jesus Christ, for without Him, nothing else matters.

Last time I mentioned my wife last, so this time I'd like to open by saying that without you, **Melissa**, I wouldn't be here. You are my everything and always know just what to say when I need to hear it most. You inspire me each and every day, and I so admire how you handle adversity and unknowns by always attacking the day, Starbucks in hand, and never letting anything or anyone affect you. I love you so much.

To my children, I hope that you know all those days and nights that I'm locked away, writing and editing—it's because I love you dearly and want to provide the best life possible for you all. Nobody makes me laugh harder than **Ryan Junior. Rylee**, you light up every room you walk in, baby girl. **Mitchell** has begged me to make him a villain in the next book, but he wants his name to be "Darth Vader," among a number of other requests. I'm not sure I can make that happen, but, Son, you are so very special. **Brynn**, I don't know what I'd do without you. A better big sister, there is not. You know better than anyone the work that goes into being a Book Spy, editor, and author—and for all the nights you've stayed up to watch movies with me and help me laugh and get my mind off of things, thank you. **Chase** and **Jakop**, well, you guys are "too cool" to have me write anything about you for people to read. I get it. But I love you both. You guys are my heartbeat, and I love you more than life.

To my parents, **James** and **Rhonda**, I will never be able to thank you enough for raising me the way you did, instilling a biblical foundation for me to build onto in my adult life. I am so very proud to be your son.

To **Aunt Marlene**, who is far more than just an aunt to me, but more like a second mother, thank you for always being there for me and loving me. I always know that I can call and reach you and that, no matter what, you're there to give me advice or let me vent. You mean more to me than you'll ever know.

To **Mikey** and **Emily Derhammer**, I don't know what I would do without you guys. Just as Redd calls on Mikey when he's stuck and needs a hand, the same is true for me—and Mikey is always there to help both me and my family. From fixing Brynn's van to putting my dad's riding mower together, and so much more, thank you for being a brother to me and always having my back. Same to Emily, who kept me fed and full of laughs as I slogged through writing this book and balancing my work life with everything else going on. You know I'm bad in serious situations (and, Emily, don't you ever make eye contact with me in a don't-laugh situation ever again), so while I can't look at you and say it, I hope you know how much I love you both.

Our hearts grew a little fuller this year with the addition of **baby Derhammer**, due in early 2023. My goal is to get book three done and out of the way so I can spend time with you this February. I haven't met you yet, but I already absolutely adore you. (PS: I'm the fun uncle, and when you want dirt on your parents someday, I have *so* many stories to tell!)

On top of writing *Lethal Range* and promoting and releasing *Fields of Fire*, I also hopped on Twitch and started streaming every night as a way to connect with readers and get to know them better. What a blast that's been, playing games with Mikey (aka The Hammer), Brynn (aka SlayBae), and Kurt (DialUp) every night. To that end, I am so grateful for **Box** (Shane Hall) and **Ariffraff** (Ann Feinstein), the best mods a guy could ask for. You two make it possible for me to game and have fun, even though I really don't know what I'm doing. Sincerely, though, thank you.

Building a community on Twitch has been far more rewarding than I ever could have imagined when we first started streaming. I can honestly say that seeing everyone is something that I look forward to each day. Regulars like **Jase** (Jeramie Edwards), **Jessica**, **Cate**, **Virginia**, **David**, and **Dave**—thank you so much for laughing with us and hanging out. You guys are what makes this fun. To new readers, come join us! twitch.tv/ Legit_twitch

To **Rajun** (Tony), **Ax**, **Hitterz**, and **Tuck**, much love and respect to you guys for grinding and building such awesome communities. I've learned a lot about streaming from you all and look forward to getting more games in together this year!

To our Sunday golf crew, **Jeff Derhammer** (who, when I lost taste this year and couldn't eat beef, provided me with enough venison to live off of—thanks, Jeff!), **Michael** and **Megan Howard**, plus their son **Aidan**. Thanks for letting me beat you all over and over this year. Ha! But seriously, I can't wait to hit the course again next year. (PS: Aidan, I have big plans for you in my next book, buddy.)

Nobody throws a Fourth of July party quite like **Kurt** and **Kaila Oman**. Thank you so much for inviting us this year and for treating us like family. I can't wait to see Kurt pound a few iced mochas, then rip up that water-slide next year!

To everyone at Tyndale, thank you. You guys are the best in the business, and I've loved every second of working with all of you. **Karen Watson**, **Jan Stob**, **Stephanie Broene**, **Andrea Martin**, **Andrea Garcia**, **Amanda Woods**, and **Dean Renninger**, I couldn't do this without you. I hope you know how much I appreciate what you've done both for me and for Matty Redd. I'd also like to once again single out my brilliant editor, **Sarah Rische**. Sarah, working with you is such a pleasure. I so appreciate your attention to detail, thoughtful notes, and ability to always stay on top of the many moving parts to a story. Just like the last one, *Lethal Range* is a much better book because of you.

When it comes to promoting a book, it's not easy. Thankfully, I had many author friends who were willing to read *Fields of Fire* and give me a blurb. So to **C. J. Box, Jack Carr, Mark Greaney, Brad Taylor, Brad Meltzer, Mike Lupica, Jon Land, K. J. Howe, Chris Hauty, Nick Petrie,** and **Kyle Mills,** thank you for helping me out and being among the first to meet Matthew Redd. To the fellas at **The Crew Review—Mike Houtz, Sean Cameron,** and **Chris Albanese**—thank you for having me on your show, again. Can't wait to see you next year!

To my agent, **John Talbot.** Boy, did you earn your commission this time around! I say that only partially joking, of course. But in all seriousness, John, I leaned on you hard throughout this process. Thank you for always lending an ear and having my back. I hear so many other authors complain about their agents and know how lucky I am to have you on my side. None of this would have happened without you.

And finally, to you, my **readers** . . . thank you for spending your hard-earned money on this book and for taking the time to read Matt Redd's latest adventure. I am cooking up something *big* for the next one, and I promise you, book three will blow this one right out of the water!

About the Author

Ryan Steck is an editor, an author, and the founder and editor in chief of The Real Book Spy. Ryan has been named an "Online Influencer" by Amazon and is a regular columnist at CrimeReads. TheRealBookSpy .com has been endorsed by #1 *New York Times* bestselling authors Mark Greaney, C. J. Box, Kyle Mills, Daniel Silva, Brad Thor, and many others. A resident of Michigan, along with his wife and their six kids, Steck cheers on his beloved Detroit Tigers and Lions during the rare moments when he's not reading or talking about books on social media. He can be reached via email at ryan@therealbookspy.com.

KEEP UP-TO-DATE ON NEWS
FROM RYAN STECK AT

therealbookspy.com